I0672996

The Carolina Coup

Another Rwandan Genocide?

James E. Mosimann

Brightview Press
Gainesville, Virginia

**For Tom,
Critic and Son.**

This book is a work of fiction. Names, characters, events and places are the product of the author's imagination or are used fictitiously. Any resemblance to persons, living or dead, or to actual events and places is coincidental.

Contents

Historical Note

From April to July, 1994, the "Thousand Hills" of the small country of Rwanda in Eastern Africa witnessed a modern genocide, the killing of ethnic "Tutsi's" by the "Hutu" majority. Nearly one million Tutsi's and moderate Hutu's were slaughtered. Unlike Hitler's impersonal and "scientific" gas chambers, the Rwandan killings often were personally effected by pangas (bush knives or machetes) and clubs wielded by one-time neighbors and acquaintances. Many victims knew their slayers.

In 1994 a civil war raged between the mostly Tutsi Rwandan Patriotic Front (RPF) led by Paul Kagame, and the forces of the Hutu-run Rwandan government. However the genocide was not a spontaneous mass movement, but a highly-organized plan cynically conceived by a small cadre of Hutu leaders who believed that the extermination of the Tutsi was necessary for their rule. Thus they prepared lists of Tutsis by district and imported massive quantities of pangas to distribute to local Hutu militias known as the "Interahamwe." ("Those who work together," or in context, "Those who 'kill' together.") For months prior to the holocaust, strident broadcasts of hate from the *RTLM, Radio Télévision Libre des Mille Collines* defamed and dehumanized the Tutsi.

All the plotters needed was a pretext to act.

That pretext arrived on April 6, 1994, when after a truce had been struck between the Rwandan Patriotic Front and the government, an airplane carrying the Rwandan President, Juvénal Habyarimana, a Hutu, was shot down. Hutu extremists blamed the RPF for Habyarimana's death. In turn, the RPF disclaimed all responsibility.

Whatever the truth, the Hutu plotters seized the opportunity to implement their plan and genocidal killings began the next day. Tutsi and moderate Hutu leaders were executed. Throughout the country lists of Tutsi's were distributed, and checkpoints were established where those with "Tutsi" identity

1

cards were slaughtered. Everywhere, recruiters armed Hutu civilians with pangas, clubs, and other weapons and instructed them to hack and kill their Tutsi neighbors.

The genocide continued through June, 1994, until the RTF forces were victorious. At that time, France, under the auspices of the United Nations, launched *Operation Turquoise* to create a safe haven for Hutu refugees. (The timing of this led some to believe that its mission was to protect the genocide leaders as much as refugees.) Under French protection, vast numbers of Hutus established themselves in Zaire (now the Democratic Republic of the Congo) around Goma, at the northern tip of Lake Kivu.

Inside Rwanda, the genocide was over. Its effects were not.

***

******

Prologue
July, 1994

Lieutenant Henri Duval drove the Peugeot P4 along a dirt road through the sculpted Rwandan hills. To the left and right, green banana groves offered colorful relief from the fields of dry stubble that slanted down to the roadway. Though the air was cool, Henri's forehead beaded with sweat. He wiped his brow and focused ahead. Several thin Ankole cattle with wide horizontal horns blocked his path. They refused to move, but Henri swerved onto the shoulder and passed them.

As a boy, Henri had explored the forested hills and valleys that surrounded his native town of Sousceyrac in the Midi-Pyrénées Region of France. He loved the outdoors, and normally the panorama of the rolling Rwandan hills glowing in the morning sun would have captivated him.

But not today.

This morning, as on every other for the past week, an all-too-familiar stench assailed his nostrils. The scent appeared to come from a clump of banana trees located ahead and to the left of the roadway.

Henri stopped his vehicle and got out. Before him, a dozen decaying bodies lay strewn and abandoned in the detritus between the tall banana tubes from which broad shiny leaves projected erratically upwards.

The vile odor churned his stomach. He bent down and retched, but only a few drops of yellow mucus oozed from his lips. He wiped his mouth.

Beside him, a meter to his right, a once-human face stared vacantly upwards at a mass of broad leaves that hung, suspended and lifeless, from an adjacent tube. The girl was young, thirteen at most. A panga had cleaved her cranium that now was covered by a metallic mass of blowflies. Henri swept the butt of his rifle at them, but to little effect.

He turned further right where decaying bodies, all Tutsi, lay in the shadows of low-growing palms. One, a young man whose arm was severed at the elbow, may have tried to resist. Crumpled on top of him was the body of an older gray-haired man. He had been executed from behind while on his knees, his face blown apart by the bullet's exit. A third man, skull crushed by a blunt instrument, had a tie about his neck, but his feet were bare. His shoes were now the trophy of some happy Hutu.

Some distance away, obscured by a dry banana leaf, lay a woman, hacked and barely recognizable, a mutilated infant near her knees. She had been nursing, but to the Hutu Interahamwe, she was just another "cockroach" with her filthy offspring, to be squashed.

Henri Duval swallowed and turned aside. He could take no more. He strapped his *FAMAS F1* assault rifle on his shoulder and walked back to his vehicle.

***

Henri had only a short ride back to the secure French encampment.

On the rutted roadway ahead, he saw a band of chanting youths wearing colorful patterned shirts and armed with pangas, metal pipes and wooden clubs. The leader, who held a French *FAMAS* assault weapon like Henri's, spotted the French flag painted on the Peugeot P4. He stepped aside to let Henri pass.

At that moment a young woman dashed to the car from his left. Frantic, she pressed her hands on the driver-side door, eyes wide in terror, pleading. Before Henri could react, red streaks splattered the vehicle, and the woman, head slashed, fell from view. A tall teenager, his yellow, green and blue shirt fresh with blood, appeared at Henri's left.

The youth grinned and wiped his panga free of gore. The leader pushed him aside and waved the Peugeot onwards.

Henri pressed the accelerator and careened forward, spinning dust up from the roadway.

***

4

Back at the encampment, Henri Duval went to make his report.

His superior sipped his coffee. Moving his cup aside, he placed his feet on the desk.

"*'Ah, Lieutenant, Quoi de nouveau ce matin?'* What's new this morning?"

"*'Rien, mon Capitaine, tout allait comme d'habitude, rien de spécial.'* Nothing, Captain, everything went as usual, nothing special."

But inside Henri screamed.

A word from his government and the slaughter could be stopped.

The radio on the desk was tuned to the *RTLM, Radio Télévision Libre des Mille Collines.* From it, a voice screeched in Kinyarwanda. Henri recognized the word for cockroaches, "*Inyenzi,*" the term that the Hutu Interahamwe used to dehumanize their Tutsi targets.

The Captain, perhaps unfamiliar with the propaganda of genocide, ignored the broadcast. He slumped in his chair, wiped his brow and returned to his coffee. He waved the cup at Henri in dismissal.

Back in his quarters, Lieutenant Henri Duval sat alone in glum thought. He stared at the bare walls around him.

Minutes passed. Then he made his decision.

He was eligible for discharge, and the recent offer of a job in a French company with a branch in the United States appealed to him.

Despite his apathy for things American, he would accept that offer and leave the military.

Anything to escape this Rwandan Hell!

***

******

Chapter 1
Some Years Later
Wednesday, August 15

In Manassas, Virginia, the sun had not yet risen. On the third floor of the Torbee Building, a man stood alone in a dimly lit office. He braced himself against the wall. The hall light that filtered through the opaque panel of the door failed to reach the shadows where he stood.

The man held a paper in his hand. He was not supposed to know the numbers on it, but security had screwed up and now he had them. He shined his flashlight on the wall safe. He read the combination from the paper and turned the knob.

The handle of the office door rattled.

He froze, held his breath. The rattling stopped, and footsteps disappeared down the hallway. He exhaled. Only a guard on his rounds.

He paused. If he opened this safe he crossed a line. No turning back.

But something was wrong, seriously wrong. *Damn it, someone in this office is planning mass murder.*

He thought of the men and women with access to this safe. The list was short, only three names. None was his. He gritted his teeth and checked his watch, 5:30 am. Everything was in place. He had to act.

He spun the dial to the safe.

***

The style of the three-story Torbee Building was known to its occupants as "Government-Bland." The edifice was surrounded by a razor-wire-topped fence whose only entrance was lined with concrete barriers and featured tire-shredding spikes that could be raised in seconds. At the guard post, each man wore a 9 mm Glock, and had access to a rack of M16 assault weapons.

All the windows of the building were sealed shut for reasons of national security. The closed windows had resulted in numerous memos from workers who variously reported odor-induced coughs, dizziness, headaches and other symptoms of debilitating illness. Sensitized by the possibility of a disaster like Legionnaires' Disease, the building's owners answered the cyclic complaints with periodic inspections. These always affirmed that the ambient air of the labs, cubicles and offices was safe.

All Torbee workers were aware of the surveillance cameras that swept rooms and hallways alike, but only a few knew that hidden covert cameras covered sensitive locations. Still fewer knew that the third floor housed devices to protect the building from electronic eavesdropping, as well as others capable of jamming radio and other signals.

But again, all workers knew that the entry or exit of CD's, flash drives, DVD's and other storage devices was strictly forbidden. Ditto for PDA's, personal phones, radios, etc. etc. The only way to carry information in or out of the building was in the mind, in underwear, or in a body cavity, and if the latter was suspected, an unpleasant intimate search would follow.

The Torbee Building was occupied by a company whose sole client was a little known, but highly secret, agency of the United States Government.

***

In the security center of this same Torbee Building, a red light started flashing. A tired guard named "Irv" jumped to his feet. *What the hell?*

"Bob, look at that!"

"That's the safe in 310. Harry, Damn it, check that hall monitor?"

Harry's eyes moved to the third screen from the left.

"Nothing there."

Bob chambered a round in his Glock. and started for the door."

"Come on Irv, you're with me. Harry, stay with the monitors and keep us posted. And call the chief. That's a special office. Let him know there's a problem with the safe."

Irv followed Bob out the door.

Harry, now wide-awake, stared at the empty hallways and stairwells on the bank of monitors.

***

In room 310, the man pulled back the door of the safe and reached inside.

There was no time to examine the contents, but a quick glance confirmed his suspicions. His flashlight illuminated two documents that listed numbers that surely were cryptographic keys. These he thrust into a canvas briefcase along with folders, bound reports, computer-security tokens, flash drives, and several CD's.

He fingered his Beretta, but left it holstered. The innocent security guards had families and were in no way responsible for this mess. Even if apprehended he knew he could not shoot. Still, he had only 60 seconds before the guards would appear.

And they would not hesitate to use their Glocks!

He donned a dark ski mask and ducked into the hallway. The ceilings in the Torbee Building were not high. This figured into his plan. Shielding his eyes from the anticipated mist, he stretched on tiptoe and sprayed black paint on the camera lens.

He dashed for the stairwell, entered, lifted his paint can and sprayed once more.

***

9

In the security center, the guard named Harry watched as the hallway monitor outside 310 went dark. He immediately communicated with Bob.

"Someone just knocked out the hall camera outside 310. Go to the third floor. No, wait. Camera twelve just went dark. That's stairwell eight. Now camera thirteen is out. He's headed down. You can trap him on the first floor."

***

But the man in the ski mask was no amateur. He did not continue down the stairs. Instead, he ran back to the third floor, left the stairwell and raced towards the window at the end of the corridor.

Only recently, the sealed window had been smashed to evacuate smoke from a paper fire on the third floor. A temporary panel occupied the opening. And earlier the man had loosened the bolts that locked that temporary glass in place.

Now he removed the bolts and set the glass panel on the floor. He leaned out the opening.

As he anticipated, two stories below was a long dumpster filled with clipped grass, leaves and trimmed branches ready for removal. To preserve appearances, the container had been placed against the building, behind a border of crepe myrtles.

The man grinned under his ski mask. The dumpster was in Zone B. It was scheduled for pickup this morning, in an hour.

***

The exterior grounds of the Torbee Building were divided into three zones, each entered through the guard post, and each isolated from the other two by high fences with razor wire. Zone C had the parking areas for employees and visitors. Zone A, whose loading and storage areas held weatherproofed crates of concealed contents, was most secure. Zone B, less secure, allowed entry to maintenance vehicles, like dumpster trucks.

The man zipped the canvas briefcase shut, sealed it in a waterproof garbage bag, and dropped it out the window. It landed in the dumpster, plunged through the loose network of brush and leaves on the surface, and disappeared, camouflaged by a coating of displaced leaves and grass that resettled upon it.

Satisfied with the drop, he removed the ski mask and threw it outwards. Next, the can of paint spray followed.

He had planned carefully. He would use the separation of Zone A from B to his advantage. He took a remote from his pocket and pushed a button. The remote, too, he tossed out the window into the dumpster.

Then he replaced the window, bolted it, and looked at his watch. He still had twenty seconds. Earlier he had fixed the card entry to his office. It showed that he had entered two hours ago and not left.

He counted the seconds.

It was a small explosion, but it triggered several events in the security center.

First, the monitor for loading dock AA went dark.

Then, a red light on the panel above Harry blinked on and off wildly, signaling that the steel door to dock AA was ajar.

At the same time a siren on the roof of the building emitted a whine too shrill to be ignored.

Harry reacted to all three alarms.

"Bob, the door to loading dock AA is breached, and the camera there is knocked out. The outside motion sensors have triggered the A-Siren. He's outside, in Zone A."

"Roger that, he's got no place to go now. We've got him."

***

But after an hour-long search they found no one. There was no intruder in Zone A. And elsewhere in the building were only regular employees working night hours.

Frustrated, Bob, the head of the night detail, returned to the security center and called maintenance.

"Get the damned surveillance cameras back on line and seal off the door to loading dock AA. Irv is on guard there. Divert any incoming to dock BB. The chief is on the way."

He turned to Harry.

"And keep your eyes on the monitors. If my butt gets busted, I'll see that yours does too."

Bob stormed into his cubbyhole of an office and slammed the door, rather tried to, but the pneumatic door-closer resisted and jammed his wrist. He winced. Tonight nothing was right.

***

Hugh Byrd, chief of security for the Torbee Building, bulled an angry path through the guards at the gate. He found Bob in the security center.

"Give me the list of all who were on the third floor during this mess."

Bob hit print on the computer and handed the list to Hugh.

"There are four, all with high clearance. They were all in their offices. You think it was an inside job?"

Hugh frowned. *How dumb can this guy be?* He crossed out one name on the list, and handed the paper back to Bob.

"Seal the offices of these three and bring them to the conference room on two. Hold them there until I call you."

Hugh pointed to the name he had crossed off.

"I'll talk to Mr. Hamm myself."

Bob left. Hugh Byrd punched his cell phone.

"Tom, I'm in the security center. Meet me in room 310 right away. We have a problem. His name is 'William Hamm.'"

***

******

Chapter 2
Wednesday, August 15

In room 310, Hugh Byrd went directly to the safe. He rotated the knob and pulled the door open.

Empty!

That was no surprise. When he had seen Hamm's name on the list of late workers, Hugh had guessed what happened. Somehow Hamm had found that damned decrypted memo.

Hugh went to the desk and pushed a button. The surveillance video from the covert camera revealed the shadowy figure of a man standing at the safe.

A knock interrupted the viewing. He opened the door to his aide, Tom Holder. Tom looked at the video.

"Not enough light. Too bad you can't make out his face."

"No matter, I know who it is."

Tom saw that the safe was empty.

"Damn! You mean he took everything? We're screwed."

Hugh nodded. Tom's eyes ranged from one side of the room to the other, as if expecting a third presence.

"Tom, calm down. There's no way the documents have left the building. And without them the guy has nothing. Besides, he's still here. Where's your Glock?"

Tom produced the weapon from under his jacket.

"Good, chamber a round but keep your weapon out of sight. Follow me. We're going to visit 'Mr. Hamm.' His office is on this floor."

Hugh locked the door.

Tom, Glock ready, followed him down the hallway.

***

But "Mr. Hamm" was not in his office. Hugh dialed the guard at the gate.

"This is Byrd, did William Hamm, ID #A17-1663, leave the grounds."

"Yes Sir, a half hour ago."

"Driving?"

"No Sir, he said his car wouldn't start. He was walking, went in the direction of the 7-Eleven down the road. We're searching all cars like you said. Maybe he saw how long it takes. Anyway his car is still in the lot. I can see it from here."

"Did he have anything with him. A package, a briefcase, anything?"

"No Sir, I patted him down myself. I have my orders. But he had a Beretta, and a permit. That's about it."

"All right. Put a guard on his car. We'll take it apart if we have to. I'll come down to meet you in five minutes."

Hugh turned to Tom Holder.

"If he hid those documents in his office, find them. Trash the place if you have to, but find them. They must be on the grounds. I'm going downstairs to search Hamm's car."

***

The dumpster truck arrived on time at the 7-Eleven where the driver habitually took a morning coffee. William Hamm was waiting.

He spoke to the driver. His price was high, one hundred dollars, but after a few minutes, Hamm had the canvas briefcase in his hand. Included in the price was a ride in the truck as far as Prince William Hospital in Manassas.

At the hospital, Hamm tipped the driver another twenty, stepped down from the cab and went through the hospital doors.

As soon as the driver left, Hamm stepped back out and crossed the street. He walked down the road to a car rental agency. There he presented the clerk with a drivers license with his photograph and the name "Walter Harmon." Then he selected a Honda Accord, paid cash, and left.

His next stop was the Manassas Post Office.

There he rented an oversized postal box into which he squeezed the supple briefcase. Then he took an envelope, placed the key inside along with a note, and mailed it to a "Dr. Jeannine Ryan."

That done, he drove to nearby Gainesville, Virginia. There he took a room in the Hampton Inn. He needed to rest and plan his next move.

Bill Hamm was a formerly covert CIA agent who knew how to disappear with the Agency's assistance, but now he was on his own. The authorities would be looking for him.

He would be hunted by good and bad alike.

***

Hugh Byrd was frustrated. The searches of Hamm's car and office had yielded nothing.

His cell phone vibrated. He picked up. It was "the woman," Denise Guerry. He feared this call.

She spoke with a French accent.

"Is it true? Are the contents of the safe missing? Tell me you have found them, that they are secure."

Hugh grimaced and stayed silent.

Who on his staff had informed her? Bob? Damn him!

She interpreted his silence correctly.

"So Hamm has them. Idiot! Find out everything you can about him, his assignments before Austria and the Torbee, everything. And locate his women. Get back our papers and those security tokens! You and Holder will do nothing else. Find Hamm and get them back."

She lowered her voice and spoke, barely above a whisper.

"Have you forgotten our clients? These Africans have no patience. If they see any danger of failure, they will make sure that you and I never existed."

"Don't disappoint me, Byrd. My uncle said I could trust you."

"Click."

***

Whatever his faults, Hugh Byrd was an experienced operative. He took the elevator down to the security center. Bob was no longer on duty. The head of the day-shift greeted him.

"What can I do for you chief?"

"Get me Hamm's phone records, recent calls."

"I'll pull them up."

Hugh studied the computer screen. Two numbers were more frequent than the others.

"Whose numbers are these?"

"One is a small company in Bethesda, Maryland, Ryan Associates. The other is a woman, Jeannine Ryan. Looks like it's the same Ryan, both numbers have the same address."

"Google her."

A newspaper article appeared. It featured a photo with a woman. She was incredibly attractive. Hugh Byrd studied her features.

Nice! No wonder Hamm keeps calling you. You will lead me to him!

Hugh called Tom Holder.

"Tom, there's a Dr. Jeannine Ryan in Bethesda. I want you to fix her phones for me. It's one location, one visit. Her business and personal phones are in the same house. This woman may be our key to Hamm. Get on it!"

***

16

But Hugh Byrd was not satisfied. Although the Ryan woman was a good lead, there had to be more.

Hamm was gone. Hugh was convinced that the papers too were gone. But how? How had he gotten the documents through security? They had not been on his person.

Hugh left his room, walked to the window at the end the hall, and stared out. Since his arrival, a light rain had coated the pane with droplets.

Rain from that hurricane in the Gulf?

As if in answer to these thoughts, lightning lit the sky and wind-driven drops splattered the glass. In only seconds, a torrential downpour sent water swirling down the glass in rippling waves.

Hugh watched in silence. The storm matched his mood.

He stood frozen for minutes. Then the downpour changed to a drizzle and the sky lightened as dark clouds moved to the East. The watery film settled to the base of the pane.

Hugh started. At the base of the window, water had seeped in and around the bolts.

The damn bolts are loose.

Wait! Maybe Hamm?

He stooped to remove the bolts and lifted the dripping pane onto the floor. He leaned out.

Bingo!

Suspended dripping on a branch below was a dark cloth, a ski mask.

He leaned further and saw a bare space where a dumpster usually sat. The dumpster was gone!

Only yesterday it had been full of debris. Landscaping had cleaned and cleared the grounds this week.

That's it! Damn you Hamm.

Hugh returned to his room. Within five minutes he had the name of the driver who had picked up the dumpster.

He called Tom Holder.

"Have you left for Bethesda yet? Good, you can fix Ryan's phones later. Meet me at my car. You and I are going to see a driver about a dumpster."

***

The driver of the dumpster truck, induced this time by a couple of hundred dollar bills, was more than willing to cooperate with his new benefactors. He described the ride with the stranger to Prince William Hospital and told them the exact spot where their "friend" had left the truck and entered the hospital.

Fifteen minutes later, Hugh Byrd stood in front of the hospital, in the very spot where Hamm had gotten out.

Hamm you weren't going to the hospital, why here?

Hugh trusted his hunches. He paused to survey the scene

Then he saw. Several blocks away there was a sign for a car rental agency. Of course.

Hamm was afoot!

He turned to Tom Holder and pointed to the car rental sign.

"That's where Hamm went. I know it. Come on, let's go."

Tom drove.

***

At the car agency, Hugh Byrd, flashed his government credentials. In only minutes a cooperative clerk verified that a man matching Hamm's description had rented a blue Honda Accord three hours earlier.

Hugh was elated. He now knew Hamm was driving a blue Accord, and more importantly he knew the Accord's license plate.

He congratulated himself. *Damn. I'm good at this!*

As he turned to leave, the clerk called to him.

18

"Sir, one more thing. The gentleman who rented the Accord asked me if we had an office in Gainesville. I told him we did. He might plan to return our car there."

Hugh's grin widened.

"Thanks, you've been a big help."

He strode to the car where Tom Holder waited.

"A home run, Tom. I hit it out the park!"

***

Several hours later, William Hamm sat in his room at the Hampton Inn in Gainesville, Virginia. The room was comfortably furnished, but he could not relax.

Eighteen hours ago he had stolen government secrets in order to expose Byrd and his co-conspirators. They had to be stopped.

He had to risk their wrath, but they would not be the only ones after him. The FBI and other federal agencies would be anxious to bring him in. Purveyors of stolen official secrets were not popular in these days of jihadists and international terrorism.

He had not wanted to involve Jeannine Ryan, but he could trust no one else. His enclosed note instructed her to use the key only if he did not appear within four days to retrieve it. If he was still free by that time, he would pick up the key himself.

He opened a beer and took several swallows. He settled in a comfortable chair and leaned his head back. He clicked on the TV. It had been a long day.

He needed distraction.

***

Tom Holder drove into the parking lot of the Hampton Inn in Gainesville, Virginia. This was the third area motel he and Hugh Byrd had visited since learning about the rental of the blue Accord. Tom spoke.

19

"It's been two hours. There's no Accord here, what are we going to do?"

"We're close, I feel it. Drive to the end of the lot, near those stores. If Hamm were here, he would park away from the Inn."

The car veered left. Hugh jumped in his seat.

"That's it. There's a blue Accord and that's Hamm's license plate."

Tom Holder stopped behind the Accord. Hugh Byrd spoke.

"Hamm's clever. He has a lot of years in covert ops for the CIA. It's not just Hamm we want. We need the papers or you and I are cooked. These clients don't accept failure."

He thought for a moment.

"Maybe the papers are in the Accord. We'll check it first. Can you get in without breaking anything?"

"Not a problem."

Tom produced a flexible steel shaft from the trunk. In a few seconds he was inside the Accord.

Ten minutes passed. The Accord's hood was up. Floor mats from the front and back seats as well as carpet from the trunk were strewn on the parking surface.

Tom looked at Hugh and shook his head, "No."

Then he lay on the ground and checked under the car. After several minutes he rose and came back to Hugh.

"Hugh, I've checked it all. Hamm didn't have time to hide anything in the car body and the door panels haven't been tampered with. The damn docs are not in that car."

"All right, put the stuff back in, and lock it up."

Hugh Byrd sat a moment in thought.

His own freedom was at stake. He had wanted to recover the documents, and then let the FBI apprehend Hamm. After that, Hugh would furnish the Feds with selected papers that ensured

Hamm's guilt. Then Hugh and his cohorts could continue their activities free from suspicion.

But the documents were not in Hamm's Accord. *Damn!*

"Tom, we have no choice. The documents are in Hamm's room. We have to go through him to get them."

Tom fingered his Glock. He was ready. He believed in direct action.

Hugh noticed the weapon.

"Not yet, Tom. You can 'off' him later. First we use this."

He held up a syringe tipped with a steel needle.

"This will do the trick."

Hugh smiled.

"Sodium thiopental, truth serum."

***

In his room in the Hampton Inn, a blonde talking head prattled on the TV, but William Hamm, head tilted to the side, eyes closed, had succumbed to fatigue. He slept, a half-empty bottle of beer on the end table next to him.

His was deep slumber. He was totally unaware that the handle of the door had turned. He did not hear the sharp snap as the restraining chain was severed. Nor was he aware that someone had entered the room and stood behind him.

As the needle penetrated his shoulder, he started reflexively, but only for a second. Helpless, he succumbed to the injection without waking.

***

A half hour later, Tom Holder had finished searching Hamm's room.

There were no papers. None!

Discouraged, Hugh Byrd shook his head.

"Hamm is smarter than I thought."

He slammed his fist on the table. The beer bottle rolled off, spilling amber contents onto an already-stained carpet. Hugh set his lips tight together.

"You'll take Hamm to Doctor Smets in North Carolina. Maybe he can find out what Hamm did with the papers. Now help me get him into the elevator."

Hugh and Tom bracketed Hamm and shuffled him to the elevator.

In the parking lot, Tom turned to his chief.

"What about the Accord?"

"Here are the keys. Stuff Hamm in the trunk. You drive it. I'll follow you in our car."

***

******

Chapter 3
Thursday, August 16

Hugh Byrd was both elated and disturbed. Elated, because he had caught Hamm quickly, but disturbed because he had not recovered the incriminating papers or the computer security tokens. At least Tom Holder was en route to North Carolina to hand over the drugged agent to Dr. Smets. Perhaps Smets could make Hamm tell the whereabouts of the papers.

Damn it Hamm, you should have let me alone.

Now he should call Denise and tell her that he had Hamm, but that the papers and tokens were still missing.

At their only face-to-face meeting, Hugh had been overwhelmed by Denise's beauty and sensuality. But then he had seen her eyes and lost all nerve. Those blue-gray pupils had revealed a mind as cold as his. He decided that any imagined liaison was too dangerous.

Failure was not an option with Denise, or her clients.

Hugh's stomach churned anew.

He decided to postpone the call.

***

The entire sixth floor of the shiny glass building in Chantilly, Virginia was occupied by Guerry Electronic Systems or GES. The composite structure bordered a bustling Route 28 that formed part of Northern Virginia's high tech corridor.

GES was an American subsidiary of *Systèmes Électroniques Globals Alphonse Guerry* also known as SÉGAG. The granddaughter of the deceased Alphonse, Denise Guerry, was a talented, smart and incredibly beautiful blond. Her parents had died when she was young and her uncle, Roland Guerry, the CEO and majority owner of SÉGAG, had been her guardian in Paris until she had come of age.

But the uncle had spent little time or affection on his late brother's daughter. He had been busy meeting and scheming with important government ministers and French industrialists. He paid no attention to Denise. What little time he allotted to family was devoted to his natural son, Jacques.

Uncle Roland was an atheist, and in his eyes, a modern man. But towards Denise he applied the archaic maxim that she should stay at home or join whatever the modern equivalent of a convent might be. Still his indifference worked in her favor. When Denise passed the state exams to attend university and follow her ambitions, he had not bothered her. And once she had succeeded, he had not blocked the SÉGAG board's choice to name her head of GES.

Denise Guerry's success was not due to the family name. She was an independent and forceful woman.

After several years of maturation in the United States as head of GES, and dealing with the "undisciplined" Americans, she had become the consummate professional. Her English was practiced and flawless, with the added appeal of a slurred-lilt from her native French. Outwardly remote and intolerant of failure (particularly in men) she ran GES with an efficiency that belied her age.

At this moment Denise focused on an encrypted email that had arrived in her inbox. The screen was filled with numbers.

18111824041220113726303706352620
05113827201706381606072440190502
21331110172024120504303520201815
00130502142026120425191420170632
33051721221910192519210624062113
05031125130819150013051811260912
40194027254026242725400927092306
11380807041234261040252424250419
21132340102409091115331305052137
08240715352110132619282040193421
07002520080611253408182025390813
00282408240409342209402220331804
20390811172132081204251912101107
03081914261928201111370907111119
21010602193612253327193909392239

It appeared to be a message from the Hutu leader, Maximilien Gutera. Doubtless he wanted more money. She ran a decoding program and the decrypted message appeared.

**mlle.guerry,|professor|shahruk|concerned|
explosive|charges|for|my|rockets|may|be|
defective|segag|must|test|charges|before|
september|deadline|for|shipment|to|mombasa|
also|must|have|second|payment|from|ges|
delay|not|tolerable|m.g.|8gz9hk2j3c5**

She was right. The sender, "m.g.," stood for Maximilien Gutera, a Hutu leader linked to GES. Gutera's father, Charles Hakizimana, had been an organizer of the 1994 genocide in Rwanda. Maximilien currently headed a group centered in the Carolinas and had plans to lead a Hutu return to power.

She recalled her uncle's admonition.

"Denise, the Hutu are persecuted, driven from their country by the minority Tutsi. Maximilien is a true leader. He will help these unfortunate refugees return to their homeland. Do not trouble yourself about politics. Leave that to me."

Uncle Roland viewed Maximilien as a Rwandan patriot in exile. Denise was not sure of that. She was sure, however, that her uncle's perception of Maximilien was influenced by the generous fees he received for SÉGAG's laundering of monies pillaged from Rwanda by the fleeing Hutu genociders.

As for Professor Shahruk's concern, it was baseless. SÉGAG had already checked the samples of explosives. There was nothing wrong with them.

She arranged to transfer funds to a bank in Florence, South Carolina. Then she typed her reply and encoded it. In seconds, it was on its way.

That done, her thoughts returned to Hugh Byrd and the missing items.

Hugh must recover them, and soon.

Unlike her uncle, she knew that Maximilien Gutera was unpredictable and dangerous.

***

In a spacious home in the countryside near Florence, South Carolina, Maximilien Gutera lowered the Cuban cigar from his lips and listened to his aide, Jules Habimana.

"Sir, GES has responded to your communication. The money has been transferred to your account."

"Good, but Jules, know that I am tired of having to beg our own funds from this French bitch. Soon we will make other arrangements."

"But not now, we must keep SÉGAG happy. Her uncle has powerful friends."

Maximilien nodded and waved his hand in dismissal. He did not like to be reminded of his dependence on GES and SÉGAG.

Jules left. Maximilien took two puffs on his cigar, laid his chair back, and closed his eyes.

He thought of his father. He appeared to doze, but his memories of 1994 were all too real.

***

The house stood alone atop the Rwandan hill. To the front, green groves of bananas dominated the long descent to an unpaved road. To the rear and side, more somber coffee plants lined a slope that overlooked the shimmering waters of Lac Kivu. There a Pied Kingfisher sat patiently on a branch, watching for ripples that signaled its prey. Far to the West a red sun hovered over a mountainous skyline.

Purple Bougainvillea smothered the wall next to a bench where a twelve-year old boy sat studying. Nearby a nectarine Sunbird, resplendent in its violet and red iridescent plumage, clung to a cup-like nest suspended from a small tree.

The sound of a motor disrupted the boy's concentration. He looked up to see a bulky armored vehicle rumbling up the hill.

The Renault VAB 4 by 4 had French flags painted on its sides and sported a large Red Cross to the rear. It stopped near his bench.

He put his book down and stood up.

The man in the front passenger seat beckoned to him.

"Maximilien, come quick. The Inyenzi, the cockroaches, are nearby. The French have come to protect us. They will take you to a safe place. Come."

"But Father, my new moto?"

"Leave it. You must come. There is no time. Get in now, beside me."

The boy complied. He sat in silence between his Father and the French soldier who was driving. He scarcely noticed the four armed men huddled together in the rear, each in a faded once-colorful Interahame shirt.

The VAB descended the gravel drive down the hill and turned north. The boy looked up at his father.

"We are not going to Kigali?"

But his father, Charles Hakizimana, was silent. The boy shut his eyes. Somewhere behind them he heard the rattle of gunfire.

The French soldier spoke.

"Monsieur Hakizimana, the troops of the Front Patriotique have blocked most of the routes, but the road to Goma is open. Shall I take you there?"

The boy opened his eyes and saw his father nod affirmatively.

A sudden bump jerked the boy's head to the side. He looked back. They had rolled over a body abandoned on the roadway. He looked forwards. Ahead, fresh corpses, Tutsi women and children, lay at random angles on the road and shoulder.

The French soldier cursed and swung the wheel sharply to find a smooth path through the scattered remains.

The boy rose in his seat.

"Father, that one is alive. Stop the car!"

The driver's eyes queried Hakizimana. At the latter's nod, he braked.

Hakizimana twisted aside to let his son step out the vehicle.

The boy overtook the figure as it struggled to crawl away. It was a girl, a Tutsi, no older than he. He drew a handgun from his belt. The girl, wide eyes pleading, extended her hand upwards to him. He kicked it aside.

The boy raised the 9 mm Browning and pointed.

"Crack!"

The girl slumped down. Her arm quivered and fell motionless. Her legs twitched.

"Crack!"

At the second bullet, her body flattened, motionless.

Charles Hakizimana signaled his son to come back and spoke.

"Maximilien Gutera, you did well. Remember that I chose your name carefully. 'Gutera' means 'Attacker.' Live up to your name. Be proud you are Hutu like me. Kill the Tutsi until they are all gone!"

"Yes Father."

Satisfied, Charles Hakizimana motioned the Frenchman to proceed.

"There is a government encampment ahead. I will descend there. Take the boy to this address in Goma. His uncle, Maximilien Gahuj, is there. He will take him to Paris."

Thirty minutes later they stopped.

Without a word, Charles Hakizimana stepped out the cab. He motioned to the four men in the rear. They descended and disappeared into the dusk.

The boy never saw his father again.

***

Maximilien jumped up with a start. Hot cigar ashes had fallen onto his thigh. He brushed them aside as his father's words flashed before him.

Remember that I chose your name carefully. 'Gutera' means 'Attacker.' Live up to your name. Be proud you are Hutu like me. Kill the Tutsi until they are all gone!

A worried Jules Habimana hurried to him.

"Sir, what was that noise? Are you all right?"

"Yes. Do not concern yourself. I was just thinking of our mission. Now leave."

Jules withdrew.

***

At her home in Bethesda, Maryland, Dr. Jeannine Ryan folded back the covers on her bed and smiled. Tomorrow, she and Bill Hamm planned to drive to Skyline Drive in Shenandoah National Park. This would be his first free afternoon in a month.

They needed time together.

Jeannine was a specialist in statistical forensics, the detection of fake data. She headed her own consulting firm, Ryan Associates, whose office was in the basement of her home. She and Bill Hamm had been professionally and romantically associated for several years. He worked for the CIA and was assigned to a desk somewhere in Northern Virginia. Though much closer than his last post in Vienna, Austria, still they had not seen each other as much as she would like.

And even when together, he had been worried and distant.

She pulled the covers over her. *Forget it Jeannine. Stop worrying. Tomorrow everything will be fine, like before.*

She rolled over and slept.

***

******

Chapter 4
Tuesday, August 21

Jeannine Ryan sat at her desk in the basement of her home in Bethesda, Maryland. She held a key in her hand. Her friend, Bill Hamm, had missed their date last Friday for Skyline Drive. Instead, this key had arrived in the mail along with puzzling instructions. She was to hold the key for him for four days. After that, if he had not picked it up, she was to go to Manassas, Virginia, and retrieve the contents of the postal box whose number was on the key.

She sighed. The four days had passed and Bill was missing. He must be in trouble.

And yesterday, two FBI jerks had visited her office looking for him! She had received them coldly and told them nothing. They indicated that Bill was a spy, and acted as if Jeannine, somehow were his accomplice.

Idiot Feds!

But their visit had unsettled her.

Where are you, Bill? And what is in that Post Office Box?

It was time to go to Manassas.

Her partner Aileen Harris was on vacation. She wrote her a note and clutching the key, left the house.

***

When Jeannine arrived at the post office in Manassas, nothing appeared unusual.

Inside the building, she took the key from her purse. *Damn it Bill, where are you? Why are the Feds looking for you?*

She checked the number and leaned down to examine the lower tier of postal boxes. There it was. The lock turned easily. She pulled at the canvas case that was wedged in the box.

"May I help you Miss?"

She looked up. A tall man stood behind her. She tugged hard and the case came free.

"No thank you. I'm fine."

Jeannine's red hair appealed to the man. He smiled.

She hesitated.

Is this guy a Fed?

But a small boy came running and grabbed the man's trousers.

OK, no! Jeannine get hold of yourself.

She pushed past the pair.

Damn it Bill, what is stuffed in this briefcase?

Outside, she clicked the locks, started the Subaru, and drove out of the parking lot.

She did not notice the man in the Ford Excursion parked across the street. The man (Tom Holder) put the Excursion in gear and followed the Subaru.

***

At the FBI building in Washington, DC, Stew Marks, coffee in hand, was at his desk. He had been with the Bureau for several years. He was an ex-Marine. (A misnomer, he would *always* be a marine.) After the military, he had joined the FBI and received counter-terrorism training at the academy in Quantico. That completed, at a mature 29 he had been assigned to the Washington Field Office, Joint Terrorism Task Force (JTTF.)

Yesterday Stew and his partner, Jack Marino, had interviewed Dr. Jeannine Ryan, friend of a missing CIA employee, William Hamm, who was suspected of conspiracy to deliver secrets to an unnamed foreign power.

Stew had conducted the interview rather than Jack, who, did not like CIA "Spooks" in general, and Hamm in particular. (Jack's testimony before a congressional committee investigating a terrorist attack on the Unity Pavilion in Virginia, had been thoroughly impeached by Hamm.)

From the moment he first saw her, Stew had been attracted to Dr. Ryan and her auburn hair, but she was not the first good-looking female he had questioned. He had a job to do.

And Ryan had frustrated him. No way was she interested in helping the FBI find Hamm. He was sure she knew more than she let on.

He reviewed his notes.

> *Stew: Ms. Ryan, I'm agent Stewart Marks with the FBI, and this is my partner agent Jack Marino. (Showed ID.) We'd like to ask you some questions about your friend, Mr. Hamm. May we come in? (Hesitates, Let's us in. Red hair, attractive. Seems uncomfortable, definitely edgy.)*

He had written "attractive." That was an understatement, "Stunning" was more like it. Stew frowned and read on. His next questions concerned background on Hamm. They had been tough and straightforward. Then he had probed her thoughts.

> *Stew: Are you aware that your friend may have stolen government secrets?*
> *Ryan: That's what you say.*
> *Stew: Then you support what he did?*
> *Ryan: [Silence.]*
> *Stew: Does that mean you do?*
> *Ryan: Don't try to trick me.*

Stew skipped to the last lines written on his pad.

> *...*
> *Stew: Ms. Ryan, can't you help us?*
> *Ryan: What exactly do you want to know?*
> *Stew: We were hoping you can tell us where he is?*
> *Ryan: If I did know, why would I tell you?*

Stew: Because you want to help him. It's for his own sake. He needs to come in voluntarily. Why won't you help him?

Ryan: Because I know Bill, he's sacrificed more for this country than you ever will, and he's no damned spy. Whoever told you that is wrong.

Stew: Ms. Ryan, I'm just doing my job.

Ryan: So your job stinks. Stop persecuting the innocent!

(Spunky!)

Stew smiled to himself. He had written the note *"Spunky"* when his partner had risen to accost the desirable redhead. Stew had waved to Jack to sit down and cool it, before trying a direct question.

Stew: Ms. Ryan do you know where Mr. Hamm is?

Ryan: I do not!

Stew: Will you call me if he contacts you?

Ryan: I'd have to think about it.

Stew: What does that mean?

Ryan: You've taken too much of my time. I'd like you to leave now.

Stew: All right, Ms. Ryan but we'll be back. Meanwhile, here's my number. You can best help your friend by calling me when he does contact you.

(Knows more than she lets on, is uncooperative. This is useless now. Is she in this too?)

Stew put down his notes and rolled his chair back. He finished his coffee, tossed the cup into the basket, and propped his feet on the desk.

OK, Ms. Ryan, now we have to investigate you too.

***

In her Subaru, Jeannine Ryan glanced at the sack-like briefcase on the seat beside her.

Bill, what have you done?

She frowned. She needed time to think, and she needed to be away from the FBI.

She turned her car onto the Manassas Bypass and headed for Dumphries and I-95 south to Richmond.

***

Wayne Johnson stood alone on the weathered deck of his beach house in Topsail, North Carolina. Wayne was bored, stifled by a lack of purpose that left him unchallenged.

The beach in front of his house on Topsail Island, North Carolina, fronted a monotonous gray ocean that stretched southeast to an indistinct horizon. Above him, the scene was equally uninteresting. No trace of blue pierced a continuous gray cloud layer where only yesterday flat-bottomed cumulus clusters, puffed and white, had punctuated an azure sky.

A single gull of uncertain species floated by as he stepped to a gray deck chair. He laid his head back. He tried to relax but could not.

Phyllis, his wife of long standing, had died the year before. Retired and alone, Wayne needed to be needed. He was a statistician who had thrived on studying counts and measurements from medical studies whose goal was to cure disease and alleviate suffering. To that end he had worked for and ultimately owned a statistical consulting firm, StatFind, located in Rockville, Maryland.

But StatFind now was defunct, his house in Maryland was up for sale, and his wife was gone.

Over the ocean behind him, dark clouds touched a frothy surface signaling an approaching squall.

***

The storm came fast. Heavy drops splattered the gray boards of the deck and coalesced to flow over and through the cracked wood.

Wayne dashed for shelter just as a strong gust flipped a deck chair against the railing with a splintering impact. He was dripping wet before he could force the sliding doors shut behind him.

The gusts stopped, but left behind a steady rain. He sat at the table and stared through the drizzled window at the deck outside. The fully soaked boards of the deck were now a dark gray.

The rain kept on. As he stared at the unrelenting gray sky and ocean, the room darkened, but he did not turn on the lights. Finally, Wayne's head slumped on the table and his breathing became regular.

***

In his third-floor office of the Torbee Building, Hugh Byrd's coat was off, his tie loose, his sleeves rolled up. A 9 mm Glock lay on the desk.

Days had passed since Tom Holder had delivered Hamm to the house in North Carolina. There had been no news about the missing documents. Nothing. Nada.

Hugh sat staring at the phone.

The only lead was that Ryan woman. They had fixed her phones, but to no avail. Again, nothing! And yesterday, the FBI had interviewed her in their search for William Hamm. Hugh knew the lead agent, Stew Marks, a good investigator.

But Hugh knew where Hamm was and Stew did not.

Finally the phone buzzed. Tom Holder was on the line.

"Boss, I followed Ryan like you said. After work today she drove to Virginia."

"So where?"

"To Manassas, the post office not far from the hospital where Hamm got off the truck. She carried something from the post office. It could have been a large woman's tote, or a cloth briefcase!"

Hugh jumped to his feet.

"Where is she now? Did you get it?"

The cell call broke up. Tom's answer was lost in static.

"Tom are you there? Speak up."

He heard more static mixed with words.

"What do you mean she's on I-95 south? You should have stopped her in Manassas. Speak up damn it."

The call cleared. Hugh listened a second longer and exploded.

"Ryan's smart. She's no idiot. Now she has our papers. If she connects the dots, we're in trouble. She's a threat. Follow her and get whatever she has. Get it all, then make sure she can't hurt us."

He paused and tightened his tie.

"Damn it! I don't care how. Just do it!"

Denise Guerry would call soon.

And that damned Ryan had the papers!

***

At the beach house, Wayne Johnson's head buzzed. He awoke abruptly. *What the?*

His cell-phone lay vibrating on the wooden table. He fumbled for the offending instrument.

"Yes?"

He recognized the voice.

"Jeannine, Jeannine Ryan, it's been more than a year. What's up?"

"It's about Bill, Bill Hamm."

Bill Hamm had been chief financial officer at Wayne's company, StatFind, before he had returned to the Central Intelligence Agency. Jeannine too had worked for StatFind.

"I thought Bill was in Austria?"

"He was, but his cover was blown at the Unity Pavilion attack in Virginia. Langley reassigned him to the States, a desk job. A few months ago they made him the CIA's liaison with some secret contractor in Manassas, Virginia. He's been there since May."

"How does this involve you or me?"

"Bill's missing. The Feds are looking for him. They say he stole government secrets. They say he's a damn spy."

A pause.

"They interrogated me for several hours. They think I know where he is."

A moment of silence.

"Wayne, they think I'm a spy too!"

Wayne had hired Jeannine at StatFind when she was still a graduate student. She had lost her graduate fellowship because she had exposed research fraud at her university. With no means of support, she had been forced to quit her studies and work. Wayne had recognized her talent and helped her finish her Ph.D. in mathematical statistics at another institution.

He often thought of her as his daughter though that sentiment had not been reciprocated. This phone call was unexpected.

"How did you find my number?"

"I called Mona, she gave it to me."

Mona was Wayne's longtime secretary at StatFind, right up to the sale of the company.

"Wayne, Mona told me about Phyllis. I'm sorry. I didn't know."

Wayne winced at the mention of his wife. He regrouped.

"Thanks, but why call me?"

"You helped me when I was down and out. And you told me once you thought of me as a daughter."

"That's true, and I still do. What can I do?"

"Last week I got a note in the mail from Bill. There was a key with it, a key to a box at the post office in Manassas. He said not to use it unless he didn't pick it up in four days. I waited, and he didn't show. Today after work I went to Manassas. There was a big canvas briefcase in the box. I have it with me, but I'm worried."

Jeannine took a breath.

"Yesterday, when the FBI questioned me about Bill, I had enough, and told them to leave. They said they would be back. After they left I knew I needed time alone to think, so I packed a bag. Now that I have Bill's briefcase, I'm glad I did."

"So the FBI will be looking for you. Are you using your regular cell phone?"

"No, working with Bill taught me that much. This is a prepay. And the last time I used my credit card was in Bethesda."

"Good. Maybe I'm paranoid, but we may as well be careful until we know what you are up against. Next, are you and Bill still together, I mean romantically?"

"Yes and no. I mean I hope so. Bill has changed since he's back in the States. He thinks I'm wed to my job and he is miserable with his. He craves action. You know that. He's disgusted with the agency for assigning him to a desk after he saved their butts at the Unity Pavilion. I'm happy in my career and I'm ready for more. I think I love the guy, but he's unsettled. He seems to be on hold."

"Jeannine, I understand. You know you are welcome here. You can stay as long as you like. Where are you now?"

"I'm north of Richmond. The traffic is heavy. I might not make it to Topsail tonight."

"Stop and sleep. I'll meet you tomorrow morning at my favorite restaurant, I'm sure Mona told you about it."

"She did. That's great. Thanks, Wayne. Thanks a lot."

***

Wayne put down the phone. For the first time in days, he smiled. He had no idea if he could help Jeannine, but she needed him, or thought she did. That was a good feeling.

He thought of his protégé's red hair and feminine appeal.

A daughter to be proud of? Yes! But a spy? Ridiculous!

He turned on the air conditioner, he liked to sleep cold. Once in bed, he pulled a light blanket over his shoulders and tried to sleep, but his thoughts whirled with the fan overhead.

Could Bill Hamm have soured on his country enough to betray it? *No way. But maybe?*

Something was amiss, but what?

His head sunk into the pillow. His eyes closed, but his mind still raced. He lay still and again tried to sleep, but to no avail.

He liked Bill. Surely he was no traitor. Or was he?

Finally, his mind shut down with one last thought.

At least someone needs me.

***

It was approaching midnight as Jeannine Ryan drove her Subaru on Highway 95 in North Carolina. Emporia, the last town in Virginia, was behind her. The traffic from Washington, DC to Richmond, Virginia, had been slow and she was tired.

The blue sign on her right signaled a rest stop, the North Carolina Welcome Center. She slowed, pulled off the highway, and parked in a well-lit diagonal slot.

She cut the motor and clicked to engage the locks.

Bill's nondescript canvas case lay next to her. She squeezed it under the seat as far as it would go, but its presence disturbed her. Surely, Bill never could do the things they said.

Damn you jerks at the FBI. Get it right!

In the back seat of the car, her computer, suitcase and pillow were pushed against each other. They were visible to any onlooker, but she did not care.

Jeannine pulled her pillow to the front, tilted back as best she could, and fell asleep.

She was unaware of the brown Ford Excursion that parked near her.

***

Tom Holder parked the Ford Excursion across from, and diagonally opposite to, Ryan's Subaru. He unfastened his seat belt and twisted awkwardly in his seat to study his target.

She had parked under a light, and the night traffic was considerable. Though it was midnight, cars entered and exited the area with regularity. Doors opened and thunked shut as travelers went to and came from the rest rooms.

He would wait until the crowd thinned. Ryan was asleep. He had time. He left his vehicle and headed for the rest room .

***

At the rest stop an hour later, a North Carolina patrolman stopped his car, lights flashing, behind Jeannine's Subaru. He surveyed the neighboring spaces, empty, before tapping on her window. He held his badge out and evaluated her appearance. Red hair, nice figure, very attractive, not a hooker.

"Miss, sleeping by yourself in the car is not a good idea. We've had several assaults on women alone here. It's not safe. You should get a hotel room."

Satisfied that Jeannine was alert, he stepped back to his car and saw a familiar Honda two spaces away. He knew the driver. Her professional name was "Annette" and she had customers to serve. He had chased her away before and would do so now, but first, he went to the nearby Ford Excursion.

"Sir, I don't know why you are here, but 'Johns' aren't welcome in this county. My advice is if you are looking for a woman, don't! Consider this a warning."

Tom Holder did not answer. He stared as Jeannine drove out of the rest stop and headed south.

"Officer, I was just resting. I need to go."

The policeman moved deliberately to the front of the Excursion and copied its plate number. Done, he returned to Tom.

"Sir, I have your plate number. You can leave now, but don't let me see this vehicle loiter here again."

Tom ground his teeth and cursed under his breath.

The patrolman did not notice. He headed for "Annette's" car to chase her away before her customer arrived.

***

Tom Holder was frustrated. He had waited an hour for a clear chance at his target. Then just as the opportunity came, that cop had arrived. *Lucky bitch! If it weren't for that cop.*

He pulled out of the lot onto I-95 South. Jeannine's Subaru was nowhere in sight.

Tom grunted. Ryan was tired. She would stop at the next exit to rest. He would find her there, at a motel in Wilson.

He drove fast.

***

Jeannine was exhausted. Only with difficulty could she keep her eyes from closing. She lowered the window and let the air flow over her face, but with little effect.

The ad showed a Holiday Inn Express at the Wilson exit. She took the ramp and drove there.

Inside her room, Jeannine threw the deadbolt, fastened the chain, dropped the briefcase on the floor, and kicked off her sneakers.

Still clad in jeans and sweatshirt, she stretched on the bed. In only moments, she was asleep.

***

******

Chapter 5
Wednesday, August 22

In Topsail, North Carolina, the morning sun had risen from the horizon. In the direction of the sun nothing could be discerned. No waves rippled the ocean surface and the flat waters reflected a blinding glare directly through Wayne Johnson's window. He awoke and squinted into the brightness where a shrimp boat with net booms spread was barely distinguishable.

A line of light marked the horizon, the day would be clear. Wayne scanned the quiet waters. No birds in sight and, other than the distant boat, no activity anywhere.

He slipped on a shirt and went to the sliding door. The boards of the deck now were dry with splintered worn gray ridges and cracks. Yesterday, those cracks had been rivulets fed by the steady downpour.

He drove north on the beach road, a route lined by individual houses, Topsail was a family beach. On lots between the dwellings, salt spray had stunted and rounded clumps of myrtle, bay and other plants together into an impenetrable thicket sometimes as high as a one-story house.

He arrived in Surf City at the deli where he was to meet Jeannine Ryan, pulled into the lot and parked.

Jeannine was nowhere in sight, but no problem. According to his calculations, she was not due for another hour.

***

Awake and refreshed, Jeannine left Wilson and headed for Goldsboro and Jacksonville, North Carolina. She would take the northern route to Topsail Island.

The sun was bright, and the traffic sparse. She had driven for perhaps thirty minutes when she noticed a brown car some distance behind her. It looked like a Ford, an Excursion. Jeannine thought of Bill Hamm. He was always suspicious of cars that stayed in the rearview mirror for any length of time.

She slowed. The Excursion drew no closer. A minute later she increased her speed. So did the brown car.

Was this just her imagination?

***

At the FBI building, Stew Marks saw the lights blink on his phone. It was his partner, Jack Marino.

"Stew, you remember the Ryan woman we saw day before yesterday. You were going to keep tabs on her house, starting today."

"Right, the redhead."

"Well she's gone."

"How do you know?"

"Hamm has a sister in North Carolina. Yesterday, I sent Ryan's tags to our Regional Office in Charlotte. They alerted the locals. Last night a patrolman was checking for hookers at a rest stop on I-95, near the Virginia border. He saw a lone woman in a Subaru with Ryan's tags. The woman had red hair."

"What time was that?"

"1:00 am. The officer told her to move on, it wasn't safe. That's all I've got. Do you think she's headed to Hamm's sister's house?"

"It's in Nags Head on the Outer Banks. For that Ryan would probably go through Norfolk, but she was on I-95 too late for that. She's headed further south than the Banks. Still she could cut over on route 64 or 264 for Nags Head. Call the resident agent in Elizabeth City just in case."

Stew put down the phone and frowned. Ryan would suspect that Hamm's sister's house was watched. And she was smart. She's not going there. She's headed further south.

Damn it Hamm, where are you? And Ryan, are you meeting him?

***

Somewhere in North Carolina at a location unknown to agent Stew Marks, Bill Hamm stirred. He was on his side on a hard surface. His mouth and throat were dry. His tongue was swollen, and a dull ache pulsed through his head.

Falling asleep in a chair in front of a TV was a distant dream.

Fine dust assailed his nostrils. He forced his eyes open. Bare walls slowly came into focus. Once-plastered, now they showed gaping areas of exposed vertical lath-stripping. The surface coating had fallen, leaving powdery gray slabs and fragments on the wood floor.

Wet-wall construction, this house is old and abandoned.

He felt metal on his wrists, handcuffs! He twisted his hands, but only succeeded in chaffing his skin. Too tight. *Damn!*

How long have I been here?

A man approached. He wore a surgical mask, and held a syringe. But this was no hospital. Bill stared upwards and tried to turn, but could not. He forced words through dry lips.

"Who are ...?"

"No questions, Hamm. *Tais toi.* Shut up, just be still. Time for another injection."

The man seized Bill's arm. The needle penetrated the skin. A warm swooshing feeling swamped Bill's thoughts and he fell back unconscious.

***

The sun was high in Surf City. Wayne Johnson had waited in his car for an hour, but there was no sign of Jeannine. He looked at his watch, it was after eleven.

She should be here.

He went into the deli where he ordered a hot pastrami on rye with a side of German potato salad. The sandwich arrived. He bit into it. *Delicious!* A long swallow of coke followed by more bites left him satisfied.

Finished, he scanned the parking lot outside.

Still no Jeannine.

Damn, Maybe I'm not needed after all.

Wayne rose and went to the parking. Other cars were arriving for lunch.

His phone vibrated against his thigh. It was Jeannine.

"Wayne?"

"It's me. Where are you?"

"On the road from Kinston. I'm near Jacksonville. Someone is following me. That's why I'm not at the deli yet."

"Are you sure?"

"Yes, a Ford Excursion, all the way from Wilson!"

"Is there more than one person in that car?"

"Looks like he's alone."

"All right. Here's what you do. I have a friend, Marine Captain Peter Hume. He's quartered at Camp Geiger, part of Camp Lejeune. I'll call him now. You're near the entrance. Go to the post. I'll have Peter meet you at the gate."

Wayne paused.

"And tell the guard there's a man behind you who has stalked you all the way from Wilson. The guard will stop that guy. He won't get in. Maybe even the guard will get his ID. I'll meet you at Peter's house. I'm maybe an hour away."

Jeannine took a deep breath.

"Wayne, thanks. Thanks, one more time."

Wayne smiled and hung up. *Glad to be of use.*

He dialed Peter Hume's number.

***

Tom Holder stopped the Excursion as soon as he discerned Jeannine's destination. From a distance he watched as she drove up to the guard post.

Tom picked up his phone and called Hugh Byrd in Manassas.

"Ryan's at Camp Geiger, part of Lejeune. What do you want me to do?"

"You should have gotten her at the rest stop. You blew it."

"I told you the trooper stopped me from following her. And I didn't locate her hotel at Wilson until this morning. I got there just as she pulled out of the lot."

He paused a moment.

"Hugh, maybe we should let the FBI take care of Ryan."

"Dumb ass. She has the papers now, and the NSA security token. If Stew Marks talks to her again and sees what she has, we're dead. He's sharp. I don't want him near her. Just go back to Kinston, and wait for me. I can't avoid Denise any longer. She has to know we haven't recovered anything. Just wait. I'll be there tomorrow."

"Click."

***

At the FBI building in Washington, DC, Agent Stew Marks sat in his office. Across from him stood his partner, Jack Marino.

"All right, Jack. What have you got?"

"I asked the Highway Patrol to check motels in Wilson, North Carolina, for me. That's the first town after the rest stop. A redhead checked out of the Holiday Inn Express early this morning. Seems the clerk liked her looks so he copied her license plate. It was Ryan's. IIe said that she had asked directions to Jacksonville. You want me to call our guys in Wilmington?"

"Not yet. Anything else?"

"Yes, clerks at a couple of other motels said someone had asked for a woman named Ryan, and if she had stayed with them overnight? She hadn't."

"Any idea who that 'someone' was?"

"It was a big guy, dark hair, and he had some kind of vague government ID. It wasn't Homeland Security. One clerk's guess was CIA, but from what he described I don't think so."

"Damn, maybe the NSA. Do they have active agents?"

"Who knows, but they must have security people."

Stew paused. Who else could be interested in Ryan?

And where was she going? Stew had served at Camp Lejeune, near Jacksonville and was familiar with the southern North Carolina coast. Mentally, he listed possible destinations from north to south: *New Bern, Morehead City, Camp Lejeune, Jacksonville, Surf City, Topsail Island, Wrightsville Beach, maybe Wilmington.*

He shook himself from this reverie and spoke to his partner.

"Jack, get your gear. You and I are going to North Carolina."

***

At the entrance to Camp Geiger, a tall marine officer stood waiting as Jeannine pulled up to the barrier. The officer signaled to the guard.

"It's OK, Sergeant, she's with me."

He turned to Jeannine.

"Dr. Ryan, Ma'am, I'm Peter Hume. Wayne told me all about you. He's not here yet, but we can wait at my quarters. And I told the guard about your stalker. You're safe here."

He added.

"That's my car over there."

He waved at a red convertible of foreign make.

Jeannine followed in the Subaru.

***

In a dry musty room somewhere in North Carolina, Bill Hamm lay on his side, unconscious. His breathing was heavy. His thigh and calf muscles twitched involuntarily, causing one leg to scratch against the exposed laths of the decaying wall.

A tall lean man stood over him. The man, Gilles Smets, still wore a surgical mask, but no longer held a syringe. In his hand were surgical scissors.

Smets had not expected Hamm to regain consciousness that soon after the last injection. Though Hamm's hands had been manacled, his legs had been free, a potentially costly mistake.

He wrapped Bill's ankles with duct tape, then snipped the final piece from the roll with clinical dexterity.

There! Now Hamm could cause no trouble, even if the drug wore off. Smets had kept Hamm sedated since his arrival.

He nudged Hamm's chest with his toe. There was no response. Good. The subject was helpless.

He delivered a vicious kick to the defenseless body, and stepped back to catch his breath. That felt good, but he had missed the ribs and encountered only soft tissue.

He stepped forward and kicked again. His foot felt bone. The involuntary grunt of expelled air satisfied him. He watched Hamm's chest recover its normal up and down movement.

He stepped back, breathing deeply. Too many years in a lab had left him in poor shape. *I should exercise more.*

But he felt better. His superiority over the helpless Hamm was established.

He justified his violence objectively. He had nothing personal against Hamm, but a CIA agent had no rights! He turned off the lights, turning only to sneer at the prostrate form in the shadows. Perhaps one more blow would be appropriate.

He decided against it. He took pride in his restraint. A third blow might prove he was uncivilized.

With that reassuring thought, Dr. Gilles Smets M. D. strode out of the darkened room.

***

49

Wayne Johnson guided his Buick out of Camp Geiger and turned left onto Route 17. Jeannine Ryan, clutching the canvas briefcase, sat at his side. On the back seat were her pillow, laptop and bag. She murmured.

"Your friend Peter seemed OK with keeping my Subaru for a few days."

Wayne smiled to himself. He sensed that the bachelor captain relished the excuse to see Jeannine again. The parked Subaru ensured that.

"Peter's a good guy. He doesn't mind, and I doubt whoever is following you knows me or my Buick. Or my Topsail house. Now what can I do to help?"

She lifted the briefcase. It took both her hands.

"I have these papers. Some are classified. I'm hoping they'll tell us what's going on."

"Where did you get this stuff?"

"It's all from the PO box in Manassas, the briefcase that Bill put in the locker. I don't know whose it is."

"But it's not Bill's?"

"I don't think so. Some of the memos are addressed to someone named 'Byrd.' Only a couple of them are to Bill. But it's filled with reports and documents, CD's too. Look."

Jeannine pulled out several items. Wayne whistled when he saw the logos and markings.

"Damn it, Jeannine, no wonder the FBI is after Bill. These documents are classified beyond anything I've heard of. And look at this NSA security token. If the FBI catches us with it, we'll be fried. How the hell did Bill get these things off site. Damn. Maybe the Feds are right about him?"

"They're not and I damned well don't care about them. These documents will clear Bill. Somewhere in them is the proof he's innocent. Otherwise he never would have taken them. Somebody on this project is a spy, but it's not Bill. You must help me examine them."

She caught her breath.

"Sorry, I'm tied up in knots. Bill's no damn traitor. But I can't think straight. I need your help."

Wayne grimaced. She kept on.

"Bill needs my help and I need yours. Please."

Her voice tailed off. The last words were scarcely audible.

Wayne thought for a moment before succumbing.

"OK, Jeannine, I'll help. What can I do?"

But there was no response.

Wayne looked sideways at his passenger.

The past 24 hours had taken their toll. Jeannine's eyes were closed. Her head was slumped forward over the briefcase clasped to her chest. Already her breathing was regular and deep.

The accomplished professional was gone. Here was a "daughter" in need.

Wayne hummed an oldie as he continued south towards Topsail Island.

***

In Chantilly, Virginia, Denise Guerry sat at her desk and contemplated the message on her computer. The message from Paris was several weeks old, sent August 2, well before that idiot Byrd had lost those critical documents to William Hamm.

> *d.g.|radguard|report|a|success|plant47|*
> *dismantled|rods|removed|radioactive|modules|*
> *ready|will|schedule|ship|from|le|havre|send|*
> *radguard|payment|when|you|wish|*
> *good|work|marat1|cv'p2n'glt5m*

Denise liked to reread and savor this message, a compliment from her uncle in Paris!

It was personally signed "Marat1," her uncle's code name. Any direct communication from Uncle Roland was rare. Rarer yet, he was pleased by her work with RadGuard and approved of her!

And by this time, the radioactive modules were already en route from le Havre!

She sat back in her chair and took a hidden ashtray from the drawer. This merited a cigarette. *Stupid Americans and their health.* She wished herself back in France where she could puff without condemnation. She finished her cigarette and placed the ashtray back in the drawer.

Her uncle's message was special. She wanted to keep it, but in its safe form. She clicked and the encrypted numbers appeared on the screen.

```
0936131508230010262906171019261015
2137280500063829080211382705151820
2225313519121418192022251111230823
1410380823041934301003063709090821
2011250828240818141040201018063713
0603311931141118192708071123291704
0638161415062526201206311305070700
2610402524220940242012122007371205
1507032110132619311304201933202006
0117240706262320030601232310063209
2300261308082105350119391331283612
```

She checked that no letters appeared, re-saved the coded numbers, and shut down the computer. She walked to the door and turned off the lights.

Now, if only Byrd would call to tell her he had retrieved the documents and that NSA computer token.

***

******

Chapter 6
Thursday, August 23

Hugh Byrd sat in his office on the third floor of the Torbee Building. Hugh was a damned fine security officer, and he knew it. Up to now his government career had flourished.

When William Hamm had been assigned to Hugh's unit as the CIA's representative in the management of security for the unit's current project, *Sea Turtle Navigation,* Hugh had ground his teeth. The project was a flimsy cover for the real work on missile guidance, and he had feared that Hamm would discover that something was awry.

Further, Hugh knew Hamm's reputation from his work when based in Vienna, Austria. Hamm was an operative who refused to cut corners. In short, Hamm was honest.

The last thing Hugh Byrd needed was an *honest* coworker!

But Hamm had become suspicious and stolen Hugh's secrets. Hamm was neutralized, and, unlike Stew Marks who was tracking him, Hugh knew where he was.

So now Hamm's girlfriend Ryan was the problem. She had the items Hamm had stolen. Hugh needed them back before she could discern their significance. *Damn!* Tom Holder had failed to seize the documents and neutralize Ryan on I-95 and again in Wilson. Tom was good at his trade. The Ryan woman was either lucky or exceptionally skillful.

He glanced at the clock, 7:00 am. Holder was waiting in Kinston. Hugh shut the safe, rotated the dial, locked his desk, and checked out of the building.

He headed for North Carolina.

***

In Topsail, North Carolina, Jeannine Ryan awoke to the repetitive rumblings of the waves outside her window. The door to her bedroom was cracked ajar, and the odor of fresh coffee slipped into the room along with a salty sea breeze. She shook herself awake and looked about.

OK, this is Wayne's house on Topsail Island. How long did I sleep?

As if in answer, she heard Wayne call.

"Jeannine, you've been out cold for eight hours. Time to get up. Coffee's ready. How do you feel?"

"Fine, I mean, good! I'm coming. Give me a few minutes."

By the time she walked into the great room, a hearty serving of fried eggs, thick West Virginia bacon, hash browns and warm toast awaited her. Wayne, poured her a full cup of steaming black coffee. She took a long swallow, sat down, and attacked the eggs and bacon with vigor.

Wayne waited while she ate. She took a last swallow and looked up.

"All right Wayne, what's in Bill's briefcase?"

"The first thing is a report by a company called RadGuard about Strontium-90 in soil."

"Sr-90?"

"Yes. A radioactive byproduct of nuclear fission. In the 1950's and 60's its levels were high due to atmospheric testing of nukes. They found high levels of it in the shed 'baby teeth' of thousands of children. Those born in 1963 had a level 50 times higher than those born in 1950. With those and other findings the U. S., Russia and Great Britain agreed to abandon atmospheric testing. After the ban, the level in baby teeth dropped. By 1980 the levels were pretty normal."

He took a breath.

"I found some specific numbers on the Internet for Sr-90 in milk. In New Jersey levels dropped from more than 20 picoCuries per Liter in 1963, to 8 in 1970 and to under 5 by 1980. At present, the level is about 2 picoCuries per Liter."

"So the ban works. But what about this report by RadGuard?"

"RadGuard prepared it for a French company named SÉGAG. The report features a graph that shows that the concentration of Sr-90 in the soil decreases as you go further from some source. They don't identify what kind of source, but there are still about twenty picoCuries forty miles away from it."

Wayne put the graph on the table.

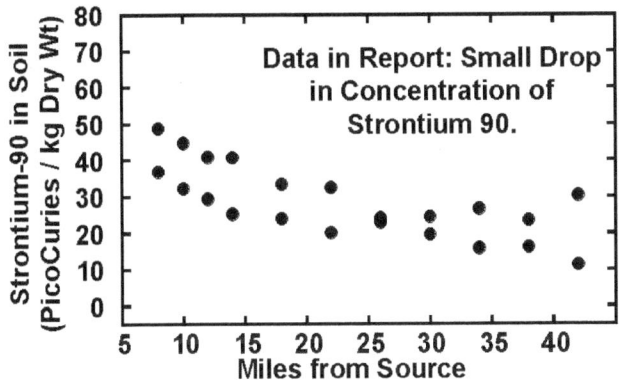

"I see that. What's your point?"

"I'm disturbed because RadGuard's CD has two sets of data for the same graph. Something is wrong. I made a graph for the second set of data. This graph is not in RadGuard's report."

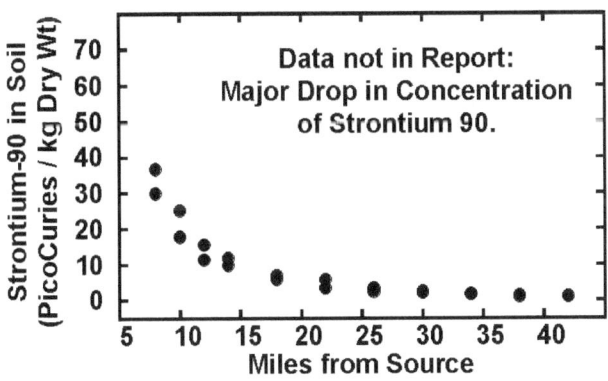

Jeannine looked. The second graph had the same labels, and a much sharper drop in Strontium-90 (to near zero) at forty miles.

Wayne spoke.

"One of these graphs is wrong! But which?"

"Let me think. Hand me that CD."

Jeannine inserted the disc into her laptop and typed.

"What are you doing?"

"I'm straightening the curve by taking logs and fitting a straight line to them. Their reported points look too symmetric. I'm betting they picked the line they wanted and then spaced points evenly around it so that when they fit the data they got the desired line back."

A new graph appeared on the screen.

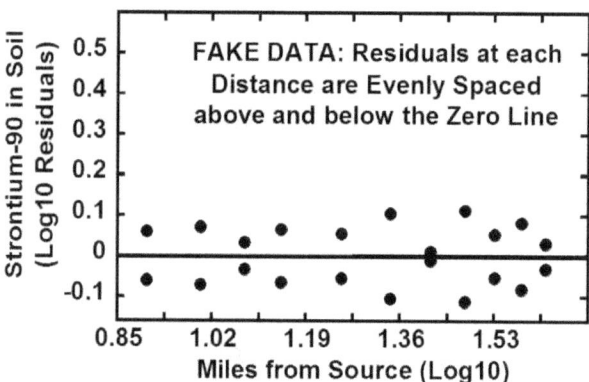

Jeannine explained.

"This graph shows the distance of each point from my fitted line. The points are perfectly symmetric about the horizontal line at zero. That's not possible by chance. The data RadGuard presented in the report are faked."

"Because the distances-above cancel the distances-below at each mile?"

"Yes, for real data, the points above and below shouldn't balance at each mile."

"What about the second data set? Did you make the same graph for those data?"

"I did, and here it is. The points above and below do not balance at each mile."

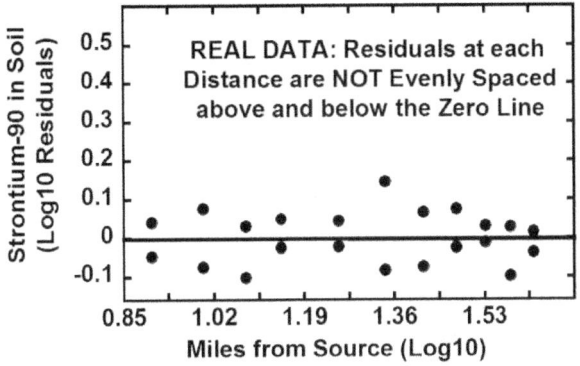

"So the points don't balance and these data could be real. But why would RadGuard report the fake data? What's their goal?"

"Apparently RadGuard wanted to show that the radioactivity is higher than it is. The fake data show that Sr-90 is still high 40 miles away, but in reality the Sr-90 level is near zero at 40 miles."

She took a breath.

"Someone wants to say that this 'source' contaminates the environment more than it really does. Maybe the source is a nuclear power plant? Or maybe even a one-time nuclear event, but I'm thinking nuclear plant."

"Could Radguard's cheaters want to show that the plant contaminates the environment so they can force its closure?"

"Sounds plausible, but if Bill were here he could tell us. He had his reasons for taking these documents. He must have the answers."

At the thought of Bill, her shoulders drooped

"Bill's in trouble, or he would have contacted me by now!"

***

Jeannine's colleague, Aileen Harris, opened the door of Ryan Associates in Bethesda Maryland. Aileen was a Ph.D. in Bioengineering and a minority owner of the company. The past week, she had been on vacation with her daughter, Mary Catherine.

Aileen stared. Jeannine's desk was clear of papers, and dry brown circles ringed the coffee pot. Jeannine survived on coffee. She had not been here for a some time.

She saw a note in Jeannine's handwriting.

Aileen,

If you are back before me, call. There's a new prepay cell phone for you in the safe. I have a new cell too. The number is in the "special" file on my computer. I changed my password, but it's just the palindrome of my old one minus one. I'm going to pick up something for Bill. He's gone and I don't know where.

Jeannine

Aileen paused. *Why the secrecy?* She went to the safe and retrieved the phone. She calculated the new password for Jeannine's computer, found the new phone number, and called. Jeannine answered.

"Aileen, you have the safe phone, good. You can expect a visit from the FBI soon. They're looking for me, and for Bill. Take your mother and Mary Catherine up to your Aunt Agatha's in Pennsylvania and stay the weekend. They probably won't track you there, but don't talk to them if they do."

"What's this all about?"

"Bill is missing and I'm with Wayne Johnson. We're looking for Bill, but so is the FBI. They think he stole government secrets. Meanwhile, I have some documents for

58

you to examine if I can get them to you. First, you should get away from the office, now. They might be watching it."

"Who's 'They? ' The FBI?"

"No, not just the FBI, they're others involved too."

Static filled Aileen's ears as the line was broken.

She hurried to leave.

***

In her office in Chantilly, Virginia, Denise Guerry, picked up the secure phone. She called SÉGAG's office in Paris's arrondissement 2.

Her uncle answered. He gave no greeting.

"What?"

"An American contact may be compromised."

"Which one?"

"The muscle man, Byrd. He's in security at the Torbee. He has lost an NSA security token as well as important documents, including RadGuard's report on Plant 47 and Strontium-90."

"You have a list of all these documents? Is Gutera's plan safe?"

"Of course I have the list, and yes, Gutera's plan should be safe. All of his messages are *Vigenère*-encoded. Byrd had copies, but no keywords."

"Denise, GES must not be linked to whatever Hamm stole. Byrd is the only connection to us. You must silence him. He's a government agent, so be careful. He should disappear, or make it look like suicide."

"But?"

"Do not question me. Henri is assigned to you. Use him for this."

"Click."

Denise Guerry glared at the phone.

He thinks I'm a killer!

She dialed again. It was a U. S. number, but the man who answered had a French accent.

"Henri, where are you."

"In North Carolina, Wilmington, like you told me."

"I want you there a few more days. Have you visited the farm yet?"

"Yesterday, it is well stocked."

"Did you check on the phony turtle lab and my new electronic equipment."

"Not yet."

"Then don't. Smets is there. You stay in Wilmington. There are important developments. I may need you, *entendu*?

"I understand."

"Click."

Denise sat at her desk, hand on her chin. She had not mentioned Byrd.

I am not a killer and that oaf Byrd might still be of use.

She needed time to decide his fate.

***

Hugh Byrd was stuck in traffic on I-95 south of Woodbridge, Virginia, when his cell phone vibrated. It was Tom Holder in Kinston, North Carolina. Byrd spoke.

"You're waiting in Kinston, like I said, right?"

"I'm here, but I have news for you. Our contact in Camp Geiger did some checking. Ryan visited the quarters of a Captain Hume. She left her car with him when some guy picked her up. They left right away."

"A guy?"

"His car had Maryland plates. I checked. He's from Rockville. His name is Wayne Johnson."

"But where were they going?"

"The guard saw that the passenger had red hair, and was a looker. The car turned south. It had a 'TI' sticker on the rear bumper, 'Topsail Island.'"

"OK, if the traffic lets up, I'll be there in four hours. Meanwhile have the office check on this 'Johnson.' Find out if he owns property on Topsail."

"Click."

Hugh Byrd pressed the accelerator and squeezed between two eighteen wheelers.

Ryan, you can run, but you can't hide!

***

Driving on Highway 17 in North Carolina, FBI agent Stew Marks watched as his partner, Jack, spoke on the phone. When Jack hung up, Stew spoke.

"Jack, did the resident agency in Wilmington have anything new for us?"

"Not really. There's no trace of Ryan since that clerk saw her in Wilson, and nothing at all on Hamm. They think he's in North Carolina too, but I think they're guessing because Ryan is here. We know as much as they do."

"Great. Now we've lost both Ryan and Hamm."

Jack was about to answer when his phone buzzed. He picked up and listened.

He turned back to Stew.

"That was Wilmington. We have a lead. A farmer found Hamm's rental, an Accord. It's burned out, but there's no body in it."

"Where?"

"In some pine woods, west of Brown Town."

"Brown Town is on 17. It's not far. Hang on."

The car lurched forward.

***

Somewhere in North Carolina, Bill Hamm, prostrate on a hard floor, stirred once again. His jaw and cheek stung. He opened his eyes in time to receive another blow to the side of his face. A man, arm raised, knelt over him ready to slap again.

"Wake up, Hamm. Wake up. I have to feed you."

Bill tried to lift his head, but his neck muscles refused to respond. His captor forced his mouth open and stuffed some fluid mush in it. At least half missed Bill's mouth and slipped down his cheeks to form a messy mixture on the old floorboards.

"You're worthless Hamm. *They* want you alive, I don't. You're lucky, if it was up to me you'd be taking a dirt nap by now."

He grabbed Bill by the shoulders and propped him against the worn plaster. He unlocked the handcuffs and fastened one to an exposed lead pipe in the wall. The other he tightened about Bill's right wrist. He perched a bowl of grits and milk on the rubble that hid the floor.

"Help yourself. Choke all you want. You'll get your injection when you're done."

Gilles Smets left the room.

Eyes blurred, Bill struggled with one hand to lift the bowl of grits to his lips.

***

******

Chapter 7
Thursday, August 23

In Kinston, North Carolina, Hugh Byrd hung up the phone and turned to Tom Holder, his assistant.

"That was Wilmington. The FBI found Hamm's Accord near Brown Town."

Hugh smashed his fist into his hand.

"I can't believe this. Dr. Smets dumped the car too close to the house."

"Boss, I told him you said to keep Hamm at the old house, but to ditch the car in Wilmington."

"The dumb-ass doctor is stubborn. He always knows best. He doesn't listen. Now we'll have to move Hamm."

"Why not kill Hamm and be done with it."

"Because I want him alive until I set up the frame. He'll take the rap for you and me."

"But why move him? All the FBI has is a burned car."

"My man reports Stew Marks is on the way. He'll find somebody who saw something. And the car is only ten miles from the house. Marks will find it. He's sharp."

Hugh's face went florid.

"Once I feed Hamm to the FBI, I'll dump the arrogant doctor. Meanwhile, that rat has to get Hamm out of that house right away. Give me the damn phone."

He stabbed Smets' number into the instrument.

***

Hugh Byrd's reasoning was dead on. Stew Marks already was at the scene of Hamm's torched vehicle. An oval area of scorched vegetation surrounded the wreck.

Stew and the farmer who had found the car stood to the side while technicians examined the charred remains for evidence. Stew spoke.

"The pines are pretty thick here. How did you find it?"

"Couple of days ago I saw black smoke above the trees. It thinned and disappeared fast and the ground was wet so I figured there was no danger to the woods. Yesterday was the first chance I had to visit. I came looking along the old fire break. And here it was. You see what I found. I didn't touch anything. This is the way it was."

"The firebreak is overgrown, my Ford made it OK, but the techs had a tough time getting the van here."

The farmer rubbed his neck.

"It was no problem for my pickup, some more scratches on the sides, nothing bad."

"Whoever lit the fire must have left in another vehicle, maybe something smaller, a motorcycle or an ATV."

The farmer smiled. *Maybe this city boy knows what he's doing?*

"Thought of that myself. Come with me. I want to show you something."

He led Stew through a thorny tangle of brush. Once clear of the bushes, there was a narrow path that reached through the pines.

The farmer pointed at a bare spot in the sandy soil where the layer of pine needles had been scattered and thrown backwards. He motioned to Stew.

"Mister, that's a bicycle, probably a mountain bike. Only one. The rear wheel spun when he took off. He must have brought a bike on the car. He set the fire and left on this trail."

Stew was elated.

"He couldn't have gone far!"

"I don't know about that, the first pavement is about five miles. Could be a car was there waiting."

"But if they had a second car, why not just bring it here. My guess is there was only one person."

"Could be, that makes sense."

"If he stuck to the woods on the bike where would he end up."

"That depends. The closest farm is the Austen's, but they're a big family. Somebody's always there. They would have noticed, and besides, I already called them. They didn't see anything. In the other direction, there's the old Maynard place. Somebody bought it about two years back. No one lives in it, most times there's nobody there."

He handed Stew a scrap of paper.

"I figured you'd want the directions."

Now Stew was truly excited. He took the paper offered with his left hand while his right seized the farmer's with a firm shake.

"You're a sharp guy. You've been a great help. Thanks a lot. By the way, I'm Stew, Stew Marks."

"Ben Rutledge and you're welcome."

Back at the wreckage, Stew pulled his partner to the side.

"Jack, you go to Wilmington in the van with the techs. Pick up a government car and meet me in Brown Town. I have to check the old "Maynard" place. It's not far, maybe ten miles direct. This shows where."

He handed Jack the paper with Rutledge's directions. Stew had committed them to memory.

Stew turned and left.

***

Gilles Smets M. D. drove slowly. He had no wish to encounter the highway police with a sedated Hamm hidden in the trunk.

He fumed at Byrd's orders to move Hamm. *Byrd, you arrogant ass, never will you talk to me as you did this morning. Never! Hamm should have been dead two days ago. I'll show you how it's done!*

He laughed and jammed the accelerator. Only this morning he had wished a perpetual *dirt-nap* for Hamm, but now he had a better idea. A perpetual *sleep with the fishes* would suit Hamm better.

And Hugh Byrd would have no say in the matter.

Smets would take care of the "Hamm Problem" his own way. He headed north for Surf City and Topsail Island.

***

Dr. Smets was not alone in reevaluating his alliances. At the same time that Smets was heading to Surf City, Hugh Byrd and Tom Holder were approaching the same intersection from the north. Hugh spoke.

"We'll go to Surf City. Smets will meet us there with Hamm. Once we have Hamm, we won't need Smets. I want you to finish him. There's a spot in Pender County where you can dump his body. No one will find him. Here's the map."

Tom, who was driving, kept his eyes on the road and stuffed the map into his pocket.

"And Tom, once we get Hamm, he mustn't see me or hear me. He's never seen you. You'll have to control him."

"No problem."

"Good. Now when we meet Smets, this is what we will do."

The sign ahead indicated left to Surf City and Topsail Island. Tom took the turn.

***

The old Maynard place was set back from the road. Stew Marks parked his car out of sight of the property and followed a path to the rear of the house.

Bingo!

There against the wall was a road-bike with freshly caked mud on its tires.

The rear door was unfastened. He chambered a round in his Beretta and stepped inside. The floor was covered with mounds of fallen plaster and dirt. The once-plastered walls were comprised of exposed slats.

To Stew's right sat several empty aquaria on a long wooden table. Tubing and supplies under the table indicated the tanks were for marine use. On the floor was a manual for the care and feeding of sea turtles.

He entered a large living area. On the floorboards was a pair of handcuffs and a cracked bowl with dried traces of hominy grits. Stains of blood splotched the bare wall that reeked of urine. A prisoner had been fastened here under miserable conditions.

To his right was another door. Stew looked in. The room was spotless. Overhead were batteries of fluorescent lights. To his right, the wall was lined by a lab bench with multiple outlets to which various electronic devices and parts were attached. The equipment appeared new and unused.

What's going on here?

***

At Wayne's house on Topsail Island, Jeannine Ryan sat slumped over a mass of papers on the table. Wayne touched her shoulder. She opened her eyes and looked up.

"I must have dozed. I'm getting nowhere."

"Damn it, Wayne, Bill's in trouble, and I can't help!"

***

******

Chapter 8
Thursday, August 23

Dusk had fallen when Dr. Gilles Smets drove through Surf City in the direction of North Topsail Beach. He had no intention of delivering Hamm to Hugh Byrd. He wanted to rid himself of this burden, and had no desire to hear Byrd lecture him on the mistreatment of his "patient."

It was not Smets' fault that Hamm was too far gone to serve Mr. Byrd's purpose. Per instructions he had kept Hamm incapacitated with low-dose injections of Sodium thiopental. Hell, even Byrd should have known that a large dose of that "truth" drug was the first of three injections in a Texas execution, and the only injection in the single-drug method used in Ohio.

Screw you Byrd and your precious hostage too. What did you expect?

He arrived at his destination, an isolated dock on a marshy creek near the Permuda Island Nature Reserve. Smets was relieved to see two wooden skiffs afloat and tied to the posts.

He opened the trunk of the car and examined his cargo. Hamm's eyes were half-open and his breathing was shallow. Smets pulled the limp form towards him.

"Come on Hamm. Wake up."

He propped Hamm upright on the rear bumper.

"Put your arm around my shoulder and stand up. We're going for a boat ride."

Hamm stared. His left arm reached for Smets' shoulder.

"Good, now lean on me. That's it, take a step. Good. Now step down, into the boat. Here hold onto me."

Eyes glazed, Bill Hamm slumped halfway on the bow seat. The skiff pitched to one side, but Smets leaned his body in the opposite direction and steadied it. He released the frayed rope, seized the oars, and pulled away from the dock.

He headed down the creek in the direction of Permuda Island, dimly discernible in the moon-lit shadows.

***

Sometime later Dr. Smets arrived at Hugh Byrd's rental in Surf City. The house did not front on the beach, nonetheless it was elevated on heavy posts that allowed cars to park under the dwelling. He drove between two posts and cut the motor.

Exterior wooden stairs led to the living level. Smets climbed them briskly. As he entered the great room, Hugh Byrd and Tom Holder stood up in unison. Hugh spoke.

"Where is Hamm?"

"You don't have to worry about him anymore."

"Enough. This isn't a game. Where is he?"

Smets' lips widened into a grin.

"He's dead, drowned. He fell off the boat in the waterway."

Hugh's Glock smashed against his face.

Smets reeled, eyes glazed, grin gone. He shuddered.

Hugh held the Glock ready.

"Smart ass. You killed him!"

Smets lifted one hand defensively. With the other, he tried to stem the blood flowing from his gashed cheek. Still, he managed a level voice.

"It was an accident. He had it coming. He was going to die anyway. Your drug was too powerful."

Hugh pointed his gun at a spot above the doctor's nose. His finger tightened on the trigger.

"You must think I'm stupid."

Smets shrank back.

"No, don't shoot. I lied. I wanted to drown Hamm, but I didn't. He's alive. He's in the trunk of the car."

Hugh's finger relaxed. He signaled to Tom Holder to go check the car.

"All right Doctor, for your sake I hope this time you're telling the truth."

Dr. Smets exhaled and slumped onto the nearby sofa.

***

But the doctor's respite was brief. Tom Holder's voice sounded up from below.

"The trunk's locked. I can't open it. Get the doc's keys."

Hugh turned as Dr. Smets tossed the keys through the air in a high arc. Hugh reacted instinctively. He lowered the Glock and stretched his free hand towards the flying metal.

In that second a desperate Smets was upon him.

Hugh Byrd was bigger and stronger than Smets, but the latter's surging adrenalin gave him a momentary advantage. The Glock was twisted from Hugh's hand and sent skittering across the floor while a ceramic lamp was seized and brought down on Hugh's head. He crumpled to the floor.

From below, Tom Holder heard the sounds of the struggle and rushed up the stairs only to find a dazed Hugh sitting on the floor amid chards of a shattered lamp and the glass doors to the deck wide open.

Tom stepped through the doors to the deck and looked over the rail. No one.

Dr. Smets had jumped. He was gone.

Tom helped the stunned Hugh to a seat. He handed him his Glock and retrieved the keys from the floor. Then he ran down the stairs to Smets' car.

He opened the trunk. It was empty.

No Bill Hamm!

***

Stew Marks was frustrated. He had found no trace of Bill Hamm at the Maynard house, though from its proximity to

Hamm's burned vehicle he was sure that Hamm had been a recent occupant. Was that Hamm's blood on the floor? Had he been the prisoner? That makes no sense, or does it?

Moreover Stew had no explanation for the new laboratory equipment he had found there, or for the marine aquaria.

The refrigerator had not been stocked with food for a lengthy stay. Either Hamm had not planned to be there long, or he had been too pressed by pursuit to stock up fully.

Curiously, Stew had found several unopened bottles of Sodium thiopental in the fridge. He knew that drug by its trade name, Sodium Pentothal. What use had Hamm for that? For the prisoner?

He called his partner Jack in Wilmington. Stew described his misgivings about the Maynard house.

"I'm sure Hamm was there, but he's gone. There was no trace of Ryan. You stay in Wilmington, Hamm may be headed that way. I'm going to spend the night on the island. My guess is that Hamm is nearby."

He added.

"And Jack, get a forensics team out there to check the house. There are some odd things about that place. I'm starting to wonder about Hamm."

"Will do, but don't wonder too much about Hamm. The guy is a rat. And the boss in DC called. He wants us to fry this scumbag. I do too. I told you what he did to me at the hearing on the Unity Pavilion."

Stew paused. For sure, Hamm *had* stolen the documents.

"OK, Jack."

But Stew did not tell Jack that there was no sign that Jeannine Ryan had been at the Maynard house, no indication of a feminine presence.

Maybe Ryan's OK? Maybe she doesn't know anything?

He shook his head clear. The woman was good looking and had spunk, but such traits were found as often in the guilty as in the innocent.

Cool it, Stew, you have a job to do. This isn't like you.

Once in his car, his objectivity reasserted itself. As he drove to Surf City, he had a single question.

Hamm, what were you doing at the Maynard house?

***

The small power boat cruised the Intracoastal Waterway near Permuda Island while Jimmy Sands scanned the dark marsh edge with the searchlight.

"Slow down Amy. I saw something. It might be a turtle."

"Jimmy, my dad wants me back by midnight. Besides it's late for turtle nesting, and anyway they nest on the beach side."

"I know, but I saw something over there by the mouth of that creek. If it is a turtle, it must be sick, stranded on the mudflat like that. Head over there, it will only take a minute. We could tow it to the turtle rehab hospital on Topsail."

"It's my dad's boat, and what you are saying will take more than a minute."

"Amy, please. Your dad will understand. Please."

At that final "please" Amy swung the boat about and slowed the engine as they entered the shallow water of the flats. In turn, Jimmy swung the search light along the border of marsh grass.

"There it is. Get closer. Pull up the motor. I'll pole us."

Amy tilted the propeller out of the water, while Jimmy pushed one of the oars into the mud and shoved.

"Jimmy, that's close enough. We'll get stuck."

Jimmy nodded and stepped out of the boat. His foot sank six inches into a muddy bottom that was topped by over a foot of water. He sloshed towards the unknown form and shone his light on it.

"Amy! It's not a turtle, it's a man!"

"Jimmy, don't joke like that."

"Amy, it's no joke. This guy is alive. His head's on a mat of vegetation and he's breathing. Toss me your life vest. If I can turn him on his back, I think I can float him to the boat."

With Amy pulling and Jimmy pushing, they managed to force the unconscious stranger over the side and into the craft.

Once again Jimmy used an oar to push the boat across the shallow flats. Several strenuous minutes later they attained the deep water of the Intracoastal Waterway.

Amy lowered the propeller and revved the motor. At full speed she headed down the waterway towards Surf City and the Urgent Care Center.

She could call her father from there.

***

At his house on Topsail Island, Wayne Johnson looked into Jeannine's bedroom. She was asleep on top of the covers. He loosened the laces of her shoes and slipped them off her feet.

He shut her door and looked out the sliding doors. The air lay still over the abandoned beach. White lines sparkled in the moonlight where the waves broke over offshore bars.

Perhaps tomorrow their analyses of the briefcase would lead to Bill's whereabouts and prove his innocence.

Wayne went to his room and turned off the light.

His last thought before he dropped off was a welcome one.

I'm useful again.

***

In his room in Surf City, Stew Marks slipped under the sheets. He lay there, studying the shadows on the ceiling. *Hamm you're lucky to have a woman like Ryan, spy or not.*

***

******

Chapter 9
Friday, August 24

At Wayne's beach house, Jeannine Ryan awoke to the aroma of fresh coffee. She slipped out of bed. Her jeans had slept-in wrinkles, but she opted to keep them on. *Who cares? I'm not going anywhere. This is the beach, right?*

At the table her laptop had been moved to make room for a plate filled with eggs, bacon and home fries. She sat and Wayne appeared with a cup of coffee.

"Wayne, you're spoiling me."

"Why not? Eat up."

Jeannine stabbed a potato chunk with her fork and spun it in the yellow yolk of an egg. She looked up as Wayne went to the door.

"Jeannine, I have to go. A neighbor says that two teens, turtle-patrol volunteers, pulled a man out of the Intracoastal Waterway last night. They took him to the Urgent Care Center in Surf City. This morning an ambulance took the guy to Onslow Memorial Hospital in Jacksonville. He's in bad shape. From his description he could be Bill."

She jumped from her chair.

"I'm going with you."

"No. You keep eating. It's going to be a long day and besides this may be a bum lead. It may not be Bill."

She glared, but he was not intimidated.

"Look, no one knows you're here. Let's keep it that way. Whoever followed you to Camp Geiger knows you have the briefcase. No one knows me, I'll go. You relax and eat."

He pointed to the documents strewn on the table.

"And work on those papers if you want to help Bill."

Jeannine wanted to argue, but he was right.

"All right, Wayne."

"Stay inside. I'll be back in two hours. If this guy in the hospital is Bill, these people are killers."

He left. Jeannine rose and threw the deadbolt on the door. She went back to the table, pushed her plate aside and replaced it with the laptop.

Bill?

***

In Surf City Stew Marks' phone vibrated. It was his partner, Jack Marino in Wilmington.

"Stew, were you asleep?"

"No matter, what have you got?"

"Zero, zip, nada! The resident agency guys are helping me, and the locals are on the lookout, but there's no trace of Hamm or Ryan. Nowhere!"

"Jack, look around Wilmington. Hamm has to be nearby. I'll check North Topsail and Jacksonville."

"What if Hamm has gone inland. We'd both miss him."

"Not likely. At Wilson, Ryan was headed for the coast, and Hamm dumped his car here. No, they're trying to meet on the coast. This is where we'll look."

As Stew clicked off, he thought of the shapely redhead. *No Mr. Hamm you are definitely near her. You're nearby.*

His facts were wrong, but his conclusion was correct.

Stew was hungry, but he would eat later in North Topsail. He had several interviews there in the afternoon. When done with those, he would take Route 210 off the island and go to Jacksonville.

***

Hugh Byrd's head throbbed. The ceramic lamp in that damned doctor's hands had left a thin red line of broken skin next to a swollen lump on top of his skull. He headed for the sink and downed two Advil.

76

He stepped into the living area where Tom Holder waited. Hugh spoke.

"Any trace of the doctor? We have his car, he can't be far."

"The neighbor across the way saw a guy jump from the deck. She thought he was drunk or high on drugs. She thinks we had a wild party. The man ran off limping, towards the beach."

"Where could he go to treat his leg?"

"He could treat himself, or there's an Urgent Care Center across the bridge."

"Smets is a whiner. He went to that clinic. Let's go."

"What about Ryan"

"Smets, first."

Byrd holstered his Glock. Ms. Ryan could wait. His beef with the doctor was now personal!

***

The nurse at the Surf City Urgent Care Center was professional. When Hugh Byrd flashed his badge, she consulted her computer

"Yes, we did treat someone with an ankle sprain last night. His name was 'Smets.' He was treated and discharged just after midnight. There's no address."

Hugh smiled.

"Thanks anyway. You've been a big help."

Hugh turned to leave as a young doctor approached the counter and spoke.

"Nurse, is Joe back with the ambulance yet?"

"Not yet. He took our 'John Doe' to Onslow Memorial in Jacksonville. It's a long way. It's lunch time, maybe he grabbed a bite to eat. Give him another thirty minutes."

"Let me know when he returns. I have another transport."

Hugh Byrd returned to the nurse.

"About your 'John Doe,' when did he arrive?"

"Last night, just after midnight. Two teens found him in the waterway. He was transferred to Jacksonville this morning."

Hugh nodded to her and left. Back in the car, he spoke."

"Smets was here. Even better, we may have found Hamm. Looks like Smets meant it when he said Hamm went overboard."

"Who do we go after? Hamm, Ryan or Smets."

"Hamm is the most important, but if that 'John Doe' is him, he'll be at that hospital in Jacksonville at least today and tomorrow. He can wait. We don't know where Ryan is. That rat Smets must be nearby. I'll settle him first."

He smashed his hand with his fist and handed Tom the keys.

"You drive, I've got a headache. There's a deli back in Surf City near the traffic light. Drive there. I need to think."

Hugh touched his head gingerly.

Damn you Smets.

He closed his eyes as Tom drove.

***

From his post across the street from the Surf City Urgent Care Center, Dr. Gilles Smets watched the Ford Excursion with Tom Holder and Hugh Byrd disappear down the street.

Smets started walking. He took out his phone and punched the number for GES in Northern Virginia.

Denise Guerry answered. Smets stammered.

"I'm in trouble. Byrd wants to kill me. He has my car keys. I have no car and I've got a bad ankle."

"You're afraid of Byrd?"

"I'm a lab person. I have no weapon, and besides, there are two of them. Holder is with him. I need help."

"And my new electronics lab?"

"Byrd made me evacuate. He said the FBI was onto us."

78

"So now my new tracking lab is lost. That equipment was valuable. It was to back up Sullivan's work at Topsail. You should have consulted me before keeping Hamm there. Damn it, Smets, you work for me, not Byrd."

"I was afraid to say no to Byrd, and he sent Hamm here with Holder. That man's a thug."

"All right. Where is Hamm now? Is he alive?"

"No. I dumped him in the Intracoastal Waterway. That's why Byrd tried to kill me. I need help."

"All right, I'll handle Byrd. Where are you?"

"In Surf City not far from the bridge."

"There's a park on the island by the Surf City bridge. Go there and wait. I'll send Henri to pick you up. He'll be there in an hour."

Smets limped towards the Surf City bridge.

***

In Wilmington, North Carolina, Henri Duval sat in the McDonald's across from the hotel and sipped his coffee.

As a Frenchman, he felt heretical eating fast food, but he had learned to enjoy American "sandwiches." The Yanks knew how to create flavor between two pieces of bread unlike in his native land where a ham sandwich might be an unadorned dry slab slapped between the halves of a baguette.

At age 38 Henri Duval was tall, fair-skinned, and a man of action. An agile 100 kilos (220 pounds) and a "silver glove" in the French kickboxing martial art, *la boxe-française Savate*. Anyone caught in a *bagarre* or street fight would be happy to have Henri on their side.

And Henri knew his weapons. For a handgun, he preferred a 9 mm Belgian-made Browning. He was equally handy with an M16 or an AK47, but his favorite assault weapon was the French rifle, *le FAMAS G2*, a modification of the *FAMAS F1* he had used during his service in *Operation Turquoise* during the genocide in Rwanda in 1994.

79

Henri had been in Wilmington a week, doing nothing, waiting for instructions. No matter, the pay was excellent. Besides, he was not far from Florence, South Carolina where his friend, Angelique Uwimana, a Tutsi from Rwanda, was studying for her Ph. D. in Computer Science at Carolina Technical University.

He had just finished his McDonald's "Quarter Pounder" when his cell phone vibrated. It was the boss, Denise Guerry.

"Henri, pick up Doctor Smets. He's in some sort of trouble with Byrd. He's at a park in Surf City, just after you cross the bridge. You must leave now. And don't let Byrd hurt Smets. If he tries, stop him, permanently if necessary."

Before Henri could respond the line was broken.

Henri Duval frowned. He did not like Dr. Smets. Smets' inability to look him in the eye plus his whiny voice told Henri never to trust the man.

Moreover, Smets, a Belgian, had worked at a government clinic in Kigali during the Rwandan holocaust. Most Belgians had fled the country after Rwandese troops murdered the moderate Hutu Prime Minister, Agathe Uwilingiyimana, along with the Belgian-UN peacekeepers assigned to protect her.

Dr. Smets could not have worked at that clinic unless the genocidal government had regarded him as a friend.

But per instructions, Henri drove to Surf City and crossed the bridge to the island. He pulled onto the shoulder and sounded the horn.

Smets rose from a park bench and limped towards the car.

"*Montez.* Get in."

"Denise told you about me and Byrd?"

Henri nodded.

Smets fell silent. Henri turned the car about and crossed the bridge back to the mainland.

***

Driving on Route 210, Stew Marks headed to Jacksonville. The low western sun was in his eyes as he crossed the bridge from North Topsail to the mainland. His phone vibrated anew. It was his partner, Jack Marino.

"Stew, where are you."

"On 210, I just left Topsail Island."

"We've caught a break on Ryan. Some years ago, she worked for a company called StatFind in Rockville, Maryland. Her boss was named Wayne Johnson. His company no longer exists, but it seems he was fond of her."

"OK, I've stopped. What's your point."

"Wayne Johnson's wife died last year, and his house in Rockville is up for sale. He has another house. It's in Topsail Beach not far from Mile Seven after the traffic light in Surf City. I think Ryan is there."

Stew's tires squealed as he swung a "U" across the highway and headed back over the bridge.

He was maybe an hour away.

Stew hammered the accelerator.

***

In the deli in Surf City, Hugh Byrd and Tom Holder took a table where Tom ordered a Reuben. Byrd ordered a coke, unfolded his phone on the table, and sat staring.

Tom's sandwich arrived. He forced his fork through the toasted rye and corned beef covered with dressing. The sandwich disappeared.

"That was good. Hugh, what's with you? You going to eat?"

Hugh Byrd felt his phone vibrate.

"That wuss Smets has called Chantilly by now. This must be Denise to tell me to lay off the rat."

He counted to five before picking up. The caller was, indeed, Denise Guerry.

"Byrd, you idiot! What did you do to Smets? He's scared witless."

"That witless rat tried to kill me."

"Only after you tried to kill him, Byrd, you will screw up the whole operation. Leave Smets alone. We need him. He's off limits."

A pause.

"Get my papers back!"

"OK, but Smets tried to kill Hamm, and failed. And I think Hamm is the 'John Doe' in Onslow Memorial Hospital in Jacksonville. I can go there if you want me to."

"No! It's Ryan who has my documents and security tokens. We found her. She's at her old boss's house in Topsail. You take care of Ryan."

She took a breath and continued.

"Here are the directions."

Hugh listened and hung up. He turned to Tom.

"Is the M16 in the trunk?"

Tom nodded.

"Extra magazines?"

"Two."

"Good. Ryan is here in Topsail, she's only minutes from here."

Tom smirked.

***

******

Chapter 10
Friday, August 24

The sun was low in the west when Wayne Johnson returned to Topsail from the hospital in Jacksonville. Jeannine jumped to her feet as he entered.

"Was it Bill?"

Wayne nodded. Jeannine grabbed his arm.

"How is he?"

"They didn't want to give me details, but when they saw I was trying to help they eased up. He's in bad shape. His blood chemistries are bad, some liver problem. He has high levels of Sodium Pentothal in his system, multiple contusions and bruises, and a severe lung infection, bacterial pneumonia."

"'Sodium Pentothal,' that's Sodium thiopental, the 'Truth Drug.' But why?"

"My guess is someone kept him captive and sedated him. The bruises would confirm that he was beaten."

"They could have been caused by a fall, like off a boat."

"It's possible, but my guess is that someone beat him."

"And the pneumonia?"

"Extended submersion, near-drowning, water in the lungs There's plenty of salt water bacteria available for an infection."

"But they think he'll be OK?"

"His condition is 'serious' whatever that means."

"It's not as bad as 'critical,' but it's not good. Does the hospital know who he is? Has the FBI showed up?"

"He's still a 'John Doe' and no they haven't yet, but they will. And there's no question of moving him. He definitely needs to stay in the hospital."

"Damn it Wayne, we have to get him out of there before the FBI."

"Jeannine, you can't just walk in there and pick him up. They won't let you. And besides, FBI or not, Bill needs to be there. There's no way he should be moved before Tuesday at the earliest."

Wayne paused.

"Besides who would you tell them you are? The FBI is looking for Jeannine Ryan."

"There has to be something we can do."

"The best thing you can do for Bill is to discover what these documents are all about. I think you should get back to work."

Jeannine said nothing.

She reached for the nearest stack of papers.

***

Not far from Wayne Johnson's house, Tom Holder and Hugh Byrd sat in their Ford Excursion. Hugh sipped his coffee.

"This damned coffee is cold."

"If you hadn't made us wait, it wouldn't be cold."

"I'll explain it again. One, we work for the government. No one must see us. Two, we saw Ryan in the house and she hasn't left. She's there. Three, when it's dark, you slip in and drop her without anyone, even her, seeing you. Four, you grab the papers and the briefcase and get out."

"What about the old guy, Johnson."

"No witnesses, clear?"

"But those cars that drove by us. Somebody may track our plates."

Hugh Byrd finished his coffee.

"Tom, anyone tracing these plates will reach a dead end. Our agency has ensured that."

Dusk settled on the island. In the dim light, a light breeze arose ocean-side to cool the interior of the SUV. Hugh Byrd fingered his Glock 9 mm. He spoke.

"It's time. Leave the lights off. The house across from Johnson's is closed for the season. Park underneath. Take the M16 and an extra magazine. I'll watch outside."

Tom started the engine.

***

Inside Wayne's house, Jeannine sat at a table covered with papers. She inserted a CD in her laptop.

"Wayne, turn on the lights, it's too dark. And come here I have something to show you."

Wayne peered at the numbers on her laptop.

3,
193371674391874652305930928006424884238338012711224574537062080912262053521320466482768666098820376112997167899457604871289298749069957987472412683257576674034708021769751187540931

He noted the number "3" followed by a much larger number.

"Jeannine, that looks like a key for RSA encryption."

"It is, and someone found the two prime factors. See."

She scrolled the screen downwards. Two numbers appeared.

439740462536567872185054745479877671835453694834744161588364635383902840114487291478823507

439740462536567872185054745479877671835453694834744161588364635383902840114487291478823633

"These last two numbers both pass the probability tests for primes. Multiplied together they give that large number. Their product and the number '3' make someone's public key."

Wayne spoke.

"But you need the private key to decode a message."

"Right, but if you know the two prime factors, like those above, you always can calculate the private key."

"Jeannine, the National Security Agency says each prime should have 2048 bits. Even a 1024-bit prime has over 300 digits. That's much more than the ninety digits that these primes have."

"Right again. And these two primes only differ in the last five places. They're too close together. This public key is weak. But whatever the number of bits, once you know the prime factors, nothing is secure and any standard is irrelevant!"

She brought up another file.

"Anyway, there are more key pairs in this file, and most meet the 2048-bit standard. And here's a file that links these keys to major members of the European Union. Their communications are not secure. An enemy would give a fortune for this list."

She rubbed her forehead.

"Some of the decoded memos are in French. They're official communications between France, Belgium and Francophone countries in Africa like Benin, Niger, Chad or Cameroon. Wait. Here are some in English. Here's one from Rwanda to the State Department."

"Jeannine, for RSA decryption, you need to factor the product of the primes. When that product is large, no computer is fast enough to factor it. Maybe someone stole these factors?"

She sat a moment before speaking.

"Yes, but who? And how did Bill get them?"

"You have to face the possibility that Bill stole them himself. He was or is a CIA agent, remember."

Jeannine flushed. Auburn hair flying, she jumped to her feet.

"I reject that. Bill is no traitor!"

Before Wayne could react, the glass doors to the deck disintegrated inwards from bursts of automatic fire.

"BrBrBrup, ..., BrBrBrup..., BrBrBrup."

The chair that Jean had left a split second earlier, shattered and splintered apart.

Wayne shouted.

"Down!"

He hit the light switch and dropped to the floor. He whispered through the darkness.

"Jeannine, are you OK?"

A low moan reached his ears.

***

Wayne's eyes adjusted to the dark. He saw Jeannine, on the floor, holding her leg. He crawled to her. An inch-long something protruded from her thigh.

"It's a piece of wood from the chair, hold still."

He felt her jeans. They were damp but not soaked.

"I don't think it hit a vessel. Hang on. I'm pulling it out."

He tore off a piece of his shirt and grasped the wood. It came out. He pressed the wound and wrapped the leg tight.

"It's stopped bleeding. Can you move?"

In answer Jeannine crawled under the table. They lay in the dark, their eyes on the shattered door and the dim deck. A slight breeze came off the ocean and rustled the wind chimes on the deck, but otherwise nothing moved outside.

They waited.

Out on the deck a shadow passed across the empty doorway. Whoever it was, was in no hurry.

Jeannine whispered.

"Wayne, do you have a gun?"

"There's a shotgun in the broom closet, and some loose shells in the dish on the shelf. He can't see us. I'll get it."

But Jeannine already had crawled to the closet. She reached up and softly turned the door handle. The door opened on oiled hinges, no squeaks. *Thank God.*

She reached inside and felt a large barrel, a 12-gauge. *Good.*

Jeannine had grown up in West Virginia and knew shotguns. This one was an old single-shot Iver Johnson. She broke it open and inserted a cartridge. In the dark she could not tell if the load was buckshot or birdshot. Whatever, it would have to do.

Wayne hissed a warning.

She looked up. The dark shadow had stepped through the gaping doorway.

Fiery flashes filled the room.

"BrBrBrup, ..., BrBrBrup, ..., BrBrBrup."

The drywall behind Jeannine crumbled and cracked along a line shoulder-high.

More three-round bursts.

"BrBrBrup, ..., BrBrBrup, ..., BrBrBrup."

This time the deadly line was only chest-high.

"BrBrBrup."

Lower still.

She heard the clank as an empty magazine hit the floor. A sharp click followed.

The shooter had reloaded.

No time to wait! She squeezed the trigger.

"Brroom."

88

The old shotgun slammed her shoulder. Buckshot rattled what was left of the sliding doors. The shadowy figure cursed, tumbled backwards and crashed against the railing of the deck.

Jeannine shoved another cartridge into the old gun. Hopefully, it too was buckshot.

Wayne signaled her not to move and crept towards the opening. Seconds passed. Finally he stood.

"You hit him good. But he had a partner. They've gone. They wanted these papers."

Jeannine limped to the table. She stuffed papers and CD's into the sac-like briefcase.

"Wayne, we have to go. They'll be back!"

"You're right, but the guy you hit needs serious patching. That'll buy us some time. I hope they didn't trash our tires."

He picked up her laptop and started down the stairs. Clutching the case and shotgun, Jeannine limped after him.

***

No lights shone from Wayne Johnson's beach house when Stew Marks drove onto the sandy driveway. His headlights shone on the wooden posts that lifted the structure one floor off the ground. There were no cars.

Stew called out.

"FBI, Anybody home?"

There was no answer. He mounted the wooden stairway, but the door at the top of the steps was dead-bolted.

"FBI, Anybody here? Anybody?"

Silence. He descended and circled to the left where a wooden walk stretched through the sea oats to the beach. At the house end, the walk rose on steps to a wide deck that fronted the dwelling. With his flashlight Stew climbed to the deck.

What the Hell?

The sliding doors had disintegrated into piles of crumbled safety glass. Gripping flashlight and Beretta together, he looked through the gaping entryway. Splintered chairs, an overturned lamp and smashed vases lay in disarray on the floor. The wall opposite was pock-marked with lines of holes.

Brass objects glinted in the beam of his light. They were 45 mm long casings, caliber 5.56 mm, either from a "Military" M16 or a "Civilian" AR15. More than two dozen of them littered the deck, surely automatic fire. But that meant the weapon was an M16, legally available only to the military, the police, and Fed types.

Inside, one of the chairs was stained with blood. Outside, abundant drips on the deck led to dark splotches on the railing where bloody hands had grasped for support.

He called Jack Marino in Wilmington.

"I need you and an FBI crime crew out here right away. This case has turned deadly."

He went back inside. Something, or someone, had dragged itself through the debris on the floor. *Ryan?* He saw strands of reddish hair in the splintered wood. His stomach knotted.

Jeannine's hurt! Where is she?

***

******

Chapter 11
Saturday, August 25

The morning sun shone through the windows of Captain Peter Hume's quarters at Camp Geiger. Jeannine limped into the kitchenette where Peter and Wayne Johnson sat at the table.

Wayne looked up.

"How's the leg? How do you feel?"

"Better, but you shouldn't have let me sleep. We have to go, I mean, I have to go."

"What?"

Jeannine looked away from Wayne to Peter.

"Can I talk to Wayne alone for a minute?"

Peter left the room.

"Wayne, I can't stay here. The FBI wants me, and I shouldn't get the Captain in trouble. What's more, I'm going to get Bill out of the hospital before the FBI gets there."

"You're right about Peter. We shouldn't involve him in our troubles. But you're wrong about Bill. Even if he is able to leave the hospital, you can't get him out without revealing who he is, and who you are. It's dangerous and it won't work."

"But it will! I found this in his briefcase. Remember, Bill was covert CIA."

She waved a passport at him.

This is issued to 'Walter Harmon,' but it's Bill's. It has his photo. I'll identify the 'John Doe' in Onslow Memorial as 'Walt Harmon' using this ID. But I have to hurry. Whoever tried to kill us is hunting for Bill, and so is the FBI. I'm taking my Subaru. It can't stay here. You can follow in your car."

Jeannine stood and rubbed her leg. Wayne took her arm.

"But you're hurt.

"So is Bill, and a lot worse than me. Are you coming?"

She pushed past him and shouted.

"Thanks for everything, Peter."

And was gone.

***

In Chantilly, Virginia, Denise Guerry punched Henri's number.

"Henri, where are you?"

"I'm at the farm in Pender County."

"Did you extract Doctor Smets."

"Yes and he's safe here. Byrd doesn't know this farm."

"Henri, listen. Byrd messed up at Topsail. Holder was shot and hurt bad. Byrd took him to the VA hospital in Fayetteville. They'll ask no questions because of Byrd's cover."

She paused and added.

"But Byrd is crazy! Ryan is on the run with my documents and all he can think of is Smets. Henri, can you assist me?"

"I'm here."

"Good. There's a 'John Doe' in Onslow Memorial Hospital in Jacksonville. Byrd thinks it's Hamm. If so Ryan may be close by. It's our only lead. How far away are you from there?"

"Over an hour, but I can leave now. What about Byrd?"

"He lost our papers and failed to retrieve them, plus he led the Feds to the new electronics lab. He's no longer of use. SÉGAG wants him eliminated. Kill him, but no one must find his body. He's a U.S. government agent."

"Understood."

She hung up.

***

Henri Duval put his "Grande Puissance" pistol into his shoulder holster. The "Hi-Power" Browning, with its 13 round magazine, was his favorite handgun.

92

Denise Guerry, had asked for his help. SÉGAG wanted him to eliminate Byrd.

"Henri, can you assist me? SÉGAG wants him eliminated."
A request, not a command!

He visualized her blue eyes, no longer aloof and imperious, but soft and alluring.

Denise was very desirable.

Perhaps?

He shook his head.

Calm yourself, Henri, you cannot trust this woman. Watch out!

Reason returned.

Why me?

Denise had others to do her bidding. Henri's job as security officer with SÉGAG was to protect people. He had taken lives, but only in defense of others or himself. He was no assassin. He guarded others from such killers.

And once SÉGAG no longer needed Henri?

The answer was obvious.

The killer of a government agent like Byrd would be tracked down, no matter the cost.

Still, the image of the beautiful Denise floated before him.

Perhaps, after all? Why not?

Done!

The drive to the hospital in Jacksonville would take over an hour. Smets would stay at the farm. The wimp would have to babysit himself.

Henri went to his car.

***

At the Onslow Memorial Hospital, a young doctor named Smith examined Stew Marks badge.

93

"FBI, what can I do for you Agent Marks?"

"Admissions told me you have a 'John Doe' on this ward."

"That's right. End of the corridor, the door on your left. Do you think you know who he is?"

But Stew was already in the corridor.

"Wait, Sir. You can't go alone. I need to go with you."

Stew reached the door as the doctor caught up. They entered the room together. The bed near the door was not occupied and the window bed was obscured by a drawn curtain.

Dr. Smith pulled it aside. Stew stared.

The rumpled sheets were rolled back. The bed was empty.

Stew Marks looked at the doctor. The latter was already in the hallway.

"Nurse Wells, where is the patient in 213?"

"You mean Mr. Harmon, Walter Harmon."

"How do you know his name?"

"His sister picked him up an hour ago. She had his passport. He was Walter Harmon all right."

"Who authorized the discharge?"

"Dr. Omani was on duty. It would have been him."

Stew Marks broke in.

"Did you see Harmon's sister? What did she look like?"

Nurse Wells glanced at Dr. Smith. He nodded approval.

She turned back to Stew.

"She had Auburn hair, quite red actually. Around thirty, dressed casually, jeans. Trim, maybe 5 foot five. She said she wanted to move her brother to a hospital close to DC."

"Did you see her car?"

"No. Sue Lacy wheeled Mr. Harmon to the front door. She might have seen it, but she's off this afternoon."

Stew turned to Dr. Smith.

"Can you get me a phone number for that nurse."

Smith nodded. Stew turned back to Nurse Wells.

"Thanks, you've been helpful. One last question, was anyone else with the sister when she picked up her brother?"

"No one that I saw."

***

Once outside the hospital, Stew Marks called his partner Jack Marino.

"Jack, I'm at the hospital in Jacksonville, The 'John Doe' *was* Hamm, but Ryan picked him up. She's probably in her Subaru. Get out a bulletin on it."

He added.

"I'm going to Surf City. I want you to leave Wilmington and meet me there in an hour."

Stew sighed. Though he had failed to find Hamm, he was relieved. Ryan had survived the fight at the beach house.

Jeannine was OK.

He was on Route 17 headed to Surf City when his partner called back.

"Stew, we have a hit on Ryan's Subaru. It's parked outside the Food Lion at the Surf City turnoff. How far away are you?"

"It's right ahead. I'll be there in two minutes."

Stew swung to the left. Seconds later, he turned right into the supermarket lot. Ahead, near the entrance was Jeannine's Subaru.

The car was empty.

***

Stew Marks scanned the lot in front of the Food Lion Super Market before calling his partner.

"Jack, I'm at Ryan's car. It's still at the Food Lion. She must be in the store."

95

At the sound of a motor he turned.

"Wait a minute, Jack. Someone's stopping. I'll call back."

A man emerged from the car. Stew started.

"Hugh Byrd, what are you doing here?"

"The same as you, looking for Ryan. This is her Subaru."

Byrd smiled. Stew frowned.

"Where is your man Holder?"

"Where is yours? Where's Marino?"

"He's on the way. Now where is Holder?"

"He had an accident. He was reassigned."

"Come clean, Hugh. Why are you here?"

"OK. Like you, I heard about a 'John Doe' at the hospital in Jacksonville. I was there when you came out empty-handed, so I figured it wasn't Hamm. I followed you here hoping you had a lead. Seems I was right."

Hugh had left his door open. Stew noted an object on the passenger-side floor.

"Hugh, is that an M16 magazine on the floor?"

Hugh slammed the door shut.

"So what if it is?"

Stew recalled the M16 cartridges on the deck of Johnson's beach house.

"Do you know Wayne Johnson?

"Johnson? Never heard of him."

"He has a beach house on Topsail Island. There was a fire fight at that house yesterday. One of the attackers was bloodied."

"What do you mean 'fire fight?' This isn't Afghanistan."

"I mean a bloody mess. And an M16 was involved."

"What are you trying to say?"

"Hugh, was Holder shot? Was that the accident?"

But Hugh Byrd was done answering questions. He strode to his car.

"Sorry Stew, that's classified."

Stew stared after him, but there was no time to evaluate Hugh Byrd's behavior.

A man was approaching Jeannine's Subaru.

***

The man opened the door of the Subaru and put his groceries on the front seat. Stew Marks stepped forward and held out his badge.

"FBI, Sir. I'm Agent Marks. May I know your name?"

"Johnson, Wayne Johnson. Is this about my beach house?"

"First, tell me where Dr. Ryan is. This is her car."

"I don't know. She's afraid for her life. You should be protecting her."

"Mr. Johnson, she's on the run. We can't protect her if we can't find her. Why do you have her car?"

"She needed mine. My tank was full, hers was near empty."

"Needed yours? And you think you're helping her! Mr. Johnson what kind of car do you drive. I need the Make, Model, Year and License Plate. Now!"

Wayne complied. Stew called Jack Marino and gave him the information about Wayne's Buick. He turned back to Wayne.

"Sir, If you really wanted to help Ms. Ryan you should have called us from the hospital. How long is it since you saw her?"

"Maybe four hours."

"And this guy Hamm is with her?"

"I assume so. Yes."

"He's a fugitive. Damn it, you both are aiding a fugitive!"

"But Jeannine's in danger. They tried to kill her."

"And you suppose she's not in danger now! What the hell were you thinking?"

A chastened Wayne mumbled.

"Maybe I need a lawyer."

At the word "Lawyer," Stew exploded.

"Damn right you do. Put your hands behind your back."

Stew cuffed Wayne.

"Sir, you are under arrest. You have the right to remain silent. You have the right to consult an attorney and to have an attorney with you when questioned. If you cannot afford an attorney, one will be provided to you at no cost. Anything you say or do may be used against you in a court of law."

Stew paused.

"Do you understand these rights?"

At Wayne's affirmative nod, Stew continued.

"Knowing and understanding your rights as I just explained, are you willing to answer my questions now, while no attorney is with you?"

The barrage of legalese had left Wayne in shock. He shook his head.

"No!"

At this point Jack Marino arrived. Stew turned to him.

"Have the Subaru towed to our lot in Wilmington, and have our forensics guys go over it. I'll meet you in Wilmington."

Stew pushed Wayne into his back seat.

"Damn it, Mr. Johnson, you should have called us. Your friend Ryan has crossed the line. I can't help her now."

Puzzled by that last comment, Wayne stayed silent as Agent Marks drove south towards Wilmington.

✳✳✳

✳✳✳✳✳✳

Chapter 12
Saturday, August 25

Hugh Byrd sped out of the Food Lion parking lot. He turned south onto Route 17, towards Wilmington.

Damn you Marks. So you think I was at the beach house with Holder, because of that damn spent magazine.

There had been no possibility of retrieving the empty casings from the house. The large number of them would have indicated automatic fire and a "Military" M16 rather than the "Civilian" AR15. Still the magazine could fit either. But Marks knew that Hugh had access to M16's.

Hugh ground his teeth.

Watch it, Marks! I'll declare you a security risk and you will be finished at the FBI.

Hugh shrugged. Forget Hamm, Ryan and Marks. He had a personal matter to attend to, that idiot Smets.

His phone vibrated, Denise Guerry's number. He picked up.

"Where are you, Hugh?"

"North Carolina, near Surf City."

"Hugh, do not harm Dr. Smets. Leave him alone, understood?"

"How could I hurt him? I don't know where you hid him."

Denise hung up.

Hugh laughed. He was a good investigator. Of course he knew about the "safe" farm.

And he was sure that Smets would be there!

***

Denise Guerry realized that she had underestimated Hugh. His complacency on the phone surely meant that he knew the "safe" farm in Pender County. He would look for Smets there. She had to act fast.

She called Henri Duval.

"Henri, where are you?"

"Near Onslow hospital, driving north on route 17."

"Turn around. Byrd is on the way to the farm. He is going to kill Smets. You have to stop him."

"But Hamm?"

"The Ryan woman picked him up from the hospital. She's headed north, probably to Maryland. I have someone waiting for her there."

Her tone shifted.

"*S'il te plaît*, Henri, do this for me. *Je t'assure*, I know how to return favors."

Her silken tone left no doubt as to what "favors" meant. Henri succumbed.

"All right, I won't let Byrd harm Smets."

But Henri had decided. He only would act in self-defense. If Byrd tried to kill the wimp, Smets, only then would he kill Byrd.

***

At a motel northwest of Wilmington, North Carolina, Angelique Uwimana knocked on the door. She was a Ph. D. student in Computer Science at Carolina Technical University in Florence, South Carolina. A Tutsi, she alone of her family had survived the Rwandan genocide.

At 28, Angelique was tall and willowy, almost statuesque. She stared at the even taller man who cracked the door open.

"Paul, let me in. Why did you want to see me?"

The man, Paul Mutabazi, opened. He ignored the question.

"Angelique, how did you meet this Duval, this Frenchman, of yours?"

"In Silver Spring, Maryland, when I was studying for my Masters at Maryland. Why?"

"You know he works for GES?"

"Of course."

"Be careful of him, GES is not on our side. Does he know you are here?"

"No, Henri thinks I'm in Florence. He was to meet me there yesterday, but he didn't show. I suppose he had business somewhere."

"Business? You mean the Guerry woman?"

She shrugged.

"Never mind, Angelique. This is the reason I asked you to meet me here."

He drew a newsprint photograph from his wallet and unfolded it. The photo was soiled, but not faded. He placed it on the dresser before her.

An involuntary cry escaped her lips. Tears formed as memories of her encounter with the man in the photo overwhelmed her. She sobbed. The years had not healed the hurt. She shut her eyes. Mutabazi's voice sounded in her ears.

"Is this the man?"

She opened her eyes and nodded affirmatively.

"Look again, this is important."

She could never forget that face. She nodded again.

"So you are sure? This is that dog, Dr. Smets?"

Angelique finally found her voice, albeit only a whisper.

"*Yego.* Yes."

Paul Mutabazi folded the photograph and replaced it in his wallet.

"*Murakoze, Angelique.* Thank you, Angelique. That's all for now."

He turned to leave the still sobbing woman.

"By the way, Smets is alive. He's still a doctor, and he is nearby, here in North Carolina."

Eyes vacant and moist, she stayed silent. He continued.

"That's all, Angelique. I had to be sure. I know you have to get back to Florence for your class. Thanks for coming."

Eyes moist she stepped to the door. His voice was a whisper.

"*Murabeho, Angelique.* Goodbye, Angelique."

She left.

Paul waited a moment until he heard her car start. Then he too left.

***

After sending Henri after Byrd, Denise Guerry called an office in Arrondissement 2, Paris. Her cousin answered.

"Jacques, Denise here. Your father wants me to eliminate Byrd."

"Can you do this without involving Gutera?"

"Yes, Henri will take care of Byrd."

"Henri Duval? He's no killer."

"He'll do what I ask."

"Why? Did you tell him you would sleep with him?"

She fell silent

Jacques had been attracted to Denise all his "grown" life, cousin or not.

"Denise, save yourself for me. Forget Duval and Byrd too!"

"Jacques, stop it! You're my cousin. That's incest. Your father wants Byrd dead."

"But you can't handle Duval. He's not a loser like the other saps you attract. He is a real man. I don't want you hurt."

"But Byrd is tough. Who else could get rid of him."

"Let me speak to my father. There has to be another way. Besides the Americans know that Henri is with GES. They will go after you if Henri kills Byrd."

"Byrd's group has deep cover inside the NSA. The Americans have full deniability. They fixed his credentials so that they can be proved forgeries from overseas. Even Byrd does not realize that."

"And Henri?"

"He doesn't know it, but we have papers proving that Guerry Security fired him two months ago. He'll look like a bitter security guard who was fired. The trail will stop here in Virginia. There will be no connection to Paris."

"All right Denise, use Duval if you must. I won't talk to my father yet, but do not sleep with Henri. Save your love for me! You love me, you know. Remember I let you beat me on the mountain."

Denise snorted. *Let me!* She always had bested Jacques on skis during their vacations at Val Thorens in the French Alps. Still, she did love him in a way.

"Jacques, you're an idiot, but thanks for worrying."

"And watch out. My father is dangerous when he doesn't get his way. He doesn't have feelings like we do."

Denise sighed. Neither of them had experienced love from her uncle Roland, his father.

She hung up.

Her thoughts turned to Henri Duval. He was a challenge.

But!

***

Henri Duval, was on Route 17, returning from Jacksonville, when his personal phone sounded. (Not the secure instrument he used to report to Guerry Security.)

At the sight of the caller's number, he immediately regretted his imagined tryst with Denise. He spoke softly.

"Angelique?"

"Henri, where are you? I waited at the restaurant but you didn't come. I called your cell and it was off. It went straight to message. Where were you?"

"I emailed you two days ago that I couldn't make our date. I'm sorry, I'm working an assignment. I guess you didn't get the email. You know I wanted to be in Florence with you."

She was agitated.

"But you should have called me. Something has really upset me. I need to talk to you in person."

"I'm sorry I couldn't make it. You're right. I should have called to make sure you knew."

"Never mind, when will I see you?"

The secure phone vibrated against his thigh. Denise!

"Angelique, It's business, I have to call you back."

"Business? You mean Denise Guerry!"

But Henri already had switched to the other phone.

"Denise?"

"Henri, how far are you from the farm?"

"Maybe thirty minutes."

"Dr. Smets is in a panic. He says someone wants to kill him. He's hiding in the old tobacco shack."

"Byrd?"

"Who else? You'd better hurry."

"Click."

***

******

Chapter 13
Saturday, August 25

At the farm in Pender County, North Carolina, Henri Duval chose not to drive up the lane to the farm house.

Instead, he parked his car by a mixed grove of native Holly, Sassafras and scrubby pines that shielded him from the gray structure where he had left Gilles Smets some hours before.

The tobacco shack was not in view, but an F150 pickup truck was parked in front of the main house. It apparently belonged to Byrd, Smets' car was still at Surf City.

Henri made his decision. He left the FAMAS G2 assault rifle locked in the trunk. He would not tip his hand with a conspicuous weapon. His Hi-Power Browning would suffice. He slipped the safety off.

As he squeezed out of the car, the prickly leaves of an evergreen Holly raked his shirt. He did not mind. The thick growth offered him concealment from the main house. He pushed forward through a mix of holly, scrubby oaks and pines.

The soil was sandy, and pine needles coated the ground to form a slippery surface.

Now Henri stood at the edge of the open weeded area that fronted the house. He studied the parked pickup, the gray porch, and the three front windows. The outlying tobacco shack was not visible from his position.

Nothing moved.

There was no sign of Smets.

***

Henri stepped into the open.

"Crack!"

The bark of the loblolly pine behind Henri splintered under the impact of the bullet.

He dove to the ground and scanned the clearing. The shot had come from the house ahead. The upper windows of the farm house were boarded shut. The shooter had to be on the lower level. The window to Henri's right was open a few inches above the sill, a window Henri had closed when he last left. The shot had come from there.

Henri rolled to the side and lay against an abandoned tractor.

"Crack, Piangg!"

The second bullet ricocheted high off the rusty frame and clipped a branch somewhere behind and to his right. Henri lay flat and peered from under the chassis in time to see the rifle's barrel withdraw from the window.

Reacting, he dashed for the pines to the right of the dwelling. No shot sounded.

From his new position, he could see the tobacco shack, perhaps fifty yards from the farm house. Was Dr. Smets in the shack?

Henri looked up.

A lone Turkey vulture was circling the field behind the shack.

As Henri watched, two more vultures appeared low over the pines to the west and headed to join the first.

Something, or someone, was dead.

***

Henri studied the scene from the cover of the pines. The slatted gray door of the tobacco shack hung open on one hinge, motionless.

There was no breeze at ground level, but over the sun-warmed field the rising air formed thermal currents on which the vultures, their number augmented by new arrivals, continued to circle.

Henri pondered exposing himself to fire, when the sound of a motor echoed from the front of the house. He dashed back through the pines in time to see the Ford pickup disappear at the end of the drive.

Henri reasoned that the shooter had been alone, still he approached the farm house with caution.

There, in the front room was the cracked-open window behind which the shooter had crouched. Henri checked the floor. Two 30-06 cartridges lay on the worn rug. His attacker had used a hunting rifle.

Henri looked out the window towards the pine near which he had stood. Either the shooter was a terrible shot, or had intentionally fired high.

At the sound of a motor, Henri jumped back from the window. A car had turned onto the drive to the house.

He held his Browning ready and waited behind the door.

***

The sound of the motor ceased and a car door opened. A voice called out.

"Hello. Anybody home?"

Henri peered around the door. Hugh Byrd, holding his Glock at the ready, stood in the drive.

"Byrd, what are you doing here?"

"Henri, Henri Duval, is that you? Relax, I'm coming in."

Henri watched as Hugh holstered his weapon and mounted the steps to the porch. Henri dropped his gun-arm to the side. Byrd spoke first.

"So you're the good doctor's baby sitter. I might have known. Where is Smets?"

"Why do you want to know?"

Henri still held the Browning, although pointed at the floor.

"Relax, Henri. Put the gun away. I'm not here to hurt the wimp, not much anyway. I just wanted to even a few things with him. The rat did this to me."

Byrd touched an elevated red area of his forehead and grinned.

"He used a lamp when I wasn't looking."

Henri did not holster the Browning. His mind raced. *Who fired that rifle at me? If it wasn't Byrd, then who?*

He returned to the present.

"All right Hugh, fasten the clip on your holster and we'll talk. Just remember, I won't let you touch Smets. Denise needs him."

At the mention of Denise Guerry, Hugh became more compliant. Besides, he was sure that Henri would shoot only if challenged. He snapped the Glock's holster closed.

"OK, but I still want to talk to him. You can understand that. Where have you hidden the good doctor?"

Henri held the Browning ready and pointed to the rear door.

"Come with me. He's out back in the tobacco shack."

***

The path to the shack was overgrown with brambles and weeds among which small prickly junipers strove to survive.

Hugh forged ahead while Henri lingered a step behind. The door hung by a single rusty hinge that squealed when Hugh pulled it wide. He leaned in.

Even standing to the side, the moldy air assailed Henri's nostrils. He did not go in, but scanned the nearby fields.

Inside, Hugh peered into the shadows as his eyes acclimated to the dim light. He turned back to Henri.

"He's not here. What are you up to Duval?"

Henri shrugged and gestured towards a dark mass in the field beyond. As if on cue, the mass split apart as two vultures launched themselves upwards, their clumsy wings flapping.

"There's something over there. Follow me."

They pushed through the knee-high broom grass and brambles and reached the body of a man, face down against the soil.

Hugh Byrd rolled the body over.

It was Gilles Smets.

His face, caked in dirt and blood, had been hacked by a sharp instrument. Deep bloody wounds on the shoulders, chest and arms evidenced repeated slashing.

Henri shuddered. *A panga?* Memories of the Rwandan nightmare swamped his brain.

He struggled to regain focus. *What was that?*

Something was tied around Smets' neck.

A vary-patterned rag faded yellow, green and blue.

Henri choked.

The torn fragment of a Hutu Interahamwe shirt!

***

Henri looked up. Hugh Byrd sported a wide grin.

"Looks like somebody besides me did not like the good doctor. How will you report this to your 'lovely' Denise?"

Henri launched a "*chasse lateral*" kick to the front of Hugh's thigh followed by an American roundhouse right hand to the jaw. Twisted with pain, Hugh collapsed.

Henri pointed his Browning at the fallen figure.

"Get up. You have no idea what this is about. Touch that Glock and you're a dead man. Now get out of here before I change my mind. Be glad it's me you're dealing with and not Denise or her uncle. Now go."

Hugh went around the side of the house to his car. Henri called after him.

"And this is not about Denise. I know she had nothing to do with this and you either. Just go!"

Henri crouched beside the body to finish his thought.

But who did?

***

An agitated Hugh Byrd drove fast down the lane from the farm house. *Byrd you're slipping. You let a damn Wop beat you. No, wait, Duval is French, a damn Frog. Hell what's the difference!*

He chuckled and settled his thoughts. Smets was dead. Someone had done him a favor.

He gritted his teeth.

Henri had bested him, but only physically. Byrd was alive, thanks to Henri's scruples. What a sap! And that pitiful effort to assure Byrd that Denise Guerry would not blame him for the doctor's death, Henri was a moralistic fool! *Don't think Denise will reward you. She needs me dead, and you let me go. Why do you think she chose you to guard the doctor?*

Byrd fingered the clip on his holster. If he'd had the upper hand, the vultures would be picking at Duval's carcass along with the doctor's.

Hugh hesitated as he thought of Smets' body, and the cloth about its neck. Duval had been shaken at the sight of the mutilated corpse. *What was that about?*

Hugh cleared his mind. Clearly his alliance with Denise Guerry was finished. Yet he and she both needed to recover the papers to protect themselves from exposure.

But Ryan had the papers and now Hamm too!

Hugh could deal with Denise Guerry later. He must recover those documents.

He set his jaw.

The Ryan woman was now the target.

***

Contrary to Denise Guerry's conclusion, Jeannine Ryan had headed south, not north.

110

Thanks to the gas in Wayne Johnson's Buick, she had reached Dillon, South Carolina, without stopping and with a few gallons to spare.

Now she guided the Buick down a tree-lined street with residences and broad front lawns that, in Spring time, featured beds of bright Azaleas shaded by dogwoods and tall pines. Next to Jeannine in the passenger seat, Bill Hamm slept, as he had for most of the drive from the hospital in Jacksonville. His breathing was regular, his limbs relaxed.

Jeannine turned into a driveway that led to a brick two-story house set back among the trees. She drove to the rear of the dwelling and cut the motor. Here Wayne Johnson's Buick was safe from prying eyes. Except for the house itself, the back yard was otherwise bordered by thick growths of tall long-needled pines.

She walked to the passenger side of the Buick and opened the door.

"We're here Bill. Let me help you."

Bill opened his eyes and leaned outwards. She seized his arm at the elbow. He hesitated.

"Where is 'here?'"

"Here is 'Dillon, South Carolina,' at Mary Dean's mother's house. Rob and Mary live in Columbia now. They rent this place, but it's not occupied at the moment."

Rob Wilson was a retired FBI agent. He and his wife Mary Wilson (née Morton, and Tom Dean's widow) had helped Jeannine and Bill to uncover and foil an assassination plot several years earlier. Tragically, Mary's mother had died at that time.

Bill offered a weak frown.

"He could get in trouble for this."

"Rob doesn't care. Besides he can deny knowing we are here."

She went to a reddish rock at the corner of the house. She leaned and turned it over. When she stood up a metallic object dangled from her fingers.

"See, I have the house key. We'll say he told us where it was a year ago."

Bill knew that phone records could prove the recent contact with Rob, but he was too exhausted to dispute the point. He dragged himself to the sofa in the front room and collapsed.

Jeannine felt his forehead. He was not feverish. She picked up a bottle of water along with a plastic vial of antibiotics that the hospital had given her at Bill's discharge.

"Bill, it's time for your medicine. Here swallow these."

Bill held his head up. She popped the capsules into his mouth. He fell back and shut his eyes. Jeannine stood by him until his breathing settled into a slow rhythm. Then she went outside to the car. She popped the trunk, and picked up the briefcase, her laptop, Wayne's shotgun and a box of shells. Carrying the load with both arms, she pushed through the door. Once inside she locked it.

Arms limp, she sat facing Bill. *God, please help him. I can't do this by myself!*

She broke the shotgun open, took a shell from the box, and shoved it into the barrel. She snapped the weapon shut and cradled it in her arms. That simple effort exhausted her.

She sat, watching Bill's chest rise and fall. In just moments, her head nodded and her eyes closed.

She slept.

***

******

Chapter 14
Sunday, August 26

The South Carolina sun was bright and high in the sky when Jeannine Ryan opened her eyes. *Bill?*

She looked about, put the shotgun aside and sat upright in the stuffed chair. She had fallen asleep watching Bill. He was still stretched on the sofa, his eyes closed. She stood up, stretched and focused.

At that slight movement, Bill rolled to one side so that one arm hung loosely off the couch, but his eyes stayed closed and his breathing remained regular. She felt his pulse. His rate was normal.

She sighed in relief.

Jeannine put her laptop on the coffee table, took several documents from the briefcase and laid them open on the table. She squinted to study the texts, but could not concentrate.

Damn. This isn't working. Coffee!

She went into the kitchen. She tried the cabinets and found the needed filters. Soon the smell of roasted Arabica beans filled the kitchen.

Cup in hand, she returned to the living room where she sat and examined the documents. Her eyes cleared, now she could read the fine print. In minutes, she was lost in thought.

On the couch, Bill did not move.

***

In her apartment in Florence, South Carolina, Angelique Uwimana threw herself on the bed and sobbed into the pillow.

She had run all the way from the Catholic church.

At Mass, she had been fine until the congregation stood to recite the "Our Father." As she began to speak the words,

"Forgive us … as we forgive those who trespass against us," her tongue had refused to move and she could make no sound.

Paul Mutabazi's photo of the Belgian doctor had released a nightmare of memories. Choking, she had pushed past the others in her pew and fled down the aisle. She had run all the way to the apartment.

God, I tried to forgive him, but I couldn't!

She had not "forgiven," but only "forgotten." When she had identified Dr. Smets' photograph, she had seen hatred in Paul Mutabazi's eyes. He was going to kill Smets, but she did not care! Old feelings of rage and revenge had overwhelmed her. Smets deserved to die.

Dear God, look at what they did to my little Augustin. I can't forgive. Help me!

Remember, I am your daughter.

Angelique's parents, overjoyed at her birth, had named her *Uwimana*, "Daughter of God."

But her father and mother were dead, both at the hands of the Interahamwe, and like her parents, she believed God's words. His forgiveness depended on hers!

But I can't, … I won't! Dear God, help. I can't handle this.

She dug her nails into her hands and closed her eyes.

***

The girl was ten years old. She was running. Behind her she could hear the horrible clatter of pangas dragged sparking against the stones of the roadway. Hutu killers! Sure of their prey, they followed purposely. The men, many clad in dirty yellow, green and blue shirts, were of mixed ages, some not much older than the girl herself.

United in purpose, they chanted in unison.

"Death to the snakes. A baby snake grows into a snake. Death to all snakes. Death to the snakes. A baby snake grows into a … ."

The girl held her little brother close. Augustin was not yet three.

She turned the corner. There, in front of her was the clinic. The Belgian doctor, her mother's friend, stood in the doorway.

She dashed forward and held out her brother. She mustered her French.

"Sauvez-nous. Mama always said you would help us."

But the doctor's eyes were cold.

"Angelique Uwimana, you are Tutsi. We do not help cockroaches here. Go away."

"But, Mama was Hutu."

"Your worthless father was Tutsi, you are Tutsi."

The doctor pointed to the boy in her arms.

"And so is that 'thing' in your arms, Tutsi."

The girl turned to run. Too late!

The killers rounded the corner with yells of triumph!

Someone tore Augustin from her arms. Angelique did not see the club that struck her senseless.

***

It was dusk when she awoke. The Interahamwe were gone.

Covered with blood, she pushed herself from under a woman's body that lay atop her. Angelique felt her head. No cuts, the blood was not her own.

She stared to the side. Augustin's body was a small mangled heap at the edge of the road.

Numb, she crawled off the roadway into the bushes.

She lay on her back, dry-eyed and trembling.

***

A groggy Angelique Uwimana lifted her head from the pillow. She had slept for over an hour, the once-soaked pillow case was now merely damp.

"Brazzzz."

That noise, stop it! But the harsh sound persisted.

"Brazzzz, Brazzzz, …, Brazzzz.

The door buzzer!"

She slid from the bed and struggled to the door. She flipped the speaker on.

"Yes? Who is it?"

"It's me, Henri Duval. Are you all right? Let me in."

"Henri. Give me a second, I'll buzz you up."

Angelique dashed to the bedroom, stepped out of her rumpled church dress and slipped into a pair of jeans. She donned a loose green blouse and returned to the door in time for Henri's knock.

She undid the safety chain and pulled the door inwards.

A breathless Henri stood before her.

"Henri, why are you breathing like that?"

"I took the stairs. The elevator is stuck up on six."

She stared. Henri's brow shone with sweat. He had come up four flights, and the stairwell was poorly ventilated.

"You're lucky the door from the stairs was unlocked."

He grinned.

"Your security is bad. Someone had wedged it open."

He took a breath.

"I thought I was in better shape. I try to run every day. Maybe I'll increase the distance."

"Come in and sit down. I'll get you some water."

She stepped to the kitchenette and took a plastic bottle from the small fridge. She handed it to him.

"He grabbed the bottle and swallowed. I don't have much time. I have to return to North Carolina."

Angelique took the bottle from him. There was a haunted shadow in his eyes she had never seen. She drew back a step, but he took her arm.

"I want you to look at this."

He held out a torn piece of bloody shirt. The cloth was faded and dirty, but the colors were clear, the yellow, green and blue of the Interahamwe!

Angelique recoiled. She gasped.

"But where? How did you get it?"

"From a dead man, in North Carolina."

"Why show me?"

"I thought you might know something. The man was chopped with a panga. This was tied around his neck."

Angelique froze. Henri kept on.

"He worked for my company. He was Belgian, a medical doctor. He ran a clinic in Kigali during the genocide. He was an ally of the Hutu government. He supported them after president Habyarimana's assassination."

She stood trembling. His tone softened.

"Angelique you told me about your baby brother, Augustin, and a Belgian doctor who turned you out to the Interahamwe. His clinic was in Kigali. Was his name 'Smets?'"

Paul Mutabazi's words echoed in her mind. *"...he is nearby, in North Carolina."*

She shuddered.

My God, Paul, you used a panga on him! Are we no better than they?

She collapsed to her knees and sobbed. Henri knelt beside her.

"Good God, Angelique, you *do* know about this! Who did it? Tell me!"

***

Hugh Byrd's phone call to Denise Guerry had gone as expected. If she was surprised that he was alive, she gave no indication of it. The conversation was brief and pointless. Each party feigned that their alliance was intact, while in fact each understood that henceforth each was on his or her own.

After that call, Hugh considered his options.

Henri Duval was still a danger, but less so thanks to his sentimentality. Hugh would exploit his misguided emotions. Stewart Marks had become a true threat now that he suspected that Hugh was involved in the attack on Johnson's Topsail house.

But the main threat, as always, was the Ryan-Hamm combo. They had evidence that could send Hugh (and Denise Guerry) to the penitentiary for the rest of their lives.

Damn you Hamm, why didn't you leave well enough alone. We weren't hurting you!

Denise Guerry had not told him, but Hugh knew that she had shifted "resources" to intercept Ryan and Hamm in Maryland. *Stupid!* Hugh had underestimated Ryan once, he would not do so again. Let others think she would retreat to familiar haunts in Maryland, Hugh knew better.

Ryan had headed south.

But where? She had not used either her or "Walter Harmon's" credit card since leaving the hospital. How much gas had been in Wayne Johnson's Buick? All right, *Wayne, you may not be the brightest bulb on the block, but you* will *lead me to Ryan.*

He grimaced.

Johnson must know where Ryan had taken Hamm.

*****

In Dillon, South Carolina, Jeannine Ryan helped Bill Hamm off the sofa and to the kitchen. She studied his eyes. They were clear and alert.

She handed him two pills and a glass of water.

"Here, take your antibiotics."

Next she placed a steaming bowl of oatmeal in front of him. He grimaced.

"Jeannine, I'm hungry. I need some real food."

She did not back off.

"This is real food, but OK, I'll sweeten the pot."

She put a fistful of wrinkled raisins on top of his mush.

Bill sighed, but after the first bland spoonful, he ate vigorously.

"This isn't bad."

Of course it isn't. I want you on your feet."

Bill emptied the bowl and looked up at her. She shook her head.

"We're not going to push it. That's enough for the moment. Do you feel well enough to talk?"

Bill rested his arms on the table. He nodded "Yes."

"Then tell me, why the briefcase? And what in the hell have you gotten us into?"

***

Jeannine poured herself a fresh cup of coffee, sat opposite Bill, and waited. He spoke.

"Are we safe here?"

"I hope so. This house belonged to Rose Morton, Mary Dean's mother. It belongs to Rob Wilson and Mary now. I called them in Columbia. He and Mary thought this would be a good place to hide while you get well. We should be OK for several days, at least. No one knows we know them."

"All right, but how did you find me, and how did you get me here?"

"I got your note with the key and waited like you told me. When you didn't show, I went to the post office in Manassas and picked up your briefcase. That was five days ago. The day

119

before that the FBI had come to my house. They said you were a spy, and accused me of being the same. After I got the briefcase, I decided I should find a place to think, away from the Feds. So I called Wayne Johnson at his house on Topsail Island. He said I could come there."

She stood from the table and paced.

"But some thug followed me to North Carolina. He must have waited at the post office."

"What was he driving?"

"A Ford Excursion."

"That would be Tom Holder. He *is* a thug. What did you do?"

"Wayne called a marine friend who put me up at Camp Geiger. Then Wayne got me to Topsail. We weren't followed by the thug or the FBI."

Jeannine stopped pacing.

"Bill, what the hell is going on?"

"Tell me how you found me first."

"When I got to Topsail, Wayne and I went over the papers in the briefcase. I have lots of questions for you about Strontium-90, and cryptographic keys, but anyway, two days ago we got word of a 'John Doe' some kids had pulled out of the Intracoastal Waterway. Wayne went to the hospital in Jacksonville. It was you."

She took a deep breath.

"When he got back to Topsail, some hood with an automatic weapon shot up Wayne's living room. We hit the floor and I bagged him with a shotgun, but he got away. Wayne and I made a run for it to Camp Geiger."

"You weren't hurt?"

"I took a splinter in my thigh, but it's mostly OK now. Anyway, the next day Wayne and I picked you up at the hospital as 'Walter Harmon,' and here we are in Dillon."

"Where is Wayne?"

"I don't know. I hope he's OK. The FBI was looking for my Subaru, so we switched cars. I have his Buick hidden out back. Now it's your turn. What is this about?"

But his eyes already were halfway closed. She took his arm.

"You're done in. I'll get you back to the couch. You can tell me everything later."

She guided him to the sofa. In minutes his eyes were shut and his breathing regular. She would have to wait for Bill to explain what he had taken from the Torbee Building.

Her thoughts turned back to Wayne.

Wayne, where are you? Are you OK?

***

In Wilmington, after no charges were filed against him, Wayne Johnson rented a car and returned to Topsail Island.

He stood amid the wreckage of his living room. The ocean view was gone, blocked by the sheets of 4-by-8 plywood that shielded the gap left by the shattered glass doors. The interior was depressing. White slabs of drywall dangled from exposed studs, while splintered chairs and broken lamps, shoveled into a heap against the far wall, offered no relief to the drab scene.

Wayne loaded a heavy-gauge plastic bag with rubble and dragged it to the top of the stairs. The 42 gallon "contractors" sack, pierced from within by pointed fragments, snagged on the top step. In disgust, Wayne kicked the heavy sack down the stairwell. It slammed into the wall and disappeared around the corner at the bottom landing.

"Hey, watch it. Hold your fire."

Wayne did not recognize the voice.

"Who are you? What are you doing in my house?"

An arm extended around the corner of the landing. It held a shiny badge.

121

"United States Government, Agent Hugh Byrd. I'd like to talk with you."

From the top of the stairs Wayne could not see letters, only a design with the spread wings of an eagle.

"If you're FBI, you can go to hell. Get off my property."

"I'm not FBI, but I know all about that jerk Stewart Marks and the hard time he gave you. I know they impounded your Subaru in Wilmington. Your arrest was bogus, they had nothing to charge you with. Marks is a disgrace and he's a cheapo. He should have reimbursed you for the rental car. I don't like him. Let me come up."

Wayne hesitated, but a smiling Hugh Byrd already had mounted the third step. Wayne relented.

"All right, but I have work to do. You have to help me if you want to talk."

"You bet. Happy to!"

At the head of the stairs, Hugh Byrd surveyed the stricken living room and chuckled.

"Mr. Johnson, this is terrible! Who did this to you?"

***

******

Chapter 15
Monday, August 27

Paul Mutabazi arrived in Florence, South Carolina, shortly before dawn. He chose a motel just off Interstate 95, but he could not sleep. He sat staring out the window.

Dr. Smets was dead!

Even in his dying moments, Smets had spewed venom at an unfair world. He had vented his hatred on Paul as the latter stood over him. And Smets' words, true or not, had sliced Paul's soul. Those words had left Paul sick and empty. Hutu extremists, former members of the Interahamwe were once more on the move. The genociders were alive and well, here in the Carolinas!

He had come to Florence to warn Angelique Uwimana about them. He pulled a paper out of his wallet.

Where is her number?

But he was too exhausted. He pulled the curtains shut across the window and lay on the bed. His lips quivered.

Not again! No. Not again!

Maybe rest a few minutes? Just a few.

His eyes closed. He half-dozed, but the memories were real.

***

The boy was eleven and alone. His parents had not come home for two days. At the noise behind him, he turned to see Mr. Mukuru, a Tutsi neighbor and friend of his father. Mr. Mukuru spoke.

"Come with me, Paul. We must go to the soccer field."

"But my mother and father aren't back yet?"

"They want you to come with me."

The boy fell silent, but only for a moment."

"Where is Angelique?"

Mr. Mukuru attempted a smile.

"She will be safe at her school in Kigali. I sent her there."

The cries and yells from the bottom of the hill grew louder as another house burst into flames.

"But you and I must go now. The government troops are at the soccer field. They will protect us."

Mr. Mukuru took the boy's hand and they climbed the hill to the field where other Tutsis had gathered. Mr. Mukuru pointed to the soldiers that lined all sides of the field.

"See, the soldiers are here. Now we are safe."

The boy followed Mr. Mukuru into the milling crowd.

Minutes later, a military car appeared at the crest of the hill. The Tutsis stood motionless at its approach. The soldiers stood at attention.

An officer stepped out of the vehicle.

Something was wrong!

Instinctively, Mr. Mukuru drew the boy back towards the center of the throng.

The commander waved a command to his men and the explosions started.

Grenades, many of them, lobbed from all sides!

Shrapnel from the multiple blasts cut down pockets of Tutsis from the panicked crowd. Some froze, unable to react. Others turned in random directions to flee the onslaught. More explosions followed and formerly isolated pockets of the fallen coalesced into large areas of moaning and twisting bodies.

Those Tutsis still able to run surged to the perimeter in a blind wave, only to be swept away by coordinated bursts of automatic fire from the encircling troops.

But the boy was unaware of that last surge. Shielded by Mr. Mukuru's fragment-pierced body, he lay unconscious and unmoving in the middle of the fallen. Likewise he was not aware of the soldiers moving through the field, silencing the survivors with single, well-placed, shots.

His first awareness was of the sound of the trucks' motors as the government troops departed. But then he heard new terrifying sounds, the cries of triumph from the Hutu gangs who prowled the field with clubs and pangas to finish the work of the troops. He kept his eyes closed, and mercifully, passed out once more.

Finally, he awoke. The silence was eerie. He lay still, eyes shut tight, too scared to move. Were the killers still here?

Thirty minutes and more the silence persisted. The boy squeezed from under Mr. Mukuru's body. The last conscious act of Angelique's father had been to fall on the boy to shield him from the executioners.

He stood. In the moonlight, nothing was real. The sports field had become a cemetery of a sort, but one without graves, only bodies, Tutsi bodies.

Tears formed. He wished them all dead; the soldiers, the Interahamwe, all of them.

Some day he, Paul Mutabazi, would avenge his parents and Mr. Mukuru, and maybe the others too!

At the sound of an approaching motor, he picked his way over the fallen forms to the edge of the field and disappeared into the bush.

He wanted justice, but first he must survive.

***

In Florence, South Carolina, Angelique Uwimana sipped her morning coffee and studied the screen of her laptop. Today she was to present her seminar, "Decoding RSA Encryption."

She was typing when the phone rang. She reached for it. The voice was familiar, but slurred as if the speaker were half awake.

"Who is this?"

"It's Paul Mutabazi. Sorry, I drove through the night. I need to see you. Is the Frenchman with you?"

"Of course not. I'm Catholic, I wouldn't do that. He left last evening."

"OK, OK, I'm sorry. No offense meant, but I need help."

"What kind of help. Dr. Smets is dead, Henri told me."

"You told Henri about me?"

"You know I wouldn't do that, but Henri found the body. He says Smets was killed by a Tutsi for revenge. He thinks I had a part in it. Paul, how could you? You shouldn't have killed him. And you chopped him with a Panga?"

"Angelique."

"No, it's murder. You're no better than the Interahamwe."

"You can't mean that. No one can forgive those murderers, least of all, you."

She recoiled.

Can I really forgive them?

Maybe Paul was right. She lowered her voice.

"All right, I'm sorry, but we must let go of our hatred. It will only destroy us."

"Angelique, I didn't kill Smets. I wanted to, but I didn't. He was dying when I found him."

His voice shook.

"Smets told me things before he died. They thought he had betrayed them, so they killed him. They were afraid he would talk."

"Them? They? Who do you mean?"

"I can't say on the phone. Can I stay with you? Only for a day or so. Please."

"Paul, what is this all about?"

"Wait, someone just drove into the motel parking. I know that face. I have to go!"

***

At the farm in Pender County, North Carolina, Henri Duval surveyed the work of Denise Guerry's "clean-up" crew. The crew was gone, as was Gilles Smets' body, never to be found by law enforcement. He would be another "missing person" whose lack of known relatives provided no incentive for further enquiry.

The field where Smets had died now was mowed and baled, so that walking was easy. Interestingly, the crew had replaced the doctor's body with the carcass of a white-tailed deer, so that the presence of vultures had a ready, and innocent, explanation.

But Henri was worried for reasons other than Gilles Smets. Angelique clearly knew more about his death than she had revealed.

And something else concerned Henri. Smets had died from a vicious assault, and such a killer would not have intentionally spared anyone who threatened him. Yet, Henri was convinced that whoever had shot at him had intentionally missed, risking detection rather than kill. And a hunting rifle was hardly the weapon of an assassin!

Henri went to the front of the house and examined the surface of the rusted tractor. The bullet's scrape proved Henri's hypothesis. The shot was way too wide. Henri had crouched at the other end. The shooter had aimed to scare Henri off, not to kill him.

His next discovery was unexpected. A large holly tree stood near the edge of the cleared front yard, near where Henri himself had first stood to spy on the house. Something fluttered from one of its branches.

As he neared the holly, he saw that it was a piece of gray cloth, apparently snagged from the shirt of someone who, like Henri, had approached the farm surreptitiously through the shelter of the woods. He recalled the spiny holly leaves that had raked his back during his approach.

But the person who had shot at Henri had not come through the woods. He had driven to the house in that pickup truck.

From the large holly, Henri followed a trail of broken and crisply clipped branches to the lane where he had parked earlier. He studied the depressed weeds. His was not the only set of tracks. Someone had parked on the lane before Henri.

Of course, the clipped branches! A bush knife!

The shooter was not the killer. The killer or killers had been at the farm before either Henri, Hugh Byrd, or the shooter.

But how would anyone know of Smets' whereabouts?

Only Denise Guerry?

But Smets? Of course! Denise wanted me to kill Byrd. She did not care about Smets!

***

Henri called Denise at the Chantilly office.

"Denise, I need the truth. You used me. You sent someone to kill Gilles Smets?"

"Cher Henri, why would you think that? Did your precious Angelique and her Tutsi friend, Paul Mutabazi, tell you that?"

"Mutabazi? What does he have to do with Smets' death?"

"Evidently your little Angelique does not trust you. Paul Mutabazi visited her. I know he was looking for Smets."

Henri was silent. *Was Mutabazi the mysterious shooter?*

Denise took the offensive.

"But Henri, you spared Byrd. How could you? I trusted you. I thought you liked me. I count on your protection."

"If you want Byrd dead, do it yourself. I'm not an assassin."

"Henri dear, I never thought you were. But Byrd is dangerous, he frightens me. Don't you want to protect me."

Henri did not believe that anything or anyone could frighten Denise Guerry. He changed the subject.

"Denise, Mutabazi did not kill Smets. It was someone else. Maybe not even a Tutsi, maybe some Hutu."

"Why would you think that?"

"Someone else knew about the farm. They went there to kill Smets. They chopped him, Interahamwe-style."

"Cher Henri, don't trouble yourself with that. I know you want to help me. Just keep Byrd away from me, that's all."

She hung up.

***

In talking to Henri, Denise had not let him know that she was as stunned as he at Smets' death.

Now, her mind was in turmoil.

Yes, Paul Mutabazi had called her about Smets, but she had told him nothing. Paul had located the farm on his own. And from the report of her "cleanup crew," it was clear that Maximilien Gutera had been at the farm.

Gutera had ordered the killing!

And he had not consulted GES before taking action. That was a bad sign. Had SÉGAG lost control of the Hutu leader?

In only minutes an encrypted message was on its way to her uncle in Paris.

***

In Florence, South Carolina, Angelique Uwimana's talk, "Decoding RSA Encryption," generated many questions and favorable comments. She was about to sit down when a man in a dark suit rose and faced her. Clearly he was not from the university. His tone was serious.

"Ms. Uwimana, if your integer factorization algorithm will work in polynomial time, you are throwing into question all current applications of RSA encryption. Is that correct?"

"My algorithm is only partly tested, and some of my results require verification. But if my calculation of polynomial time is correct and the algorithm holds, the answer is 'Yes.'"

"Ms. Uwimana, let us suppose that the U. S. government is already using a similar algorithm to decrypt communications between other governments and multinational firms. Do you have any specific knowledge of such an algorithm? Is it possible that your algorithm is based on it. Are you aware of the consequences for disclosing government secrets?

Angelique set her lips.

"Of course, I would have no information about any such government activity. What you describe would be classified far beyond the reach of a graduate student like myself. And no, my algorithm is entirely my own work."

The moderator rose from his chair.

"Our time is up. I'm sure Ms. Uwimana will be happy to answer any further questions privately. Thank you for coming."

Angelique gathered her papers from the podium, stepped to the door, and walked out into the hallway. A man, his shirt awry, approached her. Paul Mutabazi!

"Angelique, they're here. In Florence. The 'Genocide Hutus.' And that killer, Charles Hakizimana, is with them!"

✳✳✳

✳✳✳✳✳✳

Chapter 16
Monday, August 27

In Dillon, South Carolina, Jeannine Ryan sat at the kitchen table, hunched over her laptop. Beside her was a stack of papers from Bill Hamm's briefcase. She looked up as Bill entered the kitchen.

"Bill, you're walking on your own. You look better."

"I buzzed for my nurse, but she wouldn't come."

Jeannine handed him a glass of water and two capsules.

"I'm here now, and here are your antibiotics."

"But I feel good."

"Forget it. You're a sick puppy. You had bacterial pneumonia from near drowning. You have three more days of these. You can't stop, no matter how you feel. Swallow them."

Bill threw his head back and downed the pills. Jeannine looked at his face and arms.

"Your cuts are healing OK, and the bruises are fading, not bad."

She added.

"And hopefully the IV's at the hospital flushed that damned Sodium thiopental out of your system. Now maybe you'll answer questions about the briefcase. How about it?"

Bill went to the fridge and poured himself a glass of orange juice.

"All right, but have you heard from Wayne. Where is he?"

"Not a word. I don't know where he is."

The sound of a motor in the driveway interrupted the conversation.

Bill took Jeannine's shotgun from the corner and stood by the window.

A moment later a knock sounded on the kitchen door.

He held the shotgun ready and nodded to Jeannine. She peeked through the slit in the half-curtain.

A man stood on the stoop.

She turned back to Bill and grinned.

"Relax, it's Wayne!"

She swung the door wide.

"Wayne, come on in. We were just wondering about you."

She smothered him in a huge hug.

***

In South Carolina, Hugh Byrd congratulated himself. He was a damned good investigator. Once again he had outwitted his foes. The blip on the screen of his laptop was stationary.

Wayne Johnson had arrived at his destination. The blip, Wayne's car, had stopped moving.

Hugh frowned. Truly he deserved a better adversary. This had been too easy.

When Hugh had visited Wayne Johnson at the house on Topsail, the latter had said nothing of Ryan's whereabouts. Johnson had thought himself clever in not revealing anything about Ryan or Hamm. The idiot. He was unaware that Hugh had attached a location-monitoring device to the car parked outside.

The poor sap had led Hugh straight to his target.

Hugh congratulated himself. He was right. Ryan had headed south and not north.

South Carolina! Very clever Ms. Ryan, but not clever enough!

Hugh stopped his car. He must plan carefully, even a partially disabled Hamm was more dangerous than Wayne Johnson. But he could not delay, it was not wise to give Hamm more time to recover.

Hugh glanced at his laptop. The blip that was Johnson's car had not budged. Good!

***

At their "safe" house in Dillon, South Carolina, Jeannine Ryan, Bill Hamm and Wayne Johnson gathered around the kitchen table. Papers from the briefcase were spread over the surface. Jeannine, put one of them in front of Bill.

The graph was of data that she and Wayne had found were faked.

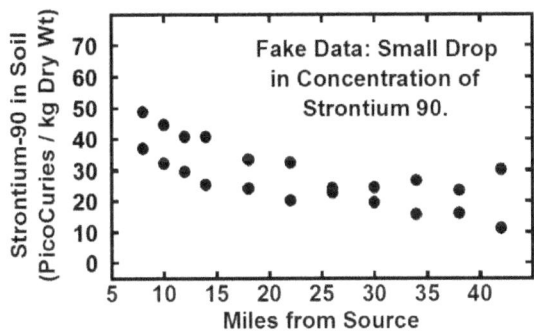

"Bill, Wayne and I know that these data are fake. They show that after some sort of 'event' the Strontium-90 levels are high at 42 miles from the source. What does all this mean?"

Bill frowned.

"In France there are about 60 nuclear reactors to generate electricity. All of their electricity is from nuclear power. Some Frenchmen are against nuclear energy. The government plans to phase out the older reactors, one half of the total, in ten years or more, but there are extreme elements that want to get rid of all the reactors. These fake data pretend that the Strontium-90 levels are worse than they really are."

He took a deep breath.

"So the RadGuard report is a lie. They used fake data to bolster their argument. Now let me see the real graph."

Jeannine put another graph in front of Bill. This time the Strontium-90 levels dropped rapidly and were near zero at 42 miles.

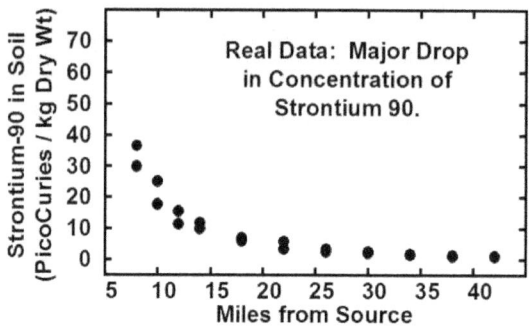

Bill whistled.

"Damn. That's a much bigger drop."

Wayne jumped in.

"It is. That explains the fake graph in the report. RadGuard made the environmental contamination from a nuclear plant look a lot worse than it is."

He hesitated, then continued.

"But so what? A little political skullduggery in France doesn't warrant a vicious attack on you, or on Jeannine and me. The other papers must be important too. Those thugs tried to kill us to get them.

A cloud blocked the sun and shadowed the window. Bill looked from Wayne to Jeannine to the window and back.

"You're right, Wayne. There's a lot more."

But Bill was tired. He settled back in his chair and spoke slowly.

"The CIA assigned me to a 'broom closet' in the Torbee Building in Manassas to get me out of the way. It was a 'nothing' assignment, but I discovered that Torbee's Chief of Security, Hugh Byrd, was allied with a corrupt group inside the National Security Agency at Fort Meade, Maryland. Through Byrd they funnel classified information from the NSA to Guerry Electronic Systems in Chantilly, Virginia. GES is a subsidiary of a French company, *Systèmes Électroniques Globals Alphonse Guerry* or SÉGAG. A French woman, Denise Guerry, is the CEO of GES. She is the granddaughter of Alphonse, and her uncle, Roland Guerry, controls SÉGAG."

He took a deep breath. Jeannine touched his shoulder.

"Bill, take it easy. Take your time."

"All right. The corrupt group inside the NSA has found a way to decrypt RSA-encrypted communications between several European governments. Moreover, they have copied their computer security tokens that give them access to their secure networks. Hugh Byrd is the group's liaison for GES and SÉGAG."

Jeannine jumped in.

"Bill, what you say is impossible. Not even the NSA can break RSA encryption. That would mean the NSA has factored many large integer semi primes. It's impossible, no way!"

Bill waved his hand at the papers on the table.

"These documents prove otherwise."

Wayne broke in.

"Jeannine, wait. What Bill says may be right."

"What do you mean?"

"I mean that special software is needed to generate the random primes that multiplied produce the semiprime, right?"

"Yes, but extended precision plus a good random number generator will do, and anybody can have access to those. Any government can generate their own random primes, and test them too."

"True, but they would want validated routines, and a superior well-tested random number generator, with thoroughly debugged code to test for primality."

"So?"

"So suppose the NSA had a way to secretly hack and tamper with the validated routines of whoever was offering them. They might be able to insert traps in the code to catch the large primes before they are multiplied to make a semiprime. That way the problem of integer factorization is avoided, and keys are easily found. A dedicated group at the NSA, with lots of smarts, time, and supercomputers at their disposable, could compromise the 'validated' software of others and trap and steal the primes as they are generated."

"Stealing the primes certainly avoids the mathematical problem, but?"

Wayne shook his head.

"No 'buts.' While mathematically it may not be possible to 'attack' and decrypt a good RSA algorithm, human flaws can always compromise its use in practice."

Bill stood up.

"You guys let me finish. A major client of SÉGAG and GES is a group of conspirators in France who want to return Rwanda to the same Hutu cabal that caused the genocide in 1994. Thanks to the decrypted communiqués, the conspirators know that several major nations, including their own France, would welcome the return of Rwanda to the Francophone circle of African nations."

He took a breath.

"I don't know how the decryption is done, but the conspirators are well-informed and flourishing. And a group of Hutus here in this country is planning an event that will tip international opinion to their cause."

Jeannine spoke.

"But Bill, what kind of event? Do you mean nuclear?"

"I doubt that, but whatever it is, we have to stop them!"

Neither she nor Wayne could answer.

***

Hugh Byrd braked his car and checked the laptop. The blip had not moved. Wayne Johnson's car was here, but it was not visible. Hugh studied the house. It was set back from the street. Doubtless, the car was parked in the back.

Hugh drove around the corner. The back yards had no fences, just broad expanses of coarse grass and azalea bushes, topped by stately pines. Hugh moved easily from tree to tree. Ahead was the Honda that Johnson had rented in Wilmington.

Hugh smiled. He would recover the papers and eliminate Hamm, Ryan and Johnson all at once.

He slipped out his Glock, chambered a round, and thumbed the safety off.

***

As Hugh prepared to move in, the back door to the house swung wide and a shapely young brunette in tight jeans and a tighter tee-shirt bounced out. *Who?*

"Jake, I'm going to get a six-pack. Watch Bobby for me."

Jake appeared at the door.

"Julie, make it Budweiser, will you? But whose Honda is that? Where's the Ford?"

"It's in the shop. I rented this from Avis this afternoon. I'm working at the club tonight, I need it."

Hugh Byrd withdrew behind a pine and leaned his forehead against the bark. *Damn!*

Evidently Johnson had returned the rental Honda with the tag to Avis in Myrtle Beach where this "Julie" had rented it.

Johnson, you lucky idiot, I'll get you for this!

He looked at his watch. The rental office was closed. Tomorrow he would visit Avis to find out what Johnson was driving. He would stay in Myrtle Beach tonight.

***

In Dillon, Jeannine covered Bill Hamm with a blanket and left him asleep on the sofa. She returned to the kitchen where Wayne waited.

"Jeannine, I'm sorry the FBI impounded your Subaru."

"Forget the Subaru. I'm glad you're here and that you're OK, but what about your Buick? Do you need it?"

"No. After they impounded the Subaru in Wilmington, I rented a Honda to go back to Topsail and secure my house. I started to come here to meet you, but I was too cramped in the Honda. I dropped it off in Myrtle Beach and rented a Buick."

He smiled.

"Bottom line, you keep using my Buick. I'll use my rental."

"Wayne, how can I ever thank you for all you are doing? Can you forgive me for getting you into this mess?"

"I'm just glad to be of use, but you look beat. Go upstairs and get some sleep. I'll take the chair and keep watch on Bill."

He retrieved the shotgun from the corner, and sat.

Jeannine was too exhausted to argue. She stumbled towards the stairs.

***

******

Chapter 17
Tuesday, August 28

In the FBI Resident Agency in Wilmington, North Carolina, Stew Marks and Jack Marino sipped coffee. Stew was quiet. His boss at the Joint Terrorism Task Force in DC was distinctly displeased with "Agent Marks" - First, because of Stew's long absence from his desk at the JTTF, and second, because Marks had not produced either the fugitive, William Hamm, or his apparent collaborator, Dr. Ryan.

Jack broke the silence. His words did little to comfort Stew.

"You didn't think that the Ryan woman would try to claim her car from the impoundment lot, did you, Stew?"

Stew threw a pained look at his partner.

"Technically, she's not a fugitive like Hamm. So why not?"

Stew still harbored the hope that somehow the attractive redhead was the evil Hamm's unwitting dupe.

Jack divined those thoughts.

"Face it, partner, Ryan got Hamm out of the hospital. She's with Hamm now. The only way she can be innocent in all this is for Hamm to be innocent too. And Hamm is a rat. Remember how he contradicted my testimony about the Unity Pavilion."

He kept on.

"Stew, you don't know the woman. What's wrong with you? You're a trained agent. Focus, damn it, focus!"

Stew thought for a moment and switched topics.

"Jack, I think Hugh Byrd is bad news. I'm pretty sure that he and Tom Holder tried to kill Ryan at the beach house. I'll bet Holder was shot. Byrd said he had an accident, no way."

"Are you that sure? Why?"

"My damn gut has been screaming at me. That great room was wrecked by a shooter with an M16. He emptied an entire 30-round magazine. You've met Holder. He's an overkill kind of guy. It was him all right, and he's Byrd's man all the way."

"So?"

"So, Byrd has access to military M16's, like were used in the assault. And we haven't seen that creep Holder since. I'll bet that was his blood on the deck? What more do you want?"

Jack thought a moment. *Proof would be nice.*

Stew continued.

"And when we entered that DNA into the data base, it was blocked. No access. Whatever group those two jerks belong to knows how to cover their official butt."

"All right Stew, suppose you are right, and Byrd and Holder are bad guys. How does that affect our mission to find Hamm."

"Think, Jack, think. Byrd found Johnson and Ryan at the beach house before we did. He's always been one step ahead of us. He has resources that we do not. Maybe if we follow Byrd he will lead us to Hamm."

"Our guys say Byrd is at a motel in Myrtle Beach, South Carolina."

"He must think Hamm is there. We need a car."

"We can get one from the pool."

Stew and Jack left the agent's lounge.

***

In Florence, South Carolina, Angelique Uwimana stepped out of her bedroom. She went to the couch where Paul Mutabazi slept and shook his shoulders.

"Paul, wake up. You must leave now. I have to go to class."

"Can't I stay here?"

"No, Henri is meeting me here later to go eat. You wouldn't want him to see you."

At the mention of Henri Duval, Paul sat up awake and swung his legs over the edge of the couch.

"There's some coffee on the counter. Grab a cup and get dressed. We're leaving in ten minutes."

"Angelique, like I told you last night, Hakizimana is alive. He is not dead. He had Smets killed. Smets told me before he died."

"Smets told you that to scare you. Troops of the *Front Patriotique Rwandais* killed Hakizimana in 1994 as he was fleeing Rwanda. It was in the papers and photos too."

"Smets was dying. His story makes sense. He said that the French helped both him and Hakizimana to escape the *FPR* and hide among the refugees in Goma. Not only Hakizimana, but a number of other leaders of the Interahamwe genocide."

"Yes but, everyone knows the leaders of the genocide were in Goma. They set up their own rule there."

"But Smets warned me that now Hakizimana and other Hutu killers live here, in South Carolina. And yesterday, I saw Hakizimana outside my motel. He and two others I didn't know."

Angelique frowned.

"Paul, you couldn't have seen Hakizimana. He's dead. Besides, after all these years who knows what he would look like"

A shadow of doubt dulled Paul's eyes.

"I saw his photo once."

Angelique stood still. This was America. Hakizimana was dead and that meant that Smets was an evil liar, dying or not.

But Paul was frightened, and Smets *had* been hacked to death. Henri Duval had seen it. The killing was real.

"All right Paul, I'll take you to a friend of mine, Milton. He's a grad student in computer science like me. I'm sure he'll let you stay in his apartment tonight."

Angelique went to the door.

"But hurry, I have to be at the university in thirty minutes."

***

In Chantilly, Virginia, Denise Guerry looked out the wide window of her office at Guerry Electronic Systems. From the sixth floor she had an expansive view of Route 28 and other tall buildings that housed various high tech enterprises. The traffic on Route 28 was light, the morning rush hour had ended some thirty minutes earlier. She punched a number on her cell.

"Henri, where are you?"

"In Florence, near Carolina Technical University."

"So you're visiting that sweet innocent Tutsi. Poor Henri, you need a real woman not a little girl."

Henri twisted in silence. Denise continued.

"Where is Byrd? Why haven't you found him?"

Again Henri chose silence.

At that, Denise threw her phone on the desk. It bounced off and slid out of sight.

Damn you Angelique, leave Henri alone. I need him.

***

Denise stared out the window. The traffic on Route 28 had slowed due to the wet road. The gray scene matched her mood.

The fallen phone buzzed from under the desk. She stooped to retrieve it.

"Henri?"

But it was her cousin at SÉGAG in Paris.

"It's your favorite cousin, Jacques. Forget Henri."

"Jacques, what do you want?"

"The RadGuard report succeeded. Plant 47 was shut down and its reactor has been completely dismantled. The rods have been made into radioactive missile modules as per your specs. The modules were shipped last week from le Havre."

142

"Jacques, that's old news. Get to the point. Why are you calling?"

"My father wants the papers back. He's mad at my beautiful Denise."

"Your Denise? Jacques, I'm your cousin!"

"So what, you're still beautiful. And I don't want you sleeping with Duval. Besides, have you dealt with Byrd?"

"I will soon, but Byrd may yet be of use. He is in South Carolina, trying to find Ryan and the papers."

"You said Ryan was in Maryland."

"I was wrong. The northern team is coming back south, and Bruno Belli is already in South Carolina, in Florence."

"Denise, don't cross father. Find those papers. He's livid!"

"Fine!"

She slammed the phone down. This time it stayed on the desk.

***

At Mary Dean's mother's house in Dillon, South Carolina, Wayne and Bill looked on as Jeannine pushed several security tokens to the side and reached in the briefcase for a document.

"Bill. this report talks about a group fighting in Africa that wants to restore Hutu rule in Rwanda."

"Right. Its leaders were responsible for the 1994 genocide. They fight in the eastern part of the Democratic Republic of the Congo, the '*DRC.*' They want to retake Rwanda. But there is also a rebellion against the *DRC*. Those rebels sympathize with the present Rwandan government."

"Bill, this is complicated. What does it all mean?"

He pointed to the briefcase.

"Messages in there show that a Hutu group under a man named Maximilien Gutera plans to commit mass atrocities in the North and South Kivu provinces of the Congo. Some members of the government in France support them. The idea is to blame the atrocities on the current government of Rwanda so that French sympathizers will ask the UN to condemn Rwanda, and restore a 'Hutu Power' government there."

"I can't believe it. That would risk another genocide? Why?"

"Why not? At the time of the first genocide, the French prime minister was a friend of the Rwandan president, Juvénal Habyarimana, whose death provided the excuse for the mass killings. And maybe some Frenchmen want Rwanda to be French-speaking again. The Rwandan Patriotic Front was started by English-speaking Tutsis from Uganda and the current constitution has a 'National' language, Kinyarwanda, and three 'Official' languages; Kinyarwanda, English and French.

Jeannine shook her head.

"No Frenchman I know would endorse racism and genocide just to restore French as the dominant language."

"I agree. But the leaders of the Hutu-Power movement have no place to go. They caused the genocide. Their only hope is to take over Rwanda. And all they need to assure French involvement is one or two highly-placed officials who use *'la gloire de la France'* as a pretext to fatten their personal bank accounts from a restored Hutu government."

Jeannine groaned. *But another genocide?*

Bill bent over. He appeared exhausted. His shoulders slumped. She steadied him.

"Bill, enough talk. Here, take your antibiotics and rest."

His fingers clasped the pills and pressed them into his mouth.

Jeannine wrapped her arms about him and settled him on the sofa. She tucked a blanket about his shoulders and stood back.

In seconds he was asleep

***

******

Chapter 18
Wednesday, August 29

In Chantilly, a frustrated Denise Guerry arrived early at the offices of Guerry Electronic Systems. She had fought her way through the heavy traffic on Route 28, most of whose cars were headed for offices in the District of Columbia.

But Denise's concern was for Henri. Was she losing her touch?

Henri, do not be distracted by that twit of a Tutsi! You need a woman, not some silly girl.

She ignored the mail in the inbox and paced back and forth. She only stopped when the phone rang. She set it to "speaker."

Maximilien Gutera's voice boomed forth.

"Mlle. Guerry!"

"I'm here."

"I informed your uncle that Dr. Smets betrayed me and that I had dealt with him. Did he notify you?"

"Of course!"

She lied. *Thanks for nothing, uncle.*

Maximilien continued.

"But now I have another problem. I just found out that a Tutsi woman is studying here in Florence. She gave a seminar at the university. She studies encryption. Would this Tutsi be associated with GES?"

"What is her name?"

"Angelique Uwimana. Some of my men attend that university. I will not tolerate a Tutsi presence there. Apparently some of them find her attractive. I will not tolerate my men being infected by such a cockroach."

Maximilien pushed ahead.

"Mlle. Guerry, your uncle informs me that you had your Dr. Belli attend Uwimana's seminar. I must repeat. Is Uwimana supported by GES?"

"She is not, but Henri Duval is and he may be with her. I insist that he not be harmed. He has a key assignment."

Maximilien ground his teeth.

She insists? How dare she!

But he held his tongue. He needed GES and SÉGAG.

"Agreed, of course, Mademoiselle. Henri will not be harmed."

He hung up. *Unless he gets in my way!*

Denise was conflicted.

Maximilien's solution for the Tutsi distraction would be extreme, but uncle Roland insisted that she not oppose the man in any way. But if Henri tried to defend Angelique from the Hutus, he could fall along with her.

Damn!

***

Denise stayed at her desk. She needed to make one more call. She punched the number of Dr. Bruno Belli. It was he whom she had sent to hear Angelique's talk.

"Bruno, are you still in South Carolina, in Florence?"

"Of course."

"Why haven't you reported to me on Angelique Uwimana's seminar on breaking the RSA encryption scheme?"

"Because I've been studying it and I had Greg go over it too. Her factorization method is clever, but it certainly will not work in polynomial time as she hopes."

"Does she suspect GES of breaking RSA messages?"

"No way. She's strictly into the math. She has no clue about how we obtain the primes for decryption. She knows nothing about manipulating human factors. Uwimana is no threat to us. Don't worry about her."

"Bruno, you are naïve. Her research alone makes her dangerous. The belief that she is correct could cause some governments to abandon RSA encryption."

"But two of the top experts in the country, one of them from Stanford, did not believe her either. Sure, they encouraged her to continue her work. She has a novel approach that has possibilities in other areas, but she cannot do the impossible. She's no threat to RSA encryption

He added.

"The bottom line is they say that her algorithm cannot be any faster than what's now available. Her approach to speed up integer factorization is flawed. It won't do that. Period!"

"Bruno, you may know math and algorithms, but you don't know people. It's like this. Gutera thinks Uwimana is a threat to his men. He is going to eliminate her. Understood?"

"You mustn't allow that. Those genociders mutilate people!"

"Talk to my uncle about that. Your problem is to make sure that Maximilien's men do not harm Henri Duval. Henri thinks he likes this Tutsi. And be careful, Maximilien is dangerous."

Bruno swallowed. *So are you!*

She hung up.

***

In Florence, South Carolina, Henri Duval sat at a secluded corner table in the small Italian restaurant. Opposite him was a beautiful African, Angelique Uwimana. Her eyes shone in the wavering candle light.

She was bubbly with the success of her seminar the day before.

"Henri, I did it, and nobody shot me down, not even that hot shot computer guru from Stanford. I have a chance, my ideas might work."

She hesitated.

"My only problem is to speed up the algorithm."

Henri was not thinking of algorithms. He reached across the table and took both her hands.

"Angelique, I knew you would. You are an extraordinary woman."

"No Henri, don't say that. I'm very ordinary."

The slightest shadow flicked across his eyes. She withdrew her hands from his.

"Henri, something is bothering you. What? Are you scared that I'm a mathematician? You needn't be. People are more important than any career. You have to know that."

Angelique 's openness endeared her to Henri who dealt mostly with deception. And she was right, he was disturbed. Denise Guerry was angry.

Still he determined not to spoil Angelique's celebration.

"I'm not worried, Angelique, and you are not only beautiful, but intelligent. Still, you must keep your career."

Abruptly the glow in her eyes dimmed.

"Angelique, what did I say wrong? I'm sorry."

"Henri, that man who just sat down. The suit and tie over in the corner. He was at my seminar. He's the one that implied that I might have stolen encription secrets from the government."

Henri looked up.

"I know him, his name is Bruno Belli. He's an Italian computer scientist who works in northern Virginia, sometimes for my company."

Inwardly, Henri shuddered. Belli at the seminar meant that Denise Guerry was monitoring Angelique and her research.

"Like you work for that 'Guerry' woman."

Henri did not answer. He stood up and signaled the waiter for the check.

"Angelique, we should leave now."

But Angelique, half-risen in her chair, froze. A tall black man had joined Bruno at his table. She whispered.

"Henri! That man sitting with your 'Bruno.' That's Maximilien Gutera, a Rwandan, a Hutu. His father was Charles Hakizimana, a leader of the Interahamwe and the genocide. Maybe Maximilien is the one Paul saw. He looks like his father."

Henri turned. Bruno and his African partner were staring in their direction.

He pulled Angelique from her chair and headed for the door.

***

Outside the restaurant, the clouds burst. Churning winds and rain splattered the street in whirling sprays that stung Henri Duval's eyes. Half-blinded, he guided Angelique on the sidewalk next to the overflowing gutters.

She clung to him as horizontal gusts lifted the water from the asphalt and flung it against their legs. He lowered his head and pulled her towards the car.

They arrived drenched.

Henri drove. Angelique, her hair damp and disheveled, leaned on the glove compartment without speaking. He could barely see through the water that cascaded against the windshield. Neither of them spoke. The rapid thump-thump of the wiper blades provided the only sound.

After a few blocks, the rain lessened, and the wipers cleared semicircles through which Henri could see. He turned to her.

"Angelique, you are in danger, you must trust me. I can help you."

She lifted her head, but before she could answer, he spoke.

149

"This 'Paul' you mentioned before. Do you mean 'Paul Mutabazi,' you know him, don't you?"

She nodded and reached for Henri's shoulder, but he kept on.

"And he was at the farm where Smets was killed, right."

She withdrew her hand. She nodded again.

Henri kept on.

"It was Mutabazi who shot at me when I arrived at the farm, wasn't it? He has a hunting rifle doesn't he?"

"But he told me he didn't try to hit you. He shot high. He only wanted time to get away. Paul is no killer. I mean he hated that man, Smets, and wanted to kill him, but when the time came he couldn't finish him."

She shook some of the moisture from her hair.

"Smets was dying when Paul found him. Whoever did it used a panga."

She sobbed, *a panga! Poor little Augustin, my baby brother.*

She bit her lips and continued.

"All right, here is what I know. Someone had told Paul of a new Hutu Power movement that wanted to restore Hutu rule in Rwanda with the aid of the United Nations. Key people in the movement were living in the Carolinas, including a Belgian doctor who lived near Wilmington. Paul saw a photo of that doctor in a local newspaper. He clipped it out."

She took a breath.

"Paul recalled that a Belgian doctor named Smets had escaped to Goma with the other killers when they were driven out of Rwanda by the FPR, and he knew that a Doctor Smets, a Belgian, had refused to shelter me and my brother from the Interahamwe, a death sentence for us."

She paused

"But I told you how they chopped my baby brother to pieces, and how God saved me, a miracle!"

She sobbed. *Augustin, why am I alive and not you?*

After a moment she continued.

"Paul showed me the photo. It was Dr. Smets, the supposed friend of my mother, the one who turned me and my baby brother away. When Paul told me that Smets was living in North Carolina, near Wilmington, I was upset. He was determined to accost Smets. He wanted to find out what Smets knew about the Hutu plot, but he was too late. Smets was chopped and dying."

Henri stopped for a red light. The water on the windshield was reduced to trickles. The rain had ceased.

"How do you and Paul know each other?"

"Nothing romantic, if that's what you think. We were neighbors in our village, but I was away at school when my father was killed. Paul was only a boy. My father and he sought help at the local soccer field, but Government troops surrounded them and several hundred Tutsis. They slaughtered them, first with grenades, then guns. As he died, my father saved Paul. He shielded him with his own body as he fell."

"Where is Paul now?"

"With a fellow graduate student, at his apartment."

The light turned to green. Henri drove off and continued.

"Angelique, this Gutera, how did you recognize him?"

"My wonderful 'diversity' university invited him to present the Hutu side of the Rwandan 'conflict,' that's their nice term for 'genocide.' I didn't go to the talk, but his photo was on the flyers. It made me sick."

"But not all Hutu … "

"Stop! There can never be justification for the genocide. You were there. You saw!"

She continued.

"Of course not all Hutus are guilty! My mother was Hutu and they killed her. But Hutu leaders corrupted my neighbors, my friends. Most of my village joined them, some out of fear. The Interahamwe killed those who befriended us."

Angelique choked on her tears.

"We have to forgive any of them who ask us. The new government's focus is on reconciliation. We have to forgive each other. There is no other choice. But Maximilien Gutera's father was one of the leaders! He belonged to the devil."

A final sob.

"And his son says it was right to kill us. We deserved it! Gutera brags that he wants nothing of the Tutsi, only our deaths."

Henri reached for her hand and squeezed, but she was not done.

"Before he died Smets told Paul that Gutera's father, Charles Hakizimana, killed him. Paul believed him."

"I thought Hakizimana died fleeing Kigali."

"He did, but some Hutus pretend he survived and anyway Smets is a liar. The French, your countrymen, helped Smets escape to Goma, but Charles Hakizimana was killed. Paul thought he saw Charles here in Florence, just yesterday, but I convinced him he was wrong. Now I know that he saw Maximilien. My God! The son is a beast like his father. And he is here to avenge him. God help us."

Henri stopped the car, pulled her close, and held her. Neither spoke.

***

Back at the restaurant, Maximilien Gutera ate his Steak Toscana while a pale Bruno Belli watched in silence. Bruno had lost all appetite. He lifted his glass to his lips, but his hand shook and he put it down. He spoke, but his voice was a whisper.

"You should have told me before setting the trap for Uwimana. Duval is with her. Denise Guerry specifically instructed me not to involve him. She will not be pleased."

Maximilien Gutera cut his steak. *Only a sirloin but the rub is flavorful and nicely seasoned.* He carefully lifted a morsel to his mouth. *Good!* His eyes returned to Bruno.

"Denise Guerry is a mere woman. We know how to deal with our enemies. Surely we have proved that to you. We will take care of this Tutsi cockroach in our own way. You do not give me orders and neither does she. Stick to your computers. We know what we are doing."

He cut a morsel from his steak and placed it in his mouth.

"Now Monsieur Belli, you should relax. Aren't you hungry? Your tortellini will be cold. Eat!"

Maximilien took Bruno's wine glass and handed it to him.

"And drink! It will calm you. My compatriots are waiting at Uwimana's apartment. I told them they could enjoy her first, before they complete their work. They will call me when done."

Bruno swallowed the Rosato in a single gulp.

Maximilien laid his cell phone on the table and continued.

"For his sake, I hope your M. Duval won't interfere. I prefer not to hurt him. My father and I owe a debt to the French."

***

Henri Duval drove. Damp arms encircled him and he felt the softness of Angelique's breasts against his side as she massaged the rippling muscles of his back and shoulders.

But as they rounded the corner to her street his muscles went taut. He drew away and stopped the car.

"Henri, what is wrong?"

The rain had lightened and he could see down the street.

"That car parked across from your apartment, do you see it? It's a Citroën C3 Picasso. How many of those have you seen in Florence?"

"I don't know cars."

153

"The last one I saw was in Chantilly, Virginia, in the parking lot at GES when some African visitors met with Denise Guerry. This Citroën could mean trouble. I'm going to see."

Damn you Denise, are you involved with Maximilien and his thugs?

He left the motor running, stepped out of the car, and motioned Angelique to move behind the wheel.

"No matter what you see or hear, if I'm not back in ten minutes drive to your friend's house, pick up Paul Mutabazi, and leave Florence. Don't tell anyone where you are going. Find a motel and pay cash. Do not argue with me on this. Please."

"Henri, don't go, you could be hurt."

Too late, Henri had jogged out of hearing.

Minutes passed.

Angelique sat quivering, staring at the rhythmic up-down, up-down, of the wipers as they swept the dripping ripples from the glass.

Henri?

***

At the restaurant, Bruno Belli had not touched his tortellini, although two more glasses of Rosato had passed his gullet. Maximilien Gutera had finished his steak, and was now enjoying a cup of coffee and a square of Tiramisu.

Bruno noted the increasing frequency with which Maximilien glanced at his cell phone as he awaited the report from his men.

Bruno was afraid to speak. A normal Maximilien was sufficient to cow Bruno, an agitated Maximilien terrified him. He kept his eyes lowered while Maximilien glared at the silent instrument on the table.

The phone was not cowed. It refused to buzz.

***
******

Chapter 19
Wednesday, August 29

In Florence, South Carolina, the shadows sheltered Henri Duval from view as he slipped through the yards across the street from Angelique's apartment building. His Browning was chambered and ready, safety off.

For a moment, he doubted himself. Surely the Citroën he had seen in Chantilly was not the only such car in the United States. Had imagination overcome his reason?

But then he looked upward. On the fourth floor, lines of light flickered from inside the windows of Angelique's apartment. The independent movements of the rays meant at least two flashlights were present.

Someone was in there!

The Citroën was parked just ahead. A large live oak, with stout horizontal branches spread wide, dominated the adjacent yard.

He crept towards it and stopped.

Only moments before the silhouette of a man had filled the driver's side of the car. Now there was only empty space. No one was in the car.

Non!

At the slight sound behind him, Henri ducked, half-falling, under the oak. His Browning spun out of his hand and skidded across the slick wet leaves.

"Krunk."

A panga smashed against the dead oak branch above Henri's head, sending a slice of bark flying before the blade met the tough interior wood and rebounded. The recoil numbed the attacker's wrist causing him to loosen his grip.

Henri seized that moment to launch himself headfirst into the midsection of his assailant. The man grunted, twisted himself free from Henri's grasp, and swung his arm high, poised to chop Henri with one lethal slash.

But Henri was quick. Leaning backwards he avoided the panga's wide arc. Then he stepped sideways and delivered a sweeping savate kick, *"un coup de pied bas,"* to the shin of his adversary. The inner edge of his shoe smashed against the man's leg fracturing the thin fibula and bruising tendons.

The attacker crumpled to the ground, his useless leg unable to sustain his weight.

But still he was not done. He flung the panga at Henri's head. Henri stepped aside and dodged the rotating object.

Satisfied that his opponent had no other weapon, Henri retrieved his Browning from the leaf litter and held it to the man's forehead.

"*'Votre nom?'* Your name?"

"*'Je m'appele Eric, Eric Nyonzima.'* My name is Eric, Eric Nyonzima."

"*'Vous-êtes rwandais? Hutu?'* You are Rwandan? Hutu?"

The fallen man nodded.

"*Oui.*"

"*'Que faites-vous ici en Caroline du Sud?'* What are you doing in South Carolina?"

Henri did not wait for the answer.

"*'Vous suivez Maximilien Gutera?'* You are with Maximilien Gutera?"

At the mention of "Gutera" a shadow of fear crossed the man's eyes. Evidently, Gutera did not suffer failure well. But the man was no coward. He glared and spoke through clenched jaws.

"*'Mais, vous-êtes français. Nous sommes amis.'* But you are French. We are friends."

That was too much for Henri.

He clubbed the man with his Browning and the Hutu fell senseless.

Still Henri was curious, *a panga?* He went to the Citroën and looked on the seat. The object of his search, the thug's handgun, was half-concealed under a bag on the floor. The man had preferred to kill Henri personally, with the panga.

Henri picked up the semi-automatic and stood still in the twilight. He studied the windows of Angelique's apartment.

Flashlights still flickered behind the curtains on the fourth floor.

What now?

Gutera's men were still there.

***

In Myrtle Beach South Carolina, Stew Marks and Jack Marino watched Hugh Byrd's motel from their car.

Stew spoke.

"Byrd must know that Wayne Johnson switched his Honda for a Buick. What's he waiting for? He's been in that motel all day."

"He gets the same alerts we do. They've been no hits."

"Hold on. Here he is. He's getting in his Excursion."

Stew started the motor as Byrd drove away. Jack intervened.

"Stew, there's no hurry. I attached the gimmick and he drove off without checking for bugs."

"Right, Jack. I'll hang back. Wait, he's stopping at that bar up ahead. We'd better wait here."

Stew pulled to the curb.

***

At a bar in Myrtle Beach, South Carolina, Hugh Byrd was angry. Yesterday, he had visited the rental agency where Wayne Johnson had returned the Honda. Johnson now was

157

driving a Buick, and Hugh knew its plates. But he had gotten no hits on them.

Hugh smarted. Wayne Johnson had outwitted him, consciously or unconsciously. And the absence of Tom Holder, against whom Hugh habitually vented his anger, exacerbated the hurt.

He chose to ease his frustration with beer. He was on his fourth draft Bud when his cell phone buzzed. He checked the number. It was the NSA.

The text was encrypted. He smiled as he decoded it.

"OK, Mr. Johnson. I've got you."

Humming, Hugh left the bar and headed for Dillon, South Carolina.

***

Near the bar in Myrtle Beach, Stew Marks sat in the car with his partner, Jack Marino. Jack studied the blip moving on the screen of his laptop and laughed.

"Stew, this guy Byrd is arrogant. He can't imagine that anyone would tag *his* car!"

"Which way is he going?"

"Inland on Highway 501, maybe Florence, maybe Dillon."

"OK, we'll follow along."

Stew put the car in "Drive" and headed for Highway 501.

***

At the Italian restaurant in Florence, South Carolina, Bruno Belli was exhausted. His back ached from sitting upright in the stiff chair. Across from him, Maximilien Gutera, a perpetual frown on his face, ignored the waiter's efforts to close out the check and instead demanded yet another refill of coffee.

During the past fifteen minutes, Gutera had not once looked at Bruno, not a glance.

Bruno squirmed in his seat. He needed to relieve himself of the accumulated fluid from the bottle of Rosato wine that he had consumed while watching the Hutu stare at his phone.

But Gutera gave no indication of dismissal and it was clear that for Bruno to leave the table without permission would be viewed as an affront.

Bruno was near despair. His legs could squeeze together no further. A urinary accident appeared inevitable, when at last the cell phone vibrated audibly.

Maximilien picked up the instrument. Bruno heard only Maximilien's half of the conversation.

"What! ... Eric's leg is broken? ... Where is Duval? ... What do you mean, 'You don't know?' ... How is that possible? Imbecile, where is Uwimana? ... What! You are an idiot. Get Jules Habimana. Put him on the line. Now!"

Maximilien held the phone to his ear and drummed the table with his fingers. He continued to ignore Bruno. Jules came on the line.

"Jules, tell me what happened. Omit nothing."

Maximilien listened in silence while, Jules gave a detailed narrative of the events at Angelique's apartment. After some time the Hutu leader exploded.

"You have achieved nothing, nothing at all! Furthermore you know nothing. Where is Duval? Where is Uwimana? They escaped you? Imbeciles! You all are worthless."

He slammed the phone on the table, and glared at Bruno.

"They are all idiots!"

Bruno squirmed in his seat. Maximilien Gutera raised himself to his full height.

"You fool, go! Go to the toilet. Run! And when you come back to the table, pay the bill."

Maximilien glowered and stormed out of the restaurant. Two bodyguards, up to now incognito at a corner table, stood up and followed.

Bruno Belli dashed to the rest room.

***

Henri Duval drove up to the entrance of the motel in Dillon, South Carolina. Next to him, Angelique Uwimana slept. They had fled Florence after she and Henri had avoided the trap at her apartment.

Henri locked Angelique in the car, and went to check in.

He returned and tapped on the window. She stirred.

"Where are we?"

"Dillon, it's near the North Carolina border. I have a room."

"A single room? I can't. Henri, that's not possible."

"Don't worry. It has separate twin beds. I won't touch you, but there's no way I'm leaving you alone tonight."

Angelique acquiesced. No way did she want to be alone tonight either.

They locked the car and went into the side entrance to the motel. They had no luggage and the climb to the second floor was effortless. Their room overlooked the rear parking. Henri went to the window. Their car was undisturbed. Then he turned back to Angelique. She put down her phone.

"Angelique, whom did you call?"

"Paul Mutabazi, I had to warn him it was Maximilien Gutera that he saw. The monster!"

She leaned over, motionless, both hands flat on the dresser.

"Angelique, what's wrong?"

"That man with Maximilien, Bruno Belli. He was at my seminar. He implied I could have stolen my ideas from the government. Why would he say that? And why was he at my seminar? I'm a lowly grad student."

She continued.

"And he works for *your* company! What do you know about that? Why was he with that horrible Maximilien Gutera? He sent those Hutus to kill me. If not for you, they would have."

She wept.

"Dear God, why?"

She collapsed in his arms. He had no answers. In fact, his questions were the same as hers. Denise Guerry despised Angelique, but how was Denise connected to Gutera, the Hutu, and what was her involvement with Bruno and cryptography?

He laid the distraught Angelique on the bed, clothes and all, and covered her with a light blanket.

Henri stood staring out the window.

Damn. Denise was helping Gutera and his murderers!

***

In Chantilly, Virginia, an unhappy Denise Guerry was on the phone with Bruno Belli.

"Bruno, what do you mean Maximilien tried to kill both Duval and Uwimana?"

"He's a madman. Even you can't control that killer!"

Normally, Bruno would never talk to Denise Guerry like this, but he was shaken from his contact with Maximilien.

"Bruno, calm yourself. What did Duval do? Where is he?"

"I don't know. Henri broke the leg of one of Gutera's Hutus. Then he and Angelique got away."

Denise was silent. Henri was helping Angelique and therefore unreliable. She would make him regret choosing that Tutsi.

As for Bruno, to ask the scientist to watch Maximilien Gutera had been her mistake. She spoke.

"Bruno, leave Gutera to me. He needs us to launder his Euros. I want you back in Topsail Beach to prepare for the missile tests. I have no more need for you in South Carolina."

The moment she hung up, the phone rang again. The caller, Ian, worked for GES.

"All right Ian, where are they?"

"I followed them like you said. They drove to Dillon and booked a motel. I'm there now, parked across the street."

"Good. Ian, as long as Henri is with that Tutsi girl, he is useless to me. This is what I want you to do."

She detailed her instructions and hung up.

***

In the motel in Dillon, South Carolina, Henri Duval abandoned his vigil at the window. All was tranquil in the parking lot. Most of the travelers had retired.

From behind him, he heard a faint rustling. Angelique was awake, her lips moving without sound.

"Angelique, what are you doing? Go back to sleep."

Eyes misty, she looked up.

"I'm praying the rosary of the Seven Sorrows of Mary. Our lady appeared to us in my country, in Kibeho. She warned us of the genocide to come, but we did not listen. All I can do now is pray, ask to be forgiven, and for myself, the strength to forgive."

Henri thought of Eric the Hutu whose leg he had smashed.

Forgive? Without that branch, my skull would be cleaved.

Angelique's eyes were shut but her lips moved. Henri knew the words. As a youth in France, he had prayed the "Hail Mary" with his mother.

He shrugged. *Why not?*

"*Je vous salue, Marie, pleine de grâce ...*"

***

******

Chapter 20
Thursday, August 30

In Dillon, South Carolina, Jeannine Ryan awoke to the smell of coffee rising up the stairs from the floor below. She slipped on her jeans and shirt and went down to the kitchen.

Alone at the table, Wayne Johnson arose and poured her a cup. She took a swallow and looked about the room.

"Where's Bill? He's not on the sofa."

Before Wayne could answer, Bill Hamm, a perspiring mixture of wrinkled running-pants, sweaty top, and bare arms, burst through the kitchen door. He slumped into the chair next to Jeannine and took several long breaths.

"That was great. I made two miles with no problem. And I could have run another two."

Jeannine tossed her head and shook the hair off her forehead.

"Very macho. But what about your antibiotics?"

Bill grinned and pointed to the empty container on the table.

"I took them before the run. That was the last of them and I'm done. I feel fine."

He jumped up, seized Jeannine by the waist, spun her out of the chair, and kissed her.

"See, I really am fine."

"OK, OK, you win, but put me down. The fun and games can wait. We have work to do."

She gave Bill a squeeze and turned to wink at Wayne. The latter laughed for the first time since his arrival in Dillon.

***

FBI agents Stew Marks and Jack Marino had just ordered their Egg McMuffins at the drive-in window when the blip on their laptop started to move.

"Hugh Byrd is on the road again. There he goes."

"Where?"

"Not Florence. He's on Route 301, near Dillon, South Carolina. Maybe he'll take I-95 to North Carolina."

Stew reached out the window to grab the bag of McMuffins. Then he handed the carton with two hot coffees to Jack.

The latter balanced the laptop on one knee, with the container on the other. He freed the cups from the cardboard, and fixed them firmly in the receptacles by the ashtray.

Stew spoke.

"I don't think Ryan is in North Carolina. My bet is she's hiding in South Carolina. If Byrd is in Dillon, that must be where she is."

"Byrd may not know any more than we do. If he knew where to find Hamm and Ryan, he would have been there yesterday. I think he has given up and is going back north."

Jack paused. The blip on the laptop had changed direction.

"Stew, wait, he's turning. Maybe he *is* stopping in Dillon."

The blip stood motionless.

"Stew, he's stopped."

Stew took the last bite of his McMuffin. Ahead were the city limits of Dillon. He turned to Jack.

"This is Dillon. Now we'll see if Byrd knows something we don't."

He turned in the direction of the blip.

***

Hugh Byrd stopped his car in the parking lot of the Walmart Supercenter in Dillon, South Carolina. He sat and watched as a steady flow of customers hustled into the entrance.

Hugh was optimistic. At his direction, the NSA was monitoring calls to Wayne Johnson's former secretary, Mona Larson, in Maryland. Yesterday, they had a hit. Wayne had called her. Triangulation from several towers indicated that the call had come from this Walmart.

So Johnson came here for groceries. Hamm and Ryan must be nearby. Wayne Johnson would not drive far from their hiding place.

He withdrew a map of Dillon from the glove compartment and spread it on the seat. He put his thumb on a nearby half-rural area. He would start there.

He reached for the ignition, but paused. *Be careful Hugh, watch yourself. Hamm is dangerous.* Only last Thursday, seven days ago, Smets had dumped the drugged Hamm into the Intracoastal Waterway, and Ryan had snatched him from the hospital the Saturday after. After a week Hamm might have recovered.

To hell with it! Weak or not I can handle him! Confident once more, he turned the key.

Hugh drove out of the lot.

***

Parked down the street from the Walmart in Dillon, Jack Marino studied the blip on his laptop. He turned to his partner, Stew Marks.

"Byrd's on the move again."

Stew looked at the screen.

"I see him. I'll hang back. We don't want him to spot us."

***

In their "safe" house in Dillon, Jeannine Ryan, Bill Hamm and Wayne Johnson sat around the kitchen table. The briefcase, the cause of many recent troubles, lay open. Jeannine handed Bill a brown folder.

"What is this folder about? It's all encrypted."

"Those documents I'm not sure about. They're from GES, Guerry Electronic Systems."

He pulled a sheet from the folder. It had a coded message.

165

*slsyemul,95,g78fsty7y|mu9s|o16yeg4jh|yyjjyet
5kr4tlunjy9tektjho8'isel'rtgg32fdlumriuyio|
uynj|zylunktygytywz|m,xs|ny8fdl4j5|u17f
tv4nxai4nfmc9ef*

Jeannine pointed.

"A name is written on the back, '*Gahuj*.' Who is that?"

"That's *Maximilien Gahuj*, the brother of Charles Hakizimana, a leader of the Rwandan genocide. Hakizimana is dead. After the genocide, his son, Maximilien Gutera, lived with his uncle, Maximilien Gahuj, in Paris. Gahuj trained the boy as a soldier, and now Gutera is the leader of a consortium of Hutu groups who seek to restore Hutu rule in Rwanda. Gutera is arrogant and violent, any competitors are gone, eliminated. Apparently Gutera is planning atrocities that will be blamed on the current Rwandan government so that he can seize control."

"What kind of atrocities? What do you mean?"

"That's what I hope these documents will tell us."

"But they're encrypted."

"Jeannine, you have to decrypt them."

She grimaced. At least the encryption was not RSA. She picked up the paper to count letters and symbols. Frequencies might help, but should she use English or French?

She started counting.

***

In Dillon, Hugh Byrd had already checked at two service stations. This was number three. Hugh handed the man behind the counter a photograph of Bill Hamm.

"Have you seen this man?"

The man laid a torque wrench on the counter and looked at the photo.

"Who are you and why do you want to know?"

"He's my buddy. We were in Iraq together."

"OK, I seen him. Big guy, a jogger, he ran by here this morning."

"You know where he's staying?"

"Nope, never saw him before today."

"That fits. He was supposed to get here yesterday. Did you see where he came from? Or which way he went?"

"Look, I work. I don't watch every rich boy who runs by to see where he goes."

Hugh handed him twenty dollars. The man called through the door behind him.

"Joe, that big jogger this morning, did you see which way he ran."

"Yeh Goose, I saw him. He turned down Azalea Road."

The man whose nick-name was "Goose," turned back to an excited Hugh.

"You're in luck, Mister. Azalea Road is a dead end."

Bingo!

Hugh tossed another twenty to "Goose" and smiled.

It was only when he was in his car that a warning flashed like neon through his brain.

Crap! If Hamm is jogging, he must be recovered!

***

At their "safe" house in Dillon, Jeannine sat alone at the kitchen table, Wayne had gone for a walk in the pine woods that bordered the rear lot.

Bill came in and fondled the hair on the back of her neck. He leaned over and kissed her.

"Bill, I know you think you're all better, but I'm trying to concentrate on this message. I don't have a clue what to do next. The letter frequencies are not helping."

He reached across the table and put another paper in front of her.

167

"Try this one. It's all numbers."

```
18111824041220113726303706282705
18192428244012202618401434292404
06310907402424090924041930101731
19112013092426190410190907142739
08180411391719060632330503112012
17082024081440202413094025241120
13101924062419242225401237231840
13242705031131093040203428051921
31132300083113051202260405053501
```

She grabbed the paper and sat down. Bill went to the window and looked out. Wayne Johnson was in the back yard.

Jeannine studied the block of numbers. There were nine rows, each with 32 digits (or 16 pairs,) making 144 pairs the block. Counting the pairs starting from the left for each row, none was greater than 39. All could be remainders that occur after division by 41.

And the Vigenère encryption method was easy to program using remainders! She stood up and paced.

To represent the alphabet, I'd need at least 26 numbers for the letters and another 10 for the decimal digits. That would make 36. Plus I might want a few punctuation marks, so 40 numbers total would be enough. And a mathematical type might work modulo a prime, like 41 for the sake of elegance. So the encrypted numbers could range from 0 to 40?

She retrieved the first encrypted sheet and studied the letters.

slsyemul,95,g78fsty7y|mu9s|o16yeg4jh|yyjjyet 5kr4tlunjy9tektjho8'isel'rtgg32fdlumriuyio| uynj|zylunktygytywz|m,xs|ny8fdl4j5|u17f tv4nxai4nfmc9ef

She sat and counted the assorted characters. There were 141 characters, not 144 pairs as in the numerical code, but close. The three extra number-pairs could be random, appended to the last line of digits to make a block with all lines the same length.

Maybe these two sheets are code for the same message?

She aligned the initial sixteen characters in the first message with the initial sixteen number-pairs in the second.

1 - 8	18	11	18	24	04	12	20	11
	s	l	s	y	e	m	u	l

9 - 16	37	26	30	37	06	28	27	05
	,	9	5	,	g	7	8	f

They do code the same message! The numbers 18, 11, and 37 have repeats matched by repeats in "s," "l," and "comma." And 05 and 06 code to "f" an "g," respectively, so the letters "a to z" code to the numbers "0 to 25." And it looks like the digits "9 to 0" code to "26 to 35."

She jumped up. The chair scraped the floor. Bill came over.

"Have you got something?"

"Bill, it could be a "Vigenère" code that uses a key word. It's easy to program on a computer using remainders. Suppose a message comprises 100 letters occupying 100 "positions." Number the positions 0 to 99 so that the first letter occupies "position 0" and the tenth occupies "position 9.""

"Whoa, you're losing me."

She was too excited to slow down.

"Look Bill, take a key word like 'watch.' It has 5 letters numbered 0 to 4. Now take a message whose tenth letter is 's.' It's in position 9. To encode that 's' divide its position 9 by the number of letters in the key word (5) so the remainder is 4. That points to the position 4 in the key word whose letter is 'h.' But the code for the letter 'h' is 7. Add this to the code for the original letter 's' (18) giving 25. Divide 25 by the prime 41 (or some larger number) so that the remainder is still 25. The encrypted number for the tenth letter 's' is 25.

Bill coughed. She looked up.

"Jeannine, I have no idea what you're talking about. I'd better let you work. Call me if you get the message decoded."

He turned to join Wayne in the back yard.

Her eyes followed him out the door. He needed results not explanations and she was far from the answer. She frowned and retreated into herself.

OK, Jeannine, that was the easy part. Now how are you going to find the key word and solve this thing?

***

Stew Marks and Jack Marino followed Hugh Byrd from the Super Walmart.

Stew drove slowly and stayed well back while Jack tracked Byrd's vehicle on the laptop.

To Stew's left were vacant lots with rusted car-bodies half hidden by weeds, and wood-frame houses with peeling paint. The lots with houses were bordered by once-plowed fields that now were fallow and brown. In contrast, on the right, two-story brick houses were set back in spacious yards punctuated with tall pines, low dogwoods, and groomed evergreen shrubs. Evidently, this highway formed an economic and social barrier.

Stew's thoughts were interrupted by Jack.

"Slow down, Stew, Byrd's creeping along like he's looking for something."

Stew pulled to the curb and stopped.

"We'll wait here a second. What's he doing now?"

"He's stopped, maybe for a light. No, wait, he's turning."

Stew swung back onto the highway and drove. Ahead on the left, he spotted a group of cars and pickups that signaled an auto garage. Farther on the right, a sign said "Azalea Road."

"Stew, up ahead, that's Azalea. That's where Byrd turned."

"I see it. Where's Byrd now?"

"He's slowed, about a mile down."

They turned on Azalea. Ahead, they watched Byrd park his car crossways in a driveway to block it. Then he stepped out and disappeared behind a tree.

"Stew, that was an M16 he's carrying."

Stew frowned.

"Damn it Jack, Byrd's not trying to arrest Ryan and Hamm. He's there to kill them. Hang on."

He accelerated down the road.

***

Alone in the kitchen, Jeannine paced.

I need that keyword.

She already had tried several free algorithms that were available on the internet. *Nothing!*

But someone had sent both the numeric and text-coded form of the same message. That was sloppy, and sloppiness had helped break more than one code.

She thought of the German "Enigma" machine in World War II. There, a U-boat sailor's "lazy" habit of turning the rotor only a few places after setting the alphabet-rings had provided an important tip to the decoders at Britain's Bletchley Park.

Wait! "Gahuj" was written on the back of the message! Gutera's uncle, Maximilien Gahuj, had sheltered the boy in Paris after the father's death. Was "Gahuj" the key?

Numbering the letters a to z, respectively, 0 to 25, she wrote down the numbers for the keyword.

g	a	h	u	j
06	00	07	20	09

She muttered to herself.

*Let's see. I can decode the first seven pairs (**18, 11, 18, 24, 04, 12, 20**) by subtracting the key letter's number from the pair's number. OK, 18-6 is 12 which decodes to "m." And 11-0 is 11 which decodes to "l." Also 18-7 is 11 decoding to "l" again, and 24-20 is 4. That decodes to "e."*

The next number was tricky.

Wait a minute, 4-9 is -5, negative, so I have to add 41 to it. OK, 41-5 is 36, which I think decodes to "."

Got it. The first seven characters translate to "mlle.gu," that's the beginning of "Mlle. Guerry," the "Denise Guerry" that Bill told me runs GES!

Smiling, Jeannine decoded the entire message.

mlle.guerry,|is|smets|farm|house|ab|ready?|
very|concerned|about|meeting|my|deadline|i|
need|second|payment|from|ges|delay|not|
tolerable|m.g.|f7w

In the last line, *"m. g."* doubtless stood for Maximilien Gutera, while the last three characters *"f7w"* were for internal verification, or perhaps just random letters to fill the line.

No matter. Once again, human carelessness, (sloppiness plus writing down the keyword) had nullified clever encryption.

She reached in the briefcase to examine other messages, but stopped.

Bill stood in the doorway. He held the shotgun.

"A car has blocked our driveway. Come on. We have to run! Quick!"

She grabbed the briefcase and laptop and dashed for the door.

Bill ran into the woods that bordered the back yard. She stumbled after him.

***

******

Chapter 21
Thursday, August 30

In Dillon, South Carolina, Hugh Byrd stood in the shelter of a large tree and studied the house before him.

Only minutes before, while driving along Azalea Road, he had spotted Wayne Johnson standing in the driveway. Before he could accost him, Johnson had disappeared around the rear of the home. Knowing that Hamm had recovered and was dangerous, Hugh had blocked the driveway with his car and taken a position behind the pine where now he stood waiting.

But there was no sign of Hamm or Ryan. *Where are you Jogger?*

Hugh studied the house. Though the masonry walls provided some protection against the 5.56 caliber bullets of his M16, even partial penetration of the rounds could send fragments of brick flying throughout the interior.

He scanned the windows at the front of the house. If Hamm were inside, he was not visible. In fact there was no evidence of any activity in the house, and certainly no sign of defensive activity in the windows.

Damn it Hamm, I know you're here with your buddy Johnson, and that Ryan woman.

Minutes passed, nothing! He must act.

Hugh dashed to the shelter of a pine closer to the house.

Still no movement.

He crept to the porch and stood to the side of the door. He heard shuffling feet, someone was inside. Hugh held his weapon at the ready, took a deep breath, stepped to the door and kicked.

The lock sprung and the door flew open. From inside, someone gasped.

M16 leveled, Hugh slipped through the doorway and stepped to the side. Wayne Johnson, empty-handed, stood before him.

"Mr. Byrd, what are you doing? What do you want?"

***

Hugh Byrd was in no mood for questions. He held his weapon pointed at Wayne.

"Shut up, Johnson. Where are they? Where are Hamm and his chick?"

Wayne stood, silent. Hugh pushed past him and went into the kitchen. He opened the back door. Two Buicks were parked in the rear.

Hamm and Ryan are still here!

At the thought that Hamm could be in the house, Hugh turned, M16 ready, but there was no movement, no sound. He returned to the living room to accost Wayne.

"Where are they, Johnson?"

Wayne started to reply, but the butt of Hugh's weapon crashed against his cheek. He stumbled and straightened back up

"What are you doing? Who are you looking for?"

Hugh smashed his face again. Wayne collapsed to the floor. Blood streamed from his cheek.

"Tell me where are they, Johnson. Answer me!"

Wayne, eyes vacuous, stared past Hugh's pointed weapon.

Hugh snorted.

"You're wasting my time. Goodbye, Mr. Johnson."

Hugh's finger tightened on the trigger. He felt a rush. He would snuff the life out of this fool on the floor. As if in a dream, he felt his finger squeeze the trigger of the M16. *Yes!*

A sharp voice behind him broke the spell.

"What in hell are you doing Byrd? Drop that weapon. Now!"

The voice was familiar. Hugh shook his head clear. Slowly, his finger released its tension on the trigger and he lowered the gun.

Of course! The voice belonged to that FBI guy, Stew Marks.

"I wasn't going to shoot. This idiot knows where Hamm and Ryan are. He would have told me if you hadn't interrupted."

"The man is unconscious Byrd, how in hell could he tell you anything."

"Don't tell me my business, Marks. He's awake, look."

Wayne Johnson had opened his eyes and was staring at the ceiling, his eyes rolled back.

At that point, Jack Marino, Beretta in hand, came into the room. He stared at Wayne, at Hugh, and finally, at Stew.

"Stew, I checked out back. There are two Buicks there, but there's no sign of Ryan or Hamm."

Byrd chimed in.

"Then they're here, maybe they're upstairs. I'd better check."

"Stop, Hugh! You're not going anywhere without me."

He turned to Jack.

"You help Mr. Johnson. Take care of his face. We'll be right back. I'm sure Hamm and Ryan are long gone."

***

As expected, the search revealed no Jeannine Ryan or Bill Hamm.

Stew Marks and Hugh Byrd descended the stairs. Wayne Johnson sat erect in a chair, a makeshift bandage on his face.

Stew turned to Byrd.

"You're damned lucky I'm not holding you on an assault charge. Now get the hell out of here."

"Marks, you touch me and the NSA will have your ass suspended before you leave Dillon. I would have had Hamm and Ryan if not for you. I'm taking Johnson and we're leaving."

"You're leaving all right, but you're not taking Mr. Johnson."

"Marks, you are obstructing a top secret investigation. You're out of your league. My boss will call you."

"Really? I kept you from murdering an innocent man. Even he can't protect you from murder. Get the hell out of my sight and leave that M16 here."

Byrd thought of the empty casings at Johnson's Topsail house. No way was he leaving this M16 with the FBI. He picked up the weapon and headed for the door.

Jack Marino moved to intercept him, but Stew waved him off.

"Forget it, Jack. That snake would start an inter-agency war."

Hugh left.

Stew watched out the window as Hugh Byrd backed his Excursion out of the driveway. Then he turned to Wayne.

"Mr. Johnson, we've proved *our* good will. Now prove *yours*. Tell us where your friends went. You still can help them."

***

Back in Dillon, Hugh Byrd stopped at the Walmart Super Center to recoup. His rapid examination of Hamm's hideaway had revealed no trace of the stolen papers. Hamm and Ryan had taken everything with them, and the FBI and Stew Marks were no nearer to the papers than Hugh.

But how did Marks find me?

Damn!

He jumped out the car, lay on the ground, and shone his flashlight under the chassis. There it was, the same government-issue he had used to tag Wayne Johnson's car. He smashed it under his heel, grinding it into the pavement.

Marks had outwitted him.

But Hugh was determined. He pulled out a map and studied the terrain. Ryan and Hamm were on the loose, but they were on foot. The woods into which they had fled narrowed to a specific tract, and he deduced where they would end up after several hours of following the dry pineland and avoiding the wet "bays" and river swamps.

He checked his watch and made a quick calculation. By car he could reach that area ahead of them.

He drove out of the lot, fast.

***

In the pine flat woods, Jeannine Ryan, leaned against a tall loblolly pine and inhaled deeply. She put her laptop on the ground and dropped the canvas briefcase at her feet. She called out.

"Bill, wait. I need a second to rest."

She sat, staring at the bracken ferns and wire grass that covered the clearing. She could hear the dry snaps of twigs and the return swish of branches pushed aside that marked Bill's path, but she could not see him through the thick undergrowth of scrubby oaks and brush under the pines. A "controlled burn" to clear the pines of unwanted undergrowth was overdue.

She called again.

"Bill, can you hear me?"

There was no answer and she could no longer hear sounds of his passage.

A light breeze tickled the tops of the tall trees and produced a whispering rustle that emanated from all directions at once. The woods were empty. She was alone.

Damn it, Bill, come back.

She listened for any sign of his return, but heard nothing but wind rustling the tips of the pines.

Afraid to shout lest any pursuers hear her, she clutched her knees in both arms and rested to regain her strength.

***

Bill Hamm broke through the brush to find himself at the edge of a swamp, drying from the August drought. Here cypress with protuberant knees and tupelos with swollen trunks shadowed dark layers of dank moldy leaves.

He hesitated. Walking on the damp surface would be easy, but if this were a flood area of the Little Pee Dee River, he and Jeannine would quickly be stopped by still-flooded lowlands.

He turned back into the pine woods and leaned his shotgun against a tree. He listened for Jeannine, but there was no sound. Minutes passed.

Damn, where is she?

Exhilarated at feeling fit after his pneumonia, he had moved fast. He had not considered Jeannine's plight, carrying the briefcase and laptop.

Hamm you are an idiot!

He picked up the shotgun and stepped back into the pines. Overhead he heard the same whispering wind that emphasized the woods' emptiness to Jeannine.

His shoes slipped silently on the long pine needles as he retraced his steps.

***

******

Chapter 22
Thursday, August 30

All day long Henri Duval and Angelique Uwimana stayed cooped up in their motel room in Dillon, South Carolina. The only exceptions were when Henri had sortied to the refreshment area on the floor below where hungry machines ate dollar bills in exchange for chips, nuts, cokes and ice.

After two such "meals," Henri was ready to risk a real supper in the motel's dining room, but Angelique was not.

She waved her arms in protest, a maneuver that Henri found graceful and stimulating.

"Non! Henri, we can't eat there. What if someone should spot us. It's too dangerous."

Henri pulled her towards him. Tall as she was, he was taller. He looked down into her eyes."

"The more agitated you are, the more beautiful."

She pulled away. Even then her movements were fluid and attractive.

"Non, Henri, Non! I'm serious. One of Gutera's spies might see us."

He drew her to him again. This time his lips pressed hers. Finally, he shook his head and spoke.

"You are beautiful, and I promise, I won't let them hurt you. I'm sure it's safe, or I wouldn't let you go there. Besides if we stay in the room, I may not be able to keep my promise to stay away from you."

She drew back. He held her at arm's length. His voice was soft.

"Dearest Angelique, if you are afraid, we can eat chips and crackers here. And I won't touch you. I respect you. I don't want you to be afraid."

"Henri, with you here, I'm not afraid. But Gutera and his thugs terrify me."

She shuddered and leaned against him.

"Are you sure it's all right?"

"No, but we cannot live in fear. We have taken precautions. They cannot know where we are. We must continue to live, otherwise, Gutera will have won. Wash those tears off, so we can enjoy an excellent supper."

With a toss of her head, Angelique disappeared into the bathroom.

Once the door closed, Henri checked the action on his "Grande Puissance" Browning before placing it in his shoulder holster, out of sight.

Unlikely as Gutera's coming might be, if he did show, Henri would be ready.

***

Hugh Byrd was not dumb. After missing Hamm and Ryan at the house on Azalea Road, he had studied a topographic map of the terrain where they had disappeared.

The fugitives would avoid the wet bays of the pine woods as well as the riparian swamps of the tributaries of the Little Pee Dee River. All "dry" routes through the pine flat woods would funnel to a spot that was intersected by an unimproved road.

Now Hugh waited at that spot, his M16 on the seat beside him. Ahead was a one-lane bridge that spanned a sluggish stream whose brown waters were too deep to ford. To his left and right were dry land with wire grass and scattered pines. Behind him the earthen roadway was underlain by large metal

180

culverts that linked low swampy areas dominated by large cypress and tupelo gum trees.

Ryan and Hamm had to cross the road along this stretch.

And he had flushed them from the house with no warning. Surely they would have the incriminating documents with them.

*Damn, Hugh, you win, in spite of that fool Stew Mark*s.

He sat back and waited.

***

Bill Hamm's search for Jeannine was impeded by the scrubby oaks and other plants that choked the lower stratum of the pine flat woods. Time and again, he broke through the brush into openings of wire grass and bracken fern, always empty!

Jeannine, Where are you? I'm sorry. I wasn't thinking.

He bulled ahead through brittle branches of scratchy oaks into an extensive clearing, carpeted with wire grass and ferns. A trail of broken bracken stems marked someone's recent passage. Nearby, was a longleaf pine with a slash mark on its bark.

Damn! I know this tree, and that's my trail.

He had walked in a circle. He looked about. The monotonous well-spaced pines gave him no hint of what direction to take to find Jeannine.

Maybe she was not lost.

But he was.

***

The sun on the western horizon was too low to be visible through the pines. Overhead, a layer of dark clouds obscured its brightness. Only diffused light reached the clearing where Bill Hamm stood. He leaned his shotgun against a fallen log and scratched his head.

At a sound behind him, he reached for the shotgun, but a voice stopped him.

181

"Touch that gun, Mister, and I'll fill your butt with shot."

Bill drew his hand back. *Who?*

"Now, Mister, step away from it and turn around real slow."

Bill turned. Protruding from a thicket was the ominous barrel of a shotgun.

The voice continued.

"Sit down on the ground, put your hands on your head and stay still!"

At that last command, the speaker, a gray-haired man of medium height, stepped from cover. He picked up Bill's shotgun and broke it open, all the while keeping his own gun pointed at Bill's back.

"Mister, I'm sick of you city fellows poaching on my land. Last week my best hound, Suzy, was shot. The vet fixed her leg, but she may never hunt again. You'll pay for that."

But he stopped.

"Whoops! What's this?"

At those words, Bill turned and saw his captor examining the cartridge from Bill's gun.

"Sir, you're mistaken. I'm not poaching your deer."

The man laughed and tossed the cartridge to Bill.

"I reckon not, unless you're dumb enough to hunt bucks with birdshot. That's a number six cartridge. Who are you?"

"My name is Hamm."

"Hamm? You're the one Rob Wilson is letting use the Morton place. What are you doing in my woods?"

Before Bill could reply, the man stretched out his hand.

"I'm Fred Middleton. Rob told me about your troubles with the FBI. It doesn't matter to me. I trust Rob, and after I heard about you and the Unity Pavilion up in Virginia, I trust you.

Rob told me all about that too. Let me guess, the Feds showed up at the Morton house and you're on the run again. Don't worry. Me, I got no love for those guys. They wouldn't let me clear and plant the woods on my south tract. One damned tupelo gum and they said it was 'wetlands.' To hell with them."

Fred did not stop.

"Say, I found a pretty redhead in the woods thirty minutes ago. She claimed she was lost. She with you?"

Bill gaped.

"Don't worry, she's fine. Made me wish I was younger. I locked her in a little hunting shack I built, nothing much. It's got cots and an old wood stove, but the pine burns too fast and makes too much smoke. She wouldn't tell me her name. Mostly she was tuckered out. I'll take you to her."

Fred cradled the pump action in his right arm while he handed Bill his shotgun and signaled him to follow.

"Come on, the shack's this way. You know I once had an old single shot just like yours. My dad bought it for me, my first gun. I got a lot of squirrels and rabbits, and my dad took me for deer too. I got a six pointer. My dad took a picture. I still have it."

Still talking, Fred Middleton wove his way through the brush with ease.

Bill tried to keep up as dusk fell.

***

At the formerly "safe" Morton house in Dillon, South Carolina, agent Stew Marks watched as a mixed FBI team from the Florence Resident Agency and the Columbia Field Office examined the scene.

Stew Marks took Wayne Johnson into the back yard.

"Look, Mr. Johnson, I have nothing against Miss Ryan. Tell me where she's going. It will be best for her. We will find her whether you help us or not."

The rest of Stew's words were lost in the roar of a helicopter whose search lights swept the back yard in broad arcs before disappearing over the pines to the west.

"Mr. Marks, I'm grateful that you saved me from Byrd, but I don't know where she is, or even if Hamm is with her."

"You seem like a good guy. Why would you help a traitor?"

"Bill's no traitor. The documents incriminate Byrd, not Bill. And it was Byrd's man that tried to kill me and Jeannine at my beach house. Hamm wasn't there. He was in the hospital."

His eyes pierced Stew's.

"Jeannine could have died."

Stew stayed silent. Wayne did not let up.

"Mr. Marks, for all his secret clearances and government power, Byrd is just a dirty rotten cop!"

A thoughtful Stew Marks retreated into the house.

***

Finally Bill Hamm caught up with Fred Middleton. The latter pointed ahead. Through the shadows Bill made out the outline of a cabin, a box-like structure made of plywood sheets.

The door was padlocked on the outside. Fred called through the door while he fumbled for the key.

"All right, Miss Redhead, I found your man. We're coming in."

Jeannine was seated on a bunk to the left. Her eyes blinked as Fred lit a kerosene lamp.

Bill embraced her.

"Are you all right"

She nodded. Fred, quiet for once, turned and lifted a hinged board to reveal a window, an opening cut in the wall with flexible screening tacked about the margins. He secured the panel above the opening by means of two hooks. Then he turned and spoke.

"That gets us some air. Now we got to get rid of the chill."

He stuffed the iron stove with kindling and added an oak log.

"That ought to do it. This spot is pretty damp. That log will do the trick. It's hardwood. We'll just let it burn down slow."

He saw Bill eye the kerosene lamp.

"Don't worry about that old lantern. Nobody can see it. The woods are thick here, and there's swamp on three sides."

Jeannine whispered.

"Bill, who is this guy? What does he know about us? Do you trust him?"

Without turning, Fred interjected.

"Don't fret Miss. Rob Wilson is my friend, and I know that your man here was a hero at that fracas up in Virginia. As for the Feds, you two are safe here for a couple of days at least."

Fred was not done.

"My home is a ways off, and it's dark. Looks like I'll be staying with you guys tonight. Sorry to spoil the honeymoon, but it *is* my cabin."

Jeannine huddled next to Bill, still whispering.

"Bill, I did it. I broke the code. Gutera and Guerry are in this together."

***

Angelique Uwimana was happy. The meal with Henri had been wonderful, and after two glasses of wine, she was relaxed for the first time since leaving Florence.

185

As Henri put the key card in the door, she pressed against him and looked into his eyes.

"Angelique? Are you sure?"

She wasn't, but she liked him close.

"Henri, I ... ."

He put a finger on her lips to silence her.

"Angelique, I know that this would not be right for you."

He pushed her inside and looked carefully about the room. Nothing appeared disturbed.

"Angelique, go to bed. I have to check something."

She took the bed by the window. After only moments, her eyes shut and her breathing became regular.

He threw the deadbolt and fastened the security chain. He was worried. That blond Irishman had stared at Angelique all through the dinner. Something was wrong.

Henri turned out the light, but he did not go to the other bed.

He sat in a chair and faced the door.

***

Hugh Byrd sat in his car. The lights were out and though there was little moonlight, the road in front of him was sufficiently illuminated. All was still. Nothing had crossed, not even a raccoon.

Hugh yawned and glanced at his watch, 2:00 am. *Damn it Hamm, hurry up, I haven't got all night.*

The night air was chill and he rubbed his arms. He thought to turn on his motor and the heater, but he did not want to alarm his prey.

He watched and waited.

***

******

Chapter 23
Friday, August 31

The rising sun blazed through the windshield of the Excursion where Hugh Byrd slept, slumped in the seat. The buzz of his cell phone woke him.

"Byrd, where are you?"

The voice was Denise Guerry's. Byrd cleared his throat.

"In South Carolina, near Dillon. Ryan and Hamm are on the run. They're on foot, in the woods."

A helicopter roared overhead. Byrd waited for it to pass.

"The FBI has helicopters in the air, searching for them."

"You led the FBI to them? Marks will find them."

"Not before me. Wait, someone's coming. I have to hang up."

Hugh slid his M16 under some newspapers on the floor just as the man arrived and tapped on the window of the Excursion.

"Mister, my name is Middleton, Fred Middleton. What are you doing sleeping on my land. Were you hunting last night?"

A pump-action shotgun was cradled in the man's left arm. The weapon was well-used. *Go slow, Hugh.*

"Sorry Mister, Isn't this a public road?"

At that response, Fred Middleton's left hand lifted the gun's barrel to point at the car door. Simultaneously, his right hand gripped the stock and his finger sought the trigger.

"Public? Very funny, Sonny. I'm sick of you poachers jack-lighting my deer. Where's your damned shotgun?"

Fred lifted the gun to a level with Hugh's nose.

"Maybe you're the one who shot my dog Suzy?"

Hugh drew back from that barrel. He held his breath. His foot nudged the M16 farther under the papers.

"Mr. Middleton, I am a Federal agent. Here, see my ID."

Fred lowered his gun.

"What kind of badge is this, Mister? You're not FBI."

"The FBI reports to us. Look Sir, I'm sorry about your hound, Suzy, but I am no poacher. Perhaps you can help me. We are looking for two fugitives, a man and a woman. She has red hair. Have you seen them?"

Fred flinched and looked aside. That was enough for Hugh.

Damn, the old guy has seen them!

"Sir, if you'll put the shotgun down, I'll leave."

Hugh started the engine. Fred stood by, shotgun lowered.

"I hope you catch your poachers, Sir. When you catch them, cut their balls off. They shouldn't have shot your hound."

But to himself. *Next time old man, I'll part those gray hairs with my Glock.*

Hugh sped away and disappeared around a bend in the road.

***

Crouched behind a thicket of scrubby oak, magnolias and bays, Bill Hamm turned to Jeannine.

"Something's wrong. Fred has been gone too long. Maybe we should have stayed at the cabin."

"But the battery on the laptop is low and there's no power there to decode Gutera's messages. We can't wait."

Before Bill could answer, Fred Middleton appeared

"Somebody was on the road, said he was a Fed. Face like a weasel. He's looking for you both. He left, but he'll be back, I'll take you across if you want, but if I were you, I'd go back to the shack. You'll be safer there, at least for one more day."

"This 'Fed,' was he FBI?"

"Some kind of badge I couldn't make out. He was driving a Ford Excursion, a brown one."

Jeannine broke in.

"That's like the car that followed me to Camp Geiger!"

"That's Holder's car. It's Byrd. He carries that anonymous ID. We'll go back to the cabin with Fred. Byrd will come for the briefcase. I'd rather face him on turf of my choosing."

"So he won't give up?"

"He can't afford to. I'm sure he's back looking for us now."

Jeannine clutched the laptop while Bill grabbed the canvas case with one hand and held the shotgun with the other. Even birdshot, if to the face, would stop any man.

He nodded to Fred. Together they started back to the shack.

***

At the formerly "safe" Morton house in Dillon, Jack Marino yelled at his partner, Stew Marks.

"Stew, what's wrong with you? You let Wayne Johnson go free. He's harbored two fugitives."

"Calm down, Jack. Johnson and I have an understanding. I've impounded his Buick. He drove the rental back to Topsail. He won't leave the beach house. I have his word."

"'His word?' I hope you know what you are doing."

The roar of a descending helicopter drowned out his words. Stew waited before speaking.

"Jack, I want you in the chopper to search the Little Pee Dee swamps. Find Ryan and Hamm and Johnson won't matter. And if you see Byrd, watch your back!"

Jack snorted and headed for the waiting chopper.

***

Hugh Byrd was still in the hunt. Once out of sight of Fred, he had parked his car and taken up his M16. The 60-round magazine plus a thirty-rounder from the trunk loaded him down, but Hugh wanted the extra firepower.

He heard a helicopter in the distance. The FBI had enlarged their search circle and the chopper was far beyond the crossing that he had guarded. They were looking for Hamm and Ryan outside the radius of the day before. *Good!*

Loaded as he was, Hugh jogged down the road to the spot where he had left Fred.

***

In an apartment in Florence, South Carolina, a Hutu woman, Agathe Muteteli, prepared breakfast. Her husband, Pierre Sehene, a graduate student in electrical engineering at Carolina Technical University, was still asleep.

But she was happy. In June, Pierre would finish his degree, and a tech company in Columbia had a position for him. They had a future. At last, they would outlive the tragedy in Rwanda.

She heard the bedroom door open and familiar footsteps.

"Pierre, you're late. You'll miss class."

"No matter. I quit. I don't need another degree. No more late night cramming. I'm done."

He leaned to grab her waist, but she pulled away.

"What do you mean?" What about your Master's degree, and the job in Columbia."

He laughed and threw a wad of bills on the counter.

"We'll have more money than you can imagine."

"Did Maximilien give you this?"

"Yes, I've joined him."

"Now you are for sale? Pierre, give it back. It's bloody. His father was a murderer and so is he."

"We all were."

"You were only twelve, a boy. You are different now, and you confessed in the Gacaca court of your village. You are forgiven. We have a new life in a new country."

"You don't understand. We are Hutu. With Maximilien, we will go back to Rwanda as rightful rulers. We are the majority."

190

"Pierre, Maximilien Gutera hates Tutsi's. He's a murderer. Don't do this!"

"Agathe, you shame yourself. You are Hutu. I am Hutu. Maximilien is our leader. It is settled."

"If you go with that murderer, I will leave you. I will not watch you throw your life away. Choose! It's me or Maximilien."

Agathe shut her eyes, hoping.

But the door slammed.

When she opened her eyes the wad of money was gone from the counter.

***

In the motel in Dillon, Henri Duval slumped in his chair, alternately dozing and watching the door. The room was dark because the curtains were drawn, but a bright sun shone through the vertical gap between the drapes. Angelique still slept.

Henri laid his head back. He must have imagined that the man in the restaurant last night knew Angelique.

His gaze fell on the floor. Next to the door was a piece of paper, evidently the bill for the room. But too early? They were to stay another night.

But it was not a bill.

Duval,

Denise Guerry sends you this message. She forgives you for your Rwandan playmate, but you must leave the girl now. She told Gutera where you are. Get out now and she will reward you personally for your service. If you don't leave the girl she will not be able to help you.

P. S. I'm the Irishman you spotted at dinner. Your friend is a tantalizing dish, but you can't save her. Save yourself. Denise will blame me if you don't. We never met but you know my name.

Ian

Henri stared in disbelief. He shook Angelique to wake her.

191

"Henri, what?"

He put his finger to his lips.

"Shsss. Gutera's men are on the way. They could be here already. We have to run."

There was nothing to pack. Angelique slipped into her jeans. Henri took his Browning from its holster and held it ready as he turned the deadbolt. He peered into the corridor.

"OK, the hall's clear. Let's go."

He seized her wrist and headed for the door to the stairwell. He stopped. Someone had moved on the other side.

Henri tried to step away, but too late. The door opened and the blond Irishman, Ian, stood before them. He pointed the Beretta at Henri's nose.

"Duval, you dumb ass, they'll kill you too."

"So you're 'Ian.' You're no assassin. Stand aside."

"Don't be a fool, Duval. Denise wants you."

Henri shifted the weight on his feet, but Ian caught the movement and his finger tightened on the trigger. Henri understood. He stopped. He had heard of Ian's prowess.

"Ian, I was in Rwanda. You will have to shoot me because I won't let Gutera's beasts rape and chop this woman."

He looked into Ian's eyes.

"And I know you are not a beast. I'd bet my life on it."

Henri opened the door and pushed Angelique into the stairwell.

Ian stared, but did not shoot.

At the first landing Henri paused and shouted upwards.

"Ian, I owe you for this."

Then he dashed down the stairs pulling Angelique after him.

Outside, they found their car and drove away.

***

The black Audi pulled up to the motel in Dillon, South Carolina. A tall African emerged from the driver side and walked to the front desk. His English was flawless.

"You have a Monsieur Duval registered here, Room 260?"

"I have a Mr. and Mrs. Duvalier in 260."

"That's them. Are they in the room now?"

The clerk shrugged and reached for the phone. The tall man, Pierre Sehene, moved effortlessly and gripped the clerk's wrist.

"It is not necessary to call them. You also have an Ian Callahan staying here, in room 160. He is supposed to meet me. Would you ring his room for me."

"I'm sorry Sir, but he checked out an hour ago."

Pierre's eyebrows shot up. He turned and strode out. At the Audi he leaned in the back window and spoke to his boss, Jules.

"Guerry's man Callahan has gone. Something is wrong."

"Take Louis Makuza and check Duval's room. Don't hurt Uwimana. Maximilien has decided to bed her before he kills her."

But Pierre and Louis returned empty handed. There was no one in room 260, and Duval's car was not in the lot. Dismayed, Jules Habimana sat in the back seat of the Audi. He shuddered. Two failures in three days! He dreaded informing Maximilien.

He signaled Pierre to return to Florence.

***

In the woods near Dillon, South Carolina, Fred Middleton led Bill Hamm and Jeannine Ryan back to the shack without incident. Inside, he looked at Bill and pointed to a shelf.

"Those are buckshot cartridges in that coffee can. You can borrow a couple. Dump that dumb birdshot. I have to get home. I got chores to do. I'll be back in the morning."

Pump action in hand, Fred pushed into the scrub and disappeared amid the shadowy pines. Jeannine watched him go.

"Bill, the laptop only has six percent power left, maybe 10 minutes. I have to stop decoding and shut down, and we still don't know Gutera's plans. Remember the Strontium graphs. He could be planning a nuclear event."

"They don't have the capability to produce a nuclear bomb."

"So, maybe only a dirty bomb? We have to leave. I can't operate from this shack, and we have to stop Gutera."

"We won't be able to stop anything if Marks locks us up."

"But we can show him these messages and other stuff."

"No one will see it. The minute they arrest us, Byrd and his men will scream 'National Security' and seize everything. And Byrd is nearby, you can bet on it."

"Great, we can't trust the good guys or the bad ones."

Dusk fell, but Bill did not light the kerosene lamp. He put a buckshot shell into the shotgun, and sat facing the door.

***

******

Chapter 24
Saturday, September 1

Stew Marks and Jack Marino sat inside a McDonald's in Dillon, South Carolina where Jack lamented the search of the day before.

"Stew, the river swamps are thick. You can't see much from the air."

"At least you know Hamm and Ryan weren't on the open river in a boat. The Little Pee Dee dumps into the Lumber River. That's one way they could get to the coast."

"They still could have been on the river. They could have heard us coming and ducked under the trees in some backwater."

"Maybe, but I'll bet they are holed up somewhere close by. I bet our helicopter spooked them from open roads, and the river too. Hamm is not dumb."

"He may not be dumb, but he's a damned traitor, a spy. And you know what the rat did to me during those hearings on the Unity Pavilion attack. Have you gone soft on him?"

"Hamm has loyal friends, like Johnson, and Jeannine Ryan. I can't believe that she is all bad."

"Damn it, Stew. That woman has messed with your head since you first questioned her. Forget her. And you trusted Johnson. You let him go! What's wrong with you? You're my partner!"

"Would you rather I trust Hugh Byrd?"

"So Byrd is a scumbag, how does that help Ryan and Hamm?"

"Jack, that is precisely what I aim to find out."

Stew took a last swallow of coffee and stood up.

"Come on Jack, you and I are going for a hike. This time we search on foot."

***

Somewhere on Interstate 26, northwest of Charleston, South Carolina, Angelique Uwimana moaned and lifted her head from a pillow made from Henri's jacket rolled into a ball.

"Henri, where are we?"

From behind the wheel, Henri, twisted to see Angelique. She was in the back seat.

"We're not to Summerville yet. I was tired and had to pull off. Are you hungry?"

Her head ached and food was far from her thoughts.

"No. But Henri, I have to meet my professor Monday morning about my thesis. How?"

"That's not possible. No way can we go to Florence, or the university. That's Gutera's turf."

"But my thesis?"

"We'll find a café in Charleston where you can email him. Meanwhile, hungry or not, I'm going to find you some food. We can't stay here."

He turned the ignition and drove onto the highway. She sat up.

"Henri, what did that man 'Ian' mean when he said Denise Guerry wanted you. Have you slept with her?"

The image of the delicious Denise flashed before him. Guilt swallowed all logic. He stammered.

"Angelique, any man would find Denise desirable, but … "

"So you would if you could."

"But I love you. That woman told Gutera where we were. She wants …"

He started to say "you," but switched.

"She wants *us* dead."

196

He twisted to look back and saw the grief in her eyes. The car swerved into the adjacent lane.

"Henri, watch the road!"

He swung back into his lane and looked in the rearview mirror. Angelique's eyes had closed. She appeared to sleep.

But Henri had another reason to watch the mirror, to look for cars following them, particularly of French, or German, make.

***

Hugh Byrd was a man of many skills, including the art of survival. Since his days on bivouac as a paratrooper, he had honed those skills. Yesterday and today they had served him well.

He peered through the brush to study the shack in front of him. The structure consisted of three-quarter-inch plywood supported, presumably, by interior two by four studs. A lone window was shuttered from within by similar plywood while a thin dwindling plume of smoke wafted upwards from the tin stove pipe at the rear of the roof.

Hugh smiled.

The smoke indicated the presence of his prey.

The shack's plywood walls were no obstacle. They were little better than paper at stopping his 5.56 caliber, 55 grain, ammo. His only worry was that the penetration might be too clean. He wanted the exiting bullets to fragment the wood into lethal splinters that would fill the room.

He studied the door. It was heavy and thick, somewhat resistant to penetration, and thereby more likely to splinter. He took a position to the front of the cabin and raked the flimsy structure with bursts of fire.

"BrBrBrup, ..., BrBrBrup, ..., BrBrBrup, ..., BrBrBrup."

At a head-on ninety degree impact, clean holes appeared in the plywood as well as the door. He continued.

"BrBrBrup, ..., BrBrBrup, ..., BrBrup."

He moved quickly and fired more bursts at an angle.

"BrBrBrup, ..., BrBrBrup, ..., BrBrup."

This time splintered holes marked the passage of the bullets. He let go again.

"BrBrBrup, ..., BrBrBrup, ..., BrBrBrup, ..., BrBrBrup."

He still had lots of rounds in his magazine. Forget the damned angle, he went to his right and raked the side walls, straight on.

"BrBrBrup, ..., BrBrBrup, ..., BrBrBrup, ..., BrBrBrup."

Again!

"BrBrBrup, ..., BrBrBrup, ..., BrBrup."

Done!

Hugh dropped the spent magazine and jammed his backup in place. Holding the M16 at the ready, he went to the front. He would grab the briefcase and leave the bodies for Marks to clean up. He pulled the door aside and looked in.

Empty!

What the hell?

He heard a step behind him and turned. Too late! The butt end of a shotgun smashed against the side of his skull.

Hugh dropped senseless to the ground.

***

In the pine woods some distance away, Stew Marks stopped to listen.

"Did you hear that, Jack? That was automatic fire."

Jack Marino turned in the direction of the sounds.

"You're right. There it goes again, three-round bursts."

Stew seized Jack's arm and pointed.

"Over that way! Hamm and Ryan don't have automatic weapons. That's Byrd. The bastard has caught up to them."

They started in the direction of the gunfire, only to find their way blocked by impassable dark waters studded with gum and cypress trees.

***

After an hour of watery dead ends, Stew halted, hand to his ear.

"Jack, those are voices ahead. That way."

Stew drew his Beretta. Jack did likewise and disappeared to the left. They moved in parallel through the pines.

Ahead Stew heard a woman.

"That's an M16. That guy tried to kill you!"

A man spoke in reply, but his words were indistinguishable.

Stew continued to his right until a voice from behind stopped him.

"Hold it, fellow. Stow the gun and tell me who you are."

The voice belonged to a man with gray hair. A pump action shotgun rested casually in his arms.

"I'm with the FBI, let me show you my ID."

"Never mind. Are you agent Stewart Marks?"

"I am."

"He told me you would come. I'm Fred Middleton. These are my woods."

"Who do you mean, 'He?'"

"Some fellow called Hamm."

"Hamm! Where is he?"

Fred shrugged. Stew persisted.

"I heard a woman's voice too. Where is Miss Ryan?"

"Ryan? I don't know. You must have heard Mary-Jean, she's a deputy sheriff. I called her to handle a problem I have. If you follow me to my cabin. I'll show you."

He pointed into the brush.

"And call your friend out here. Both of you need to see this."

Stew signaled to Jack to step into the open.

Together they followed Fred along the edge of the swamp.

***

When they arrived at Fred's cabin, Stew stopped and stared.

Bound to a stout pine, hair matted with dried blood, was Hugh Byrd.

"Stew, thank God. Tell these yokels to let me loose. Show them my ID. Tell them who I am."

But Fred stepped in front of Hugh.

"Hold on there, Mister Marks."

He pointed to a weapon leaned against the house.

"That's an M16. Your 'Fed' friend tried to kill me. See the holes in my cabin. They're more than forty. It's just luck that I saw him coming and got out first."

He glared at Hugh.

"This man is a murderer."

Jack Marino did not like Fred's tone. He stepped forward.

"Get out of the way Mister, I'm a federal officer."

A woman with a police-style shotgun stepped from behind a tree and accosted Jack.

"Back off Mister, that man is my prisoner."

Then she turned to face Stew.

"I'm Deputy Mayrant, if you want this rat, you can talk to my uncle. He's the sheriff, he ordered me to bring him in, and that is what I aim to do."

She glared at Jack.

"You're in the wrong damn county, Mister. We take care of our own here. Your friend tried to murder Mr. Middleton. He's going to sit in our jail, not some Fed country club up north."

Fred spoke up.

"Mr. Marks, Mary-Jean is the sheriff's deputy, and she's damned good at what she does."

He leaned closer and whispered.

"That shotgun has a rifled barrel. It shoots slugs. It's better not to cross her."

Hugh's eyes wandered wildly from Stew to Fred, then to Mary-Jean, Jack and back. He shouted.

"Help me, Marks."

But Stew turned to Mary-Jean.

"Deputy, I agree this is your jurisdiction. The FBI will cooperate fully. I'll notify the Field Office in Columbia, and the Resident Agency in Florence. But I would like to talk with the sheriff about ballistics on that M16. We can help there."

He added.

"And I see that you've gathered a lot of those casings. I would appreciate your giving me a couple to take with me."

Mary-Jean shook two 45 millimeter-long casings out of a plastic bag into a similar sac, and handed it to Stew.

"Thanks. Miss, your prisoner is dangerous. Keep him cuffed. Maybe Mr. Middleton will 'ride shotgun' with you ?"

Jack raised his eyebrows and approached his partner.

"Stew, what the hell are you doing? The NSA will smash you."

"Don't count on it, Jack. They won't want to 'own' this guy. I'll bet they have a 'deniability' scenario rehearsed and intact."

"Damn it, Stew, you're taking a big chance."

"Forget me. We need to get this guy off the street."

Jack stared speechless.

***

Bill Hamm and Jeannine Ryan stood, half hidden, behind the gray barn near the farm house. Those buildings, along with a remote tobacco shed, provided the only relief from the furrowed fields whose lines of brown plants stretched to the bordering pines. Occasional tufts of white cotton identified the late crop.

Bill opened the barn doors and went to an old pickup truck parked next to a new green John Deere tractor. Jeannine followed with her laptop and the canvas briefcase

Bill pulled the door open. He put his shotgun in the back, took a key from his pocket, and inserted it in the ignition.

"Jeannine, if you know any prayers, try them now."

He turned the ignition. The motor coughed, twice.

He tried again. This time there was a low drawn-out moan.

"Bill, don't let up."

He held the key firm. The motor clattered as oil reached the valve lifters.

Success!

Holding the briefcase and laptop, Jeannine got in the cab.

"OK, Bill, where to?"

"To Charleston. Byrd called there regularly from the Torbee. I believe Gutera is planning something there."

He whistled. Thanks to Fred Middleton, they had wheels!

***

******

Chapter 25
Sunday, September 2

In the hotel in downtown Charleston, South Carolina, Henri Duval awoke, rubbed his eyes and tried to focus on the fuzzy digits on the bedside clock. *Damn, 9:00 am. I slept late.*

He stared about the room. Angelique's bed was empty!

He called but no answer.

Rien! Nothing.

He stepped into his jeans and went to the window. Several stories below was an old church set apart from the adjacent buildings by an equally old cast iron fence that enclosed, also, a small graveyard. Several tourists milled peacefully among the tombstones.

Calm down Henri, think!

He had driven late, with Angelique asleep, out of sight, on the back seat. No one had followed them. And he had paid for the room with cash, furnished by GES when relations with Denise Guerry had been warmer.

No one could have found us, but?

He called the desk. A voice answered.

"May I help you?"

Before Henri could frame a question, Angelique appeared in the doorway.

"Angelique! Where have you been? What's wrong?"

Distantly, the voice on the phone pleaded.

"Sir, are you there?"

"Sorry. It's nothing."

He turned to her.

"I thought someone had grabbed you. Where were you?"

"I didn't mean to scare you. It's Sunday. I went to Mass."

She went to the window.

"That's the church down there, St. Mary's, and the graveyard is filled with French tombstones. I felt at home."

"But someone could have seen you."

"You said we must not let fear run our lives. Henri, I go to Mass to honor God."

She sat on the bed and stroked his arm.

"He saved me in Rwanda for some purpose I still don't know, and he will save me here with your help. I cannot stop loving God. And He loves you too."

He looked into Angelique's eyes. Could his pragmatism explain her goodness?

"Angelique, I was worried."

"Cher Henri!"

She embraced him.

***

In their motel in Dillon, South Carolina, both Jack Marino and Stew Marks were shaved, dressed and ready for the day ahead.

They had skipped the usual Egg McMuffins and eaten instead at the IHOP adjacent to the motel. Stew, in particular, had enjoyed the Eggs Benedict. Now with his stomach full, he peered over his coffee.

"Jack, I want you to take the car and go back to Wilmington. Wait for me at the resident agency there. You'll doubtless get a call from Washington about Byrd. I don't want you taking the blame for my hunches. You need to be free from me for a while."

"Stew, this is not good. We work together."

204

"I'm taking a few days off. For your own sake, I don't want you involved. I am not sure what I'll do."

"Stew, if it's the Ryan woman, forget her. She's bad news."

"I don't agree. That's why I have to do this on my own. Hamm may be innocent. He attracts good people, Ryan, Johnson, and even this Fred Middleton. That farmer's a shrewd judge of people. He saw through Byrd."

"You're sticking your neck way out for a damned rat and a crooked woman."

"Not for a woman, or Hamm either, for the truth."

"All right, Stew. You've made up your mind. I'll take the car back to Wilmington. Where will you be?"

"You don't need to know. It would mean problems for you."

Jack shook his head as he stood up.

"Stew, you're wrong. You're helping the bad guys. I can't support that. I'm going to nail Hamm, and Ryan too. Whatever you do, stay out of my way. Don't make me fight you."

Jack strode from the restaurant.

***

At a motel in Summerville, South Carolina, Jeannine's laptop was plugged in and charging.

She took a CD from the brown folder (now labeled "Maximilien Gutera") and scanned its contents.

She opened several files. Only numbers appeared on the screen. All the files were encrypted."

She muttered to herself.

"All right, Mr. Gutera, if you haven't changed the key word, I'll see what this is about."

She selected the first file.

```
18361315083014271921261826191414
13153816050311001708042519091903
06381614150639161012062526201206
40270640213308173911392314111119
12040012371722201119282040242422
09043200232618060117250706310905
11273928103606191220402034280505
07282005131124120505273312243806
22231919072228050627242623240620
28050611380405400619081500093410
14133702122533271939093922390518
```

She ran the numbers through her decryption program using the key word "Gahuj."

She smiled. The key worked and a message appeared

*m.g.|you|must|finish|devices|and|ship|them|
from|usa|on|l'etoile|d'afrique|to|rendezvous|
with|la|lutte.||do|not|fail|need|funds?|
contact|guerry|at|ges.|||
||jacobin5xdt2u|5d'pt,m*

"Bill. Look at this. The initials 'm. g.' stand for Maximilien Gutera, but there's a new player in the game, code name 'Jacobin' or maybe 'Jacobin5.' What do you think?"

"I think that '*l'Étoile d'Afrique*' and '*La Lutte*' are the names of ships, but what kind of device is Gutera preparing, and where is this rendezvous?"

Jeannine browsed the computer disk.

"Here's a file that has a similar name. I'll run the numbers through my program. If the key word is still 'Gahuj,' It'll only take a minute."

Bill watched as Jeannine steered the mouse rapidly, clicking occasionally. Her auburn hair drooped over her eyebrows. She flipped it up with her left hand, while the right continued to guide the mouse. He smiled. Jeannine was particularly desirable when absorbed in the computer.

She looked up and pointed to the display.

"Check this out, Bill. You wanted to know about those two ships, one of them is headed for Charleston. Look at this."

m.g.|notify|captain|of|l'etoile|d'afrique|
destination|charleston|south|carolina,|
usa,that|vessel|la|lutte|will|leave|le|havre|
as|scheduled,with|containers|with|live|rod|
modules|from|dismantled|plant|47|
moduleslabeled|shipped|fromcharleston,usa|
lalutte|will|transfer|containers|to|l'etoile|d'afrique|
international|waters|off|charleston|
at|time|agreed,||destination|mombasa.|
jacobin5xo9

Bill examined the message.

"Plant 47 must be a nuclear energy plant and the rods must be the fuel rods for the reactor. I knew the French planned to deactivate some plants, but I didn't know they had started. The modules must be radioactive units to mount on rockets. They are to be shipped to Mombasa on the ship, *l'Étoile d'Afrique*, out of Charleston. Gutera wants it to look like the modules are from the United States."

"And the rods?"

"They're highly radioactive. They're not 'spent.' The French conspirators must have hijacked the rods to make radioactive modules for dirty bombs. They won't produce a nuclear explosion, but they are still horrible. Most deaths will likely be from the explosion, not radiation, but there will be extensive contamination, and those who get sick from radiation will make a powerful political 'fright factor.'"

"But where?"

"Gutera likely will use the bombs on anti-Rwandan forces in the eastern Congo, and then blame the Rwandan government, and call for its removal. International opinion will be against Rwanda."

"And the French will say the nuclear material came from the United States. They won't be involved."

"Exactly. If the radioactive material was shipped from the U. S., that could deflect criticism from those French who support the Hutus."

"But would Gutera use the bombs against his own men?"

"He'll do anything to seize power in Rwanda. And he could warn some of his forces to withdraw from critical areas before the strike. The others would be sacrificed for propaganda photo-ops.

"But how?"

"My guess is that he'll launch missiles from Rwanda and explode them in the air over the targets in the eastern Congo. The blame will be on the Rwandan government."

Jeannine's stomach knotted. The scheme was all too plausible.

"Bill, this message is over two weeks old, with no times or dates. The *Étoile d'Afrique* could be here already."

Bill nodded and sat at her laptop.

"The Port Authority has a web page. Here it is, 'South Carolina Ports, Charleston.'"

He scrolled down the list of arrivals.

"The *Étoile d'Afrique* is expected on September 8. She is to discharge and load containers at the North Charleston terminus."

"That's this Saturday. Does it give a departure date?"

"No, but maybe three days max. We're about out of time."

***

In Dillon, South Carolina, Stew Marks paid the car rental with his personal credit card and enquired about Fred Middleton.

The receptionist handed him a map.

"This is how you get to Mr. Middleton's farm. It's about ten miles from here. I've traced the route for you."

Some time later, Stew turned onto a rutted road that passed through spent fields to a frame house and barn. Fred Middleton stood on the porch. As Stew pulled to a stop, Fred sniffed.

"You're one of those FBI men."

"Yes, but I'm on my own time. I need to ask you about Mr. Hamm and Miss Ryan. I may be able to help them too."

"I gave them the keys to my old pickup, that's all. I don't know where they went."

Fred waved Stew into the house. After several beers, Stew had gained Fred's confidence. Though neither Jeannine or Bill had revealed their destination, Fred had deduced that they were going to one of two ports, Wilmington, North Carolina or Charleston. South Carolina.

Stew smiled, both towns had FBI Resident Agencies. He rose to shake Fred's hand.

He left and headed for Wilmington.

***

In Summerville, a weary Jeannine pushed away from her computer and yawned. She turned to Bill.

"I still don't get it. Why would GES and the French plotters have Gutera prepare the explosive devices? He and his men are thugs and fighters, not engineers. Why rely on them for something that requires technical skills, and maybe even remote guidance capabilities?"

"I wondered about that myself. Maybe because they want to use batches of explosives from the U. S. that are tagged and identifiable as produced in the States? But why do you ask?"

209

"Because the French plotters are worried. Look at this."

d.g.|urgent|you|advise|paris|on|ability|of|
m.g.to|produce|remote|explosive|devices|before|
depart|of|l'etoile|d'afrique|for|mombasa|deep|
concern|here|that|m.g.unable|to|meet|deadline.|
||jacobin5hk2j3c5|s27tvp,

Bill read the message. Evidently "d. g." was Denise Guerry, while as before, "m. g." was Maximilien Gutera.

He stood and paced.

"This could be a break for us. Gutera and his men may not be ready when their ship arrives."

But Jeannine saw the look in his eyes.

"Bill, you don't think that. They'll be ready. We're in trouble."

***

******

Chapter 26
Sunday, September 2

In her office in Chantilly, Virginia, Denise Guerry slammed the phone on her desk. First Henri, and now Ian Callahan, had succumbed to that Tutsi bitch's charms. She recalled Ian's words.

"I couldn't hand her over to be raped, have her breasts hacked off, and be killed. I saw photos from Rwanda. I'll quit if you want."

But she had asked him to stay on. She needed Ian now that her connection with Henri Duval was tenuous.

Denise opened her closet to reveal a full-length mirror on the inside of the door. She stood erect and regarded herself. She knew Henri desired her. If only he were near, he would forget that little Tutsi.

She turned sideways and looked again. Curves in the right places. Whatever "It" *was*, she still *had* it."

Henri, you idiot, you don't know what you are missing!

Immediately Denise Guerry called Ian Callahan.

"Ian, where are you?"

"In Wilmington, North Carolina, like you told me to be."

"Good. Do Gutera's men know where you are?"

"I left the motel in Dillon before they got there. I drove straight here. Only you know I'm in Wilmington."

As with Henri, Denise adopted her "helpless" approach.

"Ian, there could be a problem with Maximilien Gutera, and I might need you on my side. Can I count on you?"

"I assume that's what you pay me for."

"And Ian, you may have to protect me from Duval. Would that be a problem?"

"Not if that's what you want, no."

"Good. I'll be in Wilmington tomorrow afternoon."

Denise hung up. Ian still could be useful.

***

In Charleston, Angelique Uwimana and Henri Duval left the internet coffee shop.

"Henri, thanks for letting me email my professor. I had to let him know I could not meet him. And that café was neat. All the students and the kudu horns on the wall. And the Kenyan coffee. I felt at home."

"I'm not sure I did you a favor, someone could track us."

"But it was only email, and from a public café? And sent only to my professor? I'm his student. He is harmless."

"Never mind, what's done is done."

Back at the hotel Henri watched TV, but his mind churned.

Gutera has too many men. The only person who can control him is Denise. Can I bargain with her to save Angelique?

***

In Summerville, Bill was at the Burger King while back at the motel, Jeannine hunched over her computer.

Her head ached from the tedium of decrypting Jacobin5's messages, all of which expressed doubts about Gutera's ability to obtain the guidance devices for the missiles.

She sighed and tapped "Enter." The decrypted message appeared.

*d.g.||with|regard|m.g.|and|sullivan|electronics|
holly|ridge|radar|guidance|and|timer|watch|out|
for|delay.|sullivan|electronics|now|a|
one|man|company.|critical|we|have|
delivery|in|charleston|for|etoile|d'afrique|
on|date|agreed.|jacobin5||'p2n'glt5msnsn'*

As she read, Bill and the burgers appeared. She looked up.

"Bill, this message has specifics, it's not just Jacobin5 complaining. Have you heard of 'Sullivan Electronics' in Holly Ridge."

"I know a Holly Ridge in North Carolina. It's near old Camp Davis. The U. S. Navy did missile research there after World War II. Check the web."

She tapped fast.

"I got it. Here's their web site. It seems that Sullivan Electronics has lived off of navy contracts for guidance systems for years. Wait, they've not had a renewal for several years."

"Bingo! That's it. They are supplying the guidance systems and remote control systems for Gutera's missiles. The *Étoile d'Afrique* will be in Charleston on Saturday to load them. Maybe we can stop the delivery at Holly Ridge."

"But can Fred's old truck make the trip?"

"No way. It's overheating. We'll have to chance using the 'Harmon' credit card for a rental. Pack up!"

By the time Jeannine had stuffed the CD's, security tokens and papers into the case, Bill already was outside.

***

In Florence, South Carolina, Maximilien Gutera signaled to Jules Habimana who stood at attention by the door.

"Jules, is the Audi shined and fueled?"

"Of course, just as you ordered."

"Good, Sullivan Electronics will have our missile guidance modules ready tomorrow. Mr. Sullivan will meet us at the warehouse in North Carolina, near Holly Ridge. The modules will be tested on Wednesday evening at Topsail. If the tests are successful, then we shall go to Charleston and prepare the containers for the Étoile d'Afrique."

"Understood."

"And Jules, fetch Louis Makuza and inform him he is going with us to Holly Ridge. Make sure he brings his panga."

At that point the phone rang. Maximilien picked up.

"Mr. Gutera, this is Professor Hurley, at Carolina Technical University. I'm Ms. Uwimana's doctoral advisor. You said you wanted to speak with Miss Uwimana about supporting her research. I wanted you to know that she will not be available tomorrow as I told you. She has canceled our meeting."

"Professor Hurley, do you know where she is?"

"I only have an email. It's from a WiFi café in Charleston."

"Thank you, professor. You are most considerate."

Charleston! Clever Angelique, I will enjoy your body before I give you to my men.

Maximilien rubbed his hands and rose from his desk.

"Jules, Angelique Uwimana is in Charleston. We will go there after we finish our business in North Carolina.

***

Stew Marks was near Wilmington, when his phone buzzed.

"Mr. Marks, this is Fred Middleton. I told you I'd call if Miss Ryan called me. You still want to help her?"

"Of course."

"She and Hamm are on their way to Holly Ridge in North Carolina. They rented a Town and Country minivan in Georgetown and left my truck there for me. I reckon Mary-Jean will drive me there to get it."

"Mr. Middleton, Thanks. When did she call."

"An hour ago, They were leaving Georgetown."

"Thanks again."

"Don't thank me. Just help that gal get out of trouble."

Stew sprang into action. He could easily beat Ryan and Hamm to Wilmington. He would intercept their minivan on Route 17. He would wait all night if necessary!

***

******

Chapter 27
Monday, September 3

In Chantilly, Virginia, a determined Denise Guerry arrived early at her office. She had slept fitfully, dreaming periodically of Henri Duval embracing Angelique. She recalled her own image in the mirror. How could Henri prefer a little girl to her?

Denise, you don't care about Duval. This is pure envy.

Still, Henri was a valuable asset. She must regain control of him.

GES was to test the missiles at Topsail, but after talking to Bruno Belli she was concerned. Once the tests were completed and Gutera no longer needed GES, what would the madman do?

She went to her desk drawer and retrieved her Browning Hi Power pistol. (Henri's choice of handgun was also hers.) Gun in hand, she went to her private elevator and descended to the basement. GES had leased a large portion of the basement for a private firing range, her perk for being owner and boss.

She fashioned suppressor ear muffs about her head, checked the double column 13-round magazine of the Browning, and aimed at the target.

The silhouette was that of a man. *Maximilien Gutera? Byrd? Or even Henri?*

She could trust no one. She settled herself and fired five-rounds.

"Crack ..., Crack ..., Crack ..., Crack, ..., Crack."

Two hits in the shoulder to her left, one in the neck and two misses wide right.

Damn, Denise, you can do better.

"Crack ..., Crack ..., Crack ..., Crack, ..., Crack."

Four holes appeared in the upper chest and one in the neck.

Better, and more consistent too!

She hefted the weapon and felt its natural balance. Now she was really feeling it.

"Crack …, Crack …, Crack."

All to the head!

She reloaded the empty magazine, but chose to stop shooting. She had not lost her touch. She removed the ear muffs and put the Browning in her ample shoulder purse.

She was ready to head south.

***

Denise took the elevator to her office and looked out the window at Route 28. It was early Monday and rush hour was in full swing. A misnomer, there was no "rush," the highway was clogged, a virtual parking lot.

She composed a message to her cousin, Jacobin5, in Paris and encoded it.

1500093410141337191220402034280522211
37263040252717214018181325141531130503
05201423082340130519211909231715000
13051811352833400739081914243916050201
14202617042539231940262426180820402705
03113509231906381321190014082514060
321310190638161415063109051127392810
360621262613211910101118280828081831
08250425390812201523091902111909190301
06231325142020281414201927301826242102
24402924121904252309304025242425300603
39232118072820051321372813400920262011
11153309051202260405132139080800222001
10170406280828081831081804113908130420
20371705032700091740153308080707372010
101826342205030226040539133128361225

Then she decrypted it for a final check.

jacobin5|do|not|worry|ship|l'etoile|d'afrique|
to|arrive|sept8|at|north|charleston|terminus|
depart|sept10|to|meet|ship|la|lutte.|bruno|
belli|will|test|guidance|and|detonation|
systems|wednesday|sept5|topsail|north|carolina|
m.g.|not|capable|i|will|meet|henri|duval|in|
charleston|d.g.|'glt5ms

Satisfied, she turned off the light and started out the door, but stopped and turned back. *No!* She had left the plaintext of the message on her desk.

She went back. As with many European women, she smoked, though in America she concealed her habit.

The ashtray was out of sight in a side drawer. She took it out, placed the message in it, and lit it aflame. Moments later, only a crisped black fragment remained. She pulverized that into a mass of minute ashes.

That done, she slipped her bag onto her shoulder and left.

She was ready.

The Carolinas needed "hands-on" action, hers!

***

In Onslow County, North Carolina, near the town of Holly Ridge, Jack Sullivan worked in his warehouse, a solitary building that was isolated from its neighbors by tracts of old-growth pines and marshland. The shed-like structure had a corrugated metal roof, and no external markings except for a faded sign, "Sullivan Electronics," that hung above the wide doors on its southern face.

Inside the building, to one corner, were narrow work benches topped with scrambles of coiled wires, small boxes and trays of color-coded electronic parts, wire-strippers, delicate screw

217

drivers, soldering guns and the like. Elsewhere the vast interior was filled with empty crates, pallets, and two rusted forklifts.

Jack stood at one of the benches and carefully fastened a silicon chip onto the last of the small circuit boards that covered the bench top. Done, he sighed in relief.

The computer chips were from China. They had arrived a week late, and Jack had promised his client more than two dozen guidance boards for last Wednesday. Thankfully, the client had agreed to accept shipment today.

Sullivan Electronics was a family-staffed and -owned company, founded by Jack's grandfather, Tom Sullivan. Immediately after the war, Tom had worked on the "Sand Spit" (now known as Topsail Island) as an electrician for operation "Bumblebee," the development and testing of U. S. ram jets. In 1948 when the Navy closed Camp Davis and its missile test site on the Sand Spit, Tom had started his company.

By 1960, Tom's son (Jack's father), a graduate of Johns Hopkins University, had joined the company and exploited the use of the new transistor technology and government contracts to produce a viable and profitable enterprise, one that provided employment for Jack, his older brother and a younger sister. By the late 70's the company had fully adapted to silicon-chip technology and continued to flourish.

However, the death of Jack's older brother and his father in an accident in September, 2000, coupled with his sister's emigration with her husband to California, had left Jack alone to run the company. Though an accomplished engineer, Jack was no bean counter. He detested paperwork and the company foundered.

Jack struggled to keep Sullivan Electronics alive by means of small local contracts. Then six months ago, a desperate Jack had been approached by his current client. Jack was no fool. He realized that the job was the production of a radar guidance system with timers, suitable for mounting in the ceramic cone or "radome" of a small missile.

But the money was good, enough to avoid bankruptcy, and Jack had agreed. And now that the chips from China were integrated on the boards, the shipment was ready.

Jack sat back. He shut his eyes and relaxed. Tomorrow he would bank his payment and his financial problems would be solved.

***

North of Wilmington, North Carolina, Stew Marks waited on the side of Highway 17. After last night's fruitless vigil, and armed with fresh coffee, he had resumed his place to watch for the Chrysler Town and Country minivan Hamm had rented.

After two hours, he crushed the empty coffee cup and threw it on the floor. *Where are they? I can't have missed them.*

Yawning, he focused on the oncoming cars, two pickups and a sedan, but no Chrysler Town and Country. *Damn!*

***

The brown Town and Country minivan rolled smoothly on Highway 17 north of Wilmington. Bill Hamm drove. Jeannine sat in the passenger seat. The laptop and canvas case with the documents were safe on the back seat.

"Bill, why so slow? After all those hours lost at the garage in Myrtle Beach, we need to hurry. How far is Holly Ridge?"

"Not far, and I never want to see a damned 'Check Engine' light again. We could have done better with Fred's old truck."

"But the car is fixed, why go slow now?"

"We can't risk being stopped. We're still wanted."

"I haven't seen any police cars."

"The bad ones are the unmarked ones you don't see. Look at that Honda Accord parked up ahead. If it weren't a Honda, I might think it was a cop."

219

They drove past the parked Honda in which Stew Marks sat.

Stew let several cars pass before pulling onto the highway to take his place in the line behind the slow-moving Chrysler.

***

At Sullivan Electronics near Holly Ridge, a loud banging on the wide doors of the warehouse startled Jack awake. He looked at his watch. The client was early. Jack pushed the remote.

The doors creaked and cranked upwards to reveal a tall African standing in the opening.

"Are you Mr. Sullivan? Jack Sullivan?"

"I am, but whoever you are, you are early for the delivery."

"I'm not here for a delivery. My name is Paul Mutabazi. The men you are working for are killers. They won't pay you. They'll take what you have and kill you. We need to leave."

"We? What are you talking about? I have a contract."

Metal screeched as a black Audi careened through the wide opening. The car braked, spun about, and stopped. Jack looked up as his visitor, Paul, dove behind a crate and disappeared.

The car's driver stepped out.

"Mr. Sullivan, who was that man? Why did he run? What did he want?"

Before Jack could answer, a voice came through the rear window of the car.

"Not now, Jules. Accept delivery from Mr. Sullivan, so that we can pay him for his work."

The calm voice reassured Jack. He waved at a row of taped cartons on the work bench.

"There are your guidance modules, all twenty eight of them. Give me my check and they're yours."

The Audi's driver, Jules Habimana, stepped to the bench to retrieve the boxes. Jack moved to assist him. He did not notice a second man who had circled behind him.

A fatal oversight!

The bush knife split the temporal bone behind Jack's ear. Reflexively he turned only to have a second blow cleave his cheek and mandible. Jack fell. A third blow was not needed.

Maximilien Gutera stepped from the Audi.

"Louis, wipe your panga and load those cartons in the trunk."

He continued.

"Jules, you come with me. We will look for Mr. Sullivan's shy visitor."

***

But their search of the warehouse yielded nothing.

Jules Habimana turned to Maximilien.

"Do you think that man was Paul Mutabazi?"

"Perhaps, but no matter. Mutabazi cannot harm us. We have our guidance components. We will deliver four modules to Bruno Belli for the tests at Topsail. After the tests we will take the others to Charleston for shipment to Mombasa."

Jules nodded. He drove the Audi through the wide open doors and sped away.

***

Paul Mutabazi stood behind a loblolly pine and stared at the departing Audi. His own car was parked out of sight on the north side of the warehouse. As Paul slipped through the woods to regain his car. The sound of a motor stopped him.

He ducked out of sight behind an evergreen holly as a man and a woman stepped out of a minivan.

Paul ducked down further behind the holly and waited.

***

221

Jeannine Ryan stood by the minivan and eyeballed the "Sullivan Electronics" sign that hung over the open doors of the building. She called to Bill Hamm.

"Something is wrong. The doors are wide open, but there's no one here."

"But somebody is here. That Harley hasn't been there long."

Jeannine looked to the left of the wide doors. A motorcycle gleamed in the sun. A light rain had fallen earlier and clearly the bike had not been outside then.

Jeannine stepped to the doors and called inside.

"Hello, anyone here? … Anyone?"

No answer. Bill, shotgun under his arm, stepped past her. He stopped and pointed. A bloody foot protruded from behind a crate. Bill shoved the crate aside and called to Jeannine.

"This must be Sullivan. He's been hacked. Gutera was here. That's the work of a machete."

A glance was enough for Jeannine. She looked away.

But Bill had gone to the work bench. He held up a notebook.

"We're too late. It looks like he assembled a guidance component that could fit into a small missile."

He put the notebook down and picked up a triplicate form. All three copies were present and intact.

"He had over two dozen systems ready for delivery. Evidently Gutera wasn't interested in the paperwork."

Jeannine started to reply, but Bill put his fingers to his lips and signaled her to move out of sight.

They were not alone. Someone else was in the building.

***

******

Chapter 28
Monday, September 3

All was quiet in the Sullivan warehouse. Bill Hamm crouched behind a crate and held his shotgun ready. Next to the work bench, Jeannine froze, either unable or unwilling to move.

From behind the crate, Bill pointed at a rusty forklift to the left of the door.

Jeannine stared. Someone stood in the shadows behind the machine. She glimpsed a reflection as if from metal. A gun! The man, or woman, was armed.

Jeannine found her voice.

"Who are you? What do you want?"

Bill, hidden from sight by a line of crates, crept towards the intruder. Whoever was behind the forklift stayed silent.

Jeannine called again.

"Who are you? What do you want?"

A man leaped from behind the machine, but too late. Bill Hamm was upon him.

The scuffle ended quickly with the man on the floor and Bill, a shiny .38 caliber revolver in his hand, standing over him.

Jeannine retrieved the shotgun, while Bill motioned the physically shaken intruder to stand up.

The man, a tall African, addressed Jeannine as if he belonged and she did not.

"What is your name? What is your business here?"

She gaped. *Who does he think he is?*

She turned to Bill who smiled and shrugged.

Well if Bill doesn't care, why should I?

"I'm Dr. Ryan, Jeannine Ryan. I ..."

The man's eyes widened.

"Not Dr. Ryan from Bethesda?"

"Yes. Now who are you?"

"Do you remember Angelique Uwimana, a graduate student in computer science at Carolina Tech? She wrote you about a problem some months ago. You helped her solve it."

"Yes, I remember. I'm that Dr. Ryan. Now, who are you?"

"I'm Paul Mutabazi, a friend of Angelique's. I came here to warn Mr. Sullivan, but Hutu thugs killed him. I ran away and hid."

Paul continued.

"Angelique respects you. That means you cannot be friends of Maximilien Gutera. Please tell your man to lower my revolver. Maybe we can help each other."

For the first time, Bill spoke.

"My name is Hamm, Bill Hamm. If you don't want the gun pointed at you, tell me why we should trust you?"

"Because I am Tutsi, like Angelique. And because like her, my family was killed by the Interahamwe, by thugs who followed Charles Hakizimana, Maximilien Gutera's father. Because today, if Maximilien finds me or Angelique, we are dead, if not right away, only because we will first be tortured."

Jeannine stepped forward and pointed to Sullivan's body.

"You saw Gutera do this?"

"Not Gutera, one of his men, Louis Makuza. He's an expert with the bush knife. I tried to warn Mr. Sullivan, but there was no time. They killed him and took the packages. They had a black Audi with South Carolina Plates."

Mutabazi turned to Bill Hamm.

"Mr. Hamm, if you help save Angelique from this monster, I can help you. I know how this Gutera thinks."

Bill Hamm hesitated. He doubted Mutabazi could help.

Sensing Bill's uncertainty, Paul played his trump card.

"Mr. Hamm, Dr. Ryan, do you know that someone followed you here? He is outside now, watching your minivan. I saw him take the keys out of the ignition."

Bill fumbled in his pocket. The keys were not there. *Damn!*.

"What does this man look like?"

"He's the same strong build as you, but with brown hair. He acts like the police. His car is an Accord. He hid it out of sight behind those pines."

Bill thought of the Accord by the roadside that he had thought might be a cop. Jeannine turned to him.

"'Brown hair, athletic build, your size,' that could be that jerk of an FBI agent, Stewart Marks. He thinks I'm a spy too. He must have tracked me from Washington. What will we do?"

Bill stuffed the .38 in his belt.

"I'm not going to shoot an FBI agent doing his job. We have to give ourselves up."

Paul Mutabazi grabbed Bill's arm.

"Wait. Help me find Angelique, and I can help. My car is parked in the back and there is a rear exit. We can leave that way and not be seen."

Bill pointed at Jack Sullivan's body.

"I'll be blamed for him."

"Not if your FBI man knows about Gutera and pangas."

Bill turned to Jeannine.

"Maybe this can work, come on."

"No, my laptop and the documents are in the car. I can't leave them. They're our ticket to freedom. One of us must be free to stop Gutera. That's you. I'll distract Mr. Marks. Go!"

Bill hesitated, but Jeannine grabbed Sullivan's notebook and other papers off the work bench and waved him away.

"Now!"

She waited for Bill to reach the rear of the building, before peering through the open doors.

***

The minivan was apparently as they had left it. No one was visible.

She waved the notebook above her head and stepped into the open.

"I'm coming out. Don't shoot. I'm not armed."

A man stepped from behind a pine and flashed a badge.

"Dr. Ryan, it's me, Agent Stew Marks, FBI. You've led me on a long chase."

She pointed to the minivan.

"Put the damn badge away. I know who you are. Now give me the keys to my car."

Stew smiled.

"Nice try Dr. Ryan, but you and I both know that William Hamm *aka* 'Mr. Walter Harmon,' rented this car. Your friend is a fugitive, and I have a warrant for his arrest, so drop the charade."

His words were interrupted by the sound of a motor. A car burst from around the corner of the warehouse and raced out of sight. Stew whistled.

"So that's your guy, Hamm. After you stood by him all these days, he's gone and left you to face the music. Some friend!"

He turned to face her.

"No matter, let him go. You're the one I really want."

Jeannine's mouth opened wide. She stared.

***

Jules Habimana guided the black Audi on Highway 17. He spoke over his shoulder to Maximilien Gutera seated in back.

"Why do we go to Wilmington? The tests are at Topsail."

226

"Do not question me, Jules."

Jules frowned and concentrated on the road ahead. Next to him, in the passenger seat, Louis Makuza faced forward without moving. He knew better than to question the back seat.

To Louis' surprise, Maximilien Gutera was expansive.

"Jules, you are a loyal follower. Thus I will explain. Professor Shahruk called me from Carolina Technical University. He had a question about our explosive supplier. We will meet the professor in Wilmington. If the question is resolved, then we will proceed to the test on Topsail Island this Wednesday. After that we will go to Charleston to prepare the rockets for shipment on the *Étoile d'Afrique*."

Maximilien frowned.

"Jules, I have answered you this one time only. In the future you will consider that I never act without thought."

In the passenger seat, an amazed Louis gaped open-mouthed at Jules who fixed his eyes on the highway and drove.

***

At Sullivan's warehouse, Jeannine Ryan held out her hand.

"Agent Marks, if it's me you really want to help, give me the keys to the van."

"I can't do that. Look, I'm here to help your Mr. Hamm too. He may be innocent. He might have been framed by the real spy named Hugh Byrd. I know that Byrd and Tom Holder, tried to kill you at Wayne Johnson's house on Topsail. And I know someone downed Holder with a load of buckshot."

Jeannine paled. Stew read her thoughts.

"Don't worry he's alive. He's in the hospital. Too bad, but he will recover. Byrd and he are stealing national secrets. They work for a covert group shielded by the NSA, and they are protected by ultra high clearances, unless and until the NSA disowns them."

He added.

"But you can forget Byrd for now. He's locked up in a county jail by a sheriff and his niece who are still fighting the Civil War. He'll be there a few more days at least. And Holder, he'll be in rehab at least another month. Those guys are not our problem."

Jeannine was silent. Stew continued.

"Maybe you'll cooperate if I tell you what I know? Since your friend, Hamm, emptied Byrd's safe, the FBI has been investigating both him and Byrd for passing classified information from the NSA to GES, an American subsidiary of a French computer security company. I'm not cleared that high, but I can read between the lines of the complaint. I figure that the NSA has broken some sort of encryption they call "RSA" used by the French government, and is decrypting high-level French communications on the sly.

He took a breath.

"Personally, I'm glad the NSA can decrypt French communications, but Byrd sells the NSA information to GES and they're a problem. The CEO of GES, is a French national named Denise Guerry. She sends the decrypted French communiqués to a rogue group in France that is plotting to overthrow the government of Rwanda. From the decrypted messages, the plotters know that the French government is itching to condemn the current government of Rwanda to the UN, given any suitable pretext.

Stew smiled.

"How am I doing?"

Jeannine stared. *What he says fits.*

He kept going.

"There's more. When their government fell in 1994, corrupt Hutu officials pillaged the Rwandan treasury and transferred the money to secret bank accounts in Europe. Now, GES launders money from those accounts to a Hutu group that the FBI has watched for some months. The group is in South Carolina, mostly Florence, and has connections to Carolina Technical

University. The assumed leader of the group is Maximilien Gutera. His father was a major player in the Rwandan genocide."

He paused.

"My guess is that you and Hamm have discovered this group's plans and are trying to stop them."

Jeannine continued to stare.

"Dr. Ryan, now will you believe I want to help?"

When she did not answer, Stew reflected aloud.

"Damn! I risk my job for a smart, beautiful, woman whom I want to know, but don't, whose loyalty to a friend has seen her almost killed by a rogue Fed with an M16, who gave herself up so the friend could escape, and who doesn't seem to realize she's in danger of being chopped to bits by Hutu rebels."

Stunned, Jeannine drew away, but he grabbed her wrist.

"It's true, you're smart and beautiful too, and I want to help you. Tell me who or what is in that warehouse."

Her mind raced. *Can I trust this guy? I guess I have to.*

"There's a body, Sullivan, the owner. He was hacked to death. You were right. Maximilien Gutera's men were here."

She added.

"And they took the remote guidance modules for their missiles."

Missiles!

It was Stew's turn to stare.

***

Bill Hamm sat in the passenger seat while Paul Mutabazi drove. Paul spoke.

"Where should we go, Mr. Hamm?"

Bill started. He was worried about Jeannine.

"We need to go to Topsail Beach. Sullivan's notes said that his guidance system would be tested at some missile museum there. I need to check it out."

"But I think Angelique may be in Charleston?"

"Paul, as I told you, I don't know any Angelique. If you want me to stop Gutera, we have to start at Topsail."

"Can I have my revolver back."

"You had it in the warehouse and didn't use it. It's better off with me. You think before you shoot. That can get you killed. I'll keep the gun. If we see Gutera's men, I won't hesitate."

Bill changed the subject.

"About this Angelique? Are you romantically involved."

"It's not like that. We grew up in the same village. Mr. Mukuru, her father, saved my life during the genocide."

Paul shuddered and continued.

"I was eleven years old. He pulled me under him as he fell dying. The Interahamwe thought I was dead too."

"Where was Angelique?"

"Her father had sent her to school in Kigali. He thought she would be safe. She wasn't. She was ten, her little brother was three. They chopped him to death. His name was Augustin."

"But who saved Angelique?"

"God! It had to be. There was no one else!"

"You believe that?"

"I do. Angelique is a Catholic. She lives her faith."

"And you?"

"Catholic, but not like her. I can't forgive like she does."

Forgiveness? Bill thought of Jeannine.

I'll never forgive myself if anything happens to you.

***

******

Chapter 29
Tuesday, September 4

Jeannine Ryan, untwisted her back and rolled over. Her neck ached and her legs were cramped stiff. She groaned and opened her eyes. She had fallen asleep in the back of Marks' Accord.

The driver's seat was empty, Marks was gone. She tried the door. He had disabled both door and window controls. She was a prisoner. She jammed the window button full force, but there was no response. Frustrated, she rubbed her sore calves.

A tap on the window ended that activity. Stew Marks stood outside with a cardboard tray into which two Styrofoam cups of coffee had been pressed.

"Ms. Ryan, if you had promised me last night to stay in your room and not contact anyone, you could have had a mattress to sleep on, and a bathroom. And I would not have stayed up all night driving. This must change. I'm here to help. I have to be able to trust you."

He pulled the rear door ajar, and pushed a cup through the crack.

"Anyway, here's your coffee."

Jeannine grabbed the cup and lifted it to her lips. She took a long swallow, paused, and tilted the cup upwards once more.

"All right, Mr. Marks, so you had to drive all night. Tough! Your damned 'help' has been torture. Have you tried to sleep in this car? What the hell do you expect?"

Jeannine shoved auburn locks from her forehead and stared. Stew returned the look, but she did not flinch. He noted her wrinkled sweatshirt and jeans. Though disheveled, her firm figure stood out. Stew was smitten anew. He found his voice.

"I expect you to not run away and to not contact your friends to come get you. And I need you to brief me on what you and Hamm know of Gutera's plans, how you planned to stop him."

He sighed.

"But most of all, I need you to trust me."

He wanted to add "and maybe like me too," but that was out of the question. He contented himself with a modest plea.

"I'm risking my career. I called my office. As of now I'm on leave without pay until I can get you out of this mess."

Is this guy for real? OK, Jeannine, why not give it a shot?

"All right, Mr. Marks, I won't run away or call anyone for the next twenty four hours, but that's all."

Stew Marks pulled the rear door wide.

"Done! Sit in the front with me. We're only an hour from Charleston. I know a good motel in Mount Pleasant. We'll stay there."

He added quickly.

"And don't worry, you'll have your own room."

She grimaced, but he did not notice.

"You'll have your laptop and all your papers. You can bring me up to speed when we get there."

As she took her place in the front seat, he continued.

"You said there were memos from Hugh Byrd. Good. We'll nail that bastard."

Progress!

Stew hummed to himself as he drove off.

***

Some miles removed from Dillon, South Carolina, the visitor to a county detention center stood waiting for the clerk to sign him in.

From the man's expensive suit, the clerk concluded that he was a lawyer, and one whose fees were beyond those affordable by her, or any ordinary citizen. His black Italian shoes confirmed that.

She shrugged and waved the man ahead.

The guard who opened the barred door to admit the man was more perceptive. The tailored suit coat and pants could not conceal the man's bulging biceps nor his thick thighs. Based on those muscles, and the way the visitor shifted lightly on his toes, the guard decided that the visitor was a professional football player. The guard resolved to check the photos of players from his favorite NFL team, the Carolina Panthers.

Neither the clerk's assessment nor the guard's was correct.

The man stopped at a second set of bars where another guard checked the man's thin leather case and attached pen. Satisfied, the guard admitted him into a room that was bare except for a wooden table and two chairs. There the man sat and waited.

Minutes later Hugh Byrd, clad in a blue-striped jumpsuit, entered. Hugh railed at the man across from him.

"What took you so long? This stinking hole is driving me nuts. Get me out of here, now!"

The man nodded. He slid a transparent plastic folder across the table. It contained an envelope and a sheet of paper.

"The chief sends his apologies. Read this and sign it. Seal the envelope and sign it across the seal. You'll be out in an hour. He's taken care of everything."

Hugh signed the paper and inserted it into the envelope. A few licks and it was sealed. After a final signature across the closed flap, he returned the envelope to the transparent folder.

The man retrieved it and slipped it into his case. He signaled the guard and turned back to Hugh.

"Remember, one hour. Be ready."

Under the watchful eyes of the guard, he stepped through and out of the barred passageway. Then he signed the ledger at the clerk's desk, smiled to her, and stepped towards the entrance.

A final wave to the clerk, and he was gone.

***

A bored guard walked Hugh Byrd back to his cell to an accompaniment of curses and catcalls from the cells lining the walkway. Hugh regained his accustomed swagger. Only one more hour and these miserable losers, guards and inmates both, would be out of his life.

The guard slammed the door and secured Hugh's cell. Hugh sat on his cot and smirked.

In an hour, he would resume his life, and a first priority would be to make Stewart Marks pay for his betrayal of Hugh. He would arrange an "accident" for the FBI agent, a most painful accident.

His lips tingled slightly, an effect of the sealant on the envelope. He licked them in anticipation of his revenge. The clarity that agent Marks was Hugh's enemy was the only good result of his incarceration. He never let an enemy get the best of him. Of course, Hamm too was an enemy, but he could wait.

Hamm, I'll deal with you once I destroy Marks.

An odd dizziness seized Hugh, but he shook it if off to contemplate his revenge. He rolled forward onto his cot. *Yes, Marks must be first!*

He lay back on the mattress and closed his eyes.

Revenge is sweet!

***

On a back road in South Carolina, the expensively clad "lawyer" or "football-player" approached a bridge that spanned a creek that emptied into the Little Pee Dee River. The man turned onto a weedy turnout next to the bridge.

He looked about. The absence of parked cars indicated that no fishermen were "wetting their lines" in the sluggish waters under the bridge. He was alone. Gingerly he removed the plastic folder from his case. He let Hugh's envelope fall untouched to the ground. For a brief second he looked at the sealed flap whose poison had saturated Hugh's saliva.

Then he leaned low and lit the envelope with his lighter. It charred on the edges before the entire blackened surface burst into flames. When only ashes remained, he ground them into the sandy soil with his heel and kicked the mix into the weeds that flourished at the edge of the turnout.

Then he lit a Marlboro, a brand popular in his native France. He drew deeply on it and composed a text message for Marat1 at SÉGAG in Paris. It comprised two words.

"C'est fait. It's done."

He stepped into the car. A private plane was waiting at Florence Regional Airport. It would take him to Dulles International Airport to meet his Air France flight to Charles de Gaulle Airport in Paris.

***

Hugh Byrd lay on his cot. In a few minutes he would be free. His gutless superiors had capitulated. They lacked the courage to take action against him given what he knew.

He wanted to laugh at their weakness, but his mouth and throat were too dry.

What the hell?

His tongue tingled. Numb, it rolled back clogging his throat and airways. He gagged and fell backwards on the cot. A bubbly froth exuded from his mouth.

His head spun. He grabbed for the edge of the cot, but his arms failed to respond. He rolled, face down, onto the floor. He tried to lift his head, but could not.

He gasped, but his chest did not expand. No air filled his lungs. His Paralyzed diaphragm froze and breathing ceased.

Seconds later he was dead.

***

In Mount Pleasant, across the Cooper River from downtown Charleston, Stew Marks stood up and stretched. After several hours of briefing by Jeannine Ryan, his head ached.

"All right, Ms. Ryan, you've convinced me. This proves that Guerry Electronic Systems paid Hugh Byrd for U.S. government secrets, including a highly secret NSA program that can read the French RSA messages. You have enough here to nail the bastard and GES for selling government secrets. Unfortunately, the evidence against the parent company, SÉGAG, is more tenuous."

Jeannine waved a cluster of papers at Stew.

"But look at these messages. They prove that a group of French politicians who support 'Hutu Power' paid SÉGAG for decoded communications that reveal which governments want to condemn the present government of Rwanda."

"I agree that's a likely inference, but the proof stops with GES. There is a gap between GES and SÉGAG. To get SÉGAG, we would need Byrd's cooperation. He might agree to a plea deal."

"But what about Bill? He emptied Byrd's safe and stole secrets. What about him?"

"The fox was in charge of the chicken house. Byrd was head of security. Bill had no choice. Any decent defense lawyer would be glad to defend him. It would be close to a slam dunk."

He seized her shoulders and spun her about. She stiffened.

"Jeannine, I like you, but this isn't personal. Gutera is going to ship missile components from Charleston this Saturday. We need to stop him. Call Hamm and tell him to give himself up. The FBI has documented over thirty hardcore followers of Gutera in the Carolinas. Bill can't handle Gutera by himself."

He handed her his cell.

"I know you know how to contact him. Call him."

"No!"

***

******

Chapter 30
Tuesday, September 4

In the motel in Mount Pleasant, Jeannine sat silent while Stew Marks stood over her. A full minute passed. Finally, he vented his frustration.

"Damn it woman, I'm trying to help you!"

The impasse was broken by the buzz of his phone. The caller was Stew's partner, Jack Marino.

"Stew, where in hell are you. They tell me you're on leave without pay."

"It's all right, Jack, I'm in Mount Pleasant, near Charleston."

He did not mention that Jeannine Ryan was with him.

"Stew, Byrd is dead. They killed him."

"Dead? They? Who? He was in jail."

"Right, the locals thought it was a heart attack, but the National Security Agency says different."

"The NSA killed him? They could have disowned him and let him retire."

"Not the NSA, no. It looks like an 'Op' from Paris. Byrd had a visitor. The guard says there was no contact between him and the prisoner, but Byrd licked an envelope. Maybe some sort of neurologic toxin. The NSA's doing an autopsy."

"Damn! And the mystery visitor?"

"One of the surveillance cameras malfunctioned. The NSA has the other. They're working on getting an ID."

"What makes them think Paris?"

"They're cryptic about that. Maybe your theory is right. Maybe the NSA has broken French codes. But if this hit was sponsored by their government, it adds to your problems. Stew, forget that damn Ryan woman. She has you dizzy!"

The last words were shouted. Jeannine winced.

Stew slammed the receiver down and turned to her.

"Now will you believe I'm on your side?"

***

In Wilmington, North Carolina, Denise Guerry scanned a weekly newspaper from Topsail.

Sunday, September 2

Carolina Commentary

A ceremony to commemorate the research on ramjet missiles and radar guidance systems conducted by the United States Navy at Topsail Island from 1945 to 1948 will be held this Wednesday evening at 7:00 pm at the museum in Topsail Beach. The Mayor of Topsail Beach will present an address followed by entertainment and an outdoor barbeque. Tickets will be available on site.

A special feature of the event will be the first missile firings to take place on the island since 1948. Although equipped with ordinary solid-fuel rockets, rather than the ramjet engines studied by the Navy, they nonetheless feature a radar guidance system developed locally by Sullivan Electronics currently owned and operated by Jack "Scooter" Sullivan of Holly Ridge. Jack's grandfather worked on the Navy's original project.

Visitors will be able to track the flight of the missiles on large screens set up adjacent to the museum. Radar tracking will be from a temporary facility on loan to the museum by Guerry Electronic Systems of Chantilly Virginia. As a backup, a French Oceanographic Research Vessel, "La Lutte" will track the missiles from an offshore location.

Once they reach their "Targets," the missiles will be exploded in mid air to provide a televised display that promises a fun end to an enjoyable evening.

Denise put the paper down. If Sullivan had done his assembly correctly, the tests would go well. He had done good work in the past for GES, and the odds for success were high.

And though Sullivan was dead, Bruno Belli could run the tests at Topsail as least as well or better. The public tests would provide solid evidence that the missiles for the dirty bombs had come from the United States and not France.

She thought of her uncle's words during her last visit to SÉGAG in Paris.

"Denise, do not flinch. Be proud of your work at GES. We are helping a persecuted people exiled from their homes by a ruling Tutsi minority. History will recognize Maximilien as a patriot. I am proud to help him restore Hutu rule in his homeland."

Denise wondered how her uncle would explain poor persecuted Maximilien's murderous hacking of Jack Sullivan.

Her uncle's supposed "refugee victim" was a madman.

Cher Oncle, your patriotic Maximilien is a plain murderer.

***

Ian Callahan was due at the motel at any minute. Denise balanced the laptop on the dresser to check her email. An encrypted message filled the display.

0936131508210024282705151840111
0410192004141538130620021908261
2524280524214008090810192220190
2517294018182314181120290524214
2624041825040522140308191426170
2100242827051711222323032519111
0407331309360640261204203908301
2719122040252021104012342605191
2408080707332814111803081204251
2610022137122440203431054018343
1040192408300426170805090722230
0820090812253327193909392239051

She tapped quickly to decode it. It was from her pesky cousin Jacques at SÉGAG in Paris.

d.g.|paris|plucked|l'oiseau.||upset|you|did| not|fix|l'oiseau|yourself.|why|not?|paris| records|cleaned.|urgent|you|do|same|for|the| chantilly|ges|records|now||love|me|yet?|| jacobin5|gz9hk2j3c5|s

Jacques' so-called humor irritated her. The use of "*l'oiseau*" to indicate "Bird" or "Byrd" was juvenile.

Damn it, Jacques, get serious. And love? Forget it cousin!

But Byrd was dead. SÉGAG had solved the "Byrd Problem" without informing Denise and they were upset with her for not doing it herself.

Damn you Uncle, you should have told me!

She threw the mouse on the floor. It snapped open and the battery rolled under the chair.

She supposed that her uncle was right to eliminate Byrd. He had ceased to be an asset. Perhaps she should have eliminated him herself. Mainly she was angry because she had not been consulted.

She calmed down. At least her cousin could still laugh.

"Byrd" = "l'oiseau." Juvenile, Jacobin5, but clever.

She reassembled her mouse. Her task now was to scrub all traces of Byrd from the GES records. She pulled up the files and clicked rapidly. But before she could finish, the computer beeped. She looked as the screen filled with numbers, another interruption from Jacques. She ran the decode program.

d.g.|hamm|in|charleston.|urgent|hamm|knows| shipment|date|||oncle|says|eliminate|hamm| check|gutera|missile|parts|and|explosives.| |repeat,|oncle|says|eliminate|hamm||i|say| forget|duval.|love|me|instead|jacobin5|5h4vqdt

She jumped up, face red.

Jacques you are not my keeper. Forget Duval? No way! Love you instead? Ridiculous! And I'm not killing anybody for uncle's sake. I'm done with his dirty work.

Still, she admired her cousin's flip attitude.

She would go to Charleston because Duval was a challenge to her ego, but her prime objective was to verify that Gutera's missile components worked. And she *would* kill Hamm if he interfered with the shipment, but only to defend herself.

She took pride in her work.

Cousin, I am not an idiot! And never tell me what to do!

The harsh buzz of the phone filled the motel room. Denise picked up.

"Yes?"

"Madame Guerry, this is the front desk. There's a Mr. Callahan here to see you."

Denise straightened her blouse and wiped the hair from her forehead. Then she answered.

"Fine, send him up."

She would not change her plans. Should Henri insist on clinging to his little Tutsi, Ian Callahan could handle him.

***

In Mount Pleasant, South Carolina, Jeannine Ryan made her decision. She looked Stew Marks in the eye.

"Mr. Marks, you want me to call Bill, but I will not. If you really want to help me, let me go. He and I have worked together before. We may not be able to best Gutera and his mob, but we surely can find a way to sabotage this missile shipment. Bill's good at this kind of operation, and he's not bound by regulations like you."

A shadow flicked across Stew's eyes. Jeannine softened.

241

"Look, you really do not know me, and other guys have been disappointed when they find out what I'm really like. And I don't know you at all. I'm sorry."

Stew's shoulders slumped.

"Jeannine, you are wrong. Gutera's men are too much for you and a dozen like Hamm."

He hesitated.

"But I won't force my help on you. I respect you too much for that."

He waved at the door.

"Go. I won't stop you. You are free. Go."

She turned to look at her laptop and the sack with the papers. He caught her glance.

"Sorry. I'm handing these over to my Chief. Now, if you're going, go quick, before I change my mind."

She turned, threw her arms around him, and planted moist lips on his, lingering several seconds.

Then she stepped to the table, scooped up sack and laptop, and left the room.

Stew stood and stared as the door's hydraulic closer slowly pulled it shut. Finally, the latch clicked. Bemused, he sat on the bed and muttered.

"Damn it, Marks, you let her take those papers. What's the matter with you?"

***

In Charleston, South Carolina, Henri Duval and Angelique leaned on the railing of the elevated seawall that faced towards the harbor and a distant Fort Sumter of Civil War fame. Across the street behind them, several cannon were aimed at the fort to commemorate the location of the "Battery" whose guns, along with those of Forts Moultrie and Johnson, had bombarded the Federally-held bastion in April, 1861, and initiated the four-year struggle termed, according to preference, the "War of Northern Aggression," the "War of the Rebellion," or the "Civil War." The commemorative cannon occupied the harbor-side of a park dominated by live oak trees whose branches, pendant with Spanish moss, extended over shaded paths of crushed oyster shells.

Eric Nyonzima leaned his crutches against the trunk of a live oak and peered around the thick trunk. He studied the two lone figures on the seawall. He had followed the couple from Broad Street here to the Battery.

The soft cast on his lower leg irritated the skin. He limped to a nearby bench. He would not be spotted. Uwimana did not know him and Duval had only seen him once, in the dark when he had broken Eric's leg with that vicious kick.

Eric put his crutches beside the bench and sat. He extended his aching leg to the side, and punched the number of Jules Habimana into his cell.

"Jules, tell Maximilien that I've found Angelique Uwimana. I'm watching her now on the battery's seawall. She's with that Frenchman."

"Duval?"

"Yes. He broke my leg while you were inside Uwimana's apartment."

"Where are they staying?"

"I'm not sure, but there are several hotels near where I first spotted them. What do you want me to do?"

"Don't lose them. Find out which hotel, but whatever happens, do not touch Uwimana, Maximilien wants her for himself. And Eric, good work, Maximilien could even decide to forget the tests and come to Charleston tomorrow."

The call was over. Eric glanced at the couple across the way. Arm in arm, they were in no hurry to leave. He was glad to be here for a while, he needed the rest. He shifted his stiff leg to the front and leaned on the back of the bench.

***

******

Chapter 31
Wednesday, September 5

Near Wilmington, North Carolina, Jules Habimana watched as Louis Makuza and another man finished wiping the black hood of Maximilien Gutera's Audi. Maximilien insisted that the car reflect his status, and Jules dared not imagine otherwise. Once again the daily ritual was complete. The Audi shimmered, resplendent in the early-morning sun.

Jules looked at his watch and pointed at a fast food restaurant a block away.

"That's enough, Louis. The car looks good. You have a half hour before the chief comes down. You two go grab something to eat."

Jules watched them walk down the street. He took out his cell phone and called Eric Nyonzima in Charleston.

"Eric, what news of Duval and Uwimana. Where are they staying?"

"They are not together. Duval is at a hotel on Meeting Street. He dropped Uwimana off at a small Catholic hospice not far from the cathedral on Broad Street. She's staying there with some nuns."

"What a gentleman! Duval is an idiot. How did you ever let him beat you?"

Eric ignored him.

"I can't watch both places at once."

"Stay near the hospice. It is Uwimana that Maximilien wants, not the Frenchman. Your news will please Maximilien. If Uwimana is a virgin, all the more satisfaction for him as he despoils her."

"When will he be here?"

"He has not informed me. He may watch the rocket firings at Topsail Beach tonight, or he may come to Charleston and leave the rockets to Professor Belli. Whatever, you are not to lose Uwimana. Clear?"

"Clear."

Jules hung up. He smiled to himself. Now that Angelique was located, lust would decide the issue. If Maximilien's heated loins ruled, they could drive to Charleston even today.

He sighed. He was ready.

The shiny Audi was gassed and greased for the trip.

***

In Charleston, the nuns' hospice was located in an old area of narrow streets lined with brick dwellings protected by ornate iron fences. Just down the street from the center was a public bench squeezed between two large Oleander bushes. The bench had been provided several years earlier by the town fathers who, ever conscious of tourists' dollars and sore feet, promoted walking tours of the old city.

Though not a tourist, Eric Nyonzima was grateful for the bench. His leg ached. He had left his car around the corner since the constricted street allowed no parking. From the bench, Eric had a clear view of the entrance to the hospice. He settled himself and watched.

Jules Habimana's words resounded in his mind.

"It is Uwimana that Maximilien wants."

Bum leg or not, he dare not lose Angelique.

***

In Mount Pleasant, across the Cooper river from Charleston, Jeannine Ryan was frustrated. Her only way to reach Bill Hamm was to call his pre-pay cell phone. Last night, after repeated tries, she had failed to reach him. His phone either was off or in an area with no service.

Discouraged, she had walked to a nearby hotel and booked a room for the night.

She had slept well, but again this morning, her calls to Bill produced no results. The phone was out of service.

She sat on the bed and stared at the canvas case with the stolen documents.

Damn it, in three days Gutera's ship will dock here. There's no time. Turn on your damn phone!

Jeannine heard a rap on the door. She looked about. Her room was on the second floor and the window was sealed. The windowless bathroom was next to the door. There was no other way out.

She slipped quietly to the peephole.

A man stood in the hallway. *Bill?*

Then the man turned and revealed his face.

Stew Marks!

***

Exasperated, Jeannine cracked the door, but left the chain attached.

"What the hell do you want?"

Stew noted her anger. Through the crack he saw the phone on the bed.

"So you couldn't reach Hamm? You'd better let me in."

"Why? What are you doing here? How did you find me?"

"Come on Jeannine, you need help. I never said I wouldn't follow you. Of course I did. Let me in."

She hesitated.

"Jeannine, don't be foolish. I can help you."

She sighed and undid the chain.

"All right, Stew, what can you tell me?"

"For starters, your friend Hamm is still in North Carolina. Gutera's rockets are to be tested at Topsail beach tonight. He will be there."

She drew a quick breath.

"How?"

"Don't be naive. The FBI has resources. My partner Jack called this morning."

"Has Bill been arrested?"

"No. Someone saw him in Surf City. A black man was with him, but no agent has seen him. The part about Topsail is a guess, but a good one. Bill probably saw this article. Jack faxed it to me this morning."

He put the paper in front of her.

Sunday, September 2

Carolina Commentary

...

A special feature of the event will be the first missile firings to take place on the island since 1948. Although equipped with ordinary solid-fuel rockets, rather than the ramjet engines studied by the Navy, they nonetheless feature a radar guidance system developed locally by Sullivan Electronics currently owned and operated by Jack "Scooter" Sullivan of Holly Ridge. Jack's grandfather worked on the Navy's original project.

Visitors will be able to track the flight of the missiles on large screens set up adjacent to the museum. Radar tracking will be from a temporary facility on loan to the museum by Guerry Electronic Systems of Chantilly Virginia. As a backup, a French Oceanographic Research Vessel, "La Lutte" will track the missiles from an offshore location.

...

She read it quickly.

"It makes sense. '*La Lutte*' is the ship with the nuclear rod modules. They're going to offload them onto the *Étoile d'Afrique* after it leaves Charleston. And GES is testing Sullivan's guidance system under the pretext of a 'commemorative event.'"

She looked up.

"But Stew, Gutera killed Sullivan. Why?"

Stew blinked. *She called me Stew.*

"Why does a madman kill?"

Jeannine frowned.

"Will they arrest Bill tonight at Topsail."

"If they see him, yes."

"Stew, I have to warn him. Take me to Topsail. We have time. We can be there before the celebration."

"Jeannine, you're asking me to betray my agency. I can't act against the FBI, against my buddies."

"But you know the truth now. We have to stop Gutera and his dirty bombs."

"The FBI will do that."

"Bill says that the minute you have our evidence, the NSA will seize it. The FBI will not see it until weeks later, maybe never. In any case it would be too late."

Stew paused. She was right. The NSA would use national security issues to bury the evidence, and maybe justifiably so. The prosecution of Byrd and GES would reveal the NSA's ability to decrypt RSA communications among foreign governments. Keeping that ability secret could easily outweigh any gains from the conviction of Byrd or GES.

He looked into her moist eyes. *Come on woman, don't plead like that!*

He could not say no.

"All right, Jeannine, I'll take you up north. But don't count on me once we're at Topsail."

She wanted to hug him, but held back.

Her life was complicated enough.

She need not encourage him.

***

In Charleston, Eric Nyonzima straightened his back from the iron bench. His leg felt rested, but his back was stiff. There had been no sign of Angelique. Only two nuns had left the hospice all morning, and there had been no sign of Duval. Where was he? Or she?

As Eric tried to relax, he heard a rustling behind the adjacent Oleander. Before he could turn to see the cause of the disturbance cold metal pressed against the side of his neck.

"*'Silence, mon ami, ou je tire.'* Silence, my friend, or I'll shoot."

Eric froze. He knew the Frenchman's voice.

"Duval? *'Que veux-tu?'* What do you want?"

"*'Tais-toi.'* Shut up."

Eric stayed frozen.

***

Denise Guerry was driving on Highway 17 in North Carolina when her phone chimed. She picked up. The call was from the FBI's resident agency in Wilmington. The caller was a clerk, who supplemented a low income with occasional "fees" from GES.

"Hamm was seen in Surf City. There was a black man with him. I thought you would want to know."

"Good work. You'll be paid in cash, at the usual spot."

"Thank you."

Denise hung up and turned to Ian Callahan in the passenger seat.

"Hamm will be in Topsail. I'm sure of it. And Mutabazi is with him."

"Mutabazi?"

"A Tutsi. He's not important. He's weak, but Hamm is a problem."

She fell silent a moment. *Where is Ryan? Why isn't she with Hamm?* She spoke.

"Ian, we have to go to Topsail. We must stop Hamm. Poor Bruno could never handle him. Turn right at the next intersection."

Denise studied her passenger and smiled. While he was not Henri, Ian had looks enough and was well built. She could assure his loyalty with a promise of sex. She would need him if Hamm tried to stop the tests. Besides, Ian would have to suffice until she could snare Henri from Angelique.

Something to think about.

***

Henri Duval approached the door of the nuns' hospice. Before he could ring the bell, the door opened and Angelique stepped out.

"Henri, you're late. The nuns are at noon prayer. I was supposed to leave before that."

"I was here, but something came up, a problem I had to handle."

He took Angelique's hand and led her around the corner to his car. She opened the front door and jumped back.

"Henri, the back seat! Who is that? *Mon Dieu!* What have you done?"

She put one hand over her mouth and pointed with the other. A man sat slumped in the back seat. Duct tape wrapped his wrists and a strip of the same material sealed his mouth. A pair of crutches lay on the floor.

Henri took her hand.

"He was watching the hospice, waiting for you. His name is 'Eric Nyonzima,' he belongs to Gutera."

"Then Maximilien knows where we are!"

"Yes. Help me put him in the trunk. I need to get him out of sight."

Angelique drew back.

"Will he be able to breathe?"

251

"Is that important? Hold the door open for me."

Henri seized Eric's arm and pulled him from the back. Moments later, he rolled Eric into the trunk, laid the crutches on him, and slammed the lid shut.

Mouth agape, Angelique stared at the trunk. She was not sure about this.

Henri started the motor and waved her into her seat.

***

******

Chapter 32
Wednesday, September 5

Angelique sat silent as Henri Duval steered the car through the Meeting Street traffic towards the grand Arthur Ravenel Jr. Bridge. At a height of 175 meters, and a clearance below of 57 meters, the bridge over the Cooper River allowed modern container ships access to harbor facilities north of Charleston. Angelique had no fear of heights, but she was agitated, and the long high crossing churned her stomach. She sighed with relief as they rolled down the descent to solid ground.

They drove through Mount Pleasant on Highway 17. Only when Henri took the turn north onto Route 41 did she speak.

"Henri, where are we going?"

"I want to get off the major roads. This way leads through a national forest. It's not well-traveled."

Angelique frowned.

"What about him? What are you going to do?"

"Find a deserted spot and dump him."

"You mean kill him?"

"What else. I should have done it in Florence when he tried to cleave me in two with a panga. I broke his leg, but that wasn't enough. He found us. Gutera won't be far behind."

They passed a large brown sign with yellow letters, *Francis Marion National Forest*. Ahead there were no houses, only stark forests of pines as far as they could see.

Angelique shivered.

***

Henri Duval turned off the paved route onto a sandy road that passed through open stands of long-needled pines. On all sides, open clusters of pines stretched in monotonous arrays. The only sign of human presence was the road itself.

They drove on. Angelique sat silent. Henri seemed unaware of her presence. The dirt lane narrowed and woody stems raked the sides of the car along with the window on her side.

Ahead a small tree blocked the passage. Henri stopped the car. Further progress was impossible.

A light breeze rustled the tops of the pines as Henri stepped out of the car. He had a gun in his hand.

Angelique drew a deep breath.

***

Stew Marks drove fast. He and Jeannine Ryan were on I-26 headed from Charleston towards I-95 and points north. She broke the silence.

"Will we make it to Topsail Beach in time for the celebration."

Stew nodded in affirmation. Most of the driving was on interstates. He would leave I-95 at I-40 for Wilmington and Topsail.

"Will you arrest Bill if you see him?"

Stew nodded again. But he wanted to talk about her, not Hamm.

She continued.

"You're not on duty. You don't have to arrest him."

"Jeannine, he's a fugitive and I'm an FBI agent. I have no choice."

She frowned and changed the subject.

"When can I get my Subaru out of impoundment? I need it."

He glanced sideways. Her auburn hair and good looks unsettled him. This conversation was not going the way he had hoped.

"Jack Marino is handling that now. I'm not sure. I'll do what I can."

At that response Jeannine sighed and leaned back.

Damn it Jeannine, ease up. This guy is trying to help, and he's risking his career for you. Be grateful. He really likes you.

Then a wild thought. *And he's damned good looking!*

The regular cadence of the tires rolling over the joints in the roadway soothed her. She shut her eyes and slept.

***

In the Francis Marion National Forest, Angelique stared in horror as Henri, gun in hand, opened the trunk of the car.

"Henri, non!"

"Angelique, this man was sent to kill you! He was at your apartment in Florence, and he tried to kill me. He tracked you to Charleston. He belongs to Gutera. We can't let him go."

"At least let me speak to him."

"Why? What good can that do?"

"Henri, please. Do this for me. Please."

Henri shrugged. He opened the trunk, yanked the bound Eric up and out and sat him on the rear bumper. He stripped the duct tape from his mouth and turned to Angelique.

"All right, here he is."

Angelique swallowed. *God, do not let me hate this man, but do not let me offend your justice either.*

"Where are you from?"

Eric saw Henri Duval's eyes. There was no hope there. His only chance was with the woman he had schemed to kill. And even if spared, what hope was that? He had failed Gutera twice! He lowered his eyes.

"Kirambo, Lac Kivu."

"At the university in Butare, I had a friend, Clarisse, from Kirambo, a Hutu. She was my age. Did you know her?"

"A cousin, very smart. She won a scholarship to Butare after I left Rwanda. After your *Front Patriotique Rwandais* forced me from *my* country."

"You were with the Interahamwe, why?"

"The Tutsi hate us."

"I am Tutsi and I do not hate you."

"So you say, but you are going to kill me."

He turned to Henri.

"Either you, or this traitor of a Frenchman will do it."

Eric Nyonzima stood and waited.

He closed his eyes.

The breeze fell, the rustling of the pines ceased, and all was still. Time stopped.

***

The boy's mother died at his birth, but not before she told the father the name she desired for their son, a name that meant "God is alive." The father was not of her faith, but he accepted her choice and promised to love the boy.

They were poor by the world's standards, but not by Rwanda's. His father owned a single-bedroom house on the lake, as well as a skiff, a luxury paid for by a small bean patch and an equally small coffee grove on the hillside. To the boy, life on Lac Kivu was idyllic. He would sit for hours in the boat while his father drew fish, needed protein, from the calm waters.

The boy was perhaps nine years old, when after returning from school, he posed his father a question.

"Papa, what does 'Hutu,' or 'Tutsi,' mean?"

"Why do you ask?"

"Our teacher, Mr. Jabo, told those who were 'Tutsi' to stand by the wall on the right, and those who were 'Hutu' to stand by the wall on the left."

"Did he also tell the 'Twa' to stand up?"

"Yes, but no one did."

"But you went to the left, with the other Hutus?"

"Yes, but my best friend Dieudonné went to the right."

"That's because he is different. You are Hutu. You should play with someone else, like Pascal. He is Hutu too."

"But why?'

"Because you are Hutu, like your father."

From that day, Dieudonné was abandoned, and Pascal, who was a year older, became the boy's friend along with others, all followers of Pascal. In time, the boy learned the 'proper' words for 'Tutsi,' like 'Inyenzi' (cockroach) or 'Inzoka' (snake or worm) so that by his fourteenth birthday he knew that the Tutsi were the true enemies of his country, and of all Hutus.

Only months after that birthday, in early 1994, the boy, was in his skiff on the water, watching as Pascal waved two shiny 'imipanga' (pangas) and descended the hillside to the lake.

Pascal wore a new shirt, yellow, green, and blue with a few thin stripes of red and black. As the boy stepped from the boat, his friend handed him a similar shirt. The boy donned it right away. Only then did Pascal offer him one of the pangas. The boy seized it and swung it in the air. The two embraced, each with his weapon at his side.

The boy, Eric Nyonzima, now belonged to the Interahamwe.

***

Eric Nyonzima blinked at the sound of Angelique's voice.

"Henri, someone must break the cycle of hate. We cannot kill this man. We are not murderers."

Henri stared. She looked into his eyes.

"We cannot offend God. Whatever this man has done, God will decide what to do with him. We must let him go."

Before Henri could reply, Angelique approached Eric.

"Whatever you have done, I forgive you. But God is just. Ask *His* forgiveness and accept whatever punishment comes. I will pray for you. It is His love that has spared you today."

She touched his arm.

"Do you not know that your name, 'Nyonzima,' means 'God lives.' He *is* alive and He *loves* you. All he asks is your repentance. Turn to Him."

She concluded.

"Now climb back into the trunk and pray that Maximilien Gutera will forgive you for failing to deliver me."

Eric half-rolled inside the trunk, bound hands and bad leg notwithstanding. Angelique turned to Henri.

"We will cut him loose outside the next town. Even if he dare call Gutera, we will be gone before they can react."

Wordless, Henri slammed the lid shut and got in the car. They drove through the pines back to the paved road.

To live with Angelique was to live in a different world.

***

When stressed, Jules Habimana gnawed at his nails, but now the nubs were too narrow for biting. Both Angelique Uwimana and Eric Nyonzima were missing! Calls to the nun's hospice had revealed little. The nun had informed Jules, politely, that the young African woman was no longer a guest, and that no African male had been with her. The only man she had seen was "white" with a foreign accent, possibly French.

Duval! Eric, where are you? And where is Angelique?

Jules put the phone down and sat staring at the blank wall. How would he tell his chief?

***

On I-95 in North Carolina, Stew Marks drove while Jeannine Ryan slept. Ahead was the I-40 interchange to Wilmington.

Stew looked at his passenger. Because of her would he abandon his ideals, his loyalty to the Bureau?

What if I find Hamm? Will I let him go just to please her?

***

******

Chapter 33
Wednesday, September 5

In the Francis Marion National Forest on the outskirts of Huger, South Carolina, Eric Nyonzima tore the last of the duct tape from his wrists. He picked up his crutches and hobbled towards town. Angelique's words echoed in his mind.

"Do you not know that your name, 'Nyonzima,' means 'God lives.' He is alive and He loves you. All he asks is your repentance. Turn to Him."

But the words of Pascal's father were also in his memory.

"Eric, when you cleanse the world of the Tutsi, you serve God. He wants Rwanda freed from vermin. He wants us to have our birthright, 'Hutu Power.'"

But Laurette, his neighbor across the street, had been Hutu. Her only crime had been to try to save a Tutsi friend, Nadine.

Eric liked Laurette, but he had not tried to help her. Worse, he had watched passively as his frenzied friends mutilated her body, a Hutu body. Surely God had not approved that.

And Henri Duval would have put a bullet in Eric's head, but for that Tutsi, Angelique. She had stopped the Frenchman.

I am alive because of her. She does not hate me. She forgives me.

Crutches straining, Eric pushed towards the town. He was confused. His only certainty was that Gutera must not find him.

***

The afternoon sun was high in the West, when Stew Marks turned onto Route 50 and the approach to the Topsail Island bridge at Surf City. Jeannine Ryan, until now resting in the passenger seat, opened her eyes.

She sat up.

"Sorry, I need to go to the bathroom. There's a McDonald's on the right. Can you stop there, please."

Stew nodded. He pulled into the lot and cut the motor. Jeannine dashed for the Rest Room.

He waited behind the wheel, content to be off the highway. The drive from Charleston had been hard. His eyes started to close, but he was aware that more cars had entered the lot. Half asleep, he watched a van discharge a family of four, two rowdy boys and their weary parents. Other cars had parked around the corner of the restaurant. Finally, his eyes closed, his arms slipped off the wheel, and he dozed.

A noise awoke him. Another car had parked next to his. Two giggling teens pushed out and waltzed to the McDonald's with their mother. As they entered, the mother held the door for a family that was leaving, two boys and their parents who had just eaten.

Stew blinked. It was the family that he had seen enter some time before.

How long have I been here? Over thirty minutes? Jeannine? But she was not in the car. And her laptop and the canvas briefcase were gone.

A piece of paper was taped to the passenger-side window.

Mr. Marks,

I have to go. I do not want to get you in trouble with your agency, so it's better for you this way. You have to follow your conscience but so do I. Thanks for your help, and I know that when I give you all the evidence, you will know for sure that Bill had nothing to do with Byrd's selling NSA secrets to GES. All Bill did was to expose them.

Dear Stew, you are a sweet guy, and I appreciate all you did to help me. I am sorry to leave you like this, but I did not want to wake you up. You can see it is for the best. Thanks again.

Fondly, Jeannine

Stew was torn with emotion. He was angry at her departure but he loved her signoff. She no longer detested him.

He leaned back in the seat and smiled.

***

Bill Hamm drove Paul Mutabazi's car to Topsail Beach. He had left Paul in Surf City. Paul would be of little use in a fight.

The dead Sullivan's guidance system was to be tested tonight at the ceremonial firing at the museum. Bill had read and reread the local newspaper's article.

> **... a radar guidance system developed locally by Sullivan Electronics currently owned and operated by Jack "Scooter" Sullivan of Holly Ridge.**

> **...Radar tracking will be from a temporary facility on loan to the museum by Guerry Electronic Systems of Chantilly Virginia. As a backup, a French Oceanographic Research Vessel, "La Lutte" will track the missiles from an offshore location.**

Bill parked several blocks away from the "Missiles and More Museum" and turned off the ignition. He reached into the glove compartment for Paul's .38 revolver.

The gun was gone. *Damn!*

Evidently Paul had sneaked the weapon while Bill was not looking. Bill clenched his fists and walked to a spot across from the museum grounds. He took a position behind a post in front of a small store.

The ceremonies would not begin until dark.

***

From his vantage point, Bill watched as GES technicians unrolled cables, unloaded monitors, and otherwise prepared a large tent that had been erected for the occasion.

A gray Acura sedan arrived. A man in a suit stepped out from the back. Bill recognized him as a frequent visitor to the Torbee building. He was Bruno Belli, a computer scientist and electronics specialist, as well as a GES consultant.

261

Apparently Bruno was in charge of the preparations.

Then a tall man with a fair complexion emerged from the front passenger side. He clearly represented muscle. Bill did not know him, but the blonde driver was all too familiar. Looking trim and attractive in tight jeans topped by a light chemise, Denise Guerry stepped from the car while the bodyguard watched with more than professional attention.

She straightened to full height in a smooth practiced motion. Clearly the bodyguard approved her moves. Bill had to agree.

Suddenly Denise turned and swept Bill's side of the street with a cold eye.

He jumped back. *Did she see me?*

Seconds passed before she turned away.

"Ian, Hamm is here. I feel it."

"You saw him?"

"There was movement by that store over there. I'm sure it was him."

Short as his association with Denise was, Ian knew not to disagree. But he liked certainty.

"Do you want me to go look?"

"No. Stay by me. I need to check our setup. I can ask Maximilien to handle Hamm."

Ian abhorred Gutera's ways, and Hamm, if it were him, was still an American.

"Let me go. I can handle Hamm."

Blue eyes became ice. He recoiled.

"Never mind."

He followed her to the tent.

***

In Surf City, Wayne Johnson was behind the wheel of the Buick he had rented in Myrtle Beach. Jeannine sat next to him.

"Wayne, thanks once again. You've freed me from the FBI."

"Not exactly. They've been watching my house. That Ford behind us is theirs."

"But what will I do?"

"It's all arranged. There's a vacation-style store ahead. It covers a short block. I have a rental car waiting for pickup at the end of North Topsail Drive. Here are the keys. I'll drop you at the beachside entrance and park as if I'm waiting for you. Go in and leave by the back exit. Once outside, push the remote and make the lights blink. Get in and go!"

He pulled in front of the store.

"The FBI is right behind us. I'll sit awhile to give you time to escape. The number of Bill's new phone is under the seat of your car."

She gave Wayne a huge hug. Briefcase and laptop in hand, she went into the store.

Once inside, she dashed to the rear entrance.

Wayne turned off the motor and pretended to wait.

***

Stew Marks was parked at the McDonald's near Topsail Island. He had not moved since Jeannine's departure.

At first, he had wondered how she had gone, but then he understood. Of course, Wayne Johnson had picked up his "daughter." The man was loyal.

Stew's phone buzzed. The number was Jack Marino's.

"Stew, I have a team watching Wayne Johnson. He picked up a redhead, a woman, at a McDonald's in Surf City. My men followed them onto the island, but the woman got away. She went into a store while Johnson waited. It was a trick. She sneaked out the rear entrance.

"It was Jeannine. I'm at that McDonald's. She gave me the slip too."

"You mean you were with Ryan? Damn, Stew. What's wrong with you? Work with me. We can catch Hamm at the tests on topsail tonight. Help me catch the rat."

"Jack, I'm on leave. I need time to think."

"Then stay the hell out of my way. And don't try to warn Ryan. I think you know where she went."

"Jack, you should concentrate on stopping Maximilien Gutera, not Hamm. He'll likely be at Topsail tonight too."

"Our assignment is Hamm. Damn it Stew, we can do this together."

"Sorry, Jack, I need to be on my own for a while. Besides, the NSA will tie your hands about Byrd."

"Byrd is dead."

"Yes he is, but he was only a part of Gutera's schemes. They are very much alive. Hamm and Ryan want to stop him.

"Stew, that woman is no good."

"She's a straight shooter, Jack."

Jack had heard enough. He hung up.

***

******

Chapter 34
Wednesday, September 5

In Surf City the two FBI agents assigned to follow Wayne Johnson received a phone call from Jack Marino.

"Guys, I'm betting Hamm will be at the missile museum tonight when the rockets with Sullivan's guidance systems are fired. Hamm has a stake in those rockets. He'll be there."

"What about Johnson?"

"Forget him. Meet me at Topsail Beach in half an hour. You know the spot. I'm tired of chasing Hamm. Tonight the rat will come to us."

***

In Topsail Beach, Bill Hamm watched the GES monitoring tent from a new vantage point. After the close call behind the post, he had moved to a nearby clump of junipers. Denise Guerry and the fair-skinned bodyguard were in the tent, out of sight.

Bill's phone vibrated against his thigh.

"Jeannine! Thank God! Are you all right? Is Marks with you?"

"I'm OK. I'm by myself. Wayne helped me get away."

"Where are you"

"Near Wayne's favorite place to eat."

"Do you have everything with you? And the laptop?"

"Yes and Yes."

A commotion across the street drew Bill's attention. Denise Guerry had emerged from the tent. She stood talking and waving her arms at Bruno Belli. Her bodyguard was not in sight.

"Stay there. Something's up. I got to go."

***

Across the street from Bill's hiding place, an impatient Bruno Belli stared at Denise Guerry.

"Denise, I told you I agree. with you. We don't need to encrypt the signals from the missiles. Everyone knows that we are tracking them. There is no need for secrecy. None."

He took a breath.

"Why do you keep asking me if I agree with you? You know I do. I don't understand why you keep asking?"

Denise continued to gesticulate as if arguing.

"Because, Dear Bruno, you are not a good actor. It was necessary that you thought I did not understand you. Your reaction was superb, much better than acting."

"What are you saying?"

"I'm saying that you and I are making a scene. Someone is watching us from behind those bushes. I'm sure it is that CIA fugitive, William Hamm. You and I are holding his attention while Ian Callahan smokes him out."

She frowned.

"We only need to continue our farce a few more minutes. By then Ian will have him. Now, pretend to be upset with me."

She waved her arms anew, but Bruno froze. She was right. He was a lousy actor. Fortunately further performance was not needed.

From across the street, Bruno heard a shout and a thump. He looked up. Two men grunted as they grappled on the ground. They rolled behind a thick clump of junipers. Moments later one of them emerged and disappeared along the side of a small store.

Bruno turned to Denise.

"Was that your bodyguard?"

"I don't know. The bushes were in the way."

Their uncertainty was momentary. A man crossed the street, dashing to avoid an oncoming car. Bruno saw that he held a gun.

He was not the bodyguard.

The man spoke.

"Hello, Denise."

"Bruno, I think we all met before in Chantilly, at the security conference. You remember Bill Hamm."

***

Bill pointed a Beretta at Bruno, but spoke to Denise.

"The man you sent to get me, was he the one called 'Ian'? He's good."

Denise sniffed.

"Apparently not good enough. Is that his gun?"

Bill nodded. He waved the weapon at Bruno.

"We all need to go inside the tent. It's too public out here."

When he turned back to Denise, she had twisted slightly to loosen her blouse revealing a tantalizing cleavage. His eyes stayed on her chest. She smiled.

Bill did not.

"Denise, you look great, but the bulge by your left arm worries me. I know you're a crack shot, and I assume that is your Browning. Don't test me. I can shoot too."

Blue eyes went limpid as Denise pushed her lips into a pout. She slipped sideways so that Bill could enjoy her profile and shoved Bruno towards the missile tent. She moved deliberately in front of Bill so that he could admire her walk.

Bill followed her into the tent. From behind, he could not see that those limpid eyes had frozen ice-gray.

***

Jeannine Ryan did not wait at the deli. She craved action.

She would attend the missile tests herself. She wrapped her distinctive hair in a scarf and hid her eyes behind dark glasses, not much of a disguise but better than nothing.

Then, she set forth for the missile museum and Bill.

**

In the missile-guidance tent, Bill Hamm let the Beretta hang loose and inconspicuous. He motioned Denise and Bruno towards a monotonous row of monitors that all showed the same image. Nearby, a lone technician was attaching cable to some sort of electronic box.

Denise waved the technician to leave before turning to Bill, her eyes blue and soft once more.

"All right Bill. What can I do for you? Now that Byrd is dead, there is no reason for us not to get along. He was your enemy, I never was."

Bill's surprise was genuine.

"Dead? But he was in jail in South Carolina."

"Quite so, but he was no longer of use, so Paris eliminated him. He no longer concerns you or me. Byrd was the only obstacle between you and GES. Your own government has abandoned you. Join us. We can make you rich."

She smiled.

"And I can reward you in personal ways."

Denise's mind raced. She was half sincere. Hamm had been Byrd's enemy, not hers, and GES could use Hamm's CIA experience and contacts. Plus she could justify a generous reward for him in return for the stolen items.

Besides, she might need protection from Gutera, and on the personal side, Bill obviously was superior to Ian. The small scar on his cheek spoke of covert ops and danger, things she admired.

I can control this guy and enjoy myself doing it.

"What do you say, Mr. Hamm?"

Bill's head ached from where Ian had butted him.

Does she mean this?

***

Jack Marino and his two FBI agents parked their Ford across from the missile-guidance tent in Topsail Beach. Sam, the agent sitting in back, spoke.

"Jack, that guy who went into the tent after that blonde, that was him. That was Hamm!"

Jack looked up. The man was no longer in sight.

"It's pretty far over there. Are you sure?"

Sam waved a photo in the air.

"I've been looking at this damned picture for two whole days."

Jack pointed at a car parked near the tent.

"OK, but first get me the information on that Acura. It has a Maryland plate."

"I already checked. It's leased to Guerry Electronic Systems in Chantilly, Virginia."

"That figures. They are the ones tracking the rockets tonight, and Hamm sold secrets to them. We'll wrap them up together."

Jack turned back to his driver.

"You and I are going to check that tent. Sam, you watch the car."

Jack stepped out of the Ford, Beretta in hand, and headed across the street.

***

Inside the missile-guidance tent, Bill Hamm stared at the woman in front of him. She looked great, except for those intense probing eyes. They unsettled him. He was dizzy and his headache was worse.

To his left, Bruno meekly moved near the door of the tent.

Bill tightened his grip on the Beretta, but Bruno turned back.

269

"Two men are coming. They look like police."

Denise ignored Bill's Beretta and slipped to Bruno's side.

"They're FBI. I know one of them, but I forget his name. Wait, it's 'Marino.' He belongs to Agent Marks."

She turned to Bill.

"They're here to arrest you. Decide now. There's a company pickup outside the rear of the tent. We should leave."

She headed to the opposite end of the tent. Bill hesitated. She beckoned.

"Hurry, they'll be here any second."

He followed her.

***

Denise Guerry went to a pickup truck with the GES logo on the door. The keys were in the ignition and the motor turned over smoothly. She smiled.

This is easy. I thought he'd be more of a challenge. He's just a man after all, but he's virile. I'll enjoy him.

She motioned Bill inside. He opened the door with his left hand while gripping the Beretta in his right. Denise ignored the gun. She no longer feared him.

He appeared dazed, or as she preferred 'dazzled.' Had he forgotten she still had her Browning? No matter, she did not need it.

She understood men.

As for the missile tests, Bruno could handle them. As long as Hamm was with her, he could not spoil the proceedings. The tests would take place without interruption.

She drove north. In the opposite direction, cars were backed up, heading for the festivities. She crossed the Surf City bridge to the mainland and turned south onto Route 17. She would hide Hamm at the farm where Gilles Smets had been killed. The FBI had yet to find its location. She and Bill would not be disturbed.

270

Bill still had not spoken. She smirked. Soon everything taken from Byrd's safe would be in her possession.

***

Stew Marks was experienced and smart. At Topsail Beach this evening, his experience had trumped the direct approach of Jack Marino. Not that direct action was always wrong, Stew's usual choice was to keep things simple, but with some individuals nothing was simple.

And with Bill Hamm nothing ever was.

Thus Stew had watched Jack's "frontal assault" on the GES tent with skepticism. He did not believe that Hamm could be taken by surprise. And he was right.

When Jack had "attacked" the front, Stew had placed himself at the rear to watch and wait. Hamm and Denise Guerry had appeared on schedule and left in a GES pickup. Denise had driven away behind buildings that blocked Marino's view. But not Stew's. He had followed Denise and Bill onto Route 17 south.

***

Stew kept Denise's pickup in sight. She was driving carefully, within the speed limit. But knowing Hamm was in the front seat disturbed him.

Damn. Hamm's presence confirmed his guilt. That posed a problem for Stew. He did not want to risk losing the little affection that Jeannine had shown for him and if he arrested Hamm, he would forever be the object of her scorn.

Hamm nauseated Stew. Denise Guerry was most desirable. Men wanted her and Hamm had her. *Hamm, you scumbag, how could you betray Jeannine? She deserves better!*

That decided Stew.

No matter what Jeannine thought of him, he would take down Hamm for good!

***

Denise Guerry drove the truck south on Route 17. Ahead was the road that led to the "Smets" farm, but she drove past without slowing down. A Honda Accord had occupied the rear view mirror since Surf City.

The Accord had a lone driver, a male Caucasian.

Could it be that ass Jack Marino? No. Another agent had been with him at the tent and he would not be alone. *Besides Marino is clueless.*

A single possibility remained, Stewart Marks, the only FBI agent Denise respected, and feared.

She glanced sideways. Bill was no longer upright. He had slumped over, chin against his chest. His eyes had closed. He was unconscious. A red welt had grown on his forehead.

A head butt? Before going down, Ian had left his mark.

Apparently Bill had been dazed during the entire ride, due, perhaps, to pressure from a clot or sub cranial swelling, and not from anticipation of her sensuous body pressed against his.

OK, Mon Cher Hamm, maybe you're not as malleable as I thought. Denise, you were over confident. You know better. Watch yourself.

She reached over and took the Beretta out of his loose grip. Hamm might still be an enemy.

That resolved, she looked once again in the rear view mirror.

The Accord was still there.

***

In Topsail Beach, Ian Callahan limped to the Acura. One eye had closed completely, and his right arm hung limp, straight from the shoulder. There was an Urgent Care Center in Surf City, not far from the bridge. He headed for it.

As he struggled to remain conscious, one thought was clear. His service with Guerry Electronic Systems was done.

***

272

Maximilien Gutera had decided to avoid the ceremonies at Topsail Beach. Rather, with a small cadre of his followers, he would pass the evening at the "Smets" farm, courtesy of Guerry Electronic Systems. He cared little about the high-precision guidance systems. All he required of his rockets was that they explode over the eastern region of the Democratic Republic of the Congo and not over Rwanda. Accuracy was not a problem.

It was only to appease his French sponsors that the tests at Topsail Beach were being held. He had resolved to proceed no matter their outcome. He was in North Carolina solely to show his sponsors that he was "serious."

He sipped his expensive Bordeaux, leaned back in his chair, and sent puff after puff from his cigar to the ceiling. He opened his eyes as his phone chimed. Jules Habimana answered.

"It's Mademoiselle Guerry, do you wish to speak with her?"

Maximilien seized the instrument and listened briefly. He returned the instrument to Jules.

"Someone is following Mlle. Guerry. She would like us to rid her of him. Post two men with AK-47's out of sight across the road from our entrance. She is driving a gray GES pickup truck. They are to let her pass and to stop whoever follows."

He yawned.

"Take Louis Makuza with you and wait by the old tractor on the left under the trees. You will welcome Mlle. Guerry. Keep my phone. She will call you before she arrives."

He emptied his glass and leaned back in his chair. Once again gray puffs floated upwards in vague spirals.

Jules left to find Louis Makuza.

***

The sun was low in the West. Stew Marks focused on the gray GES pickup ahead of him and its driver, Denise Guerry. *Where is she going? We'll soon be in Wilmington.*

Stew checked the gauge on the dash. *Half a tank. OK.*

He looked up to see the pickup skid, wheels-locked, across the sandy median to land in the other lane in the opposite direction. Then motor roaring and wheels spinning, it sped back the way it had come.

Stew hit the brakes to cross the median, but his turn was slow. His wheels slowed in the sandy soil. Finally they reached the hard surface and he started after the gray pickup, barely visible ahead.

Denise was retracing her steps, but why?

No matter, Bill Hamm was in that pickup.

Stew had no choice but to follow.

***

******

Chapter 35
Wednesday, September 5

At Topsail Beach, Bruno Belli sat back and relaxed for the first time in 48 hours. The tests were successful. The rockets had exploded as planned over the target areas, and the flight data had been recorded with only one hitch, a few records from a non-critical part of the flight were lost due to a buffer overflow.

Bruno, called Denise Guerry. The planners in Paris would be happy. She should notify them. Her phone rang, but she did not pick up. *Strange!*

He hesitated to leave a message. It would be better to try again in a few minutes. He waited and tried once more.

Again, no answer.

Bruno was puzzled. Denise had insisted that he notify her immediately with the results of the tests. Paris was waiting.

He tried again. No Denise.

Outside, a boisterous group was celebrating around a keg of beer. Bruno spotted an attractive technician with a frothy mug in her hand. She smiled as he joined her. He stopped worrying.

***

At the "Smets" farm, It was dark when Denise Guerry brought the pickup to a halt near the rusted tractor. Jules Habimana stood tall and smiled while at his side Louis Makuza, panga in hand, stared impassively.

Jules smiled with an effort. He was sick of this domineering woman. His chief tolerated her only because he needed his French backers. If the French wished to bow down to weak women, Maximilien (and Jules) would accommodate them, but only for a time, and from necessity.

Jules' consolation was that in a few days the radioactive modules would be transferred from the French ship *La Lutte* to the *Étoile d'Afrique*. After that, Maximilien's Hutus would be in control of the weapons and their own destiny. And once the dirty bombs had exploded over the eastern Congo, their French friends would have no choice but to condemn Rwanda and back Maximilien's bid for power. They could not back out without losing face.

Denise stepped from the pickup.

"Where is Maximilien?"

"He will be available soon. I am to serve your needs."

Denise looked at Louis Makuza and saw the panga.

"Tell him to put that bush knife away."

Jules nodded to his aide who obeyed and stepped back. Denise spoke.

"Jules, I have someone with me. His name is Hamm. He will be joining me at GES. You are not to harm him, understood."

Jules stared as Bill Hamm, his eyes glazed, stepped out of the pickup. Jules had heard of this dangerous man.

He turned back to Denise.

"As you wish. Now, please hand me your Browning and that cell phone. Maximilien does not allow such things in his presence."

Denise complied. But something in Jules' manner disturbed her. She was thankful that Ian Callahan's Beretta was stuffed in the back of her jeans. She waved for Bill to join her.

But Jules intervened.

"No. he cannot see the chief. He must wait here with Louis."

Simultaneously, Jules winked and motioned Louis to withdraw his panga from its sheath.

Denise started to protest, but stopped at the sound of gun fire from the direction of the entrance hundreds of meters away.

"BrBrBrup, ..., BrBrBrup..., BrBrup."

Jules paused and listened as more automatic fire erupted.

"BrBrup, ..., Brup, ..., Brup."

Then silence.

He smiled. The last four rounds doubtless had been insurance. Maximilien's trap had worked.

Jules seized Denise's arm and pulled her towards the farm house.

***

In the darkness, Stew Marks lay on the ground on the driver's side of his bullet-riddled Accord. *What happened? Who ambushed me?*

He smelled gas behind him. The gas tank had been hit. He needed to get away from the car. He crawled into the bushes at the side of the road.

Just in time.

Flames erupted from the rear of the vehicle. They lit the landscape, momentarily silhouetting two dark figures against the glare. Each carried a weapon with a long curved magazine, AK-47's. Stew flattened himself further. *What the hell? Who are these people?*

The flames reached the gas tank.

The rear of the car exploded sending metal flying on all sides. An orange ball of fire soared skywards. The shock wave rolled Stew further into the brambles, and sent one of the dark figures airborne, his weapon spinning away.

The figure crashed in a heap of bones and flesh onto the roadway, not far from Stew.

Stew waited. The lumped torso did not move. Stew crawled forward through the bushes, feeling his way with his hands.

His fingers touched the AK-47. *Good!* Stew, still prone, felt the magazine. It was bent and twisted. The weapon was useless. Stew laid it aside and drew his Beretta from its holster.

From the other side of the roadway someone shouted in a strange language.

Stew lay motionless and waited.

***

Jules Habimana was on the porch of the farm house when the explosion sounded. He pulled Denise to the door.

"Maximilien has rid you of your pursuer, and his car. You should be grateful."

"I am. But you are not he. Now let go my arm and never touch me again, *sale cochon*, 'dirty pig.'"

The last epithet was too much for Jules. Soon they would no longer need this woman. He punched her face, full force. She flew sideways. Her back slammed against a post and she fell in a twisted heap on the porch.

He kicked her thigh. There was no response.

Jules exhaled. He had waited for this moment. He hissed through his teeth.

"Bitch, you will respect us. We are Hutu. Save your haughty airs for your own countrymen."

He grabbed her torso and tore her chemise to expose her chest.

"You serve us, not we you. Now, Maximilien will decide if you are still useful. If not, you will serve every man here and I will be the first."

But Jules could not wait. She was helpless and he was the master. He would subdue her with pain. Then he would work his will on her.

He pulled her upright and reached for her exposed breast. He would twist until she screamed.

His hand never touched flesh. Something metal pressed against his abdomen. *A gun? I took it from her. No!* He heard and felt a muffled crack. His body was pushed backwards, away from the pressing metal. *You French bitch!*

He tried to grasp her throat. Now he would strangle her.

But she had stepped back beyond his grip.

Ian's Beretta was not muffled now.

"Crack!"

Another hole appeared in Jules' chest. His heart, pierced, stopped.

Still again.

"Crack!"

A hole formed in his forehead.

Dead, Jules fell backwards off the porch.

Denise, still gripping the Beretta, slumped down.

Her eyes closed. She lost consciousness.

***

For the first time since Ian's head butt, Bill Hamm's mind was clear. He had watched as the African called "Jules" pulled Denise away with him. More to the point he had caught Jules' wink to Louis Makuza.

Bill did not wait for Louis to unsheathe his panga, but dove backwards behind the tractor. Pointed holly leaves tore at his shirt and arms as he scrambled through the stiff brush. He rolled on the ground. He heard the swish of chopped branches falling as his pursuer cut a path towards him.

There was little moon light. In a dark recess between two large pines Bill hunched and waited.

In the distance someone shouted. Bill heard twigs crack and branches rustle in the direction of the shout. Apparently the call was a summons. Louis had gone.

Bill exhaled and waited. Then he crept back towards the rusty tractor.

Ahead, a lone light shone from the porch of the farm house.

There were no voices.

No sounds came from the house.

***

Stew Marks lay on the ground by the side of the road. Behind him, the frame of the Accord smoldered. Scattered flames persisted, but their light could not penetrate the dark bushes.

With his Beretta ready, he crawled towards the entrance lane.

"Snap!"

The sound came from across the road. Someone had stepped on a twig.

Stew froze.

Moments passed. Nothing.

He resumed his crawl towards the entranceway. His elbow pushed against a dead branch. Leaves rustled.

A voice whispered from across the road.

"Patrice, is that you?"

Stew hugged the ground.

***

Bill Hamm stood by the abandoned tractor and peered at the porch. Under the light he made out the motionless form of Denise Guerry. He could not see her face, but he knew her chemise and jeans.

On the ground near the porch steps sprawled the body of a man, Jules. Even in the shadows away from the porch light, Bill knew he was dead. The awkward angles of neck and limbs confirmed that.

Bill dashed across the open space to the porch and knelt.

"Denise, wake up. We need to get out of here."

He lifted her head, one eye opened. The other was dark and swollen.

"You?"

"Yes, me. Can you stand?"

"Where is Jules? He has my Browning and the phone?"

"You finished him. He's dead."

"Bon! The bastard."

She groaned, but rose to her knees, pulling her chemise together. He lifted her by the waist. She leaned against the wall and shoved the Beretta into his hand.

"Take this. Now get me my gun."

Bill helped her off the porch and leaned over the sprawled corpse. He handed her the Browning and pocketed her phone.

She clung to his shoulder. He held her waist and they stumbled through the yard to the old tractor at the edge of the pines. She collapsed next to the hunk of rusted metal. Bill pulled her behind it. She gripped his arm, her head on his shoulder. They huddled out of sight of the house.

Just in time.

Maximilien Gutera roared from inside.

"Claude, Alain, go find Jules? Damn him. He should have reported by now!"

Footsteps resounded on the porch, followed by cries of dismay and anger.

"Jules is shot! Jules is dead!"

More men came out of the house.

Beams of spotlights crisscrossed the grounds.

***

At the entrance to the farm, Stew Marks lay behind a Holly and peered into the shadows. There was no gate and as far as he could see no house, at least no lights shone from that direction.

For some minutes now, Stew had heard nothing from across the road. He decided to move. To his right was a thicket of Sassafras. He would crawl there.

He held the Beretta ready and shifted his weight onto his left elbow.

"Snap!"

The broken twig was directly behind him. Stew tried to turn, but before he could the butt end of the bush knife crashed against his skull.

He blacked out.

***

******

Chapter 36
Wednesday, September 5

Louis Makuza stood over the fallen FBI agent. He lifted his panga high. He would behead this worm of a spy. A hand grabbed his arm.

"Louis, no!"

Louis turned. The Hutu behind him he knew only as "Claude."

"Why?"

"Jules Habimana is dead, shot. Maximilien will want to question this man."

"Where is the French cow?"

"We do not know. We are searching for her."

Louis frowned and sheathed his weapon. Claude continued.

"Maximilien will let you have him after he is done. Put him in the woman's truck and take him to the shack behind the farm house. Maximilien will 'converse' with him there. But where are Patrice and Pierre? They can help us move him."

"Patrice is dead, killed in the explosion. Guerry's man escaped me. I sent Pierre back to look for him."

Claude grunted.

"All right, I'll help you lift him in the truck. We must hurry. Maximilien is not happy."

***

At her room in Surf City, Jeannine Ryan settled into her bed.

At the celebration in Topsail Beach, she had not seen Bill, but she had watched that FBI jerk, Jack Marino, from a distance. His evident anger told her that he had not captured Bill. But that was the sole comfort of the evening. The tests had been successful and one less obstacle remained to Gutera's using his dirty bomb.

Jeannine was upset for another reason. Were she and Bill still on the same page? Recently, their relationship had been strained. She loved her work and he hated his, at least the "desk" part. And Stew Marks' infatuation flattered her.

The last thought was only momentary. Bill had not met her at the deli as planned. Where was he?

She leaned back on her pillow and stared at the ceiling.

Bill, Are you all right?

***

At the Smets farm, Denise Guerry leaned her head on Bill's shoulder.

Why do I trust this man? But I do. I can depend on him.

Such feelings were strange to her. She could not handle them. She shook her head clear.

No, I can't.

Bill leaned over her.

"Are you all right? Can you get up?"

She opened her good eye. His were kind.

Damn it Denise, get a grip on yourself.

He touched her arm.

"Denise, we need to go."

She nodded. He lifted her to her feet. Gripping his hand, she stumbled into the dark pines. Behind them the lights and cries of Maximilien's searchers had moved away, in the direction of the road.

Bill guided her through the woods that bordered the fields at the rear of the house.

Her head spun. She trusted no one, least of all a man. And this man is the enemy.

But I do trust him.

Her head spun anew.

284

Denise, stop. You are a fool!

She slipped on the pine needles underfoot.

His strong arm steadied her.

Hmmmm!

***

The sound of a motor interrupted Denise Guerry's thoughts. She stopped.

"Bill, what's that noise?"

"It sounds like your pickup truck."

He disappeared through the pines to her left. Moments later he returned.

"It *was* your truck. Gutera's men had someone in the back. They threw him in the old shack. Whoever he is, I wouldn't want to be him."

After Jules Habimana's savagery, Denise was ready to change alliances. Her rescuer deserved the truth. Her voice was low.

"It's that FBI man, Stewart Marks. He followed us. I asked Gutera to stop him."

Bill's eyes hardened.

"What!"

"I'm sorry."

Denise surprised herself. She wanted to please this man, to have his respect, sentiments new to her. She swallowed and spoke slowly.

"I was wrong. It was all so abstract, supporting Gutera. Uncle Roland liked him, so did his wife. They raised me and they own half the company. They told me that Maximilien was a refugee, that he was persecuted."

She lowered her eyes and stammered.

"It was like a game to me. I wanted to win."

Bill stared. She kept on.

"My God. Maximilien and his men are not human. They are monsters. I cannot help them anymore."

She looked at Bill.

"What will they do to Marks?"

But she knew the answer. She spoke before he could.

"Bill, we have to help him."

Bill continued to stare.

A scream pierced their ears. It came from the old shack

***

Bill Hamm hefted the Beretta. Judging from its weight, only several rounds remained. He looked at Denise. She clung to her Browning Hi Power.

"I'll cover you Bill. I have thirteen rounds, and I don't miss."

He nodded and pulled her to her feet. Adrenalin surged and she stood erect.

"I'm ready."

Bill moved quickly to the edge of the woods. She struggled after.

They looked out from the cover of the pines. Three men stood outside the shack. Suddenly a group burst from inside. The leader was a large man. He strode to a car parked at the rear of the farm house followed by three others. He paused, illuminated by the light next to the door.

Denise whispered.

"The big one, that's Gutera."

The big man stepped into his Audi. The three men followed. Denise recognized the one who sat in back with his chief.

"The one next to Gutera is called Claude, Claude Senteli."

She added.

"And the driver is Pierre Sehene, an electrical engineer. I don't know the other one. His name might be Alain."

The Audi roared away.

Bill looked at Denise. Their odds had improved, but three men remained in front of the shack in which Marks was held. Had he survived the interrogation?

He had to act now.

Gun drawn, he signaled Denise to follow, and rushed through the weeds towards the shack.

***

Surprised at the sight of two individuals running at him, Louis Makuza stepped into the shack. He would finish his victim. The others could deal with those foolish attackers.

Louis looked in the corner where Maximilien had interrogated the captive. The FBI man was no longer there. *Where?*

Louis stepped to the other side of the shack.

Just in time. Several rounds penetrated the boards of the shack where he had stood.

Louis heard a rustling. There, the man was huddling in the far corner. Louis paused to listen. The shooting outside the shack had ceased. Good, he would not be interrupted. He raised the panga high, for a two-handed stroke.

His last conscious act.

Crack!

The panga clattered to the floor. A split second later, Louis Makuza fell dead on the worn planks.

In the doorway stood Denise Guerry her Browning in her hand. A gray curl of smoke drifted upwards from the aperture of the gun. Exhausted, she collapsed and sat with her back against the door frame.

Outside, Bill Hamm examined the AK-47 by the man he had shot. The weapon had jammed. He sighed.

Better to be lucky than good!

But it was not luck that had killed the other Hutu who lay dead among the weeds. Blood oozed from his forehead. Denise was as accurate as she had claimed.

Bill went to the door and pulled her to her feet.

Together they peered into the shack.

***

In the Audi a few miles away, Maximilien Gutera was furious. The "relaxing" evening at the farm had been a disaster.

A fatalist, he counted his losses. Patrice had been killed in the gas-tank explosion. Far worse, his trusted right hand, Jules Habimana was dead, killed by that bitch and former ally, Denise Guerry.

He shifted to the present. The two men with him were skilled warriors. Of the two, Claude Senteli was more knowledgeable. He would replace Jules as Maximilien's right hand.

The third man, the driver, Pierre Sehene, had been a "chopper" as a boy in the Interahamwe. Now trained in electronics, he could prove useful.

And back at the farm the ever-loyal Louis Makuza would finish that meddling FBI agent. When Maximilien had found that Marks had discovered the farm on his own and without backup, he had lost interest in the agent. Louis would slash and cut him until he bled out.

As to Denise Guerry and Hamm, Louis and the other Hutus still at the farm would dispatch them too.

Satisfied with his analysis, Maximilien relaxed. He was in control once more. He spoke to his driver.

"Pierre, take us to Charleston!"

***

At the farm, Bill helped the ailing Stewart Marks to the house. The latter opened his eyes.

"Is that you, Hamm?"

"It is, but you don't need to talk. I'm going to reset your shoulder. Maximilien's men jerked it out of the socket. It's dislocated."

"But?"

Bill stuffed a rag into Stew's mouth.

"Quiet. Bite on this. I'm going to pull. Denise, hold him down."

Stew did not scream, but his teeth cut through the cloth and into his gums. He groaned. Blood appeared on his lips. Then his eyes closed and he fell back, unconscious.

Denise looked at Bill.

"You realize that when he comes to, he'll arrest you, or try to."

He studied her eyes. *She's concerned. Is this for real?*

"I can't leave him alone. Gutera may come back."

She touched his arm.

"Trust me, Bill. Gutera will not return. This farm belongs to GES. No, he has gone to Charleston to meet his ship, the *Étoile d'Afrique*. Agent Marks will be safe here."

"Then I'm going to Charleston to stop Gutera and his dirty bombs."

He glanced sideways at her.

"Your dirty bombs."

She flushed. All at once a Congo contaminated by radioactivity was real, not abstract.

Children and old people would vomit and die. *What's wrong with me? Why do I care?*

She recalled Jules' savagery. *This is no game. It is real. This American is real.* She found her voice.

"Bill, let me come with you. I may be able to help you stop Gutera. Let me try."

Bill swallowed. *This is crazy. This woman is dangerous.*

289

But she looked up, blue eyes misted.

"Bill, I have to try."

He was stunned to hear his own words.

"All right, Denise, I'll trust you."

They lifted Stew Marks on the living room couch. Denise fashioned a pillow under his head.

Then they left the farm in the GES pickup.

She rested her head on his shoulder as he drove.

***

In her room in Surf City, Jeannine tossed in her sleep. She sat up, half awake.

Bill! Where? Are you all right?

But something was not right!

Bill?

***

Seated in the back of his Audi on Interstate 95, Maximilien Gutera was troubled. Louis Makuza had not answered his calls.

Something was wrong!

And the French cow, Denise Guerry, could pose a problem. He still needed the cooperation of SÉGAG, her family's parent company in France, at least until the French vessel *La Lutte* off-loaded the radioactive modules onto the *Étoile d'Afrique*. After that his Hutus would be in full control.

Had a lone man and a weak woman defeated the men he had left at the farm? Was Denise now the enemy?

Maximilien considered his options. Denise's influence with SÉGAG was not unlimited. Her uncle Roland was subject to political forces in France that would object to any attempt to halt SÉGAG's support of Hutu Power. Denise might possibly prevail, but only in days, not hours.

The transfer of the radioactive modules at sea was to take place on Monday the tenth. Maximilien did not hesitate.

He made two phone calls off-shore, one each to the *Étoile d'Afrique* and the ship *La Lutte*. Then he called the North Charleston Terminal. In less than an hour the matter was settled.

The captain had agreed to dock the *Étoile d'Afrique* in North Charleston on Thursday Evening, more than a day early. The port superintendent, suitably bribed, would obtain the necessary clearances from the authorities so that the containers with the rockets would be loaded immediately. The ship would remain in port overnight and depart Friday morning to rendezvous with *La Lutte* at noon on Saturday. The transfer at sea would take place two days ahead of schedule.

Satisfied, Maximilien leaned back in the seat and relaxed. Denise could not stop him.

"Pierre, the interchange with I-26 is ahead. Take the turn towards Charleston."

***

As the early sun pierced the branches of the pines that edged the Smets farm, Agent Jack Marino stepped out of his car, avoided the twisted body of the African on the steps, and entered the house. He saw Stew Marks on the couch.

"Jack, how did you find me?"

"I was on the way to Wilmington when they called from the Resident Agency. They're sending backup and an ambulance is almost here."

"But how did they know where?"

"Your guy Hamm called from a pay phone in Wilmington. He must want a plea bargain. He said we'd find you and some bodies. What the hell were you doing Stew? This place is like a war zone. Who are all these people?"

"Rwandans, or they used to be. They're genocidal Hutus led by a killer named Maximilien Gutera. He wants to restore Hutu Power in their country. The woman you despise, Ryan, put me onto them. She has evidence that they ..."

"Ryan! You found her? Is she with Hamm?"

"I don't know where she is now. Yes I found her, and no, she wasn't here. Denise Guerry was with Hamm."

"They're in this together. That settles it. The rat is selling secrets to GES!"

Stew tried to rise.

"No Jack, that's not the way it was."

But the pain was too much, he fell back his teeth clenched. At that moment two EMT's pushed a gurney into the room. They lifted Stew onto it.

***

******

Chapter 37
Thursday, September 6

In Surf City, Jeannine Ryan felt a buzzing under her pillow. *What? Where?* She fumbled for the phone and pushed it against her ear.

"Bill?"

"Jeannine, it's me, Wayne."

"Oh."

He coughed.

"Sorry, I haven't heard from Bill either. This is about something else. I just received a call from Carolina Tech in South Carolina, a Professor Hurley in Computer Science."

"I know him. He did a project for us at Ryan Associates, 'Non-random digits in RSA messages.' What does he want?"

"He wants you to be on the doctoral committee of his student, 'Angelique Uwimana.' He called Maryland and couldn't find you. Someone told him I might be able to reach you."

"This is bizarre! The world is maybe falling apart, and you call me about a doctoral student?"

"The world has to go on, and you need a normal life, too. Besides, Hurley told me that you had encouraged her about her project."

"What was her name? You woke me up, I didn't catch it."

"Uwimana."

"I remember. She wanted to factor semi primes for RSA decryption. No way, but her ideas could work elsewhere."

"OK, now you know. I've done my duty. I told Hurley I would call you. Now you have his number. It's up to you whether to call him or not."

"Wayne, I didn't mean to be grumpy. I'll never be able to thank you enough, but I'm worried about Bill. We were to meet at the deli in Surf City after the rocket launch. He didn't show."

She hesitated.

"I'm going to Charleston without him. If he's able, that's where he'll be. We have to stop Gutera and his killers."

"Do you want me to come with you?"

"No, that wouldn't work. The FBI is watching you."

"Jeannine, don't go. You're in as much danger as Bill.

"Thanks, but I have to."

As she hung up, she remembered.

Uwimana said she was from Rwanda!

She sat on the edge of the bed and punched a number into her phone.

"Professor Hurley, this is Dr. Ryan, Jeannine Ryan. I hear you tried to call me."

***

At a coffee shop in Charleston, South Carolina, Henri Duval savored rich dark coffee, while Angelique Uwimana tapped vigorously on her laptop.

"Angelique, I don't understand you. Why come back to Charleston? They found us here once. And you're back at the same coffee shop!"

She kissed his cheek.

"Henri thanks for humoring me. We are safe. The Lord protected us before, and He will again. Maximilien's men won't think that we would return here, and the kudu horns on the wall remind me of Africa. Besides, I like Kenyan coffee, it's almost as good as Rwanda's."

She looked at his cup, now empty, and smiled.

"I see you like it too."

She touched his hand.

"And I need to email Professor Hurley. He is setting up my doctoral committee so I can finish in June. I need one more member, a 'Dr. Ryan.' I talked to her once before. She's a statistician in Maryland. He's trying to locate her."

Henri shrugged. He worried about Maximilien Gutera tracking emails.

Angelique's computer pinged. She read and grinned.

"This is an email from my Professor. Dr. Ryan called him. She's agreed to be on the committee. She told him she was on her way to Charleston. He told her I was in Charleston too, but the only place he knew was this coffee shop."

Angelique bubbled on.

"She wants to meet me to discuss where I am on my project. She'll meet me here at the coffee shop this evening."

Henri frowned. A known place at a specific time was dangerous.

"What's Dr, Ryan's first name?"

"Jeannine, Dr. Jeannine Ryan?"

Henri's frown deepened.

Jeannine Ryan? According to Denise Guerry, Jeannine Ryan had shot Tom Holder at Topsail. And Holder had not seen action since.

"Angelique, Denise knows about your Dr. Ryan, and says she is dangerous. You must be careful. This is not a good idea."

"Henri, why do you care what that woman thinks? I thought you had forgotten her."

"Angelique, I don't care about Denise. I only care that she or Maximilien may track Ryan to you! This meeting is not safe."

Angelique looked into her coffee cup.

"The doctorate is important to me. I can't believe that Dr. Ryan is dangerous. She helped me before, and she's a professional, a scientist. I have to meet her."

Henri fell silent. Dr. Ryan might be trustworthy, but Denise and Maximilien were not.

He stared at the Kudu horns. Angelique followed different rules. How she had survived thus far mystified him. He had seen the genocide first hand. Despite the thoroughness of the Interahamwe, she was alive and thriving.

When he was a boy in Sousceyrac, his mother had trusted God. He had never understood that, but her love for Henri had been real. He did not understand Angelique either. She too lived as if God were real. *Maybe she's right. Maybe she should meet Dr. Ryan this evening?*

His stomach knotted. No matter, right or wrong, he knew.

Whatever he said, Angelique would be at the coffee shop to meet Dr. Ryan.

***

In North Charleston, at the yard of *Kenya-Carolina Apex Distributors*, Maximilien Gutera watched as company workers drove the final screws into the frame of his fourth crate.

When the crate was closed, the foreman rested his lithium power tool on a stand and stood back to inspect his work.

There were four crates, each contained three solid-fuel rockets with their explosive-packed components already attached. A detached ceramic nose, the "radome," lay alongside each rocket. The radomes housed Sullivan's guidance modules, like those that had proved themselves in the test at Topsail Beach.

The ceramic radome could be attached to its rocket only after the radioactive module was secured to the explosive component. These final steps would take place after the *Étoile d'Afrique* docked in Mombasa. German technicians, mercenaries, were to extract the radioactive modules from their heavily-shielded container and then complete the final assembly.

Satisfied, the foreman turned to Maximilien.

"Sir, the crates are secure. All four will fit into one container."

"They will be immobilized?"

"Yes Sir, the fittings have already been mounted. Once they are locked, your crates will not budge."

The foreman waved to a forklift operator who hoisted the first crate onto a bed of rollers in the container where several workers pushed it to the rear and locked it in place.

Maximilien stepped into the manager's trailer.

"Is all paper work ready? My container must be at the terminal at North Charleston today before it closes at 18:00. The *Étoile d'Afrique* will arrive this evening. I want this container loaded on board as soon as the terminal opens tomorrow at 07:00. I have already arranged details with the superintendant at the terminal."

The manager, who would receive the second half of a most generous bribe only when the container was loaded on the ship, waved his hand casually. He had no intention of botching such a lucrative transaction.

"There will be no problem. The container will arrive at the terminal before six. And Sir, if you have future shipments, please contact me. It has been a pleasure to serve you."

Maximilien smiled. He stepped to the door and saw the last crate disappear into the container. He gave the manager's hand a single shake and walked to his Audi.

All twelve rockets would be aboard the *Étoile d'Afrique* tomorrow morning! She could sail that afternoon and meet the *La Lutte* on Saturday.

No one can stop me now, least of all, you, Denise Guerry.

No weak woman would ever have power over him again. And woe to Denise should they meet!

***

The early morning sun shone on the pines of the Francis Marion National Forest. On the outskirts of Huger, South Carolina, Eric Nyonzima rested his crutches by the pay phone.

He dialed Pierre Sehene's number in Florence. Pierre's wife, Agathe Muteteli, answered.

"Hello."

"Agathe?"

"Yes, who is this?"

"Eric, Eric Nyonzima."

"Pierre is not here!"

She slammed the phone on its cradle, but missed and it fell on the table. As she retrieved it, she heard Eric's voice.

"No wait, don't hang up. Please. It's you I need to talk to."

"You killed Laurette! What do you want of me?"

"I didn't kill your sister."

"But you stood by and watched. You didn't stop them. And she was a Hutu. All she did was try to protect Nadine. Eric, you are a murderer. You and all your friends!"

Her condemnation lit his memory.

Time stood still. He saw the bloody dismembered body of Laurette lying among the weeds, within sight of her front door. Nearby, Pascal danced and waved a bloody panga in a demand for Eric's approval. Eric sweated. He lifted his arm to block the sun, and Pascal, from his eyes.

At that vivid recollection, Eric sweated anew under the Carolina sun. He sobbed into the phone.

"Agathe, you are right. And I am so sorry. How could you ever forgive me. I swear to you by God, I was wrong, horribly wrong. May God help me."

Agathe was silent. Out of fear, her father had excused the killing of Laurette, his own daughter. She recalled his words and her response.

"Agathe, Laurette should never have hidden Nadine. All Tutsi are the enemy. They are snakes who would kill us, kill you. Be strong."

"But Laurette was my sister. And Papa, she was your daughter!"

The memory brought tears to Agathe. She struggled to speak.

"Eric, we were teenagers. Whether I can forgive you or not does not matter. God will have to do that."

Eric's mumbling was indecipherable.

"Eric, stop sobbing and tell me why you called?"

He regained his composure. There was a restaurant across the street from the phone. He described it to her. If she agreed to help him, they could meet there.

They spoke for several more minutes. Then the conversation was over.

Eric leaned against the wall and sighed. Agathe had agreed to help him escape Maximilien. She would bring her car and meet him at the restaurant.

After two kind acts, Angelique sparing him and Agathe's promised help, his world was upside down.

Maybe God was real, but why would He forgive me?

Help!

***

In Summerville, South Carolina, not far from North Charleston, Bill Hamm stepped from the GES pickup truck. He compressed the sandwich wrappers and bag into a crumpled sphere and tossed it into the garbage container from ten feet away. *Swish!* He smiled.

In the passenger seat, Denise Guerry hung up her phone.

Bill spoke through her window.

"All right. What did your 'Oncle Charles' say?"

"You know Paris is six hours ahead of us."

Bill had served years in Europe as a covert operative for the CIA. He knew time zones. His voice rose.

"Stop stalling. What did he say?"

"First dump this for me. It's gross."

She lowered the window and handed Bill a soggy mix of bread, pale compacted meat and drooping lettuce.

Bill stepped away and threw the mix into the plastic-lined container.

"Damn it Denise, you have to eat."

"But surely not that."

"Forget it. What did your uncle say?"

"He was not happy with me. He and his associates were at a late lunch and could not be interrupted. He will call me after."

"Damn it, Gutera is going to contaminate hundreds of square miles of the eastern Congo, and your uncle won't interrupt a luncheon. Call him back."

She stopped posturing and pleaded.

"Bill, try to understand. He's the patriarch. He won't take my call. All I can do is wait for him to call me back."

Angry, Bill strode to the driver's side of the car and got in.

Forget the French addiction to food.

He fastened his seat belt and spoke to the windshield.

"I'm going to the library. I need a computer to check the listings of the Port Authority."

He drove off without waiting for an answer.

Denise knew to stay silent.

***

At the public library in Summerville, South Carolina, Bill Hamm sat and studied the computer screen while Denise Guerry, her blouse pinned over, wandered through the stacks nearby.

The web site for the Port of Charleston appeared on his display. He clicked the list of vessels expected in the next thirty days.

That's odd. The Étoile d'Afrique is no longer listed to arrive on Saturday. What's the delay?

He scrolled through the later arrivals. The *Étoile d'Afrique* was not listed.

Puzzled, Bill clicked back to the previous pages, hopeful that something "bad" had happened to the vessel.

Damn!

He stared at the screen in disbelief.

The *Étoile d'Afrique* was to arrive at 22:00 this very evening. And worse, the ship was to depart tomorrow afternoon at 15:00, not on Monday as previously planned.

He was out of time!

***

In a motel in North Charleston, Maximilien Gutera relaxed. His stay in the United States would soon be over. The change in arrival for his ship was accomplished.

He sat back in a cushioned chair, sipped his brandy and. puffed on his Cuban cigar. The room was "Non-Smoking," but the rules for commoners did not apply to a leader of his stature. He chuckled.

Then he frowned. There was still an unresolved problem.

Angelique Uwimana.

The image of the beautiful Tutsi haunted him. But her escape from his men in Florence could not spoil his mood. He chuckled again and puffed once more, but stopped.

Or could it?

He frowned and called Professor Hurley at Carolina Technical University in Florence.

"Professor Hurley, Maximilien Gutera, here. I still have money put aside for Miss Uwimana's Research award. I was hoping to meet with you and her."

After a few minutes of conversation, Maximilien Gutera hung up and chuckled yet again. The professor was naïve. Angelique was to meet Ryan in Charleston this afternoon.

When Angelique arrived at the café in the old city this afternoon, his men would be waiting!

Maximilien exhaled and watched as a thin ephemeral circle of smoke wafted upwards, lost form, and disappeared. He leaned back.

He shut his eyes.

After he was done with Angelique, she too would disappear.

But first he would enjoy her. It would be good, very good!

***

******

Chapter 38
Thursday, September 6

It was nearly noon in Huger, South Carolina, when Agathe Muteteli stopped the Toyota Corolla in front of the roadside restaurant. Through the window, she saw Eric Nyonzima seated at a booth. She beeped twice. Seconds later Eric appeared at the door and waved her inside.

She stepped out of the car and went in. He was in the booth by the door. She sat opposite and waited for him to speak.

"Agathe, you're a lifesaver. Thank you for coming, but where is Pierre?"

"Pierre! I thought you knew. He left me. He's joined Maximilien Gutera and his thugs."

Eric winced.

"I didn't know. You didn't tell him I called, did you?"

"I haven't spoken with him since he left a week ago."

"Agathe, I'm sorry."

She shrugged.

"Maximilien is the devil. Pierre has chosen to serve the devil."

She frowned and stared at Eric.

"And you, Eric? Whom do you serve?"

A familiar image flashed through his mind.

A bloody dismembered body lay among the weeds, My God, Laurette!

He wanted to throw up. He hid his face in his hands and choked.

303

"Agathe, I am so sorry about Laurette. You are right. We were devils. We weren't human."

"My sister called you her boy friend."

He choked anew, unable to speak. She continued.

"Eric, you were a boy then. What have you done as a man? Why do you want to leave Maximilien?"

"Why? Because if he finds me, he'll kill me, and because of Angelique Uwimana, do you know her?"

"The Tutsi? She and Pierre were in a graduate algebra class together. I met her."

"She saved my life. She talked about God."

Eric spoke fast. He recounted how, at Gutera's command, he had tried to kill the Frenchman, Duval, but suffered a broken leg instead. How he and Gutera's men would have raped and killed Uwimana in her apartment had they found her! How later, Duval had trapped him in Charleston. How in the lonely pine woods, Angelique had stopped the Frenchman from killing him. How she had spoken to him of God's love and forgiveness.

At the end of his revelations, Agathe reached and touched his arm.

"Eric, we all are wounded. We watched our Tutsi neighbors, Hutu too, die horribly. We stood silent while you and your gangs killed and raped our friends and neighbors, while you looted and pillaged their homes."

She searched his eyes.

"Eric, I have no answers, but God does. You must ask Him to forgive you. He is your only hope, our only hope."

Agathe sighed. She leaned back and stretched. Then she stood up.

"Eric, it was a long drive from Florence. I have to go to the bathroom. When I come back, we'll see where you want to go. You need to leave the East Coast. Think about where."

Agathe was trim, and energetic. Eric watched her stride to the rear of the dining area and pass through double doors to the Rest Rooms.

He waited in the booth and shut his eyes.

Chopped arms and legs among the bloody weeds, Laurette!

He covered his head with his hands.

***

In the rest room, Agathe stood in front of the mirror. She rubbed her hands together as she hummed a simple refrain that took sufficient seconds to ensure thorough cleansing.

She moved to the electric drier and held her hands under the blower. The noisy fan drowned out the sounds from the dining area.

The whirring stopped and Agathe stepped out the door to a cacophony of screams and shouts.

Near the door several men stood together. She followed their eyes to the first booth.

Eric lay slumped there, the back of his head pressed against the blood-smeared window. Blood oozed from a single hole in his temple.

Disjointed sentences reached her ears.

"A black man shot him. With a Glock, just like the cops carry."

"The guy just sat there in the booth, looking up. He didn't care if they killed him."

"I know guns. I tell you it wasn't a Glock."

"It was a Glock, and They left in an Audi, a gray one."

"Did you see the tag number?"

"They left too quick."

Agathe wanted to throw up. She ducked through the kitchen and slipped out the rear door to her Toyota.

The long arm of Maximilien had found Eric!

***

Agathe Muteteli drove north on Route 52. A half hour passed before her head cleared. She arranged her thoughts.

Prior to his phone call, she had not heard that Eric was in the United States. She had not spoken to him since the nightmare in Rwanda when they were both young.

A single phone call! How did they find us that quickly?

The truth appeared with awful clarity. Her husband, Pierre Sehene, was with Gutera all the way. He had let them bug her phone. *The bastards!*

Agathe rarely used profanity, but she was distressed, and not only because of their spying.

Suppose Pierre repented and desired her once more, wanted to return to her, to start anew their life together? They would have no chance.

No one could quit Maximilien Gutera. He would have Pierre killed, like Eric.

Life with Pierre was lost, and they had come so close to realizing their dreams, in only a few more months he would have graduated!

Agathe sobbed.

She jammed her foot on the accelerator.

***

In Wilmington, North Carolina, Stew Marks sat up in his hospital bed. He heard the phone buzz, reached his good arm to the side, and grabbed the instrument. The caller was Jack Marino.

"How's the shoulder Stew? And the bruises?"

"My left arm is dead, my eye is bandaged, and I ache all over. Otherwise, I'm fine. What's up?"

"I'm on my way to South Carolina. A man was murdered in Huger, a town north of Charleston. I should say 'executed,' an African named Eric Nyonzima. The Columbia office had a file on him. He was one of Maximilien Gutera's men."

Jack continued.

"Maybe that Ryan woman told you right. There could be a Hutu plot going down, along with a weapons shipment from Charleston to Africa."

"Jack, do you know where Jeannine is?"

"We know she left Topsail, that's all. Maybe she's OK, but that doesn't help your man, Hamm. The rat's with the Guerry woman. He's guilty as hell. Look, gotta go."

"Jack, thanks for the info."

In seconds, Stew Marks was on his feet. He went to the closet for his pants. He struggled to put them on with one hand.

No more hospital!

He was going south.

***

Before Stew Marks finished dressing, his phone buzzed again. This time the caller was a surprise.

"Stew, this is Jeannine Ryan, are you all right?"

"Who gave you this number?"

"Nobody, I called the resident agency in Wilmington. They said you were injured and on sick leave. They wouldn't say more. This is the third hospital I've called."

"I had a brush with Maximilien Gutera. He won. Your pal Hamm rescued me, he and that woman, Denise Guerry."

"Denise Guerry? She was with Bill?"

Jeannine knew about Denise's good looks. She had seen her photograph in the briefcase. She stared at the phone.

"How did they get together?"

307

Stew collected his thoughts.

"I wouldn't know. When they saved me from Gutera, I was only half conscious."

He added.

"She helped Bill escape from Jack Marino and the FBI at Topsail Beach. I followed her into a trap set by Gutera's men. Look, I'm all mixed up. They saved me. I don't know what to say."

At her silence, he changed the topic.

"Jeannine, if you know where Bill is now you must tell me. The plot he has uncovered is real. Besides, he needs to clear himself if he can. And why is he with Denise Guerry?"

She wanted to know the answer to that herself!

"I don't know where Bill is, but he will surely go to Charleston. That's where Gutera will be."

He was silent. After a moment, she made her decision.

"Stew I have to be in Charleston this evening to meet someone. Are you able to travel? Would you come with me?"

Would he!

"I can come, but I can't drive."

"I'll do that. I'm parked outside the hospital. If you come down now, we'll leave right away."

A stunned Stew shed his slippers and put on his shoes. He left them untied and slipped into the corridor.

No one! And the nurse at the station had her head down.

He entered the stairwell and started down the stairs.

Despite his aches, he was a happy man. He would be with Jeannine. And she liked him, or at least trusted him.

***

At the library in Summerville, South Carolina, Bill Hamm searched for Denise Guerry in the stacks. He found her at a computer in a secluded cubicle. She was staring at an encoded email.

He watched as she took a thumb drive from the pocket of her jeans, and inserted it into the library's computer. She tapped a key. The decoded message appeared on the screen.

*d.g.la|lutte|captain|is|french,|but|hutu|
sympathizer|captain|of|etoile|d'afrique|is|
hutu|and|loyal|to|maximilien|gutera|his|crew|
hutu|too.|at|mombasa|paid|german|techs|to|
finish|assembly|and|smuggle|rockets|to|
southern|rwanda.launch|from|there.
jacobin|5|m|*

"Denise, who is Jacobin5. What's this about?"

"Jacobin5 is my cousin. He can be a pain, but we trust each other. He doesn't like his father, my uncle, any more than I do. I hoped we could call the captain of *La Lutte* and stop him from offloading the radioactive modules, so I sent my cousin a message. This is the answer."

She looked up at him.

"The captain of the *La Lutte* is committed to Gutera. He would never cooperate with us. And the *Étoile d'Afrique* is loyal to Gutera too. We can't stop the modules from reaching Mombasa."

"But in Mombasa, maybe we could pay the German techs to not complete the rocket assemblies?"

"They are strictly independent mercenaries, chosen because they're not French. We could never outbid my uncle's Euros."

The computer dinged. Another email had arrived.

```
0936131508261309311305172131091903062529230821402705221539160524
2140081304060109191925193320060621090810062822050524202208040639
1224402927092540102812052421400809140639230507153206054029202808
0706032326170638281015021916104015380809002026132314273804050907
2223070820193905403913312836122 5
```

"Denise, what are these numbers?"

"I'm not sure. It must be another message from my cousin. I'll decrypt it."

She typed rapidly on the keyboard. After a few moments the decrypted message appeared.

d.g.|uncle|roland|furious|with|you|he|wants|
you|back|in|france|tds|what|did|you|do|to|him?||
watch|your|step.|he|is|dangerous.|
jacobin|5||31ww.ff

Bill read fast.

"What does 'tds' mean?"

"It stands for 'tout de suite.' It means 'right away.' My uncle wants me back in France, now! That's not good."

She set her lips and continued.

"Maximilien knows I killed Jules and that I'm with you. He has told SÉGAG. I'm a danger to them, and a problem for my uncle too."

Her eyes misted. She looked up at Bill.

"Now do you trust me?"

She leaned on his shoulder.

***

******

Chapter 39
Thursday, September 6

In North Charleston, Maximilien Gutera stubbed the Cuban cigar in the ashtray. Tomorrow morning the container with the rockets would be safely on board the *Étoile d'Afrique*. He had paid a high price to several port officials, but the paperwork for his container was now in order. He awaited only the arrival of his ship.

The phone rang. Claude Senteli picked up. After a brief interval he hung up and turned to his chief.

"Eric Nyonzima is dead. But they missed Pierre Sehene's wife."

"No matter. She's not important. Denise Guerry has betrayed us. I have called France and informed our backers of her treachery. She is now the enemy. Inform Pierre and the others."

He continued.

"That means GES will no longer launder our funds. We shall receive them from another company. We have sufficient monies for those remaining in Florence. For those of us sailing on the *Étoile d'Afrique* to Mombasa, our money will be there when we arrive."

Maximilien sighed. As supreme leader, he was as good in disposing of details as in formulating the grand plan. He leaned back in his chair and signaled Claude to hand him another cigar.

How fortunate his people were to have him.

***

Jack Marino and his temporary partner, Sam Smith, were on Interstate 26 in South Carolina when the phone buzzed.

Sam answered. Moments later he turned to Jack.

"That was Wilmington, your friend Stew Marks left the hospital four hours ago without checking out."

Jack frowned.

"That's just like Stew. So what?"

"A nurse saw him get into a car with a woman. They drove off together. The woman had red hair."

"Ryan! Damn that woman, and damn Stew. What the hell is he doing? Do I have to arrest him too?"

Sam did not speak. He did not share Jack's impatience with Stew Marks.

Jack grew silent. He stared at the road ahead, his hands tight on the wheel.

They were still twenty miles from Charleston.

***

On Meeting Street in Charleston, Jeannine waited for the traffic light to change. The café where she was to meet Angelique was in the heart of the old city, near the College of Charleston. She turned to Stew Marks in the passenger seat.

"We're late, but we're almost there. How's the eye?"

"It's fine, but my shoulder is a problem. I won't be much good in a fight, and I don't have a gun. I'm pretty much useless."

Jeannine glanced sideways at him. The man was muscular and his one good arm was stronger than both of hers. Aside from Bill, there was no one she would rather have as backup.

"Jeannine, why do you want to meet this woman. What can Uwimana tell you?"

"I'm not sure. She's a grad student at Carolina Tech, where some of Maximilien Gutera's sympathizers congregate, and she's from Rwanda."

"But she's a Tutsi and they are Hutu. It seems she would avoid them."

"That's logical."

"What you really hope is that she has information that could lead to Bill. Am I right?"

"You read me pretty well, Stew. That's what I hope. I'll take any lead I can get. Bill and I go way back. I'm worried."

Stew worried that Hamm was nearby. He would prefer him to be on the way to France with Denise Guerry.

Stop it Stew, you don't want to see this woman hurt.

He stayed silent as Jeannine turned onto Calhoun Street.

The café where Angelique waited was only blocks away.

***

At the café, large Kudu horns hung on the wall near where Angelique Uwimana sat with her laptop. Fun-filled and relaxed after their afternoon classes, students filled most of the tables. High-pitched chatter and laughter rose and bounced off the ceiling.

Angelique was grateful for the crowd. Henri Duval's warnings had lessened her confidence, and the abundance of carefree youths provided her a measure of safety. But she was not too concerned. Henri had surveyed the occupants of the café before withdrawing outside to watch the entrance.

She looked about the room. Several African women, wrapped in colorful robes, chatted in English at a nearby table. Angelique surmised that they were from West Africa, probably Ghana.

Then in the far corner, two African men, emerged from the rest room. Their expressive gestures showed that they could be speaking French.

Mon Dieu!

She recognized one of them. He belonged to Maximilien!

They must have been in the Men's Room when Henri had inspected the clientele.

They headed towards her.

Angelique hunched down at their approach, before a voice from behind startled her.

"Miss Uwimana? Angelique Uwimana?"

She turned. The speaker was a tall man whose left arm was in a sling.

"I am Angelique."

"My name is Marks, I'm an FBI agent and a friend of Dr. Ryan. She was to meet you here."

"Do you have ID?"

Stew waved his FBI badge in front of her.

Angelique looked across the room. Maximilien's men had seen the badge and stopped. She caught her breath.

Stew followed her glance. He recognized one of the men from his FBI photo. *Damn.*

"Miss Uwimana, those are Gutera's men. You should come with me."

She grabbed her laptop and stood. Stew pulled out his cell.

"Jeannine, drive around back. Angelique is here but so are Maximilien's men. We're coming out through the kitchen."

Stew pushed Angelique through the crowd towards the rear of the café.

***

Jeannine Ryan had the motor running as Stew Marks and Angelique Uwimana slipped out the rear door and into the alley. They boarded quickly.

"What happened in there, Stew? What went wrong?"

"Ask Angelique. Two of Maximilien Gutera's men were there. They were after her."

Jeannine spoke over her shoulder.

"It's good to see you again, Angelique. But tell me, why is Gutera after you? Is it your thesis?"

"Dr. Ryan, I can't leave. My friend, Henri Duval, is waiting for me outside the café."

"Call me Jeannine, and I'm sorry, but it's too dangerous. Stew doesn't have his gun and we can't fight Gutera's men.

314

You see his arm. Gutera did that. He's lucky to be alive. We have to go."

She continued.

"But why is Gutera after you?"

"He hates Tutsis. His father helped organize the genocide, and the son is just as bad."

"Do you know a company called GES, and Denise Guerry?"

I should, she wants to bed my Henri!

She replied with caution.

"My friend, Henri Duval works for her."

"What about Bruno Belli?"

"Henri says Mr. Belli works for GES. He was at my seminar on RSA factorization. He implied I knew government secrets. He knows Gutera. They were together at a restaurant when Gutera's men tried to kill me. Henri saved my life. That's all I know."

Jeannine eased off.

"Thanks, and by the way, I would be happy to serve on your doctoral committee."

Stew broke in.

"Angelique, we think that Maximilien Gutera is plotting to take over your country and restore Hutu Power. Denise Guerry and GES are involved."

Dear God, not another genocide!

She froze in horror. She needed to tell Henri, but she could not recall his cell number.

She shook uncontrollably.

***

Across the street from the café entrance, Henri Duval waited. He rubbed his arms in frustration. Half an hour had passed and no woman with red hair had gone in.

Something was wrong, Dr. Ryan had not come. He was about to go inside, when two Africans stepped out of the café.

Claude Senteli! Where did you come from? Where were you when I checked the crowd?

Henri did not know the other man, but clearly, he too was one of Maximilien's thugs. The man called 'Claude' took out his phone and punched a number. Henri strained to listen.

"He had a badge and took her. He could have been that FBI agent. They left out the back. There were too many people. Just pick us up out front."

A gray Audi rounded the corner and stopped. Claude and his companion got in and the car roared away. Henri dashed across and into the café.

Angelique was indeed gone. The authorities had her.

He had to find her, but how? He only knew one person who could help, but that individual despised Angelique.

Denise Guerry.

***

In Summerville, Bill Hamm gripped the wheel of his car while Denise Guerry seated herself at his side. She spoke.

"What do we do now? Where should we go?"

Bill noted her "we." He chose "I."

"I'm going to the North Charleston container terminal. It's on Remount Road. The *Étoile d'Afrique* is scheduled to arrive there this evening. I need to study the layout"

Denise touched his arm.

"Let me help you."

Bill felt a vibration against his thigh. It was Denise's phone that he had taken from the dead Jules. A man spoke.

"Who is this? Where is Denise?"

Bill clicked the phone to "Speaker" and held it in front of her.

"Henri?"

"It's me, I need your help?"

Denise responded in French. Bill understood some words, but they spoke too fast. Finished, Denise turned to him.

"Bill, do you find me attractive? Do you like me?"

He jerked the car onto the shoulder and stopped. He kept the motor running.

"Denise, what was that call about? Who is this Henri?"

"Are you jealous?"

Bill seized her arm.

"Damn it woman, get real! Stop thinking of yourself. I have to stop Gutera before his ship leaves with those missiles."

She pulled away. His tone softened.

"Yes, you are attractive. Now who was that?"

Denise recounted Henri's infatuation with a Tutsi named Angelique who was missing, that Maximilien's men were hunting her, and that Henri wanted Denise's help.

Bill understood more from her tale than she had intended.

"So you are jealous of this 'Angelique,' and angry that this 'Henri' would prefer her to you. Denise this is not a game. You can use your beauty and your body to twist men like Henri to your will, but you won't find love that way. Henri is a person, not just a man. He has a will and an intellect, as much as you do."

She turned to him. But she had heard only the words she wanted to hear.

He thinks I'm beautiful and he admires my body!

But he kept on.

"Truth is, Denise, you are selfish. You think only of yourself!"

She sulked. *Zut! Why should I care what this man thinks?*

She fell quiet.

Bill pulled back onto the highway. Moments later, he turned onto Remount Road and headed for the North Charleston terminal.

He noted her silence and reflected. She had helped save Stew Marks, and without her accurate shooting, Bill himself might be dead in that field behind the shack, the target of circling vultures.

He softened.

"Denise, I'm grateful, I am. Without you, I might not be alive."

Her smile returned.

"Bill, this Henri who called is like you. He was a soldier in Rwanda. He's a man you would want on your side in a fight, and he knows Maximilien's ways, the ways of the Interahamwe. He can help us."

"I don't think you should tell him what we're doing."

She stopped him.

"It's too late. I told him we're going to the terminal. He's on his way there now."

Bill fell silent.

Now he had to watch Denise, plus a stranger too.

***

******

Chapter 40
Thursday, September 6

Henri Duval was on his way to North Charleston to rendezvous with Denise Guerry as agreed. The traffic light in front of him turned red just as his cell phone buzzed. The call was from his superior at SÉGAG in Paris.

"Henri, listen carefully. Maximilien Gutera informed *le ministre* that Denise Guerry has joined the enemy. Her uncle is taking her off the project to protect her. He has called her back to Paris, but the minister's aide says that she knows too much."

He paused for emphasis.

"They want her dead."

Henri was silent.

"Henri, did you hear me?"

"Yes, but why me? Tell me what you want me to do."

"She knows too much, and she is linked to the missing documents. You must eliminate her."

"Will *le ministre* confirm that in writing?"

"His aide will send you a message with the authorization."

Henri felt the thumb drive in his pocket. The decryption program and key were stored on it.

"Henri, do not fail. Eliminate this woman or the minister will have both our heads. Understood?"

"Understood."

The traffic light turned green. Ahead was a Public Library. He drove into the lot.

A few minutes later he was sitting at a library computer, waiting for the message from Paris.

To Henri, the wait seemed interminable, but only a minute elapsed before it arrived. He stared at the numbers on the screen.

09362034322029011721262500018
13403119102313010637182837011
01003733183435101821171021011
37331108040711333410060513041
01062531253321063416131021051

Henri's hand shook as he plugged his drive into the USB port.

Kill Denise? I am no assassin. I protect people.

The minister's aide used the pseudonym, "Gironde1." His real name was Charles and his key was the Latin form "Carolus." Backed by *le ministre*, Gironde1 was more dangerous than Denise's uncle. For Henri to disobey would be to sign his own death warrant.

But Gironde1 was a coward and Henri hoped that the man would not commit himself in writing. Henri longed for any excuse to avoid this assignment.

Henri tapped the keyboard and the decoded message appeared.

h.duval|removal|of|d.|guerry|authorised|
by02001714112018|gironde1|||b7

The message was lethal and clear. Henri stared at the screen in disbelief.

Denise Guerry must die!

***

Jeannine Ryan stepped out of the coffee shop in Mount Pleasant, across the river from Charleston. She handed her laptop to Angelique in back, and turned to Stew Marks seated in front.

"They had WiFi. I checked the Port Arrivals. There's good and bad news."

"I'll try the good news first."

"I know where Bill will be tonight, if he's able."

Stew frowned. *Great, where Hamm will be! If that's good news, what's the bad?*

"Okay, what's the bad news?"

"The *Étoile d'Afrique* is two days ahead of schedule. It's arriving at the container terminal in North Charleston tonight at ten. If Bill is anywhere near Charleston, he will be there."

Jeannine looked at Stew.

"What do you think?"

"We need to stop Gutera's rockets before they leave the U. S."

Angelique joined in.

"Shouldn't we call the FBI Agency in Charleston."

Stew answered.

"I already did. My old partner, Jack Marino, is here in Charleston. I talked to him. He wants Jeannine and Bill Hamm to turn themselves in now, and me too. Jack is a stubborn man. He will not look at our evidence unless we come in. And my supervisor in D. C. backs him up."

Jeannine added.

"Jack is an ass. By the time he looks at the evidence, Gutera's ship will be in International waters."

She started the car. Moments later they crossed the Cooper River on the grand Arthur Ravenel Jr. Bridge to join I-26 to North Charleston.

***

In Maximilien Gutera's suite in North Charleston, his right-hand man, Claude Senteli, answered the phone. The caller was Pierre Sehene.

"Claude, let me speak to the Chief."

"Maximilien cannot be disturbed. He is taking a nap."

"Wake him anyway. That Guerry woman and some man are at the port terminal. They are checking the rows of stacked containers. They're looking for our missiles."

Claude looked at his Rolex, a perk of being Maximilien's right-hand man. It was just after 6:00 pm, the terminal was closing. And the *Étoile d'Afrique* would not arrive for four hours.

"The man must be Bill Hamm. But what can Guerry do? Tell the port guards to arrest her."

"The guards at the gate knew her. She's rich and runs GES and the cash we used to bribe port personnel came from her company. Wake Maximilien now. He has to know."

But it was too late. A growl came from the bedroom.

"Claude, who is calling? What is their problem?"

After two minutes Maximilien, fully-informed and wide-awake, had his shoes on.

"Claude, call the North Charleston terminal and get superintendant Morris on the phone. Tell him to stop Guerry. And get me a driver. We are going to the port terminal."

"Now!"

***

At the North Charleston Terminal, Denise Guerry and Bill Hamm stared in awe at the long lines of containers stacked three and four high. At random intervals, mobile Rubber Tire Gantry Cranes (RTG's) straddled the rows.

A crane operator named Tim approached and handed them hard hats and fluorescent vests. They mounted his electric cart and rolled along a line of containers that ran at a right angle to the quay on the Cooper River.

Tim was expansive.

"There are 15 rows here. We're closed for the evening. That's why the RTG's aren't moving. This place hums during regular hours. If your container is to be loaded on that African ship first thing tomorrow morning, I expect it will be here on row BH, near the wharf. There's an RTG ready at the end of the row, and I had them move an empty truck chassis there too. I'll load it for you."

(Tim was happy to oblige the visitors. Denise Guerry had handed him four crisp fifty dollar bills. He would be late for supper, but his wife would not complain once she saw the money.)

As they reached the wharf itself, Tim pointed to a huge crane that projected over the water.

"We have six ship-shore gantry cranes here. This one is a ZPMC Super Post Panamax. We have two of them. They can reach over and load a ship over twenty containers wide. The other four are IHI Post Panamax gantry's."

Bill was anxious to find Gutera's container and had no time for a tour, but curiosity overcame him.

"What does 'Post Panamax' mean?"

"It means that the crane can load a ship too large to go through the Panama Canal, maybe eighteen containers wide, but less than a 'Super Post Panamax ship.'"

"How many containers wide is a ship that can pass through the canal?"

"A Panamax ship? I'd say with normal-width containers, thirteen."

Tim stopped the cart.

"Ok, here we are. Your container should be about here."

Denise stepped out of the cart. Sure enough, there atop a three-high stack was a container on whose side was displayed, *Kenya-Carolina Apex Distributors.* She turned to Bill."

"That's it. That's the company Gutera and SÉGAG use."

Tim nodded and mounted a metal ladder to the control cab atop the RTG. He waved to Bill.

"Climb on up if you want. You might like this operation. It's not too bad if you like joysticks."

Bill looked up as he climbed. He noted that the control cab had a glass bottom.

Tim called down to Denise.

"Ma'am, you must stand clear. There's a rest room near that next line of containers. Wait by that door. This won't take long."

Denise shrugged. It had been a long day.

She stepped into the rest room.

***

The glass-floored cabin was mounted on the crane's cross bar that straddled the row of containers. On each side the cross bar was supported by steel uprights mounted on rubber tires so that cabin and cross bar could roll freely along the row.

Bill Hamm watched through the transparent floor as Tim used two joysticks and maneuvered over the desired container. When the spreader attached to the corners, he lifted the container and rolled the gantry forward over the waiting truck. Then Tim lowered the container onto the chassis.

"Clank."

Tim turned to Bill.

"Your container is loaded and ready to go. Not bad, right. This is a great job. You should try it."

Bill nodded and gave Tim two more crisp fifty dollar bills, giving him a total of $300.00 with which to pacify his wife for missing supper.

Tim handed Bill the keys to the truck.

"Tell Miss Guerry the boss wants his rig back in 48 hours."

Bill left Tim in the cabin and climbed down the ladder.

***

On the ground once more, Bill climbed into the truck and turned the key. The diesel rattled and settled into a low rumble. He stared at the door to the rest room.

Denise heard the engine and stepped out.

"Denise, the container is loaded. We're set. I'll drive the truck. You get the car and follow me to Summerville."

She started away, but her phone buzzed. She turned back to Bill.

"It's Henri. He's outside the terminal. Gutera's Audi just passed the gate. Maximilien is here on the grounds."

"We have to run. Tell Henri to meet us in Summerville."

She ran to their car.

He rammed the truck into gear.

***

******

Chapter 41
Thursday, September 6

Superintendant Ralph Morris sat at his desk in the office of the North Charleston terminal. At Maximilien Gutera's instructions he had worked late to await the arrival of the ship, *l'Étoile d'Afrique*. His neck was moist with sweat, and he tugged at his collar.

The late hour was not the cause of his discomfort. It was his visitor, Maximilien Gutera, himself. Morris shifted uneasily in his seat while looking down at the African's shoes. They were of fine Italian leather. The man had rich tastes.

Up to now Morris had avoided direct meetings with Mr. Gutera. His "cash donations" had been transmitted to the superintendant by a third party, one with only hidden links to donor or recipient.

But tonight an enraged Maximilien stood over him.

"You idiot, how could you authorize Denise Guerry to remove my container from the premises without consulting me?"

"Mr. Gutera, Ms. Guerry is the CEO of GES. It is my understanding that GES finances your programs. How could I question her authority? I assumed you knew."

Maximilien slammed his fist on the desk.

"You assumed wrong! Denise Guerry has been removed from GES. She no longer has anything to do with me or my programs. Is that clear! You should have called me. I pay you well. Do not aid my enemies."

"Mr. Gutera, I'm sorry. I had no idea. I assure you, I always follow your instructions."

"My container was to be loaded tomorrow morning. My ship cannot sail until it is recovered. You have failed miserably. I do not tolerate failure."

Morris's hands froze on the arms of his chair. *The man's mad.*

Frowning, Maximilien Gutera turned to leave.

Superintendant Morris called out.

"Mr. Gutera, wait. Ms. Guerry told me the contents were unimportant. I was a fool. But we can find the truck. It is fitted with a GPS tracker. We can tell you where it is.

Maximilien stopped. *You idiot, now you tell me.*

Morris typed furiously on his computer.

A map with a blip appeared on the screen. The truck was nearing Summerville, South Carolina.

Maximilien called Claude who was sitting in the Audi.

"We must go to Summerville. Mobilize the men to meet us there. Arm them with AK-47's and pangas."

Maximilien turned to Mr. Morris.

"You are a lucky man. You are alive thanks to your GPS device."

He strode through the doors.

Ralph Morris wiped his forehead.

***

Bill Hamm drove the flat-bed truck with Gutera's container on Interstate 26 in South Carolina. He stayed under the speed limit.

Denise Guerry followed in the car. She saw the right-turn signal of Bill's truck blink. Seconds later the truck pulled onto a wide shoulder and stopped.

Denise pulled over and walked up to the truck. She watched Bill reach under the dashboard.

"What are you doing, Bill?"

He did not answer, but continued to grope behind the panel. Finally he pulled an object from under the dash and muttered.

"Evidently the Port Authority keeps track of where their trucks are. I should have thought of this sooner. This damn thing means trouble?"

"What is it?"

"It's a GPS tracker. Your friend Maximilien ... "

"He never was my friend, and he certainly isn't now!'"

Bill did not respond. He stood, silent.

Maximilien knows where the truck is, and he wants his rockets!

Denise read his thoughts.

My God! Maximilien knows where we are!

***

Denise stood silent while Bill Hamm studied the container on the truck. The painted letters, *Kenya-Carolina Apex Distributors*, were too large and bright to alter or conceal. There was no way to conceal the provenance of the load, and no way to remove it from the flat bed.

Bill turned as a third car stopped on the shoulder behind them. His hand slipped towards his Beretta. Denise stopped him.

"No, Bill! It's Henri Duval, I told him where we were."

A man the size of Bill approached and held out his hand.

"Henri Duval. You must be William Hamm."

Bill took the outstretched hand and squeezed. Henri responded. Each returned the other's stare.

After some seconds, Denise spoke.

"Stop! Give up. It's a draw. Remember, Maximilien knows where we are."

Henri relaxed his grip. Bill did likewise. The Frenchman spoke.

"What does she mean? How?"

Bill held up the GPS device.

"Maximilien is tracking us. He wants his rockets back."

***

The guard stopped Jeannine Ryan and Stew Marks at the gate to the North Charleston terminal. He appeared nervous.

"Sorry, Ma'am, you can't enter the grounds. We closed at six pm. Come back tomorrow at seven. We open then."

"Call your supervisor. I'm sure he will let us pass. It's an urgent matter."

"Sorry Ma'am. It won't help. We had an incident earlier this evening. I have strict instructions from my supervisor to let no one enter."

"You mean unauthorized people entered earlier?"

"Sorry Ma'am, I can't say."

Jeannine shifted her ring to her wedding finger and turned the stone inwards. With teary eyes she displayed her "wedding band" to the guard.

"Please help me. I had to leave my baby with a neighbor. My sneak of a husband was here to meet his girl friend tonight and pick up a truck or a container or something. I'm sure they met here. She's a blonde bimbo who works in his office."

She swallowed and continued.

"Could the incident this evening be about a stolen truck or its load, and a man and a blonde?"

Jeannine's eyes went moist.

They carried the day. The guard stammered.

"That was it Ma'am. A guy and a blonde stole a container and took it away on a truck. Now don't tell anybody it was me that told you. Now please Ma'am, you have to go back. No one gets past these gates tonight."

Jeannine masked a smile.

"Thank you. You are kind and understanding. I won't bother you anymore."

She backed the car and turned around.

Thank God, Bill, that you have the rockets, but why are you with that woman?

Stew Marks noted Jeannine's frustration. Her playing the aggrieved lover was not entirely feigned. Denise still was with Bill.

Unsure what to say, he kept silent.

As Jeannine drove back onto Remount Road, Angelique spoke from the back seat.

"Where are you going now? I was hoping to find Henri."

"Angelique, I have no idea where your friend could be. I'm still trying to find Bill. I have one more place to try, a motel where he stayed in Summerville."

She had started to say "he and I stayed," but omitted the "I" out of deference to Stew Marks.

Damn it Jeannine, why did you do that? You don't care what he thinks.

She recoiled in surprise.

Or do you?

***

Maximilien rendezvoused with his men on the outskirts of Summerville. He and Claude Senteli rode in a gray Audi followed by Pierre Sehene and three new recruits in a black Audi of the same year and model. The two cars drove onto Interstate 26.

From his back seat, Maximilien spoke at some length with the Captain of the *Étoile d'Afrique* before briefing his headquarters in Florence on the changing situation. Finally, tongue-weary, he clicked his phone off.

It buzzed immediately.

The call was from an agitated Superintendant Morris in North Charleston.

331

"I've been trying to reach you. The line was busy. The truck is stopped northwest of Summerville, on I-26."

"How far past Summerville?"

"Far, it's close to the interchange with I-95."

"You should have called me sooner."

The superintendant stayed silent. He dared not remind Gutera that his line had been in use.

Gutera continued.

"Never mind, stay at your computer and stay on this line. Tell me if they move. You are fortunate, Mr. Morris, that they do not know we are tracking them."

Morris answered.

"I'll let you know the minute they move."

Maximilien kept his line open. Claude used his own phone to call Pierre Sehene in the black Audi.

Both cars, the gray Audi and the black, headed for the interchange with I-95.

***

Henri Duval followed as Bill Hamm sped southeast on I-26. Hamm drove fast. Evidently he was not worried about being stopped by the highway patrol.

Henri needed to catch Denise Guerry alone, but that would be difficult because of Hamm. In their encounter, Henri had felt Hamm's strength. The man was a formidable opponent. He must be cautious, Hamm would protect Denise. For now, he had to wait.

His thoughts shifted to Angelique. She should be safe with the police, whoever they were, but still he was troubled. In spite of the horrors she had seen, Angelique was truly an innocent.

Damn it Angelique, Denise despises you. She would have been happy had Gutera killed you.

Ahead of him, Hamm continued to drive fast. Distracted, Henri had lost ground.

He pressed his foot on the accelerator.

***

Maximilien Gutera's gray Audi sped west on I-26. Maximilien spoke to a weary Superintendant Morris in North Charleston.

"Mr. Morris, what is the status? Where are they?"

"They have not moved. They are still on I-26 near I-95."

"Excellent. My men and I can reach that intersection in ten minutes. Make sure you keep this line open."

Maximilien turned to Claude and waved him onwards.

"Claude, go faster. We have them!"

Gutera's car leaped forward. The black Audi followed.

In his office, Superintendant Morris sighed in relief.

***

In Summerville, South Carolina, Jeannine Ryan stopped in front of the motel where she and Bill had stayed only days before.

"Wait here, Stew, I'll only be a moment."

She approached the desk.

"I'm Ms. Ryan, did anyone leave a message for me?"

The clerk handed her a paper from under the counter.

"He stopped by two hours ago. He said it was from Julius."

mhdqqlqh||zh|klg|iodwehg|zlwk|urfnhwv||||
fdq|phhw|ph|q|jhorujhwrzq|zkhuh|zh|ohiw|iuhgv|
slfnxs|wuxfn||eloo|

Jeannine smiled. Julius Caesar had used a simple cipher in the Gallic Wars. She and Bill had encountered it in a previous case. In the Caesar Cipher, each letter is replaced by the one three after it. Thus j is written as m, e as h, a as d, w as z, and starting again at the beginning, x is written as a. Jeannine worked quickly.

jeannine||we|hid|flatbed|with|rockets||||
can|meet|me|in|georgetown|where|we|left|freds|
pickup|truck||bill|

333

Bill had hidden the flatbed with its container and would meet her in Georgetown, South Carolina, where they had left Fred Middleton's truck before going to North Carolina.

Jeannine returned to Stew and Angelique.

"Bill did it. He hid the truck with Gutera's rockets. He's gone to Georgetown. We're to meet him there."

Stew sighed in relief.

***

Both of Maximilien's Audis were parked on the shoulder of I-26. They could see the interchange with I-95 ahead of them. The Hutu leader was on the phone with Mr. Morris.

"Check your coordinates. There is no truck here, only pinewoods. Where are my rockets? What game is this?"

"Mr. Gutera, those are the correct coordinates. I would never mislead you, Sir. Perhaps the truck is in the woods."

"Fool! That is impossible. I have eyes. Do not insult me!"

Sharp raps on the glass halted his outburst. Maximilien lowered the window. Claude Senteli handed him a small device.

"We found the problem, Sir. This is the GPS device, the tracker. It was over there near that big pine. They must have thrown it out the window. Our truck is gone."

"Maximilien turned his attention back to the phone.

"Did you hear that, Morris? You have failed!"

At the other end of the line Morris stayed silent.

***

******

Chapter 42
Friday, September 7

At a motel in Georgetown, South Carolina, Denise Guerry sat up and pushed back the bed covers. Bill Hamm was slumped in the chair in the corner. His eyes were closed and his breathing was regular.

After hiding the truck with Gutera's rockets, they had arrived at the motel late, and the only available room was one with a single Queen-sized bed. Initially Denise had been pleased. Even though Bill had insisted on sleeping in the chair, she had been sure that by the wee hours he would slip into bed beside her. But now the sun was bright, and she had awakened only to see Bill, eyes shut, still in the chair.

Even so she was not discouraged, she knew when a man checked her form while pretending not to, and she knew she had passed all Bill's evaluations. He would not be able to resist much longer.

Though his eyes were shut, she did not stop posing. She sat on the edge of the bed nearest him, and stretched a bare leg to its full extent before slipping it into her jeans. As the second slim limb followed, she glanced sideways.

His eyes appeared closed, but she was sure he had seen her.

She went to the dresser and turned on the small coffee maker. Dark drips coalesced into a single stream while she picked up her phone to call Henri.

The French conversation was over in a few minutes and the coffee was ready.

She took a cup to Bill and held it under his nose.

Is he really asleep?

He opened his eyes. They were wide and clear, not at all foggy.

Did he hear me talking on the phone?

That question was answered immediately.

"Was that Henri on the phone?"

She nodded. *Good, he's jealous!*

"Henri wants to meet with me, alone, without you."

His answer surprised her.

"Denise you can't do that. It's not safe. That man despises you. What did you do to him? He is dangerous."

"He wants me. He wants to sleep with me."

His answer startled her further.

"Maybe? But only to vent his anger. He would hurt you afterwards. And he likely will kill you if you meet him by yourself."

Her mind raced. Could Henri really hate her?

She thought of Angelique. Of course he could.

Her thoughts raced on. Had Maximilien already convinced Paris that she was the enemy? Had they instructed Henri to eliminate her, like they had Byrd?

Surely Uncle Roland would not permit that.

But the ugly fact was that Uncle Roland would take care of himself first. The truth appeared in high definition.

Henri now was SÉGAG's assassin and she was the target!

She stood frozen, staring into Bill's eyes.

In spite of her terror, she saw something in them, a new revelation.

My God, this man does not want me hurt.

He cares!

***

Call it a 'conversion,' an 'epiphany,' or 'whatever,' in that small motel room in Georgetown, South Carolina, Denise Guerry changed.

The rumpled bed stayed the same, the window curtains stayed partly open as before, and the dark coffee stains remained on the dresser. But Denise was not the same.

Her past choices flashed before her. She had treated others as pieces to be moved on a game board, and if necessary, sacrificed.

Her decisions had impacted real people. Intentional or not, she and GES had caused misery and brought suffering to live individuals, not wooden tokens or plastic game tiles.

Specifically, Bill no longer was merely a man caught in her seductive scheme, but a person whose eyes reflected sadness, pity, and a true concern for her. Not for her achievements, or her money, or even her body, but for Denise Guerry, the person!

His eyes had pierced her facade and he had seen the real woman, insecure, frightened and vulnerable.

And still he had not rejected her.

***

Henri Duval sat in the breakfast area of the same motel where Bill and Denise had spent the night.

When Denise had called and mentioned that Hamm still slept, Henri had proposed that they meet. Now he sipped his coffee and waited.

He was no assassin, but to kill in self defense was not murder. If he disobeyed orders and spared Denise, then SÉGAG would kill him, and without his protection Angelique would fall prey to Gutera. Besides Denise would have let Gutera murder Angelique. Yes, killing Denise was justified, otherwise he and Angelique both would die.

He glanced down at his watch. Denise was overdue.

Then he looked up.

There she was, standing in the doorway.

Striking!

Her neatly fit jeans, and discrete, but amply filled, blouse showed her form to full effect. Henri was not the only man in the room to focus on her entrance.

He pulled back a chair. *Damn, she is alluring!*

Henri steeled his will.

But poisonous!

She sat and balanced a large purse on her lap.

"Well Henri, you wanted to meet me without William Hamm. '*Me voici,*' Here I am.

Henri frowned.

"Frankly, I'm surprised that you came alone. What happened to Ian? And who is this guy Hamm? Why more muscle?"

"Henri, just tell me what you want?"

"I want you to come with me. There's something outside in my car you should see."

She recalled Bill's words: ... *[he] despises you. ... he likely will kill you if you meet him alone.*

Denise looked about. Half the tables were occupied by over a dozen individuals eating the free breakfast included in the price of the room. She was safe here.

"Henri, I will not go anywhere with you."

Sweat beaded on his forehead. He flicked his eyes to the right-hand pocket of his jacket. She caught the signal. An ominous object distended the fabric. He muttered.

"Denise, this is hard enough. Don't make it harder."

"Forget it Henri, I too have a gun."

Her right hand was in her purse. He understood.

She smiled and continued.

"I know you, Henri. You would never carry your Browning flopping loose in that pocket without the safety on. But mine has a round in the chamber and the safety is off. I will put three bullets in your gut before you can get off a shot. So, Mon Cher Henri, relax, I propose a truce."

Henri took his hand from his jacket pocket.

She smiled again.

"We should talk."

***

Denise rose from the table and went to the breakfast buffet. She put a cheese Danish on her plate and drew a cup of coffee from the urn. She returned to the table where Henri sat, his head in his hands. She spoke.

"Henri, you could never have killed me in cold blood. That is not you. I know that."

He did not look up. His head sank lower.

"Henri, something has happened to me, something I don't understand. I was wrong to support Maximilien, and I was wrong to want Angelique dead. I don't even know her. I'm sorry."

She choked.

"I know you can never forgive me. All I can say is that at that time, nothing was real to me. And now, dear God, suddenly everything is, terribly so. God help me!"

"Denise, don't invoke God. In our France, modern women don't believe in God. You know that. Don't fake it."

"You're right, I don't know about God, but maybe I should. And I've been a fake all my life. I hated unpleasant facts. I refused to listen when you tried to tell GES about the real genocide. I'm sorry."

She swallowed.

"Henri, I can never understand that horror, but I assure you I will do everything I can to stop Gutera and his men from restoring their 'Hutu Power.' And that means stop them from hurting Angelique or you."

Henri stared, mouth open.

"Denise, what kind of game is this? You would have slept with me just to get your way. You are dangerous. Because of you Angelique could have been raped and hacked to death. And now you would protect us. How dare you!"

"Henri, I know you are honorable. But I also know GES and SÉGAG want me dead. They sent you to kill me. I'm not wrong about that."

But Henri did not hear. He was elsewhere, in a banana grove.

... a once-human face stared vacantly upwards at a mass of broad leaves that hung, suspended and lifeless, from an adjacent banana tube. The girl was young, ... A panga had cleaved her cranium.

His eyes glazed over. He stood and went to the door.

Denise shifted sideways to watch him go.

But he stopped, his eyes blank. *... some distance away, obscured by a dry banana leaf, lay a woman, hacked and barely recognizable, a mutilated infant near her knees.*

Too much! He shook his head, but his eyes did not clear.

Nearby lay another mutilated woman, chopped, bleeding and barely still alive. Angelique! Gutera stood over her while Denise Guerry looked on smiling.

Henri drew his Browning and chambered a round. He turned and squeezed the trigger.

"Crack. Crack!"

Denise jerked backwards and slumped to the floor as the chair splintered and collapsed under her.

From across the room, a man jumped up and stared. At the buffet, a security guard, a Taser on his belt, looked up from his plate of eggs. Several men rushed to the fallen Denise. All eyes were on her, not Henri.

He slipped out the door. In the lobby, no one noticed him.

***

At the knock on his door, Bill Hamm opened to a middle-aged couple supporting a pale Denise Guerry, her arm bloody and hanging loose at the side.

"Denise, what happened?"

The answers flowed.

"She was with a man. The rat hit her and ran away."

"No, I tell you I heard a shot. He shot her. We should call the police!"

"Harry, there was no gun. That was the chair cracking."

"Look at her arm, that's a bullet wound."

"She ripped it on the chair, you saw the back was split apart."

Denise freed herself and stood erect to face Harry's wife.

"You're right, Madam. The chair slipped from under me and I fell. And that man was a stranger."

Harry's wife stared at her.

You knew that man, honey, and he knew you. He was angry.

Harry's wife looked at Bill and understood. Her eyes returned to Denise.

OK, so you don't want your husband to know.

She took Harry's arm.

"We should go and let her husband take care of her. There's nothing more for us here."

She and Harry left.

***

Bill looked at the red gap of torn skin on the inside of Denise's arm. Her purse was wrecked. Evidently the bullet had been deflected by something metallic inside. Of course, her Browning. He looked. The gun now was useless.

Without a word, he sat Denise in the chair, wiped the line of oozing blood from her arm, and stanched the flow.

She looked up.

"You were right, Bill, I shouldn't have gone alone. I'm sorry."

She slumped down and shut her eyes. She winced as Bill cleansed the wound. When he finished wrapping it, she shivered and closed her eyes.

"Bill, I'm cold."

He covered her with a blanket.

***

Elsewhere in Georgetown, Jeannine took a last sip of coffee outside the McDonald's while Angelique used the bathroom. She watched as Stew threw his sling on the ground and swung his arm in circular motions.

"Stew! What are you doing?

"Exercising. My shoulder feels a lot better. I'm not a cripple."

He continued to move his arm as Angelique appeared and hopped into the back seat. Jeannine called to him.

"Stew, get in. We have to find Fred's truck and Bill."

"I'm not coming with you."

"What do you mean?"

"I'm FBI. Your friend Hamm is wanted and I would have to arrest him. I called Jack Marino in Charleston. He's arranged a rental car for me. It's waiting only two blocks away. I'll walk. And he purchased a gun and ammo for me too. They're holding it at the gun shop."

"But we need your help."

"And you have it, but first I have to meet Jack and get him to stop his obsessive pursuit of you and Hamm."

"But there's no time. The _Étoile d'Afrique_ is ready to sail."

"But the rockets are not on board. He and the Guerry woman hid the Port Authority truck. Bill will be in the clear."

He kept on.

"Now we have to apprehend Gutera and his gang. You and Bill don't have the manpower for that. The FBI does."

He peered into soft brown eyes.

"You know I don't want to leave you, but this is for the best. We'll meet after Gutera is behind bars."

He looked in the back seat of the car.

"Angelique, sit up front with Jeannine. You two take care of each other."

He strode in the direction of the car rental agency.

Jeannine switched on the ignition.

"All right, Angelique, we're on our own."

***

Superintendant Ralph Morris was still at his desk. He had not slept. Rather than return home, an easy prey to that mad Hutu Chief, he had elected to spend the night within the guarded fences of the North Charleston terminal.

The *Étoile d'Afrique* had arrived as scheduled, and even now was being loaded with containers by one of his ZPMC Super Post Panamax gantry cranes. Gutera's ship was not 23 containers wide, but Morris had assigned the ZMPC to it. He wanted that ship loaded and out of his port as soon as possible.

But now Gutera's critical container, on which everything depended including Morris's life, was missing.

The Superintendant was at a loss about what to do once the loading was completed.

He was exhausted after the night's fruitless search with no sleep. His eyelids drooped. Only at the second buzz of his phone did he pick up.

"What is it?"

"Mr. Morris?"

"This is Morris."

"This is James Hyde, one of your drivers. I'm at the steak house in Santee."

"I know you, James. Is there a problem?"

"I'm not sure. One of the Port Authority flat beds is here, parked behind the restaurant. I can't find the driver. Nobody has seen him. The hood is cool. Looks like it's been here all night. Do you know about this?"

"Is it loaded?"

"Yes. The container belongs to *Kenya-Carolina Apex Distributors*. Funny thing, it's sealed and labeled like it's ready to load on board."

The rockets!

"Is it ready for the road?"

"I checked that before I called you. The passenger side tank is near empty and there's a mess of diesel fuel on the ground. Someone must have siphoned the tank. The left side fuel tank is over half full. It has an anti-siphon device. Whoever emptied the other tank couldn't siphon this one. It's ready to travel."

Morris exhaled in relief.

"James, what are you driving?"

"My Ford F150. I'm on my way to the terminal. I report at noon."

"James, do you know how to hot wire a truck"

James kept a thin steel shaft in his pickup. He was expert at flipping door locks and hot wiring ignitions, but this was the boss he was talking to. He hesitated, before he spoke.

"I can do that."

"Good. Listen to me. Leave your pickup truck at the steak house, and bring me that abandoned rig and container right away. I'll pay any speeding ticket, just get it here as fast as you can."

Morris added.

"And there's a $300 bonus for you if you make it here before eleven this morning. I need that container now.

James grinned.

"Yes Sir, I'll be there."

Superintendant Morris leaned back in his seat and shut his eyes. For the first time in hours he relaxed. He dozed.

***

In Georgetown, South Carolina, Jeannine Ryan found the parking lot where she and Bill had left Fred Middleton's gray truck.

Nothing had changed since she had last seen it. She reached under the rear bumper, and felt along the truck's frame. The key was there, inside its magnetic holder.

She stood.

"There isn't any note, Bill hasn't been here. We wait."

Absently, Angelique nodded. Her thoughts were only of Henri.

Jeannine leaned against Fred's pickup.

Neither spoke.

Each kept her thoughts to herself.

***

Pine woods lined each side of Highway I-95 where Pierre Sehene stopped the black Audi on the shoulder some miles south of the Bass Drive Interchange. He was glad to be away from the chief's ranting at the loss of the rockets. The three Hutus with him likewise welcomed the momentary respite.

Pierre just had adjusted his seat to a comfortable position when the parked Audi vibrated and shook in the wake of a passing truck. Pierre ignored the shaking and focused on the speeding vehicle.

It was a Port Authority rig, loaded and moving fast.

But it was the logo on the side of the container that caught Pierre's eye. *Kenya-Carolina Apex Distributors!*

Maximilien's rockets!

Pierre started the engine and pulled onto the interstate while thumbing his phone.

"Claude, tell Maximilien that I found the rockets. They're on a truck on I-95 headed towards the I-26 Interchange for Charleston. I'm chasing it."

He took a breath.

"And Claude, get back to me right away. I need to know what to do."

He pressed the accelerator to keep up with the speeding truck.

Ahead the rig disappeared around a wide curve.

Pierre increased his speed.

The truck came back into view.

***

******

Chapter 43
Friday, September 7

On I-95, Pierre Sehene followed the Port Authority flatbed as it sped towards the I-26 Interchange and Charleston. Small pines filled the median strip to his left, while to his right larger trees closed in on the highway.

Nervous, Pierre strummed his fingers on the wheel. He needed instructions. At last his phone buzzed, Gutera's right-hand man, Claude Senteli, spoke.

"Pierre, where are you and where is our truck?"

"I'm in the black Audi and I'm right behind it. He's turning off onto I-26."

"Is there anyone in the truck other than the driver?"

"Not that I can see."

"Good. Stop that truck and grab the driver. Hold him for Maximilien. He wants to question him. Is that Clear."

"Clear."

"We are coming up from Summerville. We will watch for you and the truck on the opposite shoulder. We will not be long. Do not fail."

"Click."

***

James Hyde hummed as he took the I-26 ramp from Highway I-95. Mr. Morris had not explained why the Port Authority rig with the *Kenya-Carolina* container had been abandoned in Santee, but James did not question the boss. The $300 bonus answered any questions he might conjure up.

He studied the road ahead. Visibility was good and I-26 was clear. There were no dwellings in sight, only thick pine forests on both sides of the highway, and no highway patrolmen were sitting on the wooded median working their radars.

Good!

Then he looked in his rear view mirror. A black Audi was approaching fast. James moved slightly to the right to encourage the speeder to pass. The Audi roared by.

James relaxed. But the Audi swung into his lane. Its rear lights flared bright as the driver braked sharply in front of James. The car's rear end with four interlocking chrome circles filled James' field of vision.

What the hell? No!

He jammed his brakes, rubber burned on the roadway as a high-pitched squeal pierced his ears. His forward motion had almost ceased when the truck's front crumpled the Audi's rear and propelled that vehicle into a small tree. James fought the wheel, but, the trailer angled from the cab and the truck skidded sideways off the road. For a brief instant, trailer and container tilted to the side, but together they rocked back into place and came to rest upright in the weeds near a row of pines.

All this in only seconds.

James exhaled. His brakes had held, and the truck and its load were upright. He was OK and the passenger compartment of the Audi appeared to be intact.

Dumb ass driver!

He stepped down from the cab as the doors of the Audi opened. Four black men emerged. Three of them brandished automatic weapons.

Crap! Those are AK-47's.

What the hell is this?

***

Two of Pierre Sehene's "soldiers" were still in their teens. Pierre motioned them to wait by the wrecked Audi. The third "soldier," his AK-47 ready, walked with Pierre towards the truck.

The driver, James Hyde, stood motionless until they arrived.

Pierre spoke first.

"Where is Bill Hamm? Why isn't he with you?"

"Who the hell are you? And who the hell is 'Hamm?' Your dumb-ass driving damn near caused me to lose my load. And tell your guy to put that gun down."

James Hyde was a big youth. He was no taller than the two Africans next to him, but he was heavier and more muscular.

And quick!

He wheeled, grasped the weapon from Pierre's guard, and hit him, hard. The man crumpled as Pierre attempted to leap away.

Not far enough!

James seized Pierre by the neck, and held him with one arm as a shield. With the other he raised the seized AK-47 and pointed it at the young Africans by the Audi. Frightened, they aimed their weapons.

James hesitated as Pierre Sehene screamed.

"No! Don't shoot. *Ne tirez pas.* You'll hit me!"

Too late! There was to be no standoff. Bursts from the panicked youths rattled the air.

"BrBrBrup, BrBrBrup, ..., BrBrBrBrup."

"BrBrBrup, BrBrBrup, ..., BrBrBrBrup."

Hostage and hostage-taker fell backwards in a heap.

"BrBrBrup, BrBrBrup, ..., BrBrBrBrup."

The final rounds were unnecessary. Pierre Sehene and James Hyde lay dead in the weeds. The bodyguard rose and ran to the two "victors."

All three bolted into the woods.

***

In Georgetown, South Carolina, Jeannine Ryan sat on the hood of Fred Middleton's pickup while Angelique Uwimana paced.

"Angelique, relax. Bill will be here soon."

349

"It's not Mr. Hamm that worries me. It's that woman."

"You mean Denise Guerry?"

"She's my Henri's boss, and I don't trust her with him."

Jeannine did not trust Denise around Bill either.

Their thoughts were interrupted by a car turning into the lot.

Jeannine jumped off the hood and grabbed Angelique's arm.

"It's Bill."

But the two women were not looking at Bill. Each had focused on the passenger side. Each sought her first look at the infamous Denise Guerry.

They stared. The woman who stepped from the car was far from glamorous. Her face was pale and her hair was awry and straggly. A bloody blouse hung loose over her right arm which was wrapped in gauze through which a dark stain grew as they watched.

Jeannine frowned. *This is the famous Denise?*

She turned to Bill.

"What happened?"

"Henri Duval shot her."

Angelique gasped.

"Henri? No! He wouldn't do that."

"Angelique, SÉGAG commissioned Henri to kill Denise. He had orders to kill her."

Angelique buried her face in her hands. Bill kept on.

"Denise is on our side now. If Gutera found her he would kill her as soon as he would you. Without her we never could have stopped Gutera's rockets from sailing. She bluffed the port superintendant into releasing Gutera's container to us. She risked her life for all of us, for you and your Rwanda."

He muttered.

"And this is her reward, a bullet from Henri."

Denise broke in.

"No, Angelique, It's not like that. It's true that I would not have cared if Maximilien killed you. I was horribly wrong. I know you can never forgive me, but don't blame Henri. He was defending you from Maximilien and me, not obeying SÉGAG's orders. Henri is no hired murderer. You must believe that."

She caught her breath and added.

"*Chère Angelique, il t'aime beaucoup.* He really loves you."

But the emotional confession had taken its toll. Denise shook uncontrollably. She looked up at Bill.

"My arm, I have to sit."

She slumped against the car. Bill lifted her and put her on the front seat. He felt her forehead and turned to Jeannine.

"She's feverish. I have to get her to the hospital right away. You and Angelique follow us."

Minutes later, Jeannine and Angelique were following Bill, to the Georgetown Memorial Hospital.

Only when the Emergency Entrance was in view, did Jeannine realize that she and Bill had not greeted each other.

***

At the North Charleston terminal, Superintendant Ralph Morris was at his desk. It was past eleven, and the guards at the gate had not seen Hyde and the truck.

The *Étoile d'Afrique* was ready to sail. Only Gutera's container remained to be loaded. Morris fidgeted.

Where was James Hyde?

***

On Highway I-26 not far from I-95, Claude Senteli stopped the gray Audi on the shoulder of the highway. Maximilien got out and stared at the damaged Audi and the *Kenya-Carolina* container on the flatbed trailer. Claude pointed to two bodies in the weeds near the truck's cab.

351

"Chief, that's Pierre. The other guy must have been Hamm's driver. They're dead, cut down, multiple hits."

"Where are Pierre's men? They should have protected him!"

"There's no sign of them. They're on the run."

He wanted to add.

They know how you treat failures.

Claude examined the Audi and returned to his chief.

"The collision jammed the Audi's rear tires. It's going nowhere, but I can drive this truck. I used to drive a rig like this."

Maximilien nodded and turned to his bodyguard.

"Alain, Claude will take the truck. You drive me and follow him."

Only minutes later the truck and gray Audi headed for North Charleston.

Maximilien hummed to himself. His plan was back on track. In only hours, he would sail with his container. And after his dirty-bomb attack on the Congo, the government of Rwanda would be sanctioned. In only months, maybe weeks, the current government would fall.

Hutu power would be restored.

***

******

Chapter 44
Friday, September 7

Stew Marks was driving on Highway 17A, near the I-26 interchange for Summerville, South Carolina, when Jack Marino called.

"Stew, the highway patrol reports two dead bodies and a wrecked Audi on I-95, north of I-26. Where are you?"

"I'm almost to Summerville. Where are you?"

"I'm on I-26 near I-95. I'll be at the scene in fifteen minutes. Take I-26 towards I-95 if you want to meet me there. We could check it out together."

"Who are the dead guys?"

"An African, Pierre Sehene, with a student visa. He's not in the FBI's Gutera file. The other guy was white. His name was Hyde, James Hyde. He worked for the Port Authority."

A red light flashed in Stew's mind. *The Port Authority?*

"Jack, was a truck involved? Any sign of a big rig?"

"There had to be another vehicle. The Audi was rear-ended, but I don't know if it was a truck? What we do know is that these two guys were shot up badly, like almost cut in two."

Now Stew's mind raced. *Automatic weapons and an African "student?"*

"On which lane of I-26 was this?"

"South bound, towards North Charleston. Why?"

North Charleston, the terminal!

"Jack, I'm on my way now. I'll see you there."

Stew Marks took the ramp to I-26 and sped northwest.

***

In Georgetown, South Carolina, Jeannine and Angelique arrived at the hospital.

Bill's car was parked, double-blinking, at the Emergency Entrance, but he was not in sight.

Jeannine left Angelique in the car with the motor running and ran inside. She spotted Bill by the Surgery Suite. She stopped breathless.

"How's Denise?"

"The wound opened up. She's lost a lot of blood. They want to operate right away. They're prepping her for surgery. It's here on 'One.' The surgeon said I could see her once she is prepped."

"Bill, that could take time. I'll move your car for you."

As he handed her the keys, his hand shook.

Bill's car still blocked the Emergency Room entrance. She jumped in and drove to the parking area. She returned to move her own car, but something was awry. Her motor continued to idle, but the passenger seat was vacant.

Angelique was gone.

***

Jeannine and Angelique were not the only persons to follow Bill and Denise to the Georgetown Memorial Hospital. Henri Duval had kept them all in sight.

He parked in the visitor parking, and entered by a side door. After a few enquiries, he passed Emergency and found Surgery. It occupied a suite on the first floor.

Henri stopped at a door marked "*Staff Only*" and slipped inside. A white lab coat, its pocket bulging from a stethoscope, hung on the wall. He slipped it on and hurried out into the hallway. He put his Browning into the free pocket. Now each pocket had a significant bulge.

He peered into the waiting room. Bill Hamm was talking to a nurse. He listened. Denise was being prepped for surgery.

Henri retraced his steps to a door labeled "*No Admittance*," the access to the preparation area. An inconspicuous switch was mounted on the wall to his right. He pressed it and the double doors parted and swung outward.

He gripped the browning in his pocket and started to enter, but heard steps behind him.

He turned to see Angelique, breathing hard.

"Henri, what are you doing? That's the surgical area. You're not allowed."

Then she noticed the stethoscope in his pocket.

"You are no doctor. Why are you pretending?"

Then she understood.

"Denise Guerry is in there. What were you going to do?"

She spotted the bulge in his right pocket. His gun!

"My God, Henri. No! You can't. You wouldn't!"

She grabbed his arm.

"Come with me. You can't do this."

He stared at her.

"Henri, where is your car. We must leave."

She yanked him away from the door and towards the exit.

"Now!"

***

On I-26, Jack Marino studied the mashed weeds and broken scrub pines near the bodies of Pierre Sehene and James Hyde. A swathe of crushed bushes and ripped earth showed that a large vehicle had skidded sideways off the road. A big rig, as Stew had surmised.

At Jack's feet was a twisted heap of uprooted Asters. Frustrated, he kicked the purplish mass skywards, but it was Stew Marks he wanted to kick. Stew's infatuation with the Ryan woman had destroyed his judgment. When this "Hamm" case was over, Jack would get a new partner.

Such were Jack's thoughts when his temporary partner, Sam Smith, approached.

"Jack, we just got a call from the Resident Agency in Charleston. They received a call from the Georgetown Police. The hospital there has a woman with a gunshot wound. And the guy with her is 'Walter Harmon' aka 'Bill Hamm.'"

"Ryan must have been shot. Sam, call the Georgetown PD. Tell them to hold Hamm until I get there."

He added.

"And call Stew Marks. Tell him we couldn't wait."

Jack signaled the FBI techs to carry on with the bodies and the wrecked Audi. Then he and Sam left for Georgetown.

So Ryan got herself shot. Good! Hamm, you damned spook, you screwed me once, but I've got you now.

***

At the hospital in Georgetown, Jeannine took the elevator to the second floor. She found Bill in the ICU waiting room. He stood up as she approached.

"The surgeon assures me that Denise won't lose the arm, but there may be nerve damage. The surgery will take two hours, with an hour in recovery. She'll be here overnight, at the least."

"Bill, Angelique is gone. She wasn't in the car."

No reaction. He had lines in his face. He was beat.

"Bill, have you eaten anything today?"

"Some coffee, that's all. I was going to eat when that couple brought Denise back to our room."

Jeannine noted the possessive "our," but chose to ignore it.

"You need to go to the cafeteria now. There'll be no news about Denise for hours."

She dragged him from the waiting room and pushed him ahead of her. As they turned the corner, she looked back. Two policemen had arrived at the door to the waiting room.

"Bill, the police are here. We must go."

"I have to see how Denise does. You can't mind that."

"This isn't about me, Bill. Denise has a gunshot wound. The police have been notified. They'll arrest you. Get in the elevator."

A policeman rounded the corner of the hallway just as Jeannine hit the button for "One."

Through closed doors she heard the shout.

"You! You in the elevator, wait!"

Arrived on the first floor, she looked back. No policeman was in sight.

She led Bill outside.

***

Henri and Angelique were blocks away from the hospital, when Angelique sat at attention. She could wait no longer.

"Tell me, Henri, did SÉGAG tell you to kill Denise Guerry?

"Angelique, you have to understand."

"Understand that you would kill someone to save your own life? No, I don't *have to* understand, and I don't."

Her tone hardened.

"SÉGAG wants Maximilien Gutera to rule Rwanda. Another genocide! And you do what they tell you?"

"It was only one job, and it was to protect you too. Denise wanted you dead."

"Denise is sorry for what she did. She told me."

"And you believe her? You are naive."

"Maybe, but I trust God, and I know he can change us. What you saw in my country, the rapes, the killings, made you bitter. I saw more and was more bitter and hate-filled than you. God took that away. I want justice for the Interahamwe, but the hate and bitterness are gone. He changed me. He can change Denise and you too."

"But, Angelique."

"No. You pretended to be a doctor to get into the surgery area. A doctor of death, not life. If I had not found you, Denise would be dead and you would have her blood on your hands. God did not want that. He sent me to stop you."

Henri could not reply. Angelique drooped, exhausted.

"I'm tired. I want my normal life back. I want to go back to the university. Take me to Florence. I have a thesis to finish."

Henri remained silent. Eyes straight ahead, he turned onto Route 521 and headed inland towards I-95, and Florence.

Has she forgotten that Gutera and his thugs are in Florence?

Moments later, Angelique leaned her head on his shoulder.

"Henri, forgive me. I should not have said all those things. You believed you were protecting me. Thank you."

He stopped on the shoulder and kissed her. She drew back.

"Henri, you must forgive Denise for my sake. She is sorry."

She beat his arm with her fist.

"And never again tell me how desirable she is!"

***

Bill and Jeannine were a block away from the Georgetown Memorial Hospital, when several police cars, sirens blaring and lights revolving, arrived. Jeannine spoke.

"That's more than a casual search. The FBI must have ID'd you. We just got away in time."

Bill did not respond. Jeannine frowned.

He's worried for Denise.

Jeannine decided to head to North Charleston.

***

******

Chapter 45
Friday, September 7

At the North Charleston terminal, Superintendant Ralph Morris sat at his desk. Tired as he was from his all night vigil, he dared not leave. He looked at his watch. It was past eleven, and the guards at the gate had yet to notify him of James Hyde's arrival. Where was he?

Morris wanted that container. The *Étoile d'Afrique* would not depart without it.

He fidgeted with the papers on his desk.

Damn it, Hyde, hurry. You'll get your bonus anyway, just get that container here.

He rose from his desk and began to pace.

***

On I-26, Maximilien Gutera stepped out of the gray Audi onto the shoulder of the highway. He stared at his motionless rig and waved his arms in desperation at the driver.

"Senteli, you fool. Why have you stopped? There is nothing here but pine woods. What are you doing?"

Claude Senteli stepped down from the cab of the container truck and examined the driver-side fuel tank. Fuel dribbled from multiple holes near the bottom of the cylinder. He turned to his chief and pointed.

"Whoever shot Pierre and that driver, hit the fuel tank. It's almost empty. This truck is going nowhere."

"Idiot, there's a tank on the other side. Surely, it was not hit."

"It was empty when we started. Hamm must have siphoned the fuel out. He did not want this truck to move."

Maximilien huffed in exasperation.

"You make no sense. He would have emptied this side too."

Claude leaned over the tank.

"He couldn't. This tank has a device that stops siphoning."

He turned back to Maximilien.

"We can unhook this truck and leave it here. Call Superintendant Morris to send us another cab to hook up to this trailer. We can still be at the terminal this afternoon. The ship will wait for us."

Normally, Claude would never have dared to address his chief with a command, but there was no time to waste. Besides he was tired of Maximilien's imperious attitude.

Maximilien grunted. He would deal with the insolent Claude after they sailed for Mombasa. For now, he complied and drew his cell phone from its pocket.

In seconds, superintendant Morris was on the line. Maximilien shouted into the phone.

"You're the superintendant. Get me another truck. Now!"

***

Claude Senteli got to work while Maximilien Gutera spewed further frustration at superintendant Morris. Time was precious.

Fortunately, Claude was no stranger to trucking.

He circled the rig and checked the parking brakes on the trailer and cab. Then he tugged the safety handle to release the jaws of the truck's "fifth wheel" and free the trailer's kingpin. He succeeded but his hand came away coated with grease.

He wiped it as best he could and cranked the landing legs down to the ground. Then he mounted the catwalk to detach the coiled "Suzies," electric and air connections, from the trailer. That done, he released the truck's air suspension to lower the fifth wheel clear of the kingpin.

There was just enough fuel in the perforated tank for Claude to start the truck and guide it down a slight slope out of the way of the trailer with the container.

Done!

Claude stood back. The trailer was ready for coupling as soon as the new truck arrived.

He turned back only to face an angry Maximilien, his face distorted in an ominous scowl. Evidently, the chief did not like to be surpassed by an underling in any capacity, even knowing how to uncouple a trailer.

Oddly, Claude was not afraid. He spoke.

"The trailer is ready for coupling as soon as Morris's truck arrives."

Gutera suppressed his anger. There would be time for that later. He nodded to Claude, and sat in the gray Audi to wait.

His bodyguard stood by the car, an AK-47 hanging loose at his side.

***

At the North Charleston terminal, Superintendant Morris stood up from his desk. How had that madman Gutera gained possession of the truck? And where was James Hyde, the driver?

Gutera had been unwilling to give Morris any information concerning James. But Morris could guess.

James Hyde was dead.

And he was equally sure that any driver he sent with a truck to aid the madman, would end up like James, dead.

Morris could not send another man to his death. *Damn you Gutera!*

No amount of kickbacks and bribes was worth another life!

The superintendant was a large man who had come up through the ranks. Though now a manager, he identified with his workers rather than his superiors. The evident death of James Hyde, his young worker, angered him. He drew a Smith and Wesson .38 revolver from the side drawer and stuffed it in his belt at the rear.

He was still afraid of Gutera, but no longer terrified into inaction. He called the garage to requisition a truck. He would drive it himself.

Fifteen minutes later he was on Remount Road headed towards the I-26 interchange.

***

When Stew Marks arrived at the site on I-26 where the bodies of Pierre Sehene and James Hyde had been found, both the bodies and Jack Marino were gone. After confirming that a big rig had been involved in the collision with the black Audi, Stew headed back southeast towards Summerville.

Rounding a curve, he spotted an uncoupled flatbed trailer on the shoulder to his right. On it was a *Kenya-Carolina* container, and parked next to it to it was a gray Audi. A tall black man peered from behind the car, apparently scanning the passing traffic.

A Rwandan? And Maximilien's rockets?

Stew continued southeast without stopping. Shortly, he found a breach in the median used by police to wait for speeders. He crossed and headed back west towards the trailer. He would use the numerous pines on the median as shelter from which to observe whatever was going down.

Opposite the trailer, he parked on the shoulder to his right and dashed across the westbound lanes to the median. There he crouched behind thick shrubby pines. The Audi was there, but the black man guarding it was gone. Stew watched, as a second man (Claude Senteli) approached, opened the trunk and drew out a large object.

A grenade launcher!

Mouth open, Stew watched as the man clicked a Rocket-Propelled Grenade in the launcher and aimed it across the highway at the tree that sheltered Stew.

Stew ducked.

Tortured seconds passed before Stew heard a shout from across the highway.

"Claude, don't shoot. Put that launcher away. Now!"

Stew could never forget that voice. Maximilien Gutera, his interrogator.

Claude obeyed. He detached the grenade from the launcher and shoved both items into the trunk. He turned, hands empty, as a police car, red-light twirling, arrived.

A state trooper, hand on holstered weapon, stepped out and walked to where Maximilien and Claude stood. The trooper addressed Maximilien.

"Is there a problem, Sir? Is that your trailer?"

Before Maximilien could answer, a Port Authority truck with nothing in tow arrived. Stew watched as a man stepped down from the cab.

"Officer, I'm superintendant Morris from the North Charleston terminal. That's my container on the trailer. They ran out of fuel, that's all. These men were watching it for me. I'm here to take it to the terminal. I've a ship waiting."

He moved to Maximilien.

"Thank you, Sir, for your help."

With no further words, Morris climbed back into his cab.

Smoothly, he backed up so that the notch of his fifth wheel was under the trailer's kingpin. He engaged the air suspension to raise the wheel, and backed a few inches more to set the safety jaws about the pin.

Morris signaled Claude to winch the landing legs up while he connected the cables for air and electricity to the trailer.

Maximilien did not speak. The state trooper watched in silence as superintendant Morris mounted the cab and prepared to drive off with the trailer and container.

Stew knew he had to intervene.

***

Stew slipped the Beretta's safety off and started to rise.

But a metal barrel pressed into his back, pushing him to the ground on top of his gun.

Who? The bodyguard!

He had not been in sight when Stew had returned.

Why doesn't he shoot? Of course! He's waiting for the trooper to leave.

The gun pressed harder against Stew's spine.

From across the highway, Stew heard Maximilien shout.

"Claude, get in that truck. Go with Superintendant Morris. Do not let him go by himself."

Moments later, both truck doors slammed, and the truck roared off.

The pressure on Stew's spine did not lessen.

***

Maximilien Gutera watched as the trailer with his rockets disappeared down the highway. He looked back, to see the state trooper leaning over the fuel tank of the truck that was left behind.

"Sir, did you see this tank. These are bullet holes. Someone shot up this truck."

Maximilien frowned. The trooper continued.

"Someone tried to hijack that trailer. What do you know about that? Was that driver really from the Port Authority?"

Maximilien stayed silent.

"Sir, help me. Answer my questions."

The trooper's face turned red. He drew his Glock.

"Sir, are you carrying a weapon?"

Maximilien panicked. He shouted across the highway to his bodyguard on the median. In fear, he reverted to a mix of the languages of his youth, Kinyarwanda and French.

Ngwino umfashe! Help me! *Lui tirer dessus!* Shoot him!"

The bodyguard shifted his AK-47 from Stew's back, and fired.

"BrBrup, ..., BrBrup."

"Crack."

The trooper's Glock discharged into the ground as he fell.

Instantly the bodyguard turned back to Stew, but the latter had rolled to his side and freed the Beretta from under his body.

"Crack, Crack."

The bodyguard was pushed backwards.

"Crack!"

Stew's last shot pierced the heart. The bodyguard toppled backwards, dead.

From across the road, Stew heard the sound of a motor. He jumped to his feet in time to see Maximilien Gutera at the wheel as the gray Audi sped away.

Left behind among the weeds on the shoulder was the crumpled form of the state trooper. A second highway patrol car had stopped behind the first. The trooper's backup had arrived too late.

Stew withdrew through the pines and crossed the opposite lanes to his car.

***

In the Intensive Care Unit at the Georgetown Memorial Hospital, Denise Guerry stirred.

Bill? Where?

The nurse checked her vitals as Denise drifted off again.

A baby was vomiting from radiation poisoning. Nearby, an African woman lay moaning and retching by the shore of a lake. Non!

Denise shook all over. The nurse covered her with a blanket.

***

******

Chapter 46
Friday, September 7

Oh Highway 17A, near Monck's Corner, South Carolina, Jack Marino slammed his phone on the dashboard of the car. From the passenger seat Sam Smith spoke.

"What's wrong, Jack?"

"The Georgetown cops missed Hamm at the hospital. Idiots."

"What do you want to do?"

"Take the phone. See if you can reach Stew Marks."

Sam complied, but there was no answer. Jack nodded.

"I'm turning around. We're going back to North Charleston."

No sooner had he spoken, than a blue Ford passed them in the other direction.

Jack gaped. The driver was a woman with red hair.

Ryan! And the man with her must be Hamm!

Jack spun the wheel. Tires screeched as Sam's shoulder was flung against the passenger door. The car swung about and ended in the opposite lanes, headed after the Ford.

Jack hammered the accelerator.

His prey were no longer in sight, but they would be soon.

***

Jeannine Ryan drove Bill Hamm's Ford on Highway 17A near Moncks Corner, South Carolina.

Bill nudged her shoulder.

"Don't look in the mirror, but someone is following us."

"What do you want me to do?"

"We'll be at Moncks Corner soon. Highway 52 turns right, and Highway 17A continues straight ahead. Take Highway 52. Maybe that car is not after us. Maybe it will stay on 17A."

Jeannine turned right onto Highway 52. Bill studied the mirror.

The car had turned with them.

Jeannine turned to Bill.

"Bill, do you have a gun? We don't know who is behind us."

"I have the Beretta I took from Ian Callahan."

Jeannine pressed her lips together and drove. Moments later her cell phone buzzed. She put it on speaker.

"Jeannine, this is Stew, is Hamm with you?"

Bill spoke.

"I'm here. What do you want?"

"Gutera got his truck back. The rockets are headed back to North Charleston. I'm headed there now, but I'm far out on I-26. Where are you?"

"We're past Goose Creek, on Highway 52. We're a lot closer than you."

"Hamm, you have to stop them while they're still in port. Marino won't notify the police or the Coast Guard. He thinks you're using Gutera and his thugs as a scapegoat. He doesn't believe there is a plot. He says you made it up as a diversion."

"Someone's been following us since Moncks Corner."

"A maroon Ford Crown Vic?"

"Yes."

"It's Marino. What will you do?"

"I'll think of something. I can't shoot back, he may be wrong-headed but he's still FBI."

"Hamm, you have to ditch him. Those rockets must not leave port."

The connection was broken.

***

Bill turned to Jeannine.

"We need to give Marino the slip. They're hanging back so we won't spot them. There's a Burger King ahead. Speed up and turn as fast as you can."

Jeannine nodded.

She spun the wheels to the right into the Burger King parking.

Bill shouted.

"Now quick, loop around back and park!"

Jeannine did.

***

In the Crown Victoria, Sam Smith looked up.

"What happened, Jack? I don't see Hamm's car. That's St. James Road ahead. Did they turn there?"

"They turned into the Burger King. We'll get them."

Jack turned into the lot. Ahead was another exit, onto St. James Road. And Hamm's car was not in sight. Jack drove out onto St. James Road.

Hidden on the other side of the Burger King, Jeannine backed out of her space and turned back onto Highway 52.

Bill pointed to the left.

"It worked. Bear left right away and turn onto Red Bank Road. That will take us to the port terminal."

Jeannine complied.

***

On I-26, Superintendant Ralph Morris drove the truck towards North Charleston. He would not relax until this damned container from *Kenya-Carolina Apex Distributors* was loaded on Gutera's ship.

He called the gate at the terminal.

"This is superintendant Morris. I'm on I-26 about thirty minutes away. I have the last container for that African ship. I know you're closing, but have Jim ready on the ZPMC crane. Tell him he'll get overtime. I want this damned container loaded right away."

But the container was not Ralph's only concern. His driver, James Hyde, was missing and that bastard Maximilien had refused to answer queries about the whereabouts of the young trucker.

Ralph turned to the African seated next to him in the cab of the truck.

"So your name is Claude, Claude what?"

"Claude Senteli."

"You know trucks?"

"I drove one in the past, yes."

Morris fell silent. His thoughts were of his driver, James Hyde.

"Tell me, what happened to my driver."

"You must ask my chief. I was not there."

"To hell with him. You know what happened. Tell me!"

Morris drew the .38 from his rear belt and pointed it at Senteli's nose. At the same time he slammed the brakes hard and stopped truck and trailer on the shoulder.

Claude stammered.

"I was not there, but we found your man dead, shot."

He wanted to add, *"and my friend Pierre Sehene too."* But there was no time. Morris screamed and waved the gun in his face.

"Dead! And you did nothing. Get out, you son of a bitch. Get out now!"

Claude backed out of the cab. He left his phone on the seat. Morris threw it at him.

"And call that chief of yours. Tell him he'd better have a good explanation for my man's death or his container will end up in the Cooper River. I'll dump it there myself."

Claude Senteli was more afraid of Maximilien Gutera than of Ralph Morris. No way would he call Maximilien and admit that he had lost the truck. And he could not allow Morris to destroy the container and its contents.

As Morris ground gears to pull back onto the highway, Claude jumped up onto the catwalk between truck and trailer and hung on as the truck pulled away.

Claude knew the function of the two "Suzies," the hoses that carried air to the trailer. In the blue hose, air pressure increased as the driver applied the brakes to stop the truck. In the red hose, over 60 lbs of constant air pressure kept the brakes unlocked. If the red hose was disconnected, the trailer's brakes would lock on, a safety feature that Claude would use to his advantage.

He held his hands on both hoses, ready to unhook them and stop the truck. He waited for a stretch where no other vehicles were on the road.

Now!

He swung the connectors upwards. They released.

The brakes on the trailer locked. It swung wildly from side to side as Morris struggled to maintain control. Claude hung on.

Truck and trailer slid sidewise to a stop on the shoulder.

Claude shook his head and struggled to his feet. He was OK. He reconnected the hoses and climbed down from the catwalk. Morris lay unconscious across the seat, a red welt on his cheek and forehead, his chest heaving in a regular rhythm.

Claude wrestled the heavy man to the passenger seat and strapped him upright in the shoulder belt.

Claude started the motor. He tried the brakes. They were unlocked. Then he looked back at the highway behind.

There was no sign of Maximilien Gutera. Perhaps the police had delayed him.

Too bad.

Claude Senteli hummed to himself as he drove off.

He had heard the superintendant's instructions. The crane operator, "Jim," would be waiting for their arrival. If only the guards at the gate would not check Mr. Morris closely, he would be home free.

***

When Claude Senteli arrived at the gate to the North Charleston Terminal, superintendant Morris was unconscious, but upright thanks to his seat belt.

The guard glanced at Morris and gave a quick wave.

Claude whistled.

Thanks to him, and no thanks to Maximilien, the rockets soon would be on their way to Mombasa.

He headed towards the dock where the *Étoile d'Afrique* was berthed.

***

At the North Charleston Terminal, Jim Rivers stood on the dock underneath the huge Super Post Panamax gantry crane and watched the crew of the African ship prepare for departure. After a long day, Jim was tired and irritated. The boss was late.

But Mr. Morris paid well, and he could not complain.

Jim yawned and closed his eyes, only to jerk awake.

A truck with a container drove up and stopped precisely at the marked pickup spot for Jim's crane.

Jim sighed with relief. Mr. Morris was in the front seat.

The truck had arrived.

***

Claude Senteli stopped the truck at the pickup mark under the huge crane and awaited the "lift-off" of the container. The rockets would soon be safely stacked on board the *Étoile d'Afrique.*

At his side, Morris stirred. Claude clubbed him with his Browning. The superintendant sagged against his shoulder strap.

Claude looked back. The crane operator who moments before had stood next to crane, had not entered the elevator to the control cabin. Instead, the man was walking to the truck, towards the passenger side. Claude frowned.

Forget your boss. Stop! Load the damn container like you were told.

But the man continued forward.

Claude grabbed his phone and spoke. The message was brief.

"Michel, I need you after all."

Then Browning in hand, he slipped out the driver-side door.

***

Jim Rivers, the crane operator, knew something was wrong. The boss was not driving and he had not acknowledged his wave. Now up close, he saw that Mr. Morris's eyes were shut.

What the hell?

He stared through the window. Was Morris breathing and unconscious, or dead?

There was no time for further observation. Jim heard a noise behind him. The butt end of Claude Senteli's Browning crashed against his skull.

Jim fell senseless to the ground

***

On board the Étoile d'Afrique, Michel Iranzi put down the phone. Claude Senteli needed him ashore.

Right away!

373

Michel was checking containers. He left the deck and descended the multiple steps to the dock.

The gantry crane that towered above him was a ZPMC, a brand he had used elsewhere. Michel knew cranes. He had worked dockside at the port of Mombasa.

He spotted Claude and ran to him

"Is this the container you want loaded?"

"This is the one. It's Maximilien's special container. The ship won't leave without it. Don't screw this up."

Michel did not need more warning. He too feared Maximilien.

He took the elevator to the cabin and sat at the controls.

He peered through the glass floor. Below him the truck was parked precisely at the mark.

Good.

He manipulated the right-hand joystick and lowered the spreader to lock onto the container.

"Clank."

The spreader locked on.

He lifted the container into the air.

The control cabin was suspended from a trolley that rolled on a boom extending from the dock to well over the ship. Suspended in the air beneath the cab the container hung motionless.

Michel checked the controls once more. Every movement needed to be precise.

From far below, Claude stared upwards with satisfaction.

Almost done!

***

******

Chapter 47
Friday, September 7

Bill Hamm and Jeannine sped down Remount Road, near the North Charleston Terminal.

"Stop here, Jeannine, I'm getting into the back seat."

Bill stepped out. Once in back, he crouched to the floor and covered himself with a blanket.

"You've got to get us through the gate. I don't care how. If they try to stop you, spin the car about so I can roll out where they won't see me. Get me inside."

Jeannine set her lips and drove toward the gate.

There a guard stopped her.

"We're closed, ma'am, we close at six."

"But superintendant Morris wanted me to meet him at the office. I have something for his birthday."

The guard had seen Morris enter only minutes before, but he was not a fan of the big man. He paused.

Is Morris human? Does he even have a birthday? This woman is too hot for that toad.

With those confused observations he turned to consult his superior. But behind him a motor revved. He turned back.

Too late!

Jeannine jammed the accelerator to the floor and rammed the gate. The wooden slat split and cracked in two.

She was through!

Immediately she turned sharp right and raced along a row of stacked containers towards two towering cranes that dominated the dock.

But a parked truck with an empty trailer blocked the passage.

She hit the brakes and spun the wheel. The car skidded sideways. Its rear end scraped the rig and stopped.

Bill rolled out of the backdoor and under the rig.

Jeannine collapsed, head on the steering wheel.

A short distance away she heard the shouts of her pursuers.

But she no longer cared.

Bill was in.

***

Bill Hamm ran along the row of containers towards the giant crane. Gasping for breath, he reached one of the thick steel legs of the huge structure. The elevator was stopped high above, but alternate access to the control cabin was afforded by metal steps attached to the steel support.

On the ground a short distance away, Bill noted a black man staring at a container, dangling high in the air. He recognized the logo, *Kenya-Carolina Apex Distributors*.

Gutera's rockets!

He was too late!

Bill dashed up the metal stairs. Halfway up, his progress slowed. At each landing (created by the change in direction of the steps) he paused to inhale. His lungs burned, but he struggled upwards.

Finally, just as his legs went rubbery, he reached the level of the control cabin. But the operator had moved the cabin away from the steps and towards the ship.

A gap of several feet separated him from the railing at the back of the cabin.

Bill looked down. The drop to the dock below was at least ten stories.

But he had to stop the rockets.

He launched himself into the air!

***

376

For the first time in over a month Maximilien Gutera was on his own. His bodyguard Alain had shot the state patrolman from ambush, and Maximilien had fled without knowing the fate of his follower. He did not know if Alain was still alive.

Nor did he care.

After himself, his only concern was for the rockets, and with Morris in charge their delivery was assured. The superintendant would not dare fail Maximilien.

Success was at hand.

He turned onto Remount Road and drove towards the entrance to the North Charleston Terminal.

But something was wrong. Port Security vehicles with rotating red lights blocked the entrance while two local police cars, bars blinking blue, had closed the exit. Several groups of uniformed men stood near the vehicles.

Maximilien stopped on the shoulder and took out his phone. He called the Captain of the *Étoile d'Afrique*.

"Is my container on board?"

"In a minute it will be. It's in the air now."

"Good."

Maximilien was about to hang up when the Captain added.

"It is Michel Iranzi who is operating the crane."

"Iranzi? Where is Morris's man?"

"I do not know. Claude Senteli is in charge."

Maximilien paused. *In charge? Senteli? He will take the credit! He is too ambitious.*

"Captain, a word of caution. You must watch Senteli carefully. He is dangerous. He has put his ego ahead of our movement."

His thoughts turned to the police vehicles surrounding the entrance to the terminal.

"And Captain, I have decided not to board the ship now. I will engage a helicopter and join the ship tomorrow morning when you are at sea."

Maximilien hung up, turned his car about, and headed away from the terminal towards Charleston.

***

Jeannine Ryan, physically and mentally exhausted, rested her head on the steering wheel.

A guard pulled the car door open. She opened her eyes to an angry glare.

"Lady, what's wrong with you? You could have killed someone."

Strong arms pulled her from the car, bruising her against the car door as she fell outwards. She stood up only to be pushed through a crowd of guards and watchmen.

Then out of the mix of hisses and angry murmurs, one voice stood out. She had heard it before, in Maryland when the FBI had first visited her.

Jack Marino had arrived.

"All right Ryan, no more of your damned tricks. Put your arms behind your back."

He did not wait for her to comply, but wrenched her arms into position. At her cry of pain, a security guard stepped forward, but Marino shoved him away.

"FBI! Stand back. The bitch is my prisoner. I've been searching for her for weeks."

He tightened the cuffs. Blood appeared on her wrist. She winced and leaned forward, but he jerked her upright.

"All right, where is that scumbag partner of yours? Where is Hamm?"

Face florid, he slapped her from behind. Jeannine fell forward, head spinning.

At that blow, a port guard grabbed Jack's arm.

"Stop it mister. She's helpless."

Jack pulled free and glared. He stepped toward the guard, fist balled.

But the voice of Sam Smith, his present partner, stopped him.

"Good God, Jack what are you doing?"

Jack straightened. He flung the helpless Jeannine at Sam. She stumbled, hands bound behind, and fell forward. Sam caught her. Jack sneered.

"All right Sam, you want her. You take care of her."

He pulled out his Beretta and glared at the encircling guards. Then he turned back to Sam.

"Stay here with the 'Ladies,' I'm going to find Hamm."

Jack turned away. Before him, long rows of containers formed an alley that led to the dock.

Gun in hand, he raced towards the river.

***

Hurtling through the air more than a hundred feet above the dock, Bill Hamm stretched to reach the railing of the moving cab.

His left hand seized a vertical bar and held.

He struggled to swing his right arm towards the rail.

"Whap!"

His right hand missed and his body swung sideways.

But his left hand held.

Once again Bill rotated towards the railing. Ian's Beretta twisted loose from his belt and fell, spinning until it clattered on the dock below.

But this time Bill's right hand gripped tight.

With both hands secure, he swung one leg upwards toward the landing. His right foot lodged between two uprights. His right ankle twisted in pain but he clung to the rail. He struggled and rolled over the rail onto the cab's metal "porch."

He lay still to gather his breath.

Below him on the dock, He saw a man brandishing a handgun.

But the man (Claude Senteli) did not see Bill. Instead, the man ran to board the ship docked below.

Bill stood up. He carefully opened the door to the cabin.

He stepped inside and looked down.

He froze. There was nothing between him and the dock below. Then he realized, the floor of the cabin was transparent. His shoe met solid support.

"Thump!"

At that sound, the man at the controls (Michel Iranzi) turned. His eyes opened wide. He reached down and picked up a gray object, mostly metallic.

A panga!

Bill reached for the Beretta in his rear belt, but his hand came away empty.

The gun was gone.

The man swung the bush knife above his head and charged.

The panga flashed in a wide arc as Bill ducked.

"Clang."

The blade crashed against the wall jarring the man's grip.

Bill seized that arm and twisted. The panga fell to the floor.

Now they were even.

But the man was strong. He shoved Bill away and kicked him in the groin.

Twisted in pain, Bill collapsed back against the door. His hand felt the latch just as the man lowered his head and rushed at him.

Bill ducked to the side and pushed the door wide.

The man flew out.

He balanced a moment over the railing.

Then he fell out of sight.

***

Bill shut the door and rushed to the controls. The container hung over the *Étoile d'Afrique*, ready to be lowered in place.

He studied the deck below. Several rows of stacked containers spanned the width of the vessel. He counted quickly. The widest row had thirteen containers, each about eight feet wide. She was a Panamax vessel, able to pass through the locks of the Panama canal.

He recalled his conversation with Tim, hours earlier. The crane he now controlled was a Super Post Panamax, it could stack a row of over twenty 8-foot containers.

He looked down. Sure enough, the boom of his crane extended well beyond the ship, and the tracks for the trolley reached near to the end. He could move the container past the deck and drop it into the water.

But how?

He leaned forward in the chair. There were joysticks on both sides as well as other levers.

If only I had paid more attention to Tim?

He strained to remember. *Maybe this?*

He pushed the stick.

Bill stared through the glass floor. Below, the container had not moved.

He tried again.

This time the trolley wheels above him rolled forwards. Cabin and container moved towards the open water of the river.

Bill held his breath.

He let go of the joysticks and looked below.

Now he was above the open water. The container swung slightly but did not detach.

He strived to visualize what control Tim had used to lift and load the same container on the trailer only hours before. Were the controls in the ZPMG the same?

He shut his eyes to visualize Tim's actions. He opened them, pushed a lever, and peered down through the glass floor.

Success!

The empty spreader dangled beneath the cab, swinging in the air while the loosened load plunged downwards.

The container hit the water, displacing magnificent plumes of spray skywards on all sides before it disappeared. Moments later, it shot back up, almost clear of the surface, only to settle sharply downwards at an angle that left only the top rear edge in view.

For some seconds a lone back corner remained visible as the container drifted down river with the outgoing tide. Finally it too disappeared, leaving only swirling eddies to mark its final sinking.

Bill struggled to his feet and looked out towards the harbor.

The container was gone.

Only swirls and spirals on the surface marked its passage.

Then even these disturbances dissipated in the out-flowing current.

And Maximilien Gutera's dream drowned in the murky waters of the Cooper River.

***

******

Chapter 48
Friday, September 7

Jack Marino ran down the lane between two rows of containers towards the crane. From the corner of his eye, he spied a black male, a gun in hand, on the ship.

Jack ignored him and ran to the truck parked under the crane. The truck's trailer was empty. A man stepped down from the cab as Jack approached. He faced Jack.

"I'm Port Superintendant Morris. Who the hell are you? Put the damn gun down. If you want to shoot someone, get that African on the ship. He knocked me out and stole my truck. And now my container is lost in the river."

But Jack was single-minded.

"Where is Hamm? William Hamm?"

Morris's head ached. He rubbed his forehead to clear his thoughts. *Denise Guerry had called the man with her "Hamm."*

"Hamm was here hours ago. Is he back?"

Morris glanced up at the crane's control cabin, suspended on its boom high over the water beyond the *Étoile d'Afrique*.

Jack caught that look. Could Hamm be up there? He looked skywards.

Was that a man dangling from the railing of the control cab?

***

High above, limp and exhausted, Bill slumped in the seat. A red streak appeared on his sleeve where the Hutu's panga had not missed. Dizzy, Bill shook his head and looked through the transparent floor at the dark waters below.

Had he imagined a noise outside the cab? He sat up and looked out the door. Below him, just visible, two dark hands clung to the edge of the metal walkway.

The crane operator!

Bill stepped out the cabin and leaned over the rail. Michel Iranzi stared upwards. His eyes, expanded in circles, pleaded as he cried out.

À moi! Help me!

Bill seized the man's wrist, and heaved upwards. Moments later a shaken Hutu collapsed trembling on the metal grid.

***

Michel looked up at the blurred form standing over him.

"*Murakoze cyane.* Thank you, much."

Then he shut his eyes, exhausted, only to feel hands grip his arms and tug him to his feet. His enemy, the man who had pulled him to safety, stood before him.

Without him I would be dead.

The man spoke in English, but Michel's English was weak. He shook his head. The man tried clumsy French.

"*Prendre la commande de la grue*? Run the controls of the crane?"

Michel managed to nod. The man pointed to himself.

"Bill."

That Michel understood. He touched his chest.

"Michel."

The man, Bill, pointed to the far-away elevator and stairs high above the dock and struggled with more French.

"*Là, Michel, nous voulons là.* There, Michel, we want there."

Michel nodded again. He followed the man into the cabin and sat at the controls, but his hands shook as he manipulated the joysticks.

He looked up. This man was not afraid of him. Oddly, Michel felt no fear either.

He calmed himself and smoothly guided the cabin back to the elevator and stairwell.

***

Superintendent Morris and Jack Marino watched as the elevator reached its lowest level from which a flight of steps descended to the ground. The door opened, and Bill Hamm and Michel Iranzi descended to the dock. Jack started forward, but Morris pushed him back and fronted Bill.

"You dumped my container in the river. It's gone! You'll pay for this!"

"Your container? So the Hutu missiles were yours. It's you who wanted to explode dirty bombs over the Congo."

Morris retreated.

"What do you mean? It was Maximilien Gutera's shipment. I had no idea what was in it."

"You approved it. You signed the papers."

"There was no radioactivity. My men checked for it. There was no reason not to sign off."

Bill started to reply, but Jack Marino broke in.

"Quit the pretense, Hamm. You are under arrest."

At the word "arrest" the superintendent backed away and Michel Iranzi left Bill's side. Bill stared.

"You must be Marino, FBI, right?"

Jack fingered his Beretta.

"That's right! And you are the damned traitor that I've been chasing for weeks."

"Calm down, Jack, put the gun away. I'm no traitor. We just stopped a plot to overthrow the Rwandan government."

"So I'm supposed to believe a dirt bag like you?"

"Call Stew Marks. He knows. He'll tell you."

At the mention of his partner's name, Jack's face went red.

"You damned liar! You conned the congressional committee about me, and you conned Stew about your supposed Hutu plot. Don't push me. I should end your miserable self now, before you conn the jury at your trial."

Jack's face went red. His knuckles whitened on his Beretta.

"Jack, stop! What are you doing? Put that gun down."

Sam Smith, breathless, had arrived with Jeannine in tow.

Jack turned. He saw that Jeannine's arms were free.

"Who took the cuffs off that woman?"

"Easy, Jack. It was me. I took them off. Stew Marks called. He's on the way now. Ryan and Hamm are the good guys. Hamm's no traitor."

"The hell he's not. He tried to load that container on that ship. He's a liar. He lied to congress about me and the FBI, and he sure as hell will lie to the judge. He's a spook gone dirty."

Jeannine jumped forward.

"Listen jackass! Do you even have a brain? Stand down."

Jack reddened. *She'll lie too and Hamm will go free.*

Jeannine moved in front of Bill, to shield him.

Too much! Jack raised his weapon.

"Hamm, the bitch can't protect you. You'll not beat this rap!"

His finger tightened on the trigger.

Time slowed. Everyone froze.

Except Michel Iranzi! He moved fast. He sprang at Jack and knocked the gun loose.

"Crack."

The Beretta discharged and clattered on the ground.

Sam Smith retrieved the weapon, after which Jack stood motionless, his shoulders slumped.

***

Seconds seemed like minutes. Michel Iranzi turned to Bill and mouthed words meant for no one else.

"*Cela nous rends égaux.* That makes us even."

Bill nodded.

The Hutu turned and ran towards his ship.

No one moved to stop him.

***

Far from the North Charleston terminal, Maximilien Gutera sped north on route 52 towards Florence.

The Captain of the *Étoile d'Afrique* had informed him of the loss of the rockets. Maximilien would not join the vessel. The French were no more tolerant of failure than he, and he could not risk a forced transfer to the French-flagged vessel, *La Lutte.* No, he would stay with his followers in Florence.

Besides, Claude Senteli was on the *Étoile d'Afrique.* His poisonous tongue was sure to blame Maximilien for the failure.

Maximilien needed to vent. A slow minivan appeared on the road ahead. *Stupid American driver! Out of my way!*

He cut sharply in front of it. The van swerved onto the shoulder. Maximilien grimaced and sped on.

***

On Interstate 95, Henri Duval drove towards Florence, South Carolina. In the passenger seat, a tired Angelique Uwimana tossed fitfully in sleep.

Henri, too, was tired. He struggled to stay awake. He switched on the radio.

In local news, South Carolina Port Authority officials refuse to comment on reports by eye witnesses that a container being loaded onto a Kenyan vessel at the terminal at North Charleston sank into the Cooper River.

Our sources indicate that the Kenyan ship will sail tomorrow morning, as planned.

Henri turned off the radio. If Gutera's plan had failed, where was the Hutu leader? Had he boarded the *Étoile d'Afrique*, or was he still in the Carolinas? If he were still here, Angelique still would be in danger. Maximilien's lust for her had nothing to do with his Hutu Power movement.

Henri normally did not believe in spirits, but he regarded Gutera's obsession with the beautiful Tutsi as demonic.

***

In the Memorial Hospital in Georgetown, South Carolina, the receptionist smiled up at the man with the foreign accent. His suit was expensive, his shoes Italian. *A lawyer?*

"I'm sorry, Sir. Ms. Guerry is still in the Intensive Care Unit. She hasn't been assigned a room yet."

The "lawyer" smiled and turned away without answering.

He walked down the corridor to the elevators. The doors opened. He entered and pushed "Two." The ICU_was on the second floor.

The surgeon had saved Denise Guerry's life.

He would end it.

***

******

Chapter 49
Saturday, September 8

The sun had risen above the spent brown fields on the outskirts of Florence, South Carolina, when Maximilien Gutera stopped his car on the shoulder of the highway.

He needed to think. Had Claude Senteli's treacherous tongue reached the ears of the Florence Hutus? Would they believe his lies?

Rather than return to his headquarters and risk a potential confrontation with his followers, Maximilien opted for caution. He was tired. He needed a safe place to rest before preparing his version of the disaster at North Charleston.

But where?

His men had taken a key from Angelique Uwimana's apartment when they had tried to trap her. Maximilien, with his superior foresight, had kept the key on his person. No one would suspect that he would go to her apartment to rest. Equally surely, she would not dare return there, but if she did, so much the better. He licked his lips.

He found the street and building with ease. Inside the apartment, he lay on the couch and shut his eyes. When he awoke, he would speak to his followers. His strategy was simple.

Blame Claude Senteli.

***

At a Starbucks in Florence South Carolina, Henri Duval watched Angelique sip her coffee and read a text on her phone.

"Henri, thanks for bringing me to Florence. This is my mentor. He likes my thesis. He has only a few changes that he wants to discuss with me."

Henri nodded, but still worried that they were in Florence.

She bubbled.

"This is great, but I need to stop by my apartment to pick up my notes."

She stood up, ready to go. Henri looked about. There were no Africans anywhere.

He followed her outside.

***

In Georgetown, South Carolina, at the Memorial Hospital, Denise Guerry stirred awake. *Where?*

Then she recalled.

My arm, the hospital, Bill?

A voice broke into her thoughts.

"You're awake, good. You're in the Intensive Care Unit, how do you feel?"

Denise tried to move her arm, the nurse stopped her.

"No, don't do that. What do you want?"

"Is anyone waiting to see me?"

"Not now, but a Mr. Hamm called this morning. He asked how you were and said to tell you that the container is destroyed. He said you would understand."

Denise laid her head back, relieved that her nightmares of irradiated Congolese babies would not come true.

She shut her eyes. She felt fine.

***

In the ICU waiting room on the second floor, a gentleman in an expensive suit sat and studied the sheen of his Italian shoes. There was no admittance to the ICU, and once inside there would be too many eyes watching.

No matter. He had time.

Denise Guerry was going nowhere. Ever!

***

In Florence, Henri drove up to Angelique's apartment and parked. She stepped out of the car.

"Wait here, Henri, I'll only be a moment."

She disappeared into the building.

Henri examined the yard across the street. There was the large live oak whose stout branch had stopped the panga from splitting his skull. Then Henri's kick had broken the assailant's leg.

He looked up. On the fourth floor were the windows where he had seen the lights of Maximilien's men.

Damn it Angelique, you should not be here, and it's taking too long!

For several minutes he stared at the entrance to her building, willing her to appear.

Angelique, we must go. They know where you live.

He looked back to the place where the Citroën had been parked that near-fatal night. Now another car was there. He looked again.

The car was a gray Audi.

Good God! Maximilien!

Henri drew his Browning and raced for the entrance. Inside, He dashed to the elevator and jammed the button. Nothing.

He looked up. The number "4" was illuminated.

Angelique's floor! It's stuck on her floor.

He ran to the stairwell.

Breathing heavily, he climbed the stairs to the landing where a large "4" was painted on the fire door.

He tried the handle. Locked.

He pointed his Browning at the handle.

"Crack."

The bullet ricocheted past his head. Undeterred, He fired again.

"Crack."

This time the lock burst and the door cracked open.

He raced down the corridor. Angelique's door stood ajar. He looked in. There stood Angelique, numb. A .38 revolver dangled from her fingers.

On the couch lay Maximilien Gutera, face down, the back of his shirt red from multiple wounds.

Henri entered, but Angelique did not move. Henri shook her shoulders.

"Angelique, what have you done?"

"I didn't."

"But the gun?"

Her answer was lost in sobs. Henri laid his Browning on the table and eased her into a chair.

"But who?"

Her eyes directed him to the bathroom. Just then a man burst from it, snatched Henri's Browning from the table, and ran out of the apartment.

Henri jumped up. But before he reached the door, he heard the whir of the elevator.

Angelique found her voice.

"Paul Mutabazi. Don't go after him. He was using my apartment while I was gone. He found Maximilien asleep on the couch. He shot him. Maximilien was dead when I got here."

Her eyes misted.

"Henri, Paul was only twelve. My father took him to the soccer field thinking the soldiers would protect them. But the military slaughtered everybody. As my father died, he pulled Paul under him. Paul pretended to be dead. The killers didn't find him."

She stared at Gutera's bullet-ridden corpse.

"Dear God, I ask mercy for this man as I ask for your mercy on all of us, including Paul and me."

Henri eased the revolver from Angelique's grip and examined the weapon. All five chambers were empty.

Paul had emptied the gun. A rage killing!

Henri understood.

Images of the genocide in Rwanda flooded his mind. He shared Paul's rage. Had Henri found Gutera his fate would have been worse. Henri's Browning held thirteen rounds.

There would be thirteen holes in Gutera, not five.

***

Henri was used to action. He wiped the revolver of all prints, and started to toss it by the couch. No. Better it should disappear. He put it in his pocket and turned to Angelique.

"Where are your thesis notes?"

She pointed to the bedroom. He checked that her path would not go near the blood-stained sofa.

"All right go get them."

When she returned, Henri took the notes from her.

"Good. Call Stew Marks and explain to him how you found Gutera dead in your apartment. Do not mention Paul Mutabazi. Marks will think that Gutera's men killed him for his failure."

He added.

"Now we are going to the university to keep the appointment with your professor. Your life will be 'normal' again."

393

Angelique called Stew Marks and informed him of finding Gutera dead.

She and Henri left.

***

In Georgetown, South Carolina, the cardiologist visited Denise Guerry in the ICU. She lay asleep. He checked her pulse, studied the bedside monitors and made notes in her chart. He turned to the nurse.

"She is still in 'afib.' Keep her in the ICU for tonight."

"Do you want to shock her out of afib?"

"Not yet, just keep her on the blood thinner. She'll likely come out of it by herself."

The doctor left as Denise slept on.

***

In the ICU waiting room, the gentleman with the Italian shoes downed his third cup of coffee. He smiled at a young mother awaiting news of her husband. Then he went down to eat lunch at the hospital cafeteria.

He scowled at the dry hamburger and thin potato chips. And there was no wine! Abominable food, but waiting was tedious and he was hungry.

No matter. He had a job to do and he would do it.

He emptied his Styrofoam plate, poured himself another cup of coffee from the machine, and left the cafeteria. Minutes later he was back on the second floor. The young mother was not in sight, evidently she had received her news, good or bad.

He sat to resume his vigil.

Soon Denise Guerry would run out of time.

He picked up a magazine.

***
******

Chapter 50
Saturday, September 8

Gray clouds hung low over Summerville, South Carolina, when Jeannine Ryan and Bill Hamm entered the Italian restaurant. They chose a quiet table for two in a secluded corner. The waiter appeared quickly. They ordered and sat back to wait for their entrées.

Jeannine twiddled the stem of her glass of Vino Rosato, while Bill sipped his Chianti. After a moment, she spoke.

"It's been a wild ride!"

Bill smiled.

"No doubt about that. What will you do now?"

"Wayne asked me to spend some time at Topsail. His place is fixed up again and he's lonely. I might even stay a month. I called Aileen Harris. She will handle Ryan Associates for me. But what will you do?"

"I thought I'd be with you."

"Come on Bill, be honest. You and I are on hold. Maybe we can fix things and maybe not. You want to see Denise Guerry and maybe you should. Maybe we both need time off from each other."

"Like for Stew Marks?"

"Maybe? I like Stew, but he's nowhere near you."

"Why not give him a chance?"

"I might, but if we agree to this time off thing, I won't see anybody for a while. I'm going to Topsail to think. Wayne wants to be a father figure for me. I need that."

She hesitated and then spoke.

"Meanwhile, you go see Denise. If that clicks, that will be a sign for both of us."

Bill gulped the remainder of his Chianti.

The waiter arrived with Chicken Marsala for Jeannine and Lasagna for Bill.

He started to speak, but lost his thought as the aroma of the interleaved cheese, meaty sauce and pasta rose from the plate. He forked a morsel of the mix into his mouth.

Jeannine put her wine down and waited. He put another bite in his mouth and refilled his glass.

"Do you mean it, about my seeing Denise?"

"Why not?"

Damn it. Why did I say that?

Bill swallowed half his wine before his eyes met hers.

"Jeannine, thanks You saved me when you got me out of that hospital. I shouldn't have dragged you into this mess."

Shouldn't have? We're supposed to share our lives, or don't you want to?

Acid hit her stomach and rose in her throat. She swallowed and stood.

Bill looked up, puzzled. She forced a smile and blew a kiss in his direction

"I'm on my way to Topsail. Good luck. It's been real."

Then she turned and left.

He watched her go.

***

Bill sat a moment before turning back to his Lasagna, it was tasteless and cold.

He lifted his eyes and stared at the empty chair opposite.

My God! What's wrong with me. She's leaving!

396

He stood up, threw several bills on the table, and rushed from the restaurant.

She was still there, shoulders drooped, standing by the curb.

He spun her around, and kissed her. His hands ran down her back as he pulled her tight against him.

"Jeannine, forget Denise. Forget Stew. Forget I hate the desk job. Forget everything, but don't forget me. It's you I need. Don't leave me."

She pulled back and studied his eyes.

"I waited too long while you ran around Europe and did your thing for the Agency. And now that you're back, you're bored sitting behind a desk. You have to decide what you want. This time it has to be different. What are you willing to do?"

He tried to kiss her, but she pushed him away.

"No, Bill, I mean it, every word."

He took her hands.

"I'm stupid. I know it. I can't do without you. I will quit. Will you marry me?"

Her eyes probed his eyes.

"Do you know what you are saying?"

"Yes. When you left me at that table, I knew. Your chair was empty. I was empty. There was no purpose left. Please."

"Damn it, Bill!"

But she leaned against him, her lips moist on his ear, her voice scarcely a whisper.

"If you mean it, I'm here. It's you I want."

He pulled her against him.

A light rain began to fall.

Neither noticed.

***

In the ICU at Georgetown Memorial Hospital, Denise Guerry awoke free of pain for the first time in twenty four hours. A nurse stood writing something in a chart at the foot of her bed.

"Miss Guerry, you're awake. How do you feel?"

"Not bad, considering I'm wired up to these machines."

The nurse cranked Denise up to a sitting position.

"Maybe this will make you more comfortable."

She continued.

"And there's good news. The atrial fibrillation is gone. Your heart rhythm is normal. The doctor was going to keep you in the ICU tonight, but now he says we can move you to a regular room. We're trying to find one that's open. As soon as we get one, we'll take you there."

Denise smiled.

"Sounds good, but where is my phone? I need to see my email."

The nurse took the phone from the closet and put it in her free hand.

"Remember, keep that arm in the sling and don't overdo it. You need rest."

She turned and left the room.

***

Denise checked her email. A message, sent two days earlier, appeared. She touched her "jailbroken" app and the decoded email appeared. It was from her cousin.

> **d.g.they|want|you|dead.||both|duval|and|
> the|hammer|given|the|job.||use|latin|charles|
> to|read|two|attached|messages|jacobin5|||**

He had attached two messages.

They were encrypted.

09362034322029011721262500018
13403119102313010637182837018
01003733183435101821171021018
37331108040711333410060513048
01062531253321063416131021058

14362034263722014034182334399
02111628161921384023341537358
26401734302732190835181419198
26401106051411303407070412128
36271620193732150321070619088

"Damn it Jacques, I'm tired of numbers."

But her user-generated app did not work on the messages. It produced only gibberish. So the key was not "*Gahuj.*"

She reread Jacque's message. The Latin for "Charles" was "*Carolus!*" That must be the new key. She entered "Carolus" into the app and the first message appeared in plain text.

*h.duval|removal|of|d.|guerry|authorised|
by02001714112018|gironde1|||b7*

So Henri was ordered to kill her. But she knew that. It was the second message that made her shudder.

*m.dupre||removal|of|d.|guerry|authorised|
by|02001714112018|gironde1.|4*

The name "m. dupre" stood for *Marcel Dupré*, SÉGAG's assassin known as *le Marteau*, the "Hammer." It was he who had killed Hugh Byrd.

And the Hammer never failed.

She lay back and shut her eyes. Both authorizations came from Gironde1, the code name for Charles, a top aide of the Minister. Cousin Jacques must have deduced the key, *carolus*, from his name. But Gironde1 outranked her Uncle Roland. The latter could not help her even should he want to.

Her hand shook as it felt for the cup of water on the side table. She had taken her first sip when the nurse came in.

"Good news Miss. Guerry, a room just opened up in East Nursing, on this floor. We're moving you there right away. You'll be able to see all the visitors you want."

Denise choked. The Hammer would have easy access to a room outside the ICU. And his visit would be her last.

With her good arm she reached for her smart phone.

***

In Summerville, South Carolina the rain had ceased. Bill Hamm and Jeannine, hand in hand, strolled towards their car.

Bill's phone vibrated. He listened, and turned to Jeannine.

"Denise needs help. She's in the hospital. She's terrified. SÉGAG has sent an assassin to kill her."

"Henri Duval?"

"Not him, a professional. Someone called the "Hammer.""

Jeannine bit her tongue.

"Jeannine, without Denise we could not have stopped the rockets from reaching Mombasa. She convinced that port superintendant to release the container to us."

"Bill, I can see you have to go, but you're not going without me."

"We have to leave, we're an hour or more away."

"Can you get there in time?"

"I have to try."

***

******

400

Chapter 51
Saturday, September 8

Marcel Dupré, the "Hammer," stood by the elevator on the second floor of the hospital. The door to the Intensive Care Unit was down the hall, only steps away. Across from him was a full-length mirror, presumably provided to divert impatient visitors from the slowness of the elevators.

He ignored his reflection. He was calm and focused. He would snuff out the life of the Guerry woman with hardly more emotion than it took to snuff out a candle.

He looked down at his shoes. The rich sheen of their Italian leather soothed him.

The door to the stairwell was three steps away from where he stood, and the stairwell door on the first floor was unlocked. He had checked. He would leave by the stairs when his task was done.

He stood with his eyes on his shoes, his ears waiting for the opening click of the ICU doors.

**

In the ICU, Denise Guerry closed her eyes as the attendant strapped her onto the gurney. The nurse laid a chart and papers on top of her as the large attendant pushed her out from the room.

Just past the nurses' desk and to its right, a bright exit sign hung above the double doors that led from the ICU to the main corridor.

The attendant hit the wall panel to open the doors.

"Click. Click."

The doors fanned wide open.

Denise lifted her head at the sound of a man behind her. He spoke to the attendant.

"Sir, don't move. Stop the stretcher. Don't go into the corridor. Stay here."

The attendant stopped and turned. The speaker was a man in his late twenties.

"Excuse me, who are you? I must take this patient to her room. What do you want?"

The man took out a phone. He spoke with a French accent.

"Just a moment. I'll explain everything after I send this message."

This time Denise recognized the voice.

She gasped.

The speaker was "Jacobin5," her cousin, Jacques.

***

On the second floor of the Memorial Hospital, the assassin known as the "Hammer" heard the ICU doors click open. He took a step towards the now-open doorway, but his phone vibrated. He stopped and touched an icon.

An email of encrypted numbers appeared. He touched his decoding app to display the plain text.

> **m.dupre|urgent|cancel|removal|of|d.|guerry||**
> **repeat|cancel|removal|of|d.|guerry|authorised|**
> **by02001714112018|gironde1|||.67t'onj**

He stared. The Hammer hated confusion and sudden change, but the message was clear and the authorization code was correct.

The hit was off!

He dared not disobey Gironde1.

He tapped an expensive shoe on the tile floor, spun about, and took the elevator down to the lobby.

***

At the exit to the ICU, Denise's cousin, Jacques, peered into the corridor. He saw no one. He pointed to Denise and spoke to the hospital attendant.

"Sorry for the interruption. This patient is my cousin. You can take her to her room now."

The attendant rolled Denise down the hall to East Nursing.

At her room, the attendant, aided by a nurse, transferred Denise from the gurney onto the bed. He left and, after some chores, the nurse followed.

Denise spoke.

"Jacques, what are you doing here? I got your message. I'm scared. The Hammer is after me."

"Not now he isn't."

"But the message you forwarded ordered him to kill me?"

"True, but just now I sent the Hammer my own message complete with Gironde1's confirmation code. It cancels the hit on you. The Hammer has been called off."

"How did you get Gironde1's confirmation code?"

Jacques shrugged.

Denise sat up in the bed and reached out with her free arm.

"Give me a hug, Jacques. What would I do without you?"

"Nothing, I hope. Now get dressed. We're leaving."

"What?"

"We have to go. The FBI is on the way to arrest you and the Hammer will soon find he's been duped."

"But I have a friend coming. I have to see him."

"You mean Hamm? Forget him. You'll never get him away from that redhead. He's not for you. Besides, I've had it with your foolish infatuations and machinations. Your body is not a weapon to use against "stupid" men. You need someone like me. Someone who will share himself with you alone."

"Jacques, what are you saying?"

"Nothing. We must leave."

Oddly, she didn't mind his lecture or his commands. He made her feel secure.

He helped her into her clothes. As he arranged her blouse over the injured arm, she felt his warm breath on her neck. She leaned away.

"Forget it, Jacques. I like you, but I'm not into incest! We are first cousins, remember."

He laughed.

"I'm not into incest either, OK?"

He took her arm. They went down to the lobby and marched out the entrance without checking out.

Once outside, he helped her to his car.

***

At the hospital, Stew Marks, followed by Sam Smith, strode to the reception desk. Stew flashed his badge.

"FBI. What room is Ms. Denise Guerry in?"

The woman consulted her computer.

"Check with the nurse in East Nursing, on 'Two.' Take the elevator by the gift shop."

"Thank you."

Stew and Sam went to the elevator. On the second floor, a nurse led them to Ms. Guerry's room.

The bed was not made, but the room was empty. The nurse went to the closet.

Denise's clothes were gone.

The nurse called the administration, listened a moment, and turned back to Stew.

"She did not check out, but apparently she's left the hospital."

Stew's face grew red. He turned to leave, but the door was blocked by new arrivals, Bill Hamm and Jeannine Ryan.

"Damn it Hamm, did you help Denise get away? Where is she?"

Jeannine interceded.

"Stew, we just got here. We don't know any more than you."

Stew turned to Sam.

"She can't be long gone. Maybe we can still catch her."

Stew started to the door. His disappointment at not finding Denise was increased by seeing Jeannine with Hamm. *Damn. She's sticking with him.* As he stepped out he leaned towards her.

"Jeannine, Denise is wanted for selling government secrets. Please don't help her. That's aiding and abetting, and I don't want to have to arrest you."

He leaned closer and whispered.

"If you get tired of this guy, give me a call. I'm still here and I'm not giving up yet."

He looked at Bill.

"You're a lucky man Hamm."

Stew left. Sam followed.

Jeannine turned to Bill. She studied his eyes.

"Are you disappointed that Denise didn't say goodbye?"

He pressed Jeannine against the wall and kissed her hard and long.

The nurse averted her eyes and stepped out into the hallway.

***

At a small commuter airfield near Georgetown, South Carolina, Jacques Guerry parked the rental car.

"Jacques, what are you doing? Where are you going?"

"Not me, us. We're flying to Atlanta and then to Martinique."

He handed her two passports. The photos were theirs, but the names were M. and Mme. Devineau.

"Husband and wife? What are you planning? I told you, we are cousins."

"So what. I'm going to make love to you. I've waited all these years, and those passports prove we are married. Besides, I know you like me."

"Damn it Jacques, don't be an idiot!"

"Wait, you need to look at this."

He smiled and drew a paper from his jacket. He unfolded it and handed it to her. She took it and read.

"My God! Jacques, what does this mean?"

"It's clear enough. You are adopted. The man you called 'father' was sterile. He was not your biological father. He and your mother adopted you but were afraid to tell anyone, particularly his older brother, your uncle Roland, my father. They knew he controlled the money and the company. They did not trust him. They wanted to assure you of your inheritance."

She lapsed silent, stunned.

He took her hand and led her, stumbling, onto the tarmac.

She finally found her voice.

"How long have you known? How did you find out?"

"That's not important."

He put his arm around her shoulder.

"Come on, the pilot is ready. We have a connection to make in Atlanta."

He guided her to the waiting plane.

***

In Arrondissement 2 in Paris, Gironde1, the minister's close aide, paced about his desk.

His chosen instrument, "le Marteau," had failed. Gironde1 smashed his hand on the polished desk.

And where was Gutera! The rockets were lost, and the ship la Lutte was ordered back to le Havre. Why hadn't Gutera contacted him? Where was the Hutu leader?

He smashed his fist again on the walnut desk top.

It hurt.

***

In a motel in Georgetown South Carolina, in far less elegant surroundings, Marcel Dupré kicked the wall of his room.

Duped by that dumb Jacques Guerry!

And his boss, Gironde1, was not pleased with his gullibility. Not at all!

He kicked the wall again.

Damn!

Now his Italian shoes were scuffed!

***

Hours later, as the Airbus left Atlanta to fly over the waters of the Caribbean, Denise turned to Jacques Guerry.

"But what will we live on?"

"I have millions of Euros stashed in the Cayman Islands. SÉGAG had a huge surplus. Think of it as our share of the inheritance. Dear old Alphonse!"

"Jacques, something happened to me. I don't want money like I used to. I mean, I do, but there there's a lot I regret doing. I've been wrong. About many things!"

"You've got the money anyway. Half the accounts are in your name."

"Dear Jacques, you've always stuck by me, even when I was mad at you."

He laughed.

She gripped the arms of the seat and switched to the more troubling issue.

"You say we are not related?"

"Not genetically anyway. And I want you to know I'm glad. I think I've loved you since we were little together."

She frowned.

"Jacques, you always joke. Get serious."

He looked deep into her eyes. She turned away. *Dear God, he means it.*

She thought of all the shared times in their youth. *He knows me better than anyone, and he still likes me or thinks he does!*

"This is too fast, Jacques, I can't handle this."

But he pulled her towards him. She leaned her head on his shoulder and shut her eyes.

Good old Jacques. You always make me feel safe. But love?

She felt his arm tighten about her shoulders.

Who knows? Maybe?

***

******

Chapter 52
Epilogue

All charges against Bill Hamm were dismissed. He and Jeannine Ryan are engaged but have not set a date. Plans are for Aileen Harris to be the maiden of honor. Wayne Johnson will give the bride away. His house on Topsail is available for the honeymoon.

Angelique Uwimana received her Ph.D., but turned down a position at Ryan Associates to return to Rwanda to work with orphans of the genocide. She joined an order of Catholic nuns devoted to the education and healing of child survivors (as well as perpetrators) of the 1994 holocaust.

With much difficulty, Henri Duval accepted Angelique's decision to remain single for God's work. He retired to Lyon, France, where he enjoys the cuisine of the region. He and Angelique exchange notes every Christmas.

Paul Mutabazi disappeared. He has not been heard from.

Jack Marino was placed on administrative leave from the FBI. He has since left the government. Stew Marks, with his new partner, Sam Smith, returned to the Joint Terrorism Task Force of the Washington Field Office.

The documents and other items taken from the Torbee Building by Bill Hamm were returned to the National Security Agency by the FBI. At the urging of the NSA, who feared that the publicity of a trial would reveal their ability to read RSA-coded communications, Federal prosecutors did not press charges against Denise Guerry and Guerry Electronic Systems.

In France, SÉGAG lost the support of a certain government Minister who resigned, purportedly because of financial scandals. Roland Guerry, SÉGAG's CEO and principal owner, sold the floundering company. Monsieur Guerry retired due to a liver ailment attributed to the excessive consumption of alcohol.

Denise Guerry, aka "Denise Devineau," married her childhood admirer, Jacques. M. and Mme "Devineau" reside in Martinique and have a boy. His name is *not* Roland.

The body of Marcel Dupré, the Hammer, was found in the Seine near the Isle de la Cité. In spite of an apparent bullet wound in his back, his death was ruled a suicide.

Fred Middleton still lives on his farm near Dillon. Poaching on his lands has ceased.

Port Superintendant Morris was told to resign or be prosecuted. He chose the former and lives on James Island in Charleston County, South Carolina.

The Carolina cadre of Hutu militants dissolved due to lack of funds and political support.

***

******

Envoi

The house stood alone atop the Rwandan hill. To the front, green groves of bananas filled the long descent to an unpaved road. To the rear and side, coffee plants lined a slope that overlooked the shimmering waters of Lac Kivu where a Pied Kingfisher sat patiently on a branch, watching for ripples that signaled its prey.

Purple Bougainvillea smothered the wall next to a bench where Angelique Uwimana sat. Nearby a pair of nectarine Sunbirds, resplendent in their iridescent plumage, fluttered by a cup-like nest suspended from a small tree.

Angelique looked up as several nuns guided their charges, young adults traumatized as children during the genocide, to their new rooms in the recently acquired mansion. She read the mail. The first letter was from Florence, South Carolina.

Dear Mother Angelique,

I had my first tests in Computer Science last week and my professors said I succeeded. They remember you, and send you their best wishes.

Thank you, my dear adopted mother, and all the nuns for your love and training. My studies with you prepared me well for university here.

In love and thanks, Augustin.

The second letter, was from the nuns' lawyer in Kigali.

Dear Ms. Uwimana,

With reference to your query concerning the anonymous donor who purchased the Hakizimana estate for your nuns, she permits me to disclose her name: Mme. Denise Devineau, of Martinique. She asks your prayers.

Be assured, Ms. Uwimana, of my continued devotion and respect. Sincerely,

Louis Kamanutsi.

Angelique looked up as a sunbird flew in glistening circles above her. *Merci, Denise.*

She stared as several more traumatized children, now adult-sized, arrived at the mansion. Their dull blank eyes brought back her own memories.

She clasped her hands and lowered her head.

"*Seigneur prends pitié de nous tous!* Lord have mercy on us all!"

***

******

About the Author

James E. Mosimann is a retired biostatistician who spent many years at the Computer Division of the National Institutes of Health. He has a Ph. D. in Zoology from the University of Michigan, and a Masters in Biostatistics from the Johns Hopkins University. After NIH, he joined the Office of Research Integrity of the Public Health Service, where he was a scientist-investigator for cases of research misconduct. He has numerous publications and one text. This is his fourth novel.

He and his wife, Barbara Jean, live in Virginia. They have eight children, all adult.

Author's Note

This is the fourth book in a series that follows the activities of Jeannine Ryan, a specialist in statistical forensics. Like the others, it was a family project. Thanks again to my wife for her support and to my adult children for their assistance. As before, Tom's many hours of careful reading and editing significantly improved the manuscript, as did comments by Joseph, John, Theresa, Michelle, Mary and Madeleine. Finally Kateri, provided the cover graphics and design.

Note that in Kinyarwanda, the second name does not denote an individual's family.

Carolina Technical University is an imaginary institution. All characters in this book are fictional (including Charles Hakizimana, his son, Maximilien Gutera, and Angelique Uwimana.) However, Angelique's character was inspired by the experiences of Immaculée Ilibagiza as described in her book, *Left to Tell*, 2006, Hay House, Inc. Carlsbad, CA.

Jeannine Ryan's previous exploits are narrated in three novels: **Misconduct's Deadly Denial, The Assassin Chip, The**

Prague Plot. This book, *The Carolina Coup*, is the fourth in this series.

Those wishing to read more about the 1994 genocide may consult Wikipedia's entry *Rwandan Genocide*. Stephen Kinzer's book, *A Thousand Hills*, 2008, John Wiley & Sons, Inc., Hoboken, NJ, gives a history of Rwanda along with many references. The personal experiences of a survivor, Immaculée Ilibagiza, are told in her book, *Left to Tell*, 2006, Hay House, Inc. Carlsbad, CA. The frustrations of the United Nations commander in Rwanda at the time, Lt. General Romeo Dallaire, are revealed in his book, *Shake Hands with the Devil*, 2003, Carroll and Graph Publishers, New York, NY.